"Laurelin Paige writes a [...] sexy that draws the read[...] after the last page is rea[...]"

—K. Bromberg, *New York Times*
bestselling author of the Driven series

"Edgy sex and pulsating mystery make this fast-paced and sensual story impossible to put down."

—Jay Crownover,
New York Times bestselling
author of the Marked Men series

"Laurelin creates a romance that comes in many touches. Romance from her best friend, their bond, their past. Romance from her lover, their connection, their future. Each chapter leads you deeper into mystery, twisting what you knew, making you love who you're meant to hate. A fascinating read!"

—Pepper Winters, *New York Times* bestselling
author of the Pure Corruption series

"*First Touch* is a heart-chilling page-turner from a master storyteller—and the hottest thing I've read this year, hands down."

—M. Pierce, bestselling author of
the Night Owl trilogy

"Dark, intense, and incredibly sexy, *First Touch* kept me on the edge of my seat from page one up to the very last word."

—*Shameless Book Club*

"Gritty, edgy, dark, and compelling. *First Touch* pulls no punches and just might leave you reeling."

—Megan Hart, *New York Times* and *USA
Today* bestselling author of *Tear You Apart*

"Laurelin is a must-click author . . . after reading *First Touch*, we're obsessed." —*The Rock Stars of Romance*

"This spellbinding story will have you glued to the pages from the first page to the last. Paige's best work yet. Thrilling, captivating, sexy, and shocking. I am in love with this story." —Claire Contreras, *New York Times* bestselling author of *Kaleidoscope Hearts*

"*First Touch* is shocking, stunning, and intense with a heat level that can only be measured on the Kelvin scale." —C. D. Reiss, *USA Today* bestselling author of *ShutterGirl*

"*First Touch* is a deliciously dark and sinfully sexy story that had me up way past bedtime. Laurelin Paige knows exactly what a woman craves, and I'm craving more Reeve." —Geneva Lee, *New York Times* and *USA Today* bestselling author

"*First Touch* will make your blood pressure skyrocket with its wicked and deliciously depraved plot. It will leave you on pins and needles, breathless and begging for more. Laurelin Paige has delivered her finest work yet." —Jen McCoy, *The Literary Gossip*

"A beautifully executed maze of suspense, seduction, and ridiculously hot sex." —Alessandra Torre, *New York Times* bestselling author

"A dazzling mystery to unravel . . . wicked and yet sensual. Decadent in her ability to weave a captivating story from beginning to end, Laurelin Paige has another hit on her hands." —Kendall Ryan, *New York Times* bestselling author

LAST KISS

KISS

LAURELIN PAIGE

St. Martin's Paperbacks

This is a work of fiction. All of the characters, organizations, and events portrayed in this novel are either products of the author's imagination or are used fictitiously.

LAST KISS

Copyright © 2015 by Laurelin Paige.

For information address St. Martin's Press, 175 Fifth Avenue, New York, NY 10010.

ISBN: 978-1-250-16032-4

Our books may be purchased in bulk for promotional, educational, or business use. Please contact your local bookseller or the Macmillan Corporate and Premium Sales Department at 1-800-221-7945, ext. 5442, or by e-mail at MacmillanSpecialMarkets@macmillan.com.

Printed in the United States of America

St. Martin's Griffin edition / June 2016
St. Martin's Paperbacks edition / March 2018

St. Martin's Paperbacks are published by St. Martin's Press, 175 Fifth Avenue, New York, NY 10010.

10 9 8 7 6 5 4 3 2 1

TO FRIENDS
WHO KILL SPIDERS

ACKNOWLEDGMENTS

To my family—this one was tough. We made it. I think.

To my editor, Eileen Rothschild—As always, you remain my hero. Please don't ever leave me!

To the team at St. Martin's Press—you've changed while I've been working with you, but each and every incarnation is fabulous. Thanks for all you do to make us all look good.

To my agent, Rebecca Friedman—you're my soul sister. I love you.

To Bethany, Kayti, and Melanie—through spiders, trapped farts, and bears (oh my!), you're definitely the only reason I lived past October 2015. Thank you for being fellow sNAkes.

To Jenn—yep. Writers are crazy. You're just as crazy to want to work with us. And, man, am I grateful.

To all of you authors and bloggers who read and blurbed and pimped this series—I'm so honored and humbled to have such incredibly talented, creative people say nice words about my books. You all truly amaze me. Thank you!

To my girls—Fab Four, Domination, Wrahm, Snatches, FYW, Order. You guys get me. Thank God someone does.

To my readers—I never knew what a sadist I was until I read all your e-mails and private messages cursing me about that wicked cliffhanger. Gee, that was fun. Thank you so much for reading and loving Emily and Reeve's story. You truly make it worth the work.

To my God—always first and last and everything in between.

LAST

KISS

P R O L O G U E

Amber took her sweet time saying good-bye to Rob that Sunday afternoon after my seventeenth birthday. She'd kissed and cooed over him at the door of his convertible while I stood at the curb, knee bouncing, worried we'd miss our bus if we didn't run for it soon. Worried that my mother would find out that we spent my birthday shacked up with Amber's rich "uncle." Mom's wrath would have been tolerable, but the fear that she might keep me from spending time with Amber made me fiercely anxious. That weekend was the first time I'd explored my sexuality. The first time I'd felt sensual. The first time I'd experienced real desire. Now my life had possibilities; I didn't want to go back to before.

"Amber." I'd meant to nudge her gently, but I couldn't mask my anxiety. Her name was both a prayer and a curse.

She'd twisted her head sharply in my direction, the arch of her eyebrow letting me know she hadn't appreciated be-ing rushed. She'd worn that expression only a few seconds before her features had relaxed and her lips slid into a playful grin.

"Emily," she'd called to me, sugar dripping from her voice. "Don't you think Rob deserves a decent kiss for all he's done for us?"

"Of course he does." I'd matched her sweetness, though I'd been pretty sure that most of what had been "done" had been done for Rob, not that I'd objected. It had been fun and he'd bought us pretty things and given us pretty drugs and that had been well worth the blow jobs and the aching thigh muscles. "Just, the bus . . ."

She either hadn't heard me or hadn't been as concerned about the time because she beckoned me closer with a nod. "Come say good-bye to him, Em. Come kiss him."

At her request my pulse had begun to race, my cheeks flushed, and heat barreled between my thighs, and not simply because I'd wanted one last kiss. My concern about the bus had faded into the distance, so I'd taken the three steps over to them, then tilted my chin up and met his mouth with mine, letting my tongue dot against the tip of his before sliding it along the curve of his upper lip.

"Jesus, Em. The bus is about to leave. We have to run." Amber's inflection had been teasing, proving she'd been aware of my distress all along. Grabbing my hand, she'd tugged me away from our "uncle." She'd waved to him once more before we broke into a run, making our ride just as the doors had been about to close.

We'd taken a seat in the back, and, once we'd caught our breath, lost it again in a fit of giggles. "He's great, isn't he?" she'd asked after we'd settled down, but before I could respond, she'd bounded on. "I knew you'd like him. You didn't mind when I got bossy back there, did you? When I told you to kiss Rob good-bye?"

"Not at all. I liked kissing him." It had felt like a lie, or at least, not the whole truth. I had liked everything we'd done that weekend together, the three of us. Every new experience. But half the reason I'd enjoyed that last kiss so much hadn't been because of what it was—the feel of lips on lips, the twining of the wet, thick muscles of tongues—but because Amber had told me to do it . . . ordered me out of equal parts playfulness and love.

It wasn't the first time I had recognized my desire to submit. When we'd met several months before, Amber had uncovered my longing to yield. To please. To surrender.

But this time her command had also awoken my sexual tastes. She had summoned a creature to life inside me—a deeply seated beast with an appetite for carnality and a desperate need to be stroked as she knelt at the foot of the one who would feed her.

It was then I caught the first glimpse of the person I would become, and the role Amber would play in my life as the first master I wanted to please.

CHAPTER

1

My feet moved automatically, pulled by a force that couldn't be simplified with a label of compassion or curiosity or obligation. I crouched in front of Reeve and took Amber's limp wrist into my hands. My body was present, going through the motions of a concerned friend, but my head was in a fog. The smell of sex still lingered in my nose, the orgasms Reeve had given me still rang through me, low and wide, like the faintest waves sounding off a tuning fork.

Then there had been Reeve's declaration. He'd hinted both that he loved me and that he knew who I was, knew that I'd been Amber's friend. That had sent me into shock long before I'd been confronted with her ghost in the flesh.

She was supposed to be dead.

I was confused. I was relieved. I was more than a little scared.

Around me there was a buzz of voices, discussing Amber, but nothing they said made sense. All I heard was a steady drone and her whimpers softer than when I'd first seen her and barely audible. She didn't seem to be conscious, whatever pain she carried was so great that it slipped out in her sleep.

Reeve tried to get her eyes to open, slapping gently at her face with the same hand that had caressed me earlier in the evening, had been inside my mouth and cunt. The concern etched on his face and the tight emotion in his tone as he coaxed her were mirrors of the way he'd spoken to me in our most intimate moments.

"Emily. It's you," Amber whispered.

My focus snapped to her. I was aware now—of her, of her injured state, of the frenzy occurring on her behalf. Aware that Reeve now knew conclusively that *his* Amber was also *my* Amber.

"Yes, it's me." I stroked the length of her arm, forcing my gaze not to zoom in on her black eyes, her bruised nose, the sallow color of her skin. She'd been beaten badly. Her body was stick thin, her wrist fragile under my hands. I wrapped my fingers around it and registered a pulse, stronger than I'd expected from the near skeletal figure before me. This couldn't be the confident, vibrant woman that I'd known, and yet she couldn't be anyone else. My shoulders threatened to sag with guilt and grief, and my throat felt coarse like I'd swallowed sand.

But she needed strength, and I was a good actress. So I held my head high and made my voice a balm. "I'm here."

Her lip was too fat and bloodied to smile, but the corners of her mouth turned up slightly. "It *is* you." Her words were labored, her breath short. "Joe said you'd sent him. To save me. I—"

I glanced back at Joe as she broke into a coughing fit that tried to curl her torso in, but she couldn't manage to lift her head, the exertion too much for her.

"Save your energy. We're going to get you to a bed, Angel." Reeve nodded at his men.

Angel. Was that what he called her or simply an endearment he was using now? Either way it felt private. Like I'd walked into the middle of another couple's love scene.

"I need a few things from my office," Jeb said to one of the security guards. "An IV kit, my bag. There are painkillers in the safe."

He continued to issue orders, and I stood to get out of the way as Reeve gathered Amber in his arms. I turned to Brent, the ranch manager. "Shouldn't we call a doctor?" I was sure Jeb was good at what he did, but he was a veterinarian.

Brent shook his head. "Jeb's got all the training we need and we don't want to raise any unwanted attention."

I started to protest, but Amber called out, drawing my attention back to her.

Reeve was standing now, Amber in his arms, headed for the stairs, but he paused and spun so that she could see me easily.

"I'll be right there, Amber," I promised. "I'm just going to talk to Joe for one minute while they're making you comfortable."

She nodded, her lids closing as though they were too heavy to keep open.

I turned to the man who held her. Who moments ago was *my* man—now I wasn't so sure. His expression was hard and unreadable. But when his gaze caught mine, the room tilted. His eyes held a dark brew of emotion, so murky and filled that I couldn't determine *what* he was feeling, only that he *was* feeling. And that he wanted to share it with me. Even though it was obvious now just how much I hadn't shared with him.

My chest tightened, and I looked away, breaking the intense connection. It was all too much. I pivoted toward Joe, aware of Reeve behind me as he held his position a second longer before taking Amber upstairs.

I forced my full attention on Joe. I'd seen him as I'd come into the room, before I'd noticed the battered girl in Reeve's arms, but I hadn't gotten a chance to study him. Now I scanned him for similar injuries, for any sign that her rescue had caused him harm. When I saw nothing, I asked, "Are you okay?"

"Besides being exhausted, yeah. I'm fine."

I let out a shaky breath of relief. "I told you she was alive."

Joe chuckled. "You did."

In the beginning, I did, I'd insisted on it until he'd shown me the autopsy report of a Jane Doe that had matched Amber's description, a woman who bore the same V tattoo that Amber had on her shoulder. I'd found the same report in an e-mail to Reeve when I'd been snooping on his computer, which had further ended any hope that she was still alive.

"How did this—?" I wasn't sure how to ask the question. "How is she not dead?"

He ran a hand through his hair. "I don't know. I think we were deliberately thrown off." His expression told me exactly who he'd thought had done the throwing—Reeve Sallis. Joe had never trusted him, and with good reason. Reeve's reputation was shady at best. Five years before, his girlfriend, Missy, had mysteriously died while with him on his island in the Pacific. He'd been cleared from any blame in the crime, but my friend Chris Blakely, who had been close to Missy, had painted her relationship with Reeve as volatile. Chris was convinced that Reeve had killed her and had even gone so far as to hint as much on a recent talk show.

I wasn't sure which side of the fence I sat on. Reeve had assured me he'd had nothing to do with her death, and while I didn't know if I believed him, I'd decided the answer didn't matter. Now that Amber had returned, I had less reason to doubt him.

Joe, it seemed, was still skeptical. After months of investigating, he'd only found more incriminating evidence. Evidence that tied Reeve to the Greek mafia and a sex slave ring that Joe had been certain Amber had wandered into.

I thought of her bruises and shuddered. Joe was probably right.

"What happened?" I asked him, not wanting to know but needing to all the same. "Where did you find her?"

"With Vilanakis."

Michelis Vilanakis, the mob boss who I had pinned as a lowlife villain. It was the name I'd expected. Amber was last seen with him. Reeve was also connected to him—I'd seen pictures of the two at various events, as well as a few e-mails to Reeve from him.

"You just swooped in and rescued her from his house in Chicago? Or . . ." I left the question open-ended, not able to imagine what the scenario had been.

"I got lucky actually." He shook his head, demonstrating his incredulity. "Really lucky. I'd been tailing Michelis for three days before I saw her. I didn't even realize who she was at first. But while I was in my car watching, she ran out of his house, upset about something. He followed after her, Emily. He grabbed her by the hair and yanked her back so hard I swore he was going to break her neck. Then he went off on her. Fucking pounded her face in while she struggled and cried. I don't know how her screams didn't draw a crowd."

I felt sick. "Maybe his neighbors are scared shitless of him. They ignore what goes on." Where I grew up everyone turned a blind eye. No one mentioned the drug dealer that lived next door. No one bothered looking in on me when my mother was passed out drunk in the front yard.

No one intervened when Amber and I would arrive home with newly purchased designer clothes and unexplainable cash in our pockets.

"Probably so. He left her like that in his driveway. Whether he was leaving her for dead or planned to come back and get her later, I don't know. I grabbed her and took off."

"Why didn't you go to a hospital? Or the police?" I understood why Reeve's men would be wary, but Joe had more faith in the legal system.

"She refused to go anywhere but here. She was insistent and scared. She'd been to the doctor before, remember? With other bruises, and somehow she ended up back with her abuser. I didn't know who to trust. So I brought her here."

He tilted his head and studied me. "Didn't figure I'd see you here when I arrived."

"Yeah, well." I'd hired Joe to investigate Amber's disappearance, but I hadn't always been forthcoming with him about my own snooping. At the moment, I didn't want to think about the circumstances of my presence at Reeve's Wyoming ranch let alone talk about it. "How did you know to look for her there? How did you realize she was still alive?"

"I didn't. She's not why I was following him."

I wrinkled my forehead. "Then why . . . ?"

He gave me an incredulous glance, one that said he couldn't believe I had to ask. But I did have to. I needed him to say it.

And he did. "I was looking for you."

There was affection in the way he held my gaze, his expression so much easier to read than Reeve's had been, but equally hard for me to bear, for such different reasons.

I lowered my eyes to the floor. "Thank you, Joe. For finding her. For bringing her here." I couldn't manage to thank him for what he'd done for me. He'd gone willingly into danger, after I'd eluded him and been uncooperative. When I'd put myself in the damn situation after his countless warnings. I didn't deserve his concern. I couldn't condone it with gratitude.

He took a step toward me. "Emily, there's something else you should know." He waited until I looked up before he went on. "The tattoos. I found out what they mean."

"The V tattoos?" Besides Amber and the Jane Doe from the autopsy, I'd also seen one on an employee of Reeve's in Los Angeles. "Doesn't it just stand for Vilanakis? I figured it was some show of mob support. Like a gang tattoo."

"It does stand for Vilanakis. But the tattoos aren't inked voluntarily. They're like a brand. Anyone wearing the mark belongs to Michelis." In case I didn't get the picture, he clarified. "As in indentured servant."

"That's not even legal." Which was a ridiculous thing to say since I knew the mob didn't care much about the law. My throat grew thick. "What does that mean anyway? She got away. She's safe now. Right?"

"My impression is that Michelis brands people when their debt to him is too great to pay back in a lifetime. Which, if that's true, if Amber owes him that big, then he's—" He broke off at the sound of footsteps.

I wanted to know more, but when I turned I found Reeve approaching. I forgot about branding and servitude, and got swept up in the confusing mix of emotions that rose at the sight of him. There was so much unsettled between us—and that was without anyone else involved. Amber and Joe only complicated things that much more.

"She's asking for you, Emily," Reeve said, his eyes pinned on Joe. "She's in the suite next to yours." It was a dismissal that left little room for refute.

Besides, I really did want to be with Amber, so I nodded and headed upstairs, despite knowing that Joe could very well reveal all my secrets. Maybe it was time for those secrets to come out anyway.

If she really had been asking for me, she wasn't by the time I arrived upstairs. Now the only thing on her mind was getting something for the pain. Her shirt was off, and there were several bruises down her chest and arms, some yellowed and fading, others were much newer. Several near-black angry splotches lined one side of her torso. Jeb was pressing on them when I walked in, and though his touch seemed tender, the examination had her in tears.

I ran to hold her hand and stroke her hair, but she was in such agony, I wasn't sure how much my presence helped. Jeb finished tracing the lines of her ribs before looking up at me. "Emily, would you mind going down to the kitchen and making some ice packs? If there's some frozen peas or something, that would work just as well."

"Sure. Broken?" I'd had broken ribs before. I knew that pain.

"Just fractured, I think. But her breathing's not great. I'd like to get her on some oxygen so that she doesn't develop pneumonia."

"We have some for emergencies in the main office," Brent piped in. "I'll call down and have it brought up. And, Emily, there's ice compresses in the small freezer in the pantry."

I bent to kiss Amber's forehead. "Hang in there. We'll get you feeling better soon." She squeezed my hand so I knew she'd heard me, although I'm sure it was hard to believe in her current state of discomfort.

The men Jeb had sent for supplies were coming in as I left the room and by the time I returned with ice packs, Amber had been hooked up to an IV and fluid was dripping down the line into the vein at her wrist. Her eyes were closed. She was either asleep or almost there so I didn't disturb her. Instead, I handed Jeb the compresses, then sat on the love seat near the bed and watched, helpless.

I was actually grateful for that helplessness. Of the myriad complex emotions that were weighing on me at the moment, helplessness was the easiest to carry. It was the one I knew.

Brent returned with the oxygen tank as well as a heart rate monitor. Reeve came along with him, taking a perch on the opposite arm. Together we watched as Jeb and Brent hooked Amber up to the machines. We didn't speak or look at each other. Tension buzzed between us like a fly caught in a closed room. I was desperate to know what he was thinking and feeling. Was he as focused on her as he appeared to be? Or was his mind as caught up in us as mine was?

The longer I sat without his acknowledgment, the more my anxiety grew.

It was just after three when Jeb gestured for us to follow him out to the hallway for a powwow.

"Well?" Reeve asked, impatience in his voice.

Although he'd shut the door behind him, Jeb kept his voice low. "She's bruised up mostly. Her ribs are tender, but they seem to be just fractures. Her wrist is sprained and she has a concussion, all of which can be healed with time."

Reeve rubbed at the back of his neck, nodding, taking it in.

"When she wakes up," Brent said, "she might be wanting some kind of upper, if you know what I mean. She was pretty fond of the white stuff when she was here last."

Reeve shook his head. "Joe—the guy who brought her here—said he thinks she's not into that right now. He's pretty sure she's moved onto opiates."

So that's what he'd talked to Joe about. He was looking out for Amber, and I was grateful. And I was also selfish because it was disappointing to realize he hadn't been asking about me.

Jeb considered, raising a brow. "Heroin?"

Reeve shook his head again. "Codeine. Oxy maybe. She got beat up pretty bad, but he said she's been begging for a pill every two hours."

"Do you know if he gave her anything?" Jeb asked.

"Some Vicodin. He said he gave it as directed to help with her pain. The last was about four hours ago."

Jeb seemed to do a mental calculation. Satisfied with his result, he said, "I just put some morphine in her IV as well as something to help her sleep. We'll have to watch the clock carefully and only give her what she needs rather than what she asks for. In the morning I'll see if I can get my hands on some methadone."

Brent clapped a hand on Reeve's back. "I'm going to go check on security, make sure we're covered in case—"

Reeve cut him off. "He won't come here looking for her."

"With all the other activity lately, are you sure?"

Reeve hesitated, then said again, "He won't come here. But extra security is a good idea."

A chill ran through me as I thought about what Joe had said about Amber's tattoo. But I trusted Reeve's perception of danger. If he said he didn't think Vilanakis would come around, I believed him. The additional security was likely just a measure of precaution.

As soon as Brent left, Reeve addressed Jeb again. "What do we need to do for her tonight?"

I nodded, wishing I'd asked first.

"There's nothing you can do at this point." Jeb looked at his watch. "She's probably going to be out for a while. I'd take this opportunity to get some sleep. I'll stay with her until the morning in case she wakes up."

"I could take the first shift." Again Reeve spoke before

I could. His offer rubbed me in places that I didn't know were raw. I told myself it was simply because I wanted to be the one by her side.

Well, if he was going to stay, so was I.

But then Jeb said, "I'd rather it be me. I want to be there in case she has any strange reaction to the medicines or in case she takes a turn."

Reeve hesitated before conceding. "Come and find me if there's any change."

"Will do, boss."

"Then I'll see you in a few hours." Without even a glance at me, he turned on his heels and headed for his bedroom.

Jeb gave me a tight smile then opened the door to Amber's room, leaving me in the hallway, alone.

CHAPTER
2

I remained in the hallway for a handful of seconds before following Reeve into his bedroom.

He'd left the door open—whether that was to be available for Amber or an invitation for me, I wasn't sure. I was afraid it wasn't the latter. But I traipsed in anyway. I needed answers. I needed assurance. I was prepared to demand both.

Until I crossed the threshold and saw Reeve undressing.

He peeled off his shirt and tossed it on an armchair then sat on the bed and began tugging at one boot. The sight of his half-naked body made my own body react with a rush of desire, every time, current circumstances notwithstanding. That he was stripping with no sexual intention was somehow even more arousing, the intimacy of it shocking and surreal. As if he and I were actually a couple, and not a sham, despite Amber's return.

That realization did things to me. *He* did things to me. Things that no man had ever done, no matter how deep inside of me he'd been.

"I'm tired, Emily," he said, without a glance in my direction. "It's been a long night. For both of us. So whatever it is that you want to discuss, it's going to have to wait until we've gotten some sleep."

Well, that burst the bubble of affection swelling in my chest. How the fuck was he able to brush me off without giving me even a crumb? With barely an acknowledgment, after everything we'd shared? How could he sleep when the woman he'd cared so much about was broken and beat-up in the next room? And how could he not want to question me about the secrets I'd withheld as much as I wanted to question him?

He knew.

It was the only thing that made sense. Somehow, he *knew.* That I wasn't simply Emily Wayborn, actress and professional girlfriend. That I was Emily Wayborn, formerly Emily Barnes, Amber's best friend. Emily Wayborn, liar. He knew and I was caught and I could barely see straight, could barely get air inside my lungs.

"You knew," I whispered. I'd lied, and he knew, and I needed to hear from him what that meant for us.

He stood to step out of his jeans then pulled back the bedcovers. "I said we'll talk about this in the morning."

I couldn't wait even another minute, not when our entire relationship was on the line. "You knew and you didn't say anything." I'd spent months worrying he'd discover that I'd gotten close to him only to learn what had happened to Amber. Months of monitoring what I said and did, weeks and weeks of keeping my guard up, and he'd already known.

The more I thought about it, I wasn't just anxious but angry. "You knew and you let me go on pretending. How could you?"

He spun toward me, his eyes narrowed with incredulity. *"You're* mad at me? You were the one who came into my life under false pretenses. To use me. And you're mad at *me*?"

My stomach twisted with the guilt, and even though I deserved the accusations, I suddenly didn't have the will to defend myself. "You're right. Let's talk about this in the morning."

I spotted the pile of my clothes I'd left in front of the bathroom earlier and crossed to gather them, already thinking ahead, already planning the picture that I wanted Amber to see. She wouldn't be able to understand without my explanation that I'd hoped she was alive when I began things with him, or that I only let myself fall for him when I believed she wasn't.

That last part was a lie—I never *let* myself anything with him. I never had any control. Now it was obvious—he had been manipulating *me,* not the other way around.

A fresh wave of rage rolled through me. Clutching my clothing to my chest, I swung toward him. "I thought she was dead, Reeve!"

He'd climbed into the bed. Now he sat up, his head tilted as though confused. "Dead?"

"How could you let me believe that?" My throat choked on a sob and I noticed my cheeks were wet. I hadn't realized I was crying.

He took a moment to process. "I had no idea," he said finally, softer than before. Even though he was a skilled liar I had a feeling he was telling the truth. "Why did you think that?"

"Because Joe showed me an autopsy report." *Why the hell didn't* you *think that?* He'd had the same report in his e-mail. But I wasn't ready to let him know that I'd snooped through his things.

His brow furrowed. "The autopsy of that anonymous woman from the Dumpster last fall? How the hell did Joe get ahold of that?"

"He's good at his job," I said snidely, not exactly remembering where Joe had said he'd gotten it.

"Yeah, I guess he is. Except that it wasn't actually a report about Amber, was it?" The hardness was back in his tone, and, instead of regretting that I'd pushed his kindness away, I was grateful that I'd succeeded. I knew what to do with harsh. I didn't know what to do with compassion.

"The description matched her to a T. Including the tattoo on her shoulder." I shuddered remembering how well the report had depicted Amber. I hadn't wanted to believe it was her. I'd fought it as hard as I could. Until I couldn't anymore, and I had to accept it. "I mourned her, Reeve."

Tenderness flickered across his stone features and then disappeared. "If you had bothered to talk to me about it, I could have saved you that grief. But you didn't."

I rolled my eyes and bent to scoop up the panties I'd missed. "Like I could talk to you about that."

"Right. Because I wasn't supposed to know that you were her friend."

"Yes, that was one of the reasons."

"What were the others?" He twisted toward me, throwing his legs off the bed. "Did you think *I* killed her?"

My lips parted, taken aback by his reaction and by how fast he'd jumped to the correct conclusion.

When I took too long to respond, he stood and took an aggressive step toward me. "Tell me, Emily, is that what you thought?"

I shrunk back, holding my clothes to my chest as though they could protect me from him. He started to ask again, and I blurted out, "No. But I thought you might have had someone else kill her."

"The whole time? The whole time we've been together, that's what you thought?"

Yes, it had been what I'd thought. The terrible thing was

that it said as much about myself as it did about him. It was humiliating. That I could be the type of person who would stay with a man who might have killed someone I'd loved—it was difficult to admit.

So I didn't answer him, and that was an answer in itself.

The barely controlled fury in his eyes flared and his features turned to stone, but somehow I understood that what he was really feeling in this moment was disappointment.

I felt that disappointment, too, so vividly, both from him and from myself, and suddenly I understood that I really should have been embarrassed that I'd thought he could have done something that terrible and never talked to him about it. I'd been in a committed relationship with this man for more than two months. I'd let him in, let him consume me, and yet I'd still kept him at a distance, even when I knew he'd tried to let me in.

Now, for the first time, I cared about what I did to Reeve instead of just caring about what he did to me. I'd hurt him, and that felt shitty.

"Look." I sighed, trying to lessen the blow. "I don't know why you think that's an impossible conclusion to jump to. You've done everything in your power to keep me frightened of the things you were capable of."

He laughed, a dark *ha* that held very little humor. "You wanted me like that, Emily. You wanted me to be the man who would frighten you, and don't you try to say for a moment that you didn't."

"Just because it's what I wanted doesn't mean that's not who you really are."

"No. I guess it doesn't." His eyes met mine, and again I saw all the emotion he'd shown me downstairs, his pupils like a dark and turbulent storm. He held me in that gaze for several long seconds.

Then he took another step toward me. "I told you what happened. I told you she left here, alive. You didn't believe me? I thought you trusted me. You *acted* like you trusted me."

It was an opening—a chance for me to fix everything, and I knew it. I'd told him once that, for me, trust equaled love. He'd wanted me to trust him because he'd wanted me to love him. He wanted me to say it now.

But I *didn't* trust him. And I *did* love him. I could have told him that, and it might have made a difference.

Funny how the idea of actually admitting my affection was so much more frightening than believing he was a killer.

Somehow I managed to keep my eyes on him when I spoke next. "I never said I trusted you."

He shook his head in disbelief. "This is not when we have this conversation. Not when we're tired and stressed." He turned back toward the bed.

I swallowed the ball in my throat. "Fine." Then I headed for the door.

"Where are you going? You sleep with me."

Those were the old rules—I slept with him when he was at the ranch. Now that Amber was here, I wasn't sure what the rules were. And if I had rules, surely she'd had rules too. When they'd been together, where had Amber been required to sleep? Surely she hadn't been allowed to sleep alone either.

Jealousy tugged at the pit of my stomach. I pushed it away. "I'm not leaving her side."

"Emily, there's nothing you can—"

I swiveled back in his direction, cutting him off. "I'm not leaving her!"

There was a part of me that wanted to ignore my desperate need to keep vigil in Amber's room and stay instead with Reeve. Though we hadn't yet said everything we'd needed to, I knew enough to understand that he'd forgive me for my wrongs if I let him.

The truth was, I could probably forgive him for his wrongs as well.

But Amber's presence changed everything. I'd made promises to her long before I'd thought about making promises to Reeve. I'd vowed to never come between her and a man, and although she'd left Reeve, I couldn't climb back into his bed until I was sure she understood the circumstances.

"Fine. Don't leave her." Reeve crossed to me in three easy steps. He grabbed my upper arms and pulled me close, his touch sending an unexpected jolt through my veins. I hadn't forgotten what he'd said before she'd shown up. That he'd loved Amber's best friend, and now I was sure that he'd meant me when he said it.

The full force of that hit me now—he *loved* me. He loved me enough to say it out loud.

But he'd loved her too.

He locked his eyes with mine. "This doesn't change anything, Emily. You still belong to me."

He allowed that to settle before he let me go. Then he shut off the light and returned to the bed.

I shut the door behind me and leaned heavily against it. Closing my eyes, I let out a long slow breath, replaying his last words over and over in my head. *You still belong to me. You still belong to me.*

Yes. I did belong to him.

But I belonged to Amber too.

CHAPTER

3

I woke with a start, my heart pounding and my throat dry.

"He just left," a voice said behind me.

Turning, I found Joe sitting on a chair beside the love seat I'd camped out on. His feet were propped up on the arm of the couch, and he was reading something on his cell. The chair he was sitting on had been across the room before, and its new location disoriented me.

Stifling a yawn, I asked, "*Who* just left?"

"Sallis." Joe pocketed his phone and shifted his attention to me. "You called his name just now."

"I did?" I tried to remember what I'd been dreaming but couldn't. Judging by the angle of the light streaming in the window, I'd slept through the morning. "What time is it anyway?"

"It's a little after one." He looked me over. "Have you been here the whole time?"

After leaving Reeve's room earlier, I'd stopped by my room to dump my dirty clothes and shower. The scent of sex had still clung to me and although I was probably the only one who could smell it, I'd needed to get it off of me. Needed to hide any evidence of my relationship with Reeve—for now.

Then I changed into yoga pants and a T-shirt and came down to Amber's room. Jeb had given me the love seat and with his hat over his face, he'd snoozed in the armchair, the one Joe sat in now, when it was still across the room.

"Basically. I don't remember falling asleep." Rubbing the sleep out of my eyes, I noticed a thermos on the side table between us. "Is this for me?"

"I believe so."

Thank God. I took a sip. It wasn't hot but still warm enough to drink so I downed half of it, my eyes on the sleeping figure in the bed across from us. She looked better in the daylight, her skin less pale, her bruises less purple. "Has she woken up at all?"

"Once, when the doctor was here, but the report I got said it was only for a minute. She slept most of the drive here from Chicago too. Pretty much she wakes up to get another pill, and then she's back under. Doc's got her on some sugar water to get her some energy."

"'Doc'," I chortled. "Jeb's a veterinarian. He births cows. We should be getting her to a real M.D."

Joe leaned back in his chair and crossed his ankle over his opposite knee. "Nah. That guy's a people doctor. He might do animal medicine, but he knows what he's doing with her. Leads you to wonder why a ranch would have a full-time doctor on staff posing as a vet. What kind of regular injuries go on around here that they'd need that?"

I looked up, surprised at the implication. Then, as always when it came to anything to do with Reeve, defensive. "There could be any number of reasons."

"Guess that's just part of the Sallis mystery, isn't it?"

He was prodding me, trying to get me worked up, but I didn't have the strength. I pulled my feet up underneath me and studied his profile, his strong jawline, the tattoos that snaked out under the sleeve of his T-shirt, the same one he wore yesterday. He was scruffier than usual, his buzz haircut grown out and his face hidden behind a week-old beard. He was sexy, I noted, in a bad boy kind of way. Which should have done it for me.

Except Joe was only bad boy on the outside. He looked hard and detached, but behind that rough exterior was the heart of a puppy. He was loyal and just. Like Robin Hood—skirting the law but for a greater good.

And that was his problem—he was decent. A little *too* decent for me. I liked my bad boys with a rough core. And when they were packaged in refinement and money, I liked them even more. *Champagne taste*. Amber had taught me well.

Joe tilted his head toward me, catching me staring.

I reddened. "What are you doing here, anyway?"

His grin said he noticed my blush. Said he liked it. "It's my shift to watch Amber."

"You relieved Jeb?"

"Sallis relieved Jeb. I relieved Sallis. It's a four-hour rotation."

I looked down at the thermos in my hand, then at the chair that had been pulled up next to me. "Was that there when your turn started? Or did you put it there?"

"It was there. Why do you ask?"

Then Reeve had moved it here. To be next to me while I slept. He'd also left the coffee. Amber had returned, and he was still caring for *me*. I shouldn't like the warm hum that spread through my chest at that knowledge. Not when it was a victory that pitted me against my friend.

"No reason," I said to Joe. "I'm surprised you're still around. Thought you would have rode off into the sunset by now. Isn't that what you do?"

He chuckled. "Haven't been here long enough to see

sunset yet, have I? Reeve invited me to stay a while. Actually, he encouraged me to stay. I think he wants to figure out what I know. Probably so he can cover his tracks."

"Or so he can protect his ranch. He might not be the bad guy, you know." Those were words I maybe should have been saying to myself. Not that it mattered. His status as antagonist had not been a deterrent in my feelings for him so far.

"That's an interesting change of stance on your part. I'm not sure—"

He didn't get a chance to finish his sentence because Amber opened her eyes then. "Emily?"

I set my coffee down and jumped to her side. "I'm here." I smoothed the hair out of her eyes then said it again. "I'm here."

She cleared her throat. "Water—"

"Yep." Joe was at my side immediately, a plastic cup with a straw in his hand. I helped her sit up, and he held it as she sipped.

"Thank you." She sounded better now, her voice less scratchy.

Joe set her water cup down and propped the pillows up behind her so she could stay sitting on her own. She thanked him again then turned her eyes to me. "You look so fucking good, Em," she said, attempting a smile before remembering her lip was still fat. "Jesus, I must look like shit."

I sat on the bed next to her, grasping one of her hands between both of mine. "You're too skinny. But you were always too skinny. How do you feel?"

"Like I got kicked in the ribs a bunch of times by an asshole." She put her free hand up to her face and pressed tentatively along her cheekbones. "I feel like my face is a giant cream puff. I don't want to see it, do I?"

"Not today," I agreed. "Probably not tomorrow either."

She let out a sound that was half laugh, half groan. "You still know what I need to hear. God, I've missed you, Em." It was hard to read her expression behind the swelling and discoloration, but there was sincerity in her eyes. She maneuvered her hand so that it clutched mine, and for a minute, every bad thing that had happened between us disappeared, and the years that had passed didn't matter at all. She was the Amber I'd always loved and admired, and I was Emily, her protégée. Her best friend.

There was a rustle behind me, and I turned to find Brent at the door. "You're awake. I'll tell Reeve." He was gone again before anyone could respond.

"Nice to see you too, Brent," Amber called after him. "He's such a lackey. Anything you say to him goes straight to Reeve. Unless you're telling him you want him to stick his dick in you. Then he'll be super mum."

"Did you . . . ?" In the short time I'd spent with him, I'd gotten the impression he was a bit of a manwhore. I hadn't been interested in finding out if he'd mess with his boss's girl, and Reeve had made sure I knew in no uncertain terms that I was to remain faithful while I was with him. Had that rule been different for Amber? Or had Reeve put the rule in place because of her?

"With Brent? No way. Doesn't mean he didn't try."

"Hmm." I forced a smile at her attempt to waggle her brows. Inside, though, I felt a familiar stab of resentment. I'd forgotten that about her—forgotten how her ability to charm and seduce any and every man she met was as much a burden to our friendship as it had been a blessing.

It had been easy to forget those kinds of things when I'd thought I'd never see her again.

The seconds that followed felt taut, the strings between us pulling in opposite directions. Amber was the one who finally gave them slack. "But anyway"—she patted my hand—"tell me about you. I want to hear everything."

Everything. Such a big question and yet I could probably fill her in on my life in three sentences—*I'm a voice actress for a hit TV show. I came looking for you when you left our code word on my mother's answering machine.* And *I met Reeve.*

Everything. In a nutshell.

Joe saved me from having to stretch my three sentences into more substantial material. "Hey, I hate to intrude on your reunion, but do you mind if I ask you some questions now that you're back in the land of the living?"

In other words, Joe wanted to get intel before Reeve showed up. As much as it irked me that Joe was always on his case, there were things I wanted to hear as well.

She pulled her blood-matted hair to one side, and I silently made a note to help her bathe later. "I guess I owe you at least that much. After you rescued me and all. He's a hero, you know," she said, winking at me. "You should be proud of him."

"He knows I appreciate him." I narrowed my eyes in Joe's direction, wondering exactly what he'd told Amber about our relationship on their drive together from Chicago. Maybe she'd made her own assumptions. Whichever, I didn't correct her. That could easily lead to having to admit my relationship with Reeve, and I wasn't ready to do that. Yet.

If ever.

Joe ignored my glare. "Amber, what were you doing with Michelis Vilanakis?"

"You don't waste any time, do you?" she teased. "Why is *anyone* with Micha? He's got money and power, and he knows how to get the best drugs." She had a nickname for him. I wanted to ask if everyone called him that or just her.

But I didn't. Because I knew I was just searching for evidence that she had feelings for someone that wasn't Reeve and that wasn't helpful in the moment.

"You were with him of your own free will?" Joe asked.

"Embarrassing as it is to admit, yes. I was." She glanced at me, and I wondered if she was thinking about the men I'd been with who'd treated me similarly. The men I'd been with freely. The men I'd be with freely now. Though the man I was with now hadn't yet bruised me in any place I hadn't wanted to be bruised. And maybe that was the difference.

I interrupted Joe's interrogation. "How did you meet Michelis?"

"Through Reeve."

"They're friends?" He flicked his eyes in my direction. I could feel it even though I kept mine pinned on Amber.

"They're . . . it's complicated." She sighed, leaning back against her pillow. I'd figured out that Michelis was related to Reeve. His uncle, I'd suspected. It seemed like it should be easy to say that they were family. Who was Amber protecting by not admitting that? Reeve or Michelis?

"Is their relationship the reason you left the phone message for Emily last August?"

I lowered my head to study my hands. Reeve had already told me his version of what had happened with Amber. She'd wanted to leave him, and he'd locked her up on the ranch, kept her there against her will.

At least, that's what he'd said. I held my breath waiting for her to confirm that story.

"Uh, no. That was . . ." She trailed off and I peered up to see her gazing out the window. When she looked back at Joe, she said, "That was an overreaction on my part."

"Why are you defending Reeve? What did he do to you?"

"Joe," I warned, suddenly remembering the cameras that were in all of these rooms. Or maybe I would have warned him even if I hadn't been concerned about that. Because I couldn't bear accusations against my lover like I used to.

"I'm not protecting anyone that doesn't deserve it. It was an overreaction. I felt more desperate than I needed to. That's all." Amber's terse tone matched my own. She reached out and touched my knee. "I'm sorry I got you involved, Emily. I didn't mean to send you on a wild goose chase."

I covered her hand with mine. "But if you hadn't left that message, then Joe wouldn't have been where he was when you needed him." And I wouldn't have found you again. I wouldn't have found Reeve.

"Instead I would have been left to die," she said, and since her injuries were not severe enough to lead to death, I knew she meant she would have still been with Vilanakis then. "Right. Good thing I called."

Something about her words felt like she didn't mean them. Perhaps she had feelings for the man who'd repeatedly beat her after all. I could, unfortunately, understand that.

The bed shifted as Joe sat down behind me. I could feel his frustration before he spoke. "Amber, I'm sorry if this is uncomfortable for you to talk about, but I need some more concrete information."

Amber folded her arms over her chest and winced, the gesture probably pulling uncomfortably against her ribs. "You got me back safe. Is there something else you're after? I'm not going to press charges against Micha, if that's where you're going. That's suicide, you know."

Joe wouldn't give up. "Can you tell me anything about the sex slave ring he's involved with then? Were you at all part of that?"

"So that's what this is about. You have grand aspirations if you plan to get involved with that, Joe. It's very noble of you. I had no idea there were still noble men left. Leave it to Emily to find the last."

This time I opened my mouth to correct her.

Joe beat me to speaking. "Do you have any information at—"

"No." Her sharp response said she was frustrated now as well. "I don't know anything about it. Well, nothing concrete. I heard rumors, but that's all. I wasn't involved in it."

"And Sallis?"

Her expression bordered between skeptical and appalled. "Was Reeve involved in slave trade with Michelis Vilanakis? You're kidding me, right?" Her eyes flicked from Joe's to mine and back to Joe's. "Oh, I guess you don't know."

"Don't know what?" Joe and I asked in unison.

"Reeve would never do business with Micha. He loathes him." She looked to me, as though she thought I was the only one who might understand what she was about to say. "It was the reason I was with him. I knew it would make Reeve unhappy."

My stomach dropped. She wanted to make Reeve unhappy. She wouldn't have cared unless she still loved him.

"Amber." His voice behind me caused the ball to sink lower in my gut. In a flash, Reeve was at her side, opposite me in the bed. She reached her arms up to him, and he enfolded his around her.

"I'm so sorry. I'm so, so sorry," she blubbered against his shirt.

"Shh, Angel. You know how I hate it when you cry." He stroked her hair while she sobbed into his chest, and I sat frozen in a hell I'd never known. Whoever had decided that damnation was fire and brimstone was wrong. Hell was cold and ice and emptiness. Hell was watching the one I'd grasped so tightly slip through my fingers. Hell was realizing the one I'd come to love would never choose to love me.

I stood, but couldn't take my eyes off the scene.

"I was stupid," Amber said, and they could have been my own words. "I don't deserve this. I don't deserve for you to let me back here."

"You're always welcome here. You know that." Reeve pulled away from her. With his hands on each side of her face, he issued his own demand for the truth. "Tell me what he did to you. Tell me what he did and then just say the word and I'll fucking kill him."

Grasping at his forearms, she shook her head. "No, Reeve. You don't want to start that. This was all my fault."

"I don't care what you did. He laid his hands on you, and he deserves to pay for that. Just say the word."

I'd asked Reeve once if he was still close to his former lovers. He'd dodged the question. Now I saw the answer firsthand, and whether he was like this with all of them or just Amber didn't matter. That he was like this with her was bad enough. In fact, it was the worst.

"Before you get ahead on your revenge scheming, Sallis, let's get the girl well." Jeb's arrival was like a token sent from heaven. It broke the trance that Reeve and Amber had me in.

I stepped backward, into the shadows, barely aware of the conversation that continued.

"Please tell me it's time for more painkillers," Amber said, almost begging.

"We'll talk about that." Jeb scanned his audience. "Can we maybe have the room cleared so the patient and I can have some privacy?"

Thank God. Because I couldn't be there a moment longer.

Unfortunately, Reeve was escorted out with us, and in the hallway he stopped me before I could escape into my own room. "Jeb got ahold of some methadone. He's going to start a treatment plan that will help her with the pain, and then he can slowly wean her off dependence."

"Awesome. I'm glad you employ ranch staff with such diverse skills for occasions such as this." I couldn't keep the bitterness from my tone. Actually, I didn't even try.

Before he could say anything else, I plowed on. "Meanwhile, I'm hungry, and I believe I've missed lunch. Joe, would you mind taking me into town for something to eat?" I sent a pleading glance to my private investigator.

He darted his eyes from me to Reeve. "It's my shift with Amber. I don't know if I should."

I practically jumped on the end of his statement. "I'm sure Reeve won't mind covering it. I'll take the next shift. Tell her I'll be back in a couple of hours, will you, Reeve?" I didn't look at him. Addressing him was hard enough.

"Emily," my name on Reeve's tongue was like poisoned honey, "perhaps Joe should stay. I can take you into town instead."

I shook my head. "Now that she's awake, I'm sure that Amber would much rather catch up with you. Take the opportunity to spend time with your 'angel.'" Finally, I lifted my eyes to Reeve's. I knew what he'd see there— pain and anger and acid.

I hadn't expected to see the same in his eyes.

Unable to hold his gaze, I spun on my heels, and, this time, with Joe in tow, it was Reeve I left in the hallway, alone.

CHAPTER

4

Lunch with Joe was uneventful. After I'd responded to most of his attempts at conversation with nothing more than one or two syllables he'd gotten the hint and let me eat in silence.

On the drive back, with the possible repercussions of how I'd left things hanging over my head, I remembered something Joe had said earlier. "Reeve actually invited you to stay at the house?" It wasn't like him to trust so easily. Especially another man.

"Eh, he was sketchy at first. When you went upstairs with Amber, he had his men thoroughly pat me down. There may have been a few hostile threats thrown in as well."

"That sounds about right." I didn't add that Reeve probably also ordered a background check and that I was pretty sure we'd been followed into town by Tabor, the man Reeve had hired to watch me. "And that was all?"

Joe pursed his lips, and I could tell he was keeping something from me. "What else did he say, Joe?" My mind whirred through the possibilities, with the deals he might have had to make in order to win Reeve's trust.

"I'll tell you, but I don't want you to overreact."

My scowl told him I wasn't promising anything.

"He said I could stay as long as I agreed that I was there to protect you."

A host of reactions flew through my brain, a few of them in such opposition that I didn't know how to choose one to express. It irritated me that he'd think he should make those kinds of arrangements without my permission or knowledge, but I was also thrilled that he cared.

Or maybe that was wishful thinking, and he just wanted to be in control.

I leaned my head against the glass window and nibbled on my knuckle. "I don't know what that means," I said finally.

Joe threw a glance toward me then returned his focus to the road. "I don't either. I don't know why he thinks you might be in danger. Whether he thinks Vilanakis might come around or if he's worried that you'll do something stupid again."

"Or maybe he's passing me to you so he won't feel guilty when he takes Amber back into his arms." Immediately, I felt stupid for admitting that to Joe. "Anyway. It's fine. As long as he's letting you stay."

"It's an informal agreement, Em. He's not paying me. I can leave when I want. Likely it means nothing and is just a way to show me he's in charge. Ignore it."

Possible. But I wouldn't bet on it.

"How long are you planning on sticking around, then? If you can leave when you want, I mean." In other words, how long would *I* be allowed to stick around?

"Depends," he said, turning down the long road to the ranch main gates. "I'd like to pursue Vilanakis, but only if you're okay with that."

"Of course." Why he thought he needed my permission was beyond me. Unless he wanted me to ask him to stay, which I wouldn't. "You can go wherever you need to go for that. I'll be fine." I was actually being truthful with Joe for once. It felt more liberating than I'd imagined.

Joe surprised me with his next words. "Where I need to go for that is nowhere." He paused at the gate, not saying anything while the guard was at the window clearing us for entrance.

When we were in, I turned to him. "You don't think Reeve is still connected to that slave ring, do you?"

"I don't have a strong reason to believe he is, no. Especially not if that's why he thinks you need protection. But he and Amber know more about Vilanakis than anyone else I've come in contact with. I don't think I can get a better lead than through them."

I chewed another finger as he parked the car, trying to decide if I wanted to share what I knew with Joe, and if so, how much. I didn't want to betray Reeve but Joe had rescued Amber. I owed him, didn't I?

Grabbing his arm, I stopped him before he got out of the car. "I'll tell you this, Joe—there are cameras in every room of that ranch. So be careful what you say or do."

"I've seen them. But thanks for the heads-up."

"Also"—I took a deep breath, already having decided to spill the secret—"Reeve's mother, Elena Kaya? Her real name is Elena Vilanakis."

Joe's expression lifted with the information. "Reeve's related to Michelis?"

"Michelis is his uncle. But Elena wanted to leave the mob life. Reeve's father took her away from all of it. Changed her name. Hid her away."

"It explains the bad blood between Michelis and Sallis."

"It does." There. I wasn't throwing Reeve under the bus at all. I was actually reinforcing my opinion that Michelis was the enemy instead. "They aren't tied anymore. Blood or no blood."

"Possibly." Joe tilted his head. "Or they're extremely good at their cover."

Well, there was that. I believed Reeve probably skirted the line when it came to legal business practices, but did I truly think he could cross it?

I still didn't know him well enough to have the answer.

I didn't go up to Amber's room when we got back. Reeve would be there, and I wasn't eager to see him. I also didn't make it too hard for him to find me, settling down in the den with the remote in hand, not actually planning to watch anything at all.

I'd only just turned on the TV when he breezed through, barely glancing at me on his way. "Emily. My office. Now."

My heart pattered in the way it always did when he ordered me around, and my hands began to sweat like they always did when I feared I'd displeased him. My nerves tingled with the excitement that always accompanied both.

With only a second of hesitation, I set down the remote and followed him.

The ornate double doors to his office were open. I hadn't been in his office at the ranch before, and I was struck by the warm tones that accentuated the masculine décor, a stark contrast to the clean lines of his minimalistic LA office. This space had a homey feel to it that was absent from the other, yet it was still strongly charged with the authority and success that defined Reeve Sallis.

Especially now, when the man was standing in front of his desk in full-command mode.

"Shut the doors," he said, his tight tone an invisible string that tugged on my arousal button.

It felt like I was moving through molasses as I pushed

the heavy doors into their frame. The soft click of the latch echoed loudly in my ears as if instead it were the clang of metal hitting metal at the closing of a jail cell. Being alone in a room with Reeve wasn't necessarily like being in a prison. But it would most certainly be a trap. And I'd most definitely been caught.

When I turned to face him, Reeve's expression was cold stone as he gestured to the chair in front of his desk. "Sit down."

"I'd rather st—"

"Sit."

I sat, my face flushed from both the heat of his directive and the humiliation of how easily I obeyed. Determined to not cower, I straightened my spine. This confrontation was a long time coming. I should have been prepared.

Seemingly satisfied with my deference, Reeve leaned on the desk behind him. "Joe Cook," he said.

So we'd start there. I was tempted to spill everything, but wasn't sure exactly what Reeve was after, and I wasn't ready to show my whole hand yet. "What about him?"

The grip of his hands tightened on the edge of the desk. "Define your relationship."

I crossed my arms over my chest. "He works for me." *And he works for you, apparently.*

"Go on."

Silly as it was, I'd half-hoped that this would be more of a conversation and less of a showdown. That there would be a give-and-take in the information we shared.

But Reeve's approach was that of an interrogator. So that hope dissolved and I had to choose if I was going to be cooperative or combative.

It was the intensity of my body's reaction to him that decided my course. The way my torso automatically leaned forward to be closer to him. The way my pulse tripped at the potency of his presence. I'd be obliging. For now.

I sighed. "He's a private investigator. I hired him to help me find Amber." There they were—my first cards laid.

His eyes narrowed at me, and the vein in his neck bulged, but he said nothing, as if waiting for more.

"Jesus," I huffed, "say what you want to know already. It's so awkward to guess what you're looking for when you obviously know most of it on your—"

He cut me off. "Did you fuck him?"

"What?" I was so taken aback, the question came out before I had a chance to stop it.

"You heard me."

"Yes, I heard you." I slumped back in my chair. Really? This was where he was going first?

Of course it is, I chastised myself. It was how he'd reacted when he'd found me with Chris Blakely. Strange how it stung so much when I shouldn't have been surprised.

Even stranger that he would ask Joe to protect me if he was worried that I was sleeping with him. The man was such a bundle of contradictions, it made my head hurt.

"Well?" Reeve's impatient tone only added insult to injury.

"I love how you automatically assume I'm sleeping with every man I come in contact with. Are you going to choke me with your cock now so I learn to never have relationships with men that aren't you again?"

Even the reminder of the cruel way he'd treated me after I'd been with Chris didn't cause him to flinch. "You'd like that too much. Answer the question."

"No." I raised my chin defiantly. "I won't give you anything else until you give me something."

He let out a patronizing chuckle. "That's not how this works, Emily."

"Maybe it's not how it worked before, but it's how it's working now." Somewhat stunned by my own bravado, I barreled on before I had a chance to second-guess myself. "How long did you know that I knew Amber?"

He ticked his head dismissively. "It doesn't matter. Did you fuck Joe Cook?"

Exasperated, I dropped my hands to my side. "It doesn't matter to you, but it matters a whole hell of a lot to me. And, frankly, my question is much more relevant than whether or not I've gotten naked with Joe."

"It's relevant if I say it's relevant."

I rolled my eyes and started to stand, but Reeve sprang forward and stopped me. His hands gripped on both arms of the chair, he caged me in. "Did. You. Fuck. Him?"

He was so close. And so angry. So angry and so close. He could lean down and kiss me in the blink of an eye. Or strangle me. Or pull me to my knees, where I knew he wanted me. Where I would fall so naturally into the role I craved.

But that wasn't the best role for me at the moment, no matter how much I wanted to play it. And I'd grown with Reeve. I could be strong with him when I needed to be.

So I threw my shoulders back and narrowed my eyes. "If you have to ask, then you don't deserve to know the answer." I pushed at his arm, astonished when he let me brush it away, and stood. I turned to go.

In a heartbeat, he was at the door in front of me, blocking my exit.

"Let me go." I kept my eyes forward, refusing to meet his. I felt his pull, though. Felt the puppet string at my head, tugging my chin up to look at him, to obey him, to submit.

But I kept my eyes forward. Because if I didn't, I'd crumble. If I didn't, I'd be back under his thumb, and while I wanted to be there, I didn't want to be there like this.

Several seconds passed. Seconds that stretched and yawned and made my pulse tick higher and the back of my neck sweat. Seconds that chipped away at my resolve and began to uncover my fear.

Then, finally, he shifted, and I flinched.

But he only moved to open the door and let me out.

I made it to my room before I fell apart. There, with the wood of my own door at my back, I sunk to the floor and gasped for breath between sobs. He could have made me answer him. He could have forced me. Could have grabbed me or choked me or physically hurt me in a myriad of ways. He was that strong. He was that capable. He could have done so much.

The worst part was that he didn't.

CHAPTER
5

I managed to avoid Reeve until much later that evening. I'd spent much of my time with Amber, hoping for a chance to talk, but just as content to be near her. She'd slept off and on through the afternoon and when I thought I might have a shot, she decided she felt well enough to have more visitors. Word had gotten out among the ranch staff that she was back, and, apparently, many of them had been fond of her.

Which wasn't surprising.

Feeling the odd man out, I curled up on the love seat in her room while Brent and Parker, the stable manager, doted over her along with a handful of other cowboys I'd seen around but never spoken more than two words with. Even Cade, one of the men who worked the surveillance room, seemed to be friendly with Amber.

She'd been here longer, I told myself. Of course she'd have more friends. Of course she'd fit in as though they were her family and she wasn't just the ranch owner's fuck toy. Because she hadn't been that for Reeve like I had been. Like maybe I still was.

Joe seemed to be the only one who noticed my withdrawal. He sat on the arm of the couch next to me, and I tensed at his nearness when he leaned in and said, "She sure has a lot of fans."

I hugged my knees to my chest and smiled bitterly. "Oh, yes. Everyone always loves Amber best."

"Not everyone."

Uneasiness ran through me as I assumed he was talking about himself, but when I followed the line of his gaze, I found Reeve at the end of it. Reeve, who, despite Amber's presence in the room, was looking at me.

Around midnight, I slipped out and went to my room to shower and change for bed. Having expected to primarily sleep naked when I'd packed, I had to be creative with what to wear, settling on an oversized T-shirt that barely hit the tops of my thighs. It covered enough, I decided. The only person who might be bothered by the length was Reeve, and I didn't really mind bothering him at the moment.

Back in Amber's room, I was almost disappointed to find he'd left. Well, everyone had left, and now only Jeb was there changing her IV.

"Tomorrow," he said, tapping the line to get the fluid moving, "I want to get you on real food. If you tolerate a soft breakfast and lunch, you might be able to join everyone downstairs for dinner."

"You know how much I love dinner," Amber teased, and the way Jeb laughed made me sure I'd missed an inside joke.

I picked up the laptop on the bed next to her. "Are you still using this?"

She shook her head. "I'm done with it. Thank you."

I closed the lid and set the computer on the top of the dresser, Then I stretched out beside her in the full-size bed and waited for Jeb to finish his checkup. "I'm on shift with you until four," I said. "So I'll be over on the sofa if you need me. Unless you want me to climb under the covers with you here."

She turned awkwardly onto her uninjured side to face me, flinching slightly with the movement. "Remember when we used to share that twin at your mom's house?" Her eyes twinkled with the memory. It was infectious. "We used to stay up half the night talking."

"You need rest, not talking," Jeb scolded.

She peered at him over her shoulder. "I won't be able to keep my eyes open for longer than ten minutes, so quit your worrying. When did you turn all prison guard, anyway?"

"Maybe when you started acting like someone who needed to be kept in line."

"Fair enough." Her expression was somber when she turned back toward me, and I wondered if Jeb's comment had her thinking the same things I was. About how Reeve had "kept" her before. I didn't think Jeb had known about that, so his comment was made innocently, but it had to hit home with Amber. Did she regret that she'd ever got involved with a man who wanted to guard her? Or did she regret that she'd ever left him?

Whatever her regrets were or weren't, I didn't like seeing the pain that was now etched in her features. I preferred the glow she'd had when talking about the past.

"You used to spoon me," I said, attempting to rekindle that glow. She'd been the first person I'd ever slept in the same bed with. I could still recall the warmth of her body next to mine, how it made me feel safe and protected and cared for in ways I'd never been. In so many ways, she'd been my first love, and, while I'd never been attracted to her sexually, I'd been attracted to everything else about her. Especially to the way she'd made me feel about myself.

"I did spoon you. You hated that."

"I did not. I liked it."

She shrugged her shoulder as though she knew full well that I'd liked it and had just wanted to hear me say it. "You liked it until I'd throw my leg over you, and then you'd bitch about feeling crowded, and somehow you'd always end up on the floor."

Actually, I'd liked it when she'd done that too. Liked how it had made me feel owned. I'd only ever moved out of the bed for her—because she was a restless sleeper, and I'd always ended up feeling like I was in her way.

Those weren't things I needed to admit though. Not now. "So, I'll take the couch."

She laughed. "When I'm better though," she said, her expression suddenly serious, "I'd really like to talk to you. When I'm sure I won't fall asleep halfway through the conversation."

"I'd really like that too."

I slept fitfully on the love seat, and when Brent came to relieve me at a quarter to four, I didn't feel the least bit ready for bed. My head was too buzzed and my emotions too tangled. For several minutes, I stood outside of Reeve's closed door, wishing I had the courage to knock or just go in.

But I didn't.

Instead, I grabbed slippers and a blanket from my room, then tiptoed downstairs and out to the front porch.

It was warm for Wyoming in April, or so I'd been told, meaning that the crisp early morning temperature hovered around forty. Wrapping the blanket around me, I took in a deep breath of air and let it out with a sigh. Why did I feel so miserable? Amber was alive. And I was with her again. It was what I wanted, why I'd started down this whole path.

I leaned against the railing and stared up at the stars. If only my head could be as clear as that night sky.

"She used to talk about you."

I straightened at the sound of Reeve's voice behind me, knowing immediately the "she" he referred to. I didn't turn around, too scared that he'd stop talking when I so badly wanted him to say more.

He went on. "Bragged about you, actually. When she saw your picture in the magazines she'd beam with pride. 'That's my friend, Emily,' she'd say. 'I always knew she'd be a star.'"

She'd talked about me.

All the time I'd assumed she'd moved on with her life, never thinking about me at all.

I pivoted slowly toward his voice and found him sitting in the shadows on the porch swing. He brought a beer bottle to his mouth and took a swallow.

My cheeks warmed as I realized what else he was telling me. "Then you always knew who I was. From the very beginning." God, what a fool I'd been, thinking I'd pulled anything over on Reeve Sallis. He could have silenced me real quick if he'd wanted to. "Why did you even get mixed up with me?"

Though I couldn't make out his face, I saw his head tilt, felt his eyes piercing through me. "I knew who you were. I didn't know what your game was."

I was silent as I tried to put myself in his position. He'd had a bad breakup with Amber, and she'd left him to be with his enemy for no reason but to piss him off. Then, I'd shown up and flirted my way into his company. What the hell must he have thought I was after?

"At first I thought she'd sent you," he said, as if reading my mind. "To test me or to mock me in some way. When you started asking questions about her around the resort, I decided you were trying to pin something on me. Either on your own or with her, I wasn't sure."

"No."

"I figured that out soon enough. You were gone by then."

I'd left because he'd scared me off. No wonder he'd been such an asshole to me at his resort—he'd thought I was the one who'd been cruel.

I leaned back against the railing. "Then you bumped into me at the award show."

"I came *looking* for you at the award show. I did some investigating and tied your questions to the ones that a certain private investigator was asking and realized that you'd been looking for Amber. Which meant you didn't know where she was. I helped you out by sending the picture of her with Michelis to Joe. Do you know which one?"

The anonymous picture that Joe had received of Amber with another man. It had proved that she'd been alive after she'd left Reeve. "Yes. I know which one."

"I thought that would lead you in another direction. Get me off the hook, so to say."

"Why did you even care?"

"Because I wanted you. And I didn't want her to be the reason you wanted me."

Goose bumps skated down my skin that had nothing to do with the cold. I pulled the blanket tighter around me anyway.

I liked this, though—this talking. Sharing. Trying to understand each other. It was worth exposing myself when he was doing the same. Somehow it felt even more intimate than anything we'd done with our bodies. It made me hopeful. He was trying and that meant . . . well, it meant something.

"I'm guessing the photo didn't work." He ran his palm up and down on his thigh.

Was he warming his hand up? Or was he nervous? "It almost did. Except I recognized the ring on his finger, and I'd seen pictures of you and him together."

"Clever." He sounded impressed. But then a beat passed, and when he spoke again, his voice was low and raw. "I didn't know. I thought you'd let your search go."

He'd thought I'd been with him honestly. I was surprised how much it stung to watch him realize I hadn't been. "I'm sorry."

"You were being a good friend to someone I care about. You shouldn't apologize for that." His words were dismissive, but his tone belied them. He couldn't pretend that what I'd done hadn't affected him. He'd let me in too far, and I knew him too well.

I'd let him in too far too. So far that it prickled at me when he said he cared about Amber. So far that I was almost glad that he'd been hurt.

I moved to the swing to sit next to him. Pulling my legs underneath me, I faced him. "I *did* let my search go eventually, Reeve. I wasn't looking for her anymore." I didn't tell him that I'd only given it up a few hours before Amber had turned up. The point was that I'd been there honestly in the end. I'd been there honestly for quite some time, actually.

He put his arm on the back of the swing, his fingers resting so close to my shoulder I could almost feel them brush against me. I *wished* they would brush against me.

But he kept them just out of reach.

He studied me. "You stopped searching because you thought she was dead."

"Yes, but then I wanted to know what happened to her. And then . . ." Only the day before, I'd had Reeve's office keys in my possession. I'd planned to sneak in and watch the camera feeds of when Amber had been there, hoping they'd tell me what had happened to her.

Except, I hadn't. Because I'd decided it didn't matter. Because I'd decided I cared about Reeve more than I cared about the truth.

"And then?" Reeve prompted. Even when he was gentle, he dominated me.

"And then, there came a point that I didn't."

"But you still didn't trust me."

But I loved you.

I still loved him.

And I still couldn't say it. So I said the next best thing instead. "I trust you more than I've trusted almost anyone."

"I guess that's something."

It was so much more than just something. It was everything to me. The only other person I'd ever trusted had been Amber, and, in the end, even she'd betrayed my trust.

Maybe my statement had been wrong. Maybe I trusted Reeve more than *everyone*.

But I didn't correct myself because it didn't matter. What he really wanted to hear were the other words, the words I couldn't give. He'd danced around it, too, though. He'd suggested he loved me, but he'd never told me outright. Those words stood so prominently that they'd become a barrier between us. Either they'd been a lie, a cruel response to my scheming, or they'd been truthful—a possible doorway leading to something else. Something more.

Damn, how I wanted the more. Wanted it enough to brave broaching the subject. "You said things the other night, Reeve—"

He jumped in, turning his head to meet my eyes straight on. "I meant them."

"Oh."

Oh.

There was so much to say in response and yet nothing at all came to mind. And as wary as I was to fully trust him, I believed him. Many men had proclaimed their love for me—usually when I had my mouth around their dick—but it had never been sincere. The plethora of false variations had been enough to teach me that this version was the real thing.

But Reeve had said he'd loved Amber that night as well. And I believed that too.

"I want you sleeping in my bed, Emily."

Or perhaps I was wrong about everything, and his devotion was tied up in sex like all the other men I'd known.

I considered retorting back something sassy about not always being able to get what you want. But I wasn't quite sure that was an adage that Reeve understood. Besides, I wanted to be sleeping in his bed as well, and maybe I would be eventually. If it was really where he wanted me. If I was really the one he wanted there.

I knew I should just ask—*how do you feel about Amber now? What happens next between us?* It was on the tip of my tongue, the questions preformed in my mouth when I decided to swallow them instead. Because I wasn't sure I was ready to hear those answers—whatever they may be—and, in this moment, at least, *I* was what he desired. And maybe it was just an excuse to not have to think about her for a minute, to not worry about feeling guilty or like I'd betrayed her. As long as I didn't know, I could blame my behavior on ignorance, and I could please him too.

The swing rocked as I shifted to my knees. Ignoring the chill of the seat against my bare shins, I leaned forward and unfastened Reeve's jeans.

"This isn't my bed," he said, not moving to either help me or stop me.

"It's the best I can do right now."

He'd gone commando, a sign that he'd likely tried to sleep as well, then had thrown his clothing on when he found the effort futile. I rubbed my hands together, heating them with friction before I reached in for his cock.

Just as I lowered my lips to his tip, he said, "That 'right

now' insinuates that there will be a time that you can do more."

I didn't want to answer, afraid of giving too much of myself away. Afraid that he wouldn't like my reasons for not being with him fully or that he'd try to talk me out of worrying about Amber's place in all of this.

So I occupied my mouth in other ways that prevented talking.

I began, kissing his tip as I massaged his shaft. He wasn't ready, but it was cold. For a few minutes I wondered if it were too cold, or if he were possibly resisting me. Whether he was or not, he was certainly not participating. He kept one arm on the back of the swing and the other at his side while I licked at his head. After several swipes of my tongue, I got more aggressive, sucking his crown then taking the whole of him, heating him up in the warm hollow of my mouth.

Soon he was fully erect and pulsing against the back of my throat.

I sucked him deep, stroked him hard. I knew him well enough to know he liked his blow jobs best if I suffered a bit while giving them. That was easier to achieve when he was in charge—when he pulled at my hair and pushed my head to take him at his tempo.

Without his directing, I concentrated on his pleasure and considered any discomfort I had as a bonus. The more I gagged, the more my legs tingled and ached underneath me, the harder it was for me to breathe, the better I knew it was for him. For both of us.

He remained silent while I worked him up. When my hand started to cramp, I gripped his thighs and used only my mouth, bobbing up and down, my lips pressing tightly down the length of him. The first clue I had that my efforts were succeeding was when his muscles tensed under my palms.

The second clue was when his hand left the back of the swing and squeezed the side of my breast.

"Ah," I moaned, the sound reverberating against his shaft. He bucked up into my mouth in response. Selfishly, I fell to my side, letting the blanket fall off my shoulder to offer him better access to my tits.

He took my offer, crushing the heel of his hand into my ample flesh as he pinched at my nipple so hard that tears pricked my eyes. So hard that my moans turned to sobs. So hard that I was wet. Dripping.

Then his hand was no longer on my tit, but between my thighs. He nudged my top leg up and pushed away the cloth barrier of my panties and shoved several fingers into me at once. He wasn't gentle as he probed me, viciously stroking against the sensitive inner wall of my pussy like my itch was his own. Almost immediately, I was tightening around him. He knew what I liked too.

Or, more likely, we just liked the same thing.

I fought against the pleasure, trying to keep my focus on him, on his cock in my mouth, his crown at the back of my throat, but the more I attempted to ignore what he was doing, the harder he fucked me. My orgasm pushed against my restraint, threatening to burst like the dark clouds of a spring storm.

Just when I thought I couldn't hold back any longer, when my rhythm had begun to stutter and my concentration waned, he spoke, his voice rough and raw as he gave me permission to let go. "Do it."

At his command, I surrendered, erupting over his hand in a flood. My jaw went slack as I yielded to the pleasure, as I tumbled into ecstasy.

I was still trembling and blissed out when Reeve gathered me into his lap, facing out.

"On your knees," he said. I obeyed, putting a shaky

hand out on the arm of the swing to balance myself as he tugged my panties down my thighs. He notched his cock at my hole, then roughly pulled me down, sheathing him completely.

I cried out at the sudden fullness. He gave me no time to adjust, immediately adopting a rapid tempo that inspired my waning orgasm to rebuild. Had it really only been a day since he'd been inside me? It felt like so much longer. Like I'd been hungry for him for weeks. Like I'd been starving and now I was easily filled, easily glutted.

I fell back against his chest and succumbed to the onslaught of sensation. Every nerve in my body was alight. The blanket had been abandoned in the shift of positions and the cold air felt sharp against my hot skin. My nipples burned, goose bumps covered every square inch of my exposed limbs, and the sweat on my forehead felt like melted ice.

Reeve was lost to his own lust. With a hand over my mouth and another on my hip, he pounded into me with a relentless drive. I felt his mouth on my neck, felt his thighs tighten under mine, felt the tip of his cock reach so deep inside me that I thought he'd tear me apart.

And then he did—he hit me in a spot that sent the second orgasm ripping through me, shredding me into so many pieces that I was sure there were parts of me I'd never recover.

"You feel me," he said while my cunt clenched around him like a vice-grip. "Right now you feel me, Emily. That's where I am—inside you. All the time, I'm there. No matter whose bed you sleep in."

I let out a sob, muffled by the heel of his palm. It was a cry of both pleasure and pain, of both release and imprisonment. He'd let my body soar, let me take flight amid the stars. But then he'd anchored me, yanking me back to him with only a handful of sentences. Maybe it was selfish how he made sure that no matter how far I drifted, I would always be tied to him, but I liked it.

Reeve reached his own finish on the tail of his speech. His tempo grew ragged, then, with a final thrust, he let out a feral grunt and came.

After, we stayed unmoving, our breaths creating a small haze around our mouths as hot air expelled into near freezing night. The sting of the chill became more noticeable as I settled, as well as the tingle of my feet, which had fallen asleep in my bent position. But when I started to move off of him, Reeve wrapped his arms around me and held me tight, so tight that I could barely breathe. The gesture had both romantic overtones and an edge of desperation.

I was grateful to be facing away from him, so he couldn't see the tears pricking at my eyes. So he couldn't know how much he moved me, how much he always moved me.

We went into the house together, climbing the stairs in comfortable silence. At the top, when it was time to part to our separate rooms, we hesitated together. With his eyes he invited me again. No, it was more than an invitation. It was a strong tug at my invisible leash.

But I stood planted, and though it wouldn't have taken much additional force to pull me with him, he dropped my lead with a nod and turned toward his door.

"Reeve," I called out quietly, unable to let him leave without giving him something.

He paused, his expression masked. "Yes?"

"I didn't sleep with Joe," I said. "I've never kissed him or thought of him sexually, and I have no desire to in the future."

He smiled, a smug, knowing smile that did wicked

things to my insides. "Good." Then, without any trace of humor he said, "Because otherwise I'd kill him."

Without waiting for a response, he spun on his heels and disappeared behind his door, leaving me with a racing heart and the shuddering certainty that he'd meant what he said.

CHAPTER

6

I woke to banging on my bedroom door.

With one lid still shut, I checked the bedside clock. It was just after nine. The banging began again.

"Just a minute," I groaned. After giving myself ten seconds to blink the sleep out of my eyes, I threw the covers off and stumbled out of bed.

I cracked the door open and found Joe on the other side.

"I need to talk to you," he said, his tone tense. "Can I come in?"

I was still wearing only a T-shirt, and, though I would have been comfortable in less in front of most anyone, I thought of Reeve and knew he wouldn't approve. "Uh, give me five."

Four minutes later, I'd donned a fresh shirt and leggings and had brushed both my teeth and hair. I opened the door, and Joe took a step as if to come in.

"It would be better out there." I gestured to the hall. Reeve's door was open, I noticed, which meant he was awake and likely wouldn't ever know if Joe and I talked in my room.

But the security cameras. But the perception.

I'd learned not to make the same mistakes twice.

Joe's expression said he would have preferred privacy, but he didn't argue. "Something is going around the Internet today that I think you need to see."

"Okay. What is it?"

He looked at the phone he clutched to his chest as if he had the article or post or tweet—whatever it was—loaded to show.

Before he handed it to me, though, he paused. "I need to preface. A week or so ago, Chris Blakely was blasting social media with insinuations that Reeve might have been involved with the mafia and possibly got off with murdering Missy Mataya. I'm not sure if you were aware."

I grimaced. "I'm aware."

"If any of his accusations are anywhere close to truth, he could get himself in big trouble with the likes of Vilanakis."

"Right. But you know what? He's on his own with that. I told him to keep his trap shut, and he couldn't. Too bad for him."

"Also, too bad for you." He unlocked his phone and handed it to me. "Because now you're involved too."

With my brows pinched, I grabbed the cell from Joe's hand and studied the screen. The picture at the top of the page was of Chris and me at an award show we'd both attended in January. The photographer had caught me mid-laughter, which somehow made the photo look intimate even though we weren't even standing close enough to touch. I remembered the night well. He'd been waiting for his fiancée to return from the bathroom, and, in between flirting with me, he'd told me about his connection with Missy.

The image was innocuous, but the headline that accompanied it was concerning. *Busted: Chris Blakely and NextGen Voice Star's Torrid Affair!*

"What the fuck?"

I scanned through the rather uninformative article that claimed Chris and I had been seeing each other on the sly. Rumors about Hollywood figures were common enough, and I was just about ready to dismiss the whole thing when my eyes landed on the final image of the post—a blurry photo that showed the two of us in an embrace outside his apartment. That picture had been taken only a couple of weeks prior. It was from the day that I'd seen him for information about Reeve and Missy. The day that Reeve had shown up at my house upset about the perception I was giving the public by being alone with Chris when I was in a relationship with him.

Suddenly I had a headache.

"Where did they even get this picture?" It wasn't something that I thought Joe could answer. "And why is it only showing up now?"

He shrugged. "But if Vilanakis is connected to Missy's death in any way," Joe said, "and if he knows you're connected to Reeve, well, he might finger you as the leak to Chris because of this."

Reeve had assured me that he'd had nothing to do with Missy's tragic end, but he'd never said anything that had cleared his family of responsibility. And if Joe was right—if Vilanakis *had* caused her death—this certainly did put a bad light on me.

More urgently, if Reeve believed the article's claims, then that could mean trouble for both Chris and me.

I had to set the record straight. "Has Reeve seen this?"

"Not sure. But it's all over the gossip sites. Twitter's having a field day with it."

"Do you know where he is?"

"His office, I believe."

I handed his phone over, already in motion. Joe followed on my heels, as I bolted down the stairs and to Reeve's office. The doors were closed when we got there, but I burst in without bothering to knock.

"It's not true," I said, without any preamble. If Joe had already found the article, I was certain Reeve had as well. The only mystery was why he hadn't come to see me about it yet.

Reeve was sitting behind his desk, and he glanced up at our arrival before turning his attention back to his computer. "Good morning, Emily. Joe. Come right on in." His tone was laced with annoyance that seemed more to do with our abrupt entrance than anything else.

Perplexed by his otherwise cool attitude, I repeated my claim of innocence. "I know you saw the article, and I'm telling you, it's not true."

Reeve sat back in his chair and looked from me to Joe then back to me again. Finally, he said, "I know."

"You *know*?" I was happy that he believed me but more than a little surprised that I hadn't had to convince him. "*How* do you know?"

"Because, first of all, you're with me." Maybe Reeve had learned a thing or two about me as well. Like, when I'm committed to a guy, I'm committed.

"Secondly," he continued, "that picture in the article is one of mine. The embrace it's depicting has already been explained as innocent." He eyed me as he spoke the last part, his expression saying, *I trust you, even if you don't trust me.*

Warmth shot through me even as I recalled the spiteful manner in which he'd treated me when obtaining that explanation.

"What do you mean it's yours?" Joe asked, but I had a feeling I already knew the answer.

"It was a picture that one of my men had taken."

I'd thought I'd been followed that day. Then, when Reeve had shown up at my house in a rage over my afternoon with Chris, I'd *known* I'd been followed. He'd been jealous and mean, but, as embarrassing as it was to admit even to myself, I'd liked it.

I was pretty sure, though, that it wasn't something Joe would understand.

"A bodyguard took the photo," I said, covering for Reeve's behavior.

Reeve, however, didn't seem to think he needed me to protect him. "An investigator," he corrected. "I'd had Emily followed. These were the pictures he'd taken and e-mailed me."

Joe's gaze narrowed. "Is that something you normally do—have your girlfriends followed?" His terse, accusing tone made my spine prickle.

Reeve was quick to respond. "When I know they've hired someone to investigate me first? Yes. I do."

Just like that, Reeve had both defended his questionable actions and divulged that he'd known Joe had been hired to research him. *Impressive.* I lowered my head, hiding my grin.

"Emily is already aware of that, though," Reeve went on, "so there's no need to make it an issue now."

Feeling Joe's eyes on me, I looked up and gave him a reassuring smile.

Joe seemed hesitant, but he conceded. "No issue made. What I'm more concerned about is if this article is going to mean trouble for her."

Reeve's expression said he knew what sort of trouble Joe was referring to. "I'm handling it."

"Thank you." My gratitude was blotted with unease. Reeve's version of *handling it* would likely lead to him discovering that I *had* slept with Chris. It had been long before Reeve, but after his numerous jealous outbursts, I wasn't sure the timing of our fling would soothe him at all.

Which meant I needed to tell him myself, before he uncovered it. He might react poorly, but it would be better than waiting and worrying.

" *'Handling it,'* " Joe repeated. "Just out of curiosity, is that a euphemism?"

Reeve let a few seconds pass, which I guessed was to temper his response. "It means I'm looking into the source of the article as well as reasons it might have been released, besides for the purpose of mere fodder for the masses. I'm also feeling out my sources to see if anyone is up in arms over Blakely's other recent revelations in the media."

He glanced at me but then directed his next words solely to Joe. "But, as long as she's with me, she's safe, no matter what's discovered from my research."

Reeve's possessive words hit all my hot buttons like a mallet glissando on a xylophone.

Joe raised a skeptical brow. "Are you sure? If this was one of your guy's photos, how did someone else get ahold of it?"

"And why is this coming out now?" I added. The pictures were several weeks old, which was a lifetime in Hollywood.

"Those are exactly my questions. Either someone hacked my e-mail or my investigator's. My guess is that the photo was an accidental find by someone searching for access to my bank accounts. The hacker likely saw it and recognized an opportunity to make a little money by selling the image to the paparazzi."

Reeve's supposition was very probable. Secure databases containing private e-mails were breached every day. I supposed even a control freak billionaire wasn't immune to cybercriminal activity.

Joe was less willing to buy the theory. "Are you positive this man of yours is someone you can trust?"

"Anatolios has worked for me for over ten years and is the most faithful employee I have." Reeve's right-hand man was nothing if not loyal. "But, of course, I'm researching every possibility."

Joe's body remained tight and his expression uncertain. "I'm sure you'll understand if I want to do some research of my own."

"Of course I'll understand." Reeve's smile was smug. "I appreciate that, actually, as well as your immediate response to something you recognized as a possible threat. It means a lot to me."

Understandably, Joe didn't seem to know how to take Reeve's acknowledgment. "Yeah. No problem."

Great. Now there were two people digging into my relationship with Chris.

Joe shifted as though he were getting ready to leave, but he stopped when Reeve asked, "Emily, what's wrong?"

I hadn't realized my distress was so transparent. But perhaps it was a good thing to disclose my past in Joe's presence. Reeve would have to control his temper then, wouldn't he?

"Nothing's wrong," I said, slowly. "Exactly. Just, if both of you are going to be looking into Chris and me, then there's something I should tell you." I took a deep breath and forced my eyes to meet Reeve's. "We've been friends for several years, and, in the past, the friendship did have a . . . uh, physical nature."

A shadow fell over Reeve's face, but he disciplined his features.

Joe was smart enough to recognize the tension. "How long ago in the past?" he asked cautiously.

"Before I was ever on *NextGen*. Before he got engaged." *Before you,* I added silently, my gaze never leaving my lover. "He's made comments that have implied he'd be willing to have more now, but I've refused him."

Reeve's brow rose slightly.

"Then this might be coming from Blakely directly," Joe suggested. "A sort of attempt at wish fulfillment or a way to get back at you for turning him down."

I let go of Reeve's stare and looked to Joe. "I hadn't considered that. But no, I don't think so. Even though Chris wouldn't mind cheating on his fiancée, he wouldn't want that out in the open."

"Is that why you refused him?" It was the first time Reeve had spoken since my confession. "Because he was attached?"

"Yes." It had been the reason I'd refused him at the awards. "And then *I* was attached." Now I'd admitted that my meeting with Chris the month before had met with a proposition. It might have been a detail I regretted divulging, but there was no way I'd ever be able to trust Reeve if I didn't give him a chance to prove himself.

And also I wanted to give him a chance to really trust *me*. Wanted to see if he *could,* and there was no way that would happen if I weren't completely honest.

"Besides," I said, attempting to lighten the mood with more truth, "he never really did it for me, if you know what I mean."

"Not quite as much information as I needed, but thank you for your candidness." Joe turned to Reeve. "I'll look into the possibility of that angle as well. It's hard to guess what someone might reveal about himself if his ego has been bruised." Joe's insinuation that Reeve might behave in the same manner was thinly veiled.

Wisely, he decided that it was time to end the conversation. "Looks like I have work to do. I'll get on it." Without waiting a beat longer, he made his exit.

I turned to follow, but Reeve called after me. "Emily." He waited until I twisted my head in his direction. "Shut the doors."

My hands were shaking as I did what he asked, so I kept them behind me when I pivoted my body to face him.

He studied me. "Come here."

I took a step forward, but then stopped, paralyzed by both my attraction to him and the delighted fear of what he might say or do next. Wringing my hands together at the base of my back, I ventured, "Are you . . . mad?"

"Well." He leaned back in his chair and crossed his ankle over his knee. "I'm in a quandary about that, aren't I? Your affair with Chris happened before you met me, so I suppose I have no grounds to be angry. Though, I am extremely unhappy—again—that you chose to meet with him, and now that I know he had openly declared his interest in bedding you, I have to question your judgment."

He had a point. The problem was he didn't understand what my motivation had been, and there wasn't any good reason to keep that to myself anymore. "I met with him to see if I could get any leads on Amber. That's the only reason why."

His eyes widened in understanding. He nodded an acceptance. "And you've already promised to not be alone with him again, so I guess I have to swallow my jealousy and let it go, don't I? If I want you to know that I believe you."

It was hard not to get tripped up on his declaration of jealousy. It was something I knew about him, and it was annoying and inconvenient. Even so, it got my thighs humming in all the right places.

But more important were the words he'd said after. I'd given him the opportunity to prove himself, and here he was teetering on the brink of doing just that. I pushed him. "*Do* you believe me?"

"It's impossible to think that smarmy piece of shit could satisfy your needs. So yes, I believe you rejected his advances."

I rolled my eyes. "And *that's* why you believe me? Because you know you're a better lover than he is?" God, he was stubborn. The way he made me work for every drop of affirmation . . .

Well, I liked it. It made what he *did* give all the more genuine. All the more meaningful. So when he said, "I believe you because you say it's the truth," warmth scurried along my body, and I beamed.

"Thank you." I lowered my head to hide the flush crawling down my neck.

"While we're on the topic," his words drew my eyes up, "is there anything else you're keeping from me that I should know about?"

I paused, not because I was hesitant to answer, but because I was surprised by what my answer was. "No. I can honestly say I think you know everything now."

"Good." His smile was slight, but it lit up the dark that had rested over his face. "Now, come here."

This time I came to him. Then, when he put his foot to the floor and patted his thigh, I climbed into his lap, straddling him with my knees at his sides.

I felt giddy for no reason other than I was in his arms. It was strange how my feelings for him had changed with Amber's return, simply because her arrival disproved many of the theories that had hung in my mind. He hadn't killed her. He hadn't hurt her in any way other than the ways he'd confessed—if he had, she wouldn't have returned. Before, he'd been dark and powerful. The extent of his mastery had been unknown. Now, the curtain had been pulled back and behind it I'd found just a man.

There was still a layer of fear where he was concerned, though, mostly because he was so unpredictable. He could be mean, which was, in some ways, what made him so captivating.

And then he could be sweet, which was the most

terrifying part about him of all. Because it made me think there could be more to what we had than just satisfying sex. It made me start to dream about the possible, it made me even more comfortable in my submission, it made me trust fully, and I'd learned long ago that was the surest way to a broken heart.

But, oh, how I craved any risk the man offered—including the danger of love.

"I think last night was good for us, Blue Eyes." He stroked the curve of my jaw with the back of a single finger, and I wondered if he knew how much it felt like fire on my skin—how it kindled my lust, how it ignited my dread.

I swallowed and took a step onto ground that could be quicksand. "I think last night was good for us too."

Maybe *too* good.

"I'm having a hard time concentrating on work this morning because I keep thinking about it. I wish I had time in my schedule—I'd spank your ass red to punish you for being such a distraction."

"Reeve," I giggled.

"I love it when I make you blush." He moved his hands to my ass, pulling me closer so I could feel the hard ridge of his erection. "Almost as much as I love it when I make you come."

My breath quickened. "You're so charming today. It's throwing me off."

"I'm warming you up so that the next part of our conversation will be productive." The timbre of his voice justified my earlier wariness.

"What a lead-in. Go ahead then." I braced myself for the worst, a difficult task since I had no idea at all where he was headed.

"When I brought you here, there were certain expectations of you."

My mind raced back to the list of rules he'd gone over with me on the way to Kaya. *Don't walk around undressed. Don't miss lunch or dinner. Be available when he wanted. No arguing with him in front of other people. Sleep with him.*

So far, I'd broken all of them except the dress code, though the T-shirt I'd worn for an outfit last night on the porch might have come close to breaking that as well.

The rules had honestly slipped my mind. I cleared the rasp from my throat. "Right."

"You told me you don't want our relationship to be based on an exchange of gifts for services anymore. Is that still true?"

I'd said that just before Amber had shown up. With the recent events, it was natural that he'd question if my intentions had changed. Logical to wonder if it was still true.

"Very much so," I answered earnestly.

His lids grew heavy and his pupils dark. "I like that. A lot." He brought his hands between us and slid his fingers just under my shirt to dance across the top of my navel. While his caress was sensual, it was also without motivation—an absentminded gesture based in the need to simply touch my skin rather than the need to fuck.

"But while I'm happy about this change in our arrangement," he continued, "I hope you don't think it releases you from the expectations I've outlined."

"No. Of course not." A part of me—the stubborn, independent part—pleaded to say fuck you and wash my hands of the man who sought to train me to his liking.

But a greater part of me wanted his rules and regulations, loved them, especially because it wasn't easy for me to submit to them. Pleasing him wasn't just satisfying—it was necessary for my own happiness, just as his happiness depended on my obedience.

But I'd been defiant.

A curtain of shame fell over my mood.

He brought a hand to my face, and, grasping my chin firmly, he lifted it so my eyes would meet his. "Don't do that. We're fine. That's why we're talking."

"Okay." And in just that short admonishment, I understood that he was committed to me, that he wanted us to work.

The realization begged to notch my giddiness into full-on exhilaration, but something held my excitement at bay.

Again, Reeve's fingers stroked my belly. "What is it that's preventing you from meeting those expectations?"

And there was the something that had overshadowed my joy. "You know what. Amber." She was the only thing holding me back, the only reason I hadn't gone to his bed the night before, the only hesitation in taking any step he wanted me to take.

Before she'd returned, we'd been headed toward those things that came "next" in a relationship. I'd already explained to Reeve that our friendship had ended when she'd believed the worst of me—she'd thought I'd stolen her man, and while, instead, that man had raped me and caused the death of the baby I'd carried, I'd vowed to never take a man from her again.

Didn't he realize that if I committed to him now, I might be breaking that vow?

Then there were his feelings. He'd been devastated when she'd left him. Wasn't he interested in a second chance with her? I knew I was.

Well. This was the moment of truth. I'd spoken her name now. I'd labeled her as barrier between us. He had to decide what she meant to him. And I had to decide too.

"Yes, Amber's here," he acknowledged. "You were looking for her. She's been found. Why does that change what's going on with us?"

"How can you ask that? You *loved* her—"

"—and she left—"

"And she came back."

He let a beat pass. "She didn't come back for me."

"How do you know that? Did you ask her?"

"Emily, I don't have to ask her. I know the circumstances that we parted under. I know how she felt when she left, and, trust me—I deserved it. She's only here now because I'm the one person who can assure her safety when it comes to Michelis."

I let his words digest. They made sense, but did that automatically mean she hadn't come back to salvage what she had with Reeve too?

From everything I'd learned about him and everything I'd known about Amber, the two were not a perfect match. She liked to be adored and catered to, and, though I'd known many men who'd loved me one way while loving her another, I couldn't imagine Reeve as one of them. He would never pander. He would never bend.

Still—there was no guessing what someone might do, might become, in the name of love.

Reeve tapped a finger on my chin. "You're overthinking this, Em. She came back for protection. She's not looking to pick up where we left off."

Then I realized what his assurance was missing—what *he* wanted. "Would it make a difference if she did?"

He opened his mouth to answer, but there was a knock on the door followed by it being swung open.

"The group from Callahans is here," Brent declared without invitation. "I got them set up near the fire so we can start the branding, but there's a new guy in charge, and he won't do shit without you." It seemed it was only then that Brent saw me. "Ah, sorry. Didn't realize I might be interrupting."

Reeve threw a glare at his ranch manager. Then he let out a huff of air. "I'll go down there then."

I slid off his lap to let him stand. His brow was furrowed as he donned the jacket that had been on the back of his chair. "A new guy? First I've heard about it. What's his name?"

"Grabrian, I think," Brent said.

Reeve nodded then turned to me. Threading one hand in my hair, he placed the other at my neck. "We'll talk more later," he said, his fingers stroking firmly and possessively up and down the length of my throat. "Just know that I won't be lenient about this for long."

It should have been a statement that struck fear in me, and it did—terror and excitement twined together and ran up my body, lighting every nerve along the way. He pulled me to him for a rough kiss, causing the thousand little fires inside to spit and flare.

When he broke from me, he took off with Brent, leaving me feeling as branded as his calves, and I was sure the iron he'd used on me was twice as hot.

I let a smile linger on my just-kissed lips for several minutes before I shook the daze from my head and tried to focus on the task I'd been given. Reeve expected me to resolve the issues that were keeping me from being with him. In other words, I had to talk to Amber. While he was likely right about her motivations and intentions, I needed to be clear with her about mine. I owed her that.

CHAPTER

7

The chance to talk to Amber wouldn't come if I didn't make an effort. So after leaving Reeve's office, I went up to her room only to find her bed empty. It was the first time I'd seen her out of it since she'd returned.

The room wasn't unoccupied, though. There was a guy I didn't know dozing on the love seat, likely the person assigned to this four-hour rotation of watching over her. I nudged him awake, irritation clear in my voice. "Where's Amber?"

He startled, then sat up immediately to scan the room. "Uh . . ."

Groaning from the bathroom interrupted his guilty stutter. I scowled at the man. "You can go. I'll take over."

I didn't wait for him to leave before going to the door and knocking. "Are you okay in there, Am?"

Her answer came in the form of retching. I tried the handle, and when I found it unlocked, I went in to crouch with her on the hard tile floor. With my hands wrapped in her blond hair, a dozen memories flooded back. Other occasions where one of us—usually Amber, who liked to overindulge—ended the evening leaning over a toilet. There was a certain melancholy to the scenario now. I could still easily slip in next to her to help her out as if not a day had passed since those days, and that was enormously satisfying to me, but, how sad at the same time, that this many years later I'd still have to.

After she'd finished, she rested her cheek on the porcelain. "Thanks, babe."

"You're not hooked to the IV," I noted as I perched on the side of the tub.

"Jeb took me off this morning," she explained. "Then I had my first attempt at food. It didn't go too well."

Her skin, I noticed, had a gray undertone, and she was sweating. "Do you have a fever?" I put the back of my hand up to her forehead and found her to be cool and clammy.

"I doubt it. Just part of the process of getting this out of my system."

"Is the methadone not helping?" I'd been familiar with the aftereffects of too much coke—the depression, the irritation. It dawned on me now that I didn't know the first thing about opiate withdrawal.

"It reduces symptoms. Supposedly. If this is reduced, though, cold turkey has to be a fucking bitch." She wiped at her nose with the back of her hand then scooted back to lean against the wall. "I'd kill right now for another pill. But I never want to go through this again. This shit is the worst."

I reached over the toilet to grab her a wad of toilet paper. "So you really do want to quit? What was it you were hooked on?"

"Thank you," she said as I handed her the tissue. "It was oxy. I never meant to start taking it in the first place. You know me, I like the uppers, not the opiates." She paused, her hand at her mouth as if she'd had another wave of nausea.

I put my arms out to help her back to the toilet if she needed it, but she stayed put. There was amusement in Amber's eyes despite the ashen look on her face. A moment later, she relaxed, the bout having passed. "You're such a good nurse," she said when she could speak again. "It's one of the things I've missed the most about you."

I stood and crossed to the sink to get a washcloth to wipe her mouth, but also to busy myself because I didn't know how to respond to her comment. *Such a good nurse.* I knew what it really alluded to—that I was good at being attentive. Good at pleasing.

I *was* good at it, and I loved that it was what she'd thought of when she'd thought of me. But there was so much baggage attached to the role I'd played with her, and dwelling on it would only make it more difficult to separate the person I'd been then from the person I was now. The line had already blurred so much since Reeve had rekindled my old desires. One poker in the fire was all I could handle.

Her eyes stayed fixed on me. "I missed lots of things about you," she said, misreading my retreat. "Not just that."

I forced my gaze to hers. "I missed a lot of things about you, too."

She smiled, and I noticed she could do that now without grimacing in pain. "Anyway," she said, "I only got hooked on the oxy because Micha fed them to me like candy. First, only after he'd gotten rough, or one of his men had gotten rough. Then more often. And then I wanted them all the time because it was easier to escape that way than it was to escape for real."

My spine prickled. She'd been a prisoner to the man then. It was what Joe had believed all along.

I sat again on the side of the tub and gripped the edges with my hands. This wasn't the conversation I needed to have with her, but it was personal and intimate and I figured it might be a good lead-in. "Escape? Were you not with him of free will? I thought you said you went to him to punish Reeve?"

"At first. Yes. Reeve and I . . ." she hesitated, and I realized she was trying to figure out how much to reveal, not knowing that I already knew the story. "Well, we ended badly."

I was tired of beating around the bush. "He said he tried to keep you here."

She eyed me suspiciously. "He told you that?"

"Yeah." Well, that was one way to hint that he and I had become close. Amber knew him well enough to understand he didn't give anything freely.

But Amber came up with another explanation. "Reeve probably figured there wasn't any harm in admitting it since I was obviously not pressing charges. He's lucky I went to Micha instead of the cops." Her tone was tart and full of spite.

"He was actually pretty remorseful about it all." As soon as the words were out of my mouth, I worried I'd said the wrong thing. I'd wanted to defend him, but perhaps I should have kept silent and let her hold onto her resentment so that she wouldn't care that I was with him.

"He was?" She seemed more surprised about this news than that he'd admitted anything to me. "Well, that's something."

Her entire countenance seemed to brighten. She'd been so run-down that I was somewhat glad I could say something to cheer her, but, damn, I wished that hadn't been it.

"So, yeah, that's what happened," she went on. "He wouldn't let me leave the ranch for, I don't know, weeks. Which really wasn't as horrible as all that since he treated me like a queen the whole time, but it was still wrong. And I was pissed and vengeful and I stupidly ran to Micha

because I knew it would get Reeve worked up. I'd only
planned to fool around with him for a few weeks, you
know, let it burn. But then Micha was good to me. He gave
me a lot of things—really fucking nice jewelry, Em. You
should have seen the emeralds. And he was so attentive.
He wanted to know all about my life. I actually told him
about my dad."

"Wow." I was pretty sure she'd never told anyone but
me about the father who had repeatedly raped her until she
got fed up and ran away at sixteen.

"I know, right? And Micha said he wished he could
erase all that pain. I believed him." Her voice caught, and
she paused to blink back tears.

I moved to the floor next to her so I could put my arm
around her. "They make it easy to believe," I said, trying
to soothe her. I knew how that felt—to trust someone not
to harm and then have that trust betrayed. At least, with
Reeve, I'd found a man who could give me what I craved
without breaking me down.

Amber dried her tears off after only a minute. "God, I
sound like a Lifetime special, don't I?"

"Nah. You're definitely an HBO documentary."

She laughed. "At least I'm premium entertainment." She
leaned forward to get more toilet paper and, after dabbing
at her nose, tossed it into the can at the side of the tub. "By
the time I realized what he was really like, he'd already
assured that I was tied to him forever."

My spine tingled at the thought of her tattoo and what
Joe had said it meant. "How?"

"He found my father for me. And had him killed." Her
delivery was so matter-of-fact that I almost didn't register
what she'd said.

Then . . . shit. I was speechless.

During Joe's search for Amber, he'd found her father
had been killed while serving time for child molestation

in federal prison. Joe had believed the man who'd done the crime had been connected to the Greek mob but there had been no way to prove it.

It had been Vilanakis then. Joe had been onto something after all.

"Yeah," Amber said in acknowledgment to my stricken reaction. "Micha's not a man you want to mess with. Or get in bed with, it seems, because then he said I owed him."

She shifted to face me. "And, you know what? I was willing to accept that. Because even though I didn't ask him to do it, I wasn't at all upset that he had."

Honestly, I didn't feel any remorse either. But now she owed Vilanakis. Did she realize exactly what that meant? I wasn't even sure what it meant, and I knew it was bad.

Amber lowered her head. "You must think the worst of me."

"No. I really don't. I'm thinking the worst of *him*." Thinking the worst and getting pissed. "He breaks the law and then uses that to keep you with him. That's bullshit, Amber. Then, did he make you get that tattoo? To remind you that you owed him?"

She stretched an arm across her body and placed her hand over the place of her design. "Yeah." She tilted her head at me. "Did Reeve see the tattoo? Do you know?"

"Probably. I noticed it right away. Why?"

Her face was unreadable. "No reason. Let's not talk about it anymore, though, okay?" She didn't wait for my response before bringing her knees to her chest and burying her face.

She was shutting me out. I knew that feeling too. I'd done the same thing after she'd saved me from a dirtbag in Mexico who'd used me and nearly destroyed me in the process. I hadn't feared that my dirtbag would come after me though. I couldn't imagine how I would have moved on if I had.

I brushed a strand of hair off her forehead. "Okay. We don't have to. We can talk about something else." Perhaps it was the wrong time to segue into my relationship with Reeve, but the weight of his expectations sat heavily on me.

Amber shook her head. "I don't think I feel like talking at all right now, if that's okay." She peeked up at me. "But will you stay with me? You can help me back to bed and then we can turn on bad soaps and make fun of the plots just like old times."

I hesitated only a second before my lips slid into a smile. "Whatever you want." Just like old times.

CHAPTER

8

I stayed with Amber until she drifted off to sleep late that afternoon. Then Joe came to take his shift with her.

"You been here all day?" he asked. "Have you even eaten anything?"

As if on cue, my stomach grumbled. "No, I haven't. But I really just want to take a nap right now. Will you be good with her?"

He nodded. "Make sure you make it to dinner. You heard we're out on the deck tonight, right?"

"Not in the hall like usual?" Supper at the ranch was always a family affair—after the long day of work, the men would gather to eat in the main house. I'd eaten with them every day since I'd arrived.

"Nope. I guess there's a bunch of guests here for the next few days so Brent said that Sallis asked for a private setting for a few of us. Me and you included."

"Got it. I'll be there." It seemed strange for the arrangement to have changed when one of Reeve's expectations had always been that I ate with the men. But I was wiped out, and the only thing I wanted to think about at the moment was putting my head on my pillow followed by not thinking at all.

Though I woke up starving, the nap had been a good choice. It was the most peaceful sleep I'd had since Amber had returned, and it did wonders for my mood. I felt more relaxed than I had the entire time I'd been at Kaya. More relaxed than I had the entire time I'd known Reeve.

My steps were light as I went downstairs and headed toward the deck. The hall buzzed with the usual raucousness that accompanied the ranchmen. I peeked in and noted that the room was definitely more crowded than normal, yet there was still plenty of seating available.

A night away from the rowdy cowboys didn't sound too bad, though. Maybe that's what Reeve's thought had been as well.

He was already outside when I got there, alone, leaning against the railing, looking out over the landscape like he was an emperor surveying his land. He'd stood like that when I'd had dinner with him for the first time in Palm Springs. Even then, when I'd been shaking in my heels, scared of the lair I was walking into, desperate to find Amber—even then, the magnificence of his presence had me twisted in knots.

Now, as I took him in, my breath caught and my throat tightened, but instead of paralyzing me like he had that night in the Springs, it propelled me forward. Brought me to him.

I wrapped my arms around him and buried my face in his back.

I felt his surprise as he turned his head to glance at me. I surprised myself, actually. I'd always let him take the lead, because I liked it that way, but also because *he* liked it that way. Right now, though, I was too overcome with emotion to care about anything other than holding him.

He only allowed the embrace for a handful of seconds before he pulled me around to face him. Trapping me between his body and the railing, he threaded a hand in my hair and tugged hard enough to make me gasp.

He grinned as his other hand traced down the line of my neck. "Maybe I should cancel dinner and feast on you instead. Right here, on this deck where everyone can see."

Please. It was on the tip of my tongue, ready to fall into the tiny space of air between us like a white flag of surrender.

But as much as I wanted to be lost in him, I needed reassuring more. "Reeve, is Amber safe right now?"

He pulled back slightly, but I still noticed his body tense. "As long as she's under my protection, yes."

"How can you be so sure?"

The way he searched my eyes, I could tell he understood that I wasn't just asking about Amber's security—I was asking him to explain it all. Inviting him to tell me everything.

Yet all he said was, "Because Michelis respects me. Therefore he'll show respect for that which he perceives as mine."

I turned my head to study the horizon, hoping he didn't see the hurt in my gaze. "It didn't stop him before," I said, wondering how much of the perception he'd mentioned was based in reality.

"Before was different. She went to him on her own. I couldn't protect her when she walked into his arms."

"Then she's safe as long as she's here?" What I meant was, *Does that mean she can never leave you?*

And I couldn't tell if he understood what I was really asking when his answer was simply, "Yes."

"Looks like I'm interrupting," Joe said from behind us.

Reeve's hands fell to my sides, but he kept them on me, kept me pinned as he twisted to acknowledge the intruder. "Of course you're not interrupting." His fingers stroked my hips possessively. "Have a seat. Please." Reeve gestured to the patio table that had already been set with a white table-cloth, utensils, and cloth napkins.

I started numbly toward Joe, my head still wrapped up in Amber, but Reeve held me in place.

"Not so fast." His tone reminded me that he was the one who dictated my actions. He leaned in close, letting his breath rush hot against my ear. "I wonder, if I make him watch, will he try to rescue you when you start screaming or will he wait until I wrap my hands around your throat?" He drew back to let me see the glint in his eye. "Fascinating question, isn't it?"

My heart raced, and I forgot why I'd had even a second of jealousy. Even when he abruptly released me and went to join Joe at the table.

It took several seconds to compose myself before I was able to walk the few steps to them and even longer before I could look Joe in the face without turning scarlet. Hopefully he'd assume my flushed skin was from the fire pits that surrounded us—an elegant touch that provided both light as the sun went down and enough warmth to keep out the April evening chill.

Conversation was casual and easy—easier than I'd expected between Joe and Reeve. They chatted about the land and the ins and outs of ranching and the luxury hotels that Reeve owned. Though, while each question from the investigator seemed in line with typical small talk, I could practically hear the gears turning in his head, processing each of Reeve's answers and filing it away for later in categories with labels like *Suspicious, Follow-up,* and *Miscellaneous.*

It was hard to guess whether Reeve caught it as well.

He didn't give any indication that he was on guard any more than usual, but that was the thing about Reeve—he was subtle in the way he held his cards. So subtle, it was almost impossible to discern whether he was even playing the game.

As had been the case in Palm Springs, dinner was served from a warming cart, our plates having already been dished up in the kitchen so a staff member could place them in front of us still piping hot. Another server poured wine for each of us. There was a fourth set of utensils on the table, but no food was laid there. For Brent, maybe, who'd probably gotten caught up with the visiting ranchers.

"Joe says there are extra guests here this week?" I asked, before putting a forkful of garden salad in my mouth, the raspberry vinaigrette dressing surprising me in its decadence. The entire meal was a contradiction to the surroundings, just like Reeve was in a place like Kaya. Even in a rugged environment, he brought luxury.

He swirled the wine in his glass, the merlot thick and heavy as it spun. "Our visitors are men from another ranch." He paused, and I wondered if that was all he'd say.

But after he took a swallow of his drink, he set the glass down and went on. "They always come out for a few days for the spring branding. Since we aren't set up to handle a large herd of cattle, we sell a portion of the calves to the Callahans. We also don't have modern branding machinery, so they send up men to help us do it the old-fashioned way. We mark half with the Kaya brand and the other half with theirs. They leave with a truckload of cattle and our numbers are more manageable."

"Cowboy stuff," I said with a wink. Even with the opulent touches, it was strange seeing Reeve wearing the hat of ranch owner, though, really, it wasn't much different than the hat of business tycoon. Both roles fit his authoritative personality. Both roles looked equally good on him.

"Cowboy stuff," Reeve repeated with a chuckle. "It's an occasion the men all look forward to. Lots of drunkenness will be had in the main hall tonight, I assure you."

"Any reason we need to be concerned about any of them?" Joe voiced my own thoughts. I'd eaten with the ranchers when they'd been drunk before—when Reeve was out of town, even.

"Not at all," he answered.

Wanting more, I nudged him under the table with my leg. "Are you afraid they'll be too wild for us to be around? Is that why we're dining away from them?"

His hand fell to my knee and remained there, hidden under the tablecloth. "I'm sure that nothing's too wild for you, Blue Eyes. But I don't know all of them. Besides, I thought you might enjoy the quieter atmosphere for a change."

"Hmm," I said in vague agreement, trying not to let his touch distract me. While the setting was indeed pleasant, I sensed there was more to the alteration in our routine than simply that Reeve didn't want to mingle with strangers. He didn't trust them, it seemed. Was he protecting me from them because he wanted to be sure no one else laid a hand on me? Or because he believed they were somehow a real threat?

The question immediately left my mind when a figure appeared at the door.

"Amber!" I exclaimed, surprised to see her downstairs. Though her posture still seemed weak, her pallor was much better than when I'd left her. Relief rushed through me, and I realized for the first time exactly how terrible she'd looked and how worrying her appearance had been. It was extremely comforting to know she'd gotten through the worst of it. Reassuring to see that she would bounce back.

That feeling only lasted a handful of seconds before anxiety crept in. I wanted her well, I really did. But with the return of her health, I could no longer ignore the threat she posed to me. She was a beautiful, vibrant woman—a beautiful, vibrant woman that Reeve had once loved. Maybe even still did.

And that terrified me as much as the thought of never finding her alive once had.

Reeve twisted in his chair to look at her, his hand leaving my leg as he did. "You made it." He nodded at a servant who stepped forward and pulled out the empty chair across from Reeve.

Joe jumped up and met Amber at the door, and immediately I felt awful for not thinking of it. "Need to lean?"

She smiled, the full flirty grin I recognized from days gone by. "Why thank you, Joe." She linked her arm through his and let him lead her to her seat.

If Reeve felt remorse for not being the one to attend to her, he didn't show it. "I had a place set for you," he said, as another servant made his way toward us with the warming cart, "in case you felt up to joining us. From Jeb's last report, I didn't expect to see you here."

I fidgeted in my seat. The uncertainty of what to expect or how to behave brought such a heavy air of tension that I was sure everyone had to be feeling it as well. I glanced at the men and found them both stoic and unreadable.

Amber, however, seemed quite comfortable. She settled into her seat and unfolded her napkin as though she felt right at home. "It's interesting you get your reports from Jeb when there are other ways you could check up on me." She placed the linen in her lap, keeping her eyes pinned on the man opposite her.

Reeve arched a brow. "Meaning?"

"You haven't been by. I thought you might be avoiding me." Her delivery was light and playful. Only Amber could make an accusation sound like she was teasing. I'd forgotten that about her, forgotten how often she snuck her jabs in under dimples and flashes of ivory teeth.

"Not avoiding you. It's been a busy few days." Under the tablecloth, Reeve's hand returned to my leg, higher on my thigh this time.

I forced myself not to react, directing my attention to cutting my steak. While I always loved the way my body buzzed when he touched me, the gesture was totally inappropriate and it made me suspicious of his motives. I wanted to be his, wanted him to be open about our relationship, but if this were something else—if I were merely a pawn in a game of revenge, I wouldn't participate.

I started to push him away, but the glance he shot me told me that he wouldn't let me dictate his actions.

For the moment at least, she was unaware, and arguing with Reeve would only draw her attention. So I let his hand remain, and, truthfully, I liked it. Liked how he touched me when *she* was sitting so near.

Maybe I liked being a pawn after all.

"How are you feeling?" I asked as the server laid a plate in front of Amber and filled her empty glass with water.

"I'm actually feeling pretty okay at the moment. Much better than this morning. Jeb gave me my evening dose about forty minutes ago, which helps. I figure I have an hour or two before I start spiraling downward."

She looked pointedly at Reeve's wine as she picked up her water. "I definitely think I'm ready to not need baby-sitting anymore."

I lowered my gaze again to my plate. The underlying discord between Reeve and Amber was palpable, and it shook me up. It would be easy to decide that the contention meant that their relationship was entirely in the past, but I was smarter than that. I understood intricacies of human relationships, specifically of Amber relationships and even Reeve relationships. She wouldn't be holding on to hostility if she didn't still feel something.

And Reeve wouldn't be monitoring her beverage consumption if he didn't care as well.

Oh, God, how I didn't want him to care!

I loathed myself for that wish. Of course he should care. His concern didn't have to mean anything about me. But rationale doesn't work on emotion, and instead of understanding his compassion, I felt bitter and raw.

"Alcohol is not recommended with methadone or addiction recovery," Reeve said dispassionately. "If you want it, you'll have to find someone else to provide it." She opened her mouth to interject, but he didn't let her. "And the people taking shifts with you are not babysitters. They're there to help you."

Here, she dug in her heels. "I don't need them."

"But if you found that—"

"I don't need them and I'd prefer to not have them." Her voice lowered. "If I have any say in it." I didn't miss her innuendo, the insinuation that his care now wasn't unlike the time she'd spent here as his captive.

She'd hit him below the belt. He'd told me that had been the worst of him, that "keeping" her had been the worst thing he'd done.

I saw the struggle within him. Felt it, even. He hated to lose, and, wanting to show him I understood, I lowered my hand to cover his on my thigh.

But he pulled his hand away. Meeting her eyes, he set down the reins. "If that's what you'd prefer."

"It is." She beamed triumphantly. Then, looking down at her plate for the first time, she said, "Meat and potatoes. Of course." Her disdain was evident.

To my left, Joe's leg bounced up and down nervously.

Apparently, I wasn't the only one who felt the tension. I wondered if my unease was as obvious as his.

"The asparagus is perfect," I said, trying to lighten the mood.

As though I hadn't spoken, Reeve said tersely, "The potatoes were for you, Amber. Jeb said soft and bland for your diet. If you prefer, I can have some soup brought up."

"Potatoes are fine. Thanks." She said it as if this were her concession. She refused to be hovered over, but she'd allow him to choose her menu.

I imagined it was the way they'd been when they were together—constantly butting heads while she fought for her independence and he demanded the right to attend to her needs. That had always been the difference between her and I—she saw that sort of attention as stifling where as I'd found submission to be freeing.

But maybe Reeve enjoyed the challenge. Maybe I was too easily subdued. Wouldn't it be more of a victory to top someone who refused to be topped?

I finished off my wine and signaled for the server to bring me another glass. *My* alcohol content wasn't being monitored, thank goodness. Maybe if I had enough of it, I could drown the twin beasts of envy and insecurity that lived inside me, or, at least, lull them both to sleep.

We fell into a silence that was not at all comfortable but a hundred times preferable to the conversation that had taken place. Amber picked at her food, ignoring the steak altogether and barely making a dent in her potatoes.

Eventually, she sat back in her chair and sighed as she looked out through the deck railings to the ground below. "You got a dog?"

I followed her line of vision to see the scraggly black Lab that I'd seen around the ranch since I'd arrived. "Jenkins," I said, recalling the name Brent had used. "Isn't he a stray?" Not that I cared much about the dog, but it was a far safer topic of discussion than the previous one.

Reeve nodded. "He's hung around the last few weeks. I'm pretty sure Parker's feeding him even though he says he isn't."

"Parker." Amber waited until she caught my eye. "Have you met him, Em?"

"I have." I remembered the drunken references Parker had made to me about Amber one night. He'd referred to her as a pain in the ass and a bunch of trouble.

He'd also been in the stable when Reeve had stripped me of my clothing and bridled me like a horse. I bit back a smile at the memory.

Amber's face lit up with a naughty gleam, and I suddenly realized she had memories of her own.

Before I could wonder too long, Reeve clarified. "Emily doesn't know him like you know him."

It had been obvious in the stable that sometimes Reeve had shared his women with Parker. I'd felt pride that he hadn't wanted to share me.

Now, as it became clear that Reeve had shared Amber, I felt sick with jealousy. "Oh. No. I don't know him like that."

At least Reeve had helped keep my cover, his words shielding me from her speculation about us without being dishonest. I told myself I was, but with as much as he'd withdrawn since Amber joined us, I had to wonder if his discretion had anything to do with me.

It was also possible I was overthinking the situation.

More wine. That's what I needed. Clearly.

Amber laughed. "Well. Anyway." She chuckled again as she sat forward to put a spoonful of food in her mouth. "Good potatoes."

I concentrated on finishing my meal, focusing on the mechanics of eating, thoroughly chewing each bite before swallowing. It was tempting to race through so I could excuse myself and run away from the awful awkwardness. Thankfully, the silence resumed, but it stretched so taut I feared it would create a perilous chasm when it finally broke. A chasm that would consume me entirely.

I'd just set down my fork when Amber jutted out her chin and declared, "I have something to say." She cleared her throat. "This might not be the best moment for this, but who knows when I'll be feeling this good again, and with your busy schedule, Reeve, it might be the only chance I get."

I bristled at her use of his name, as if it were mine to use and she had no right to it. Which of course was ridiculous.

Reeve placed his napkin over his empty plate and cocked his head. "I'm listening."

"I want to say that . . ." Her lip quivered, and it hit me that she was nervous, that she'd been nervous through the entire meal. And why wouldn't she be? This was the first time she'd spent any time with her former love at length.

She cleared her throat again, then plunged forward with slightly more confidence. "I want to say I'm sorry for how I left things between us." She paused, and my pulse jolted up in speed. "And about how I reacted. Running to Micha—to Michelis—was one of the worst decisions I've made in my life, and I've made quite a few. But I deserve what he—"

Reeve interrupted, his words softer than I'd heard him use with her since the night she'd arrived. "You didn't deserve anything, An—" He stopped himself before the nickname crossed his lips completely. "You didn't deserve it."

"I disagree, but that's not what—"

He cut her off again. "No. That's not acceptable. He's the lowest of scum, and it doesn't matter what you said or did—"

She raised her voice to quash his. "The point is that I made a mistake. I was overly confident, and I was stupid to—"

"You weren't stupid. He's good at manipulating."

"He is." She let a beat pass. "Can I finish?"

"Go ahead." His voice was tight with reluctance, and I wondered if he was as apprehensive as I was.

Probably not. The interaction was intimate and, not for the first time, I felt like a voyeur. It wasn't a conversation I was meant to be part of. I debated excusing myself to let them work out their past baggage alone, but I couldn't move. I was eager for her to clear the air, even if it had nothing to do with me. Whatever she had to say to Reeve, I was interested in hearing it as well.

"I was going to say that I was stupid to leave you." She took a breath, and I stopped breathing entirely. "I still love you, Reeve, and if you have any room in your heart for forgiveness, I'd really like a second chance."

Everything around me dimmed, as though a curtain had fallen over my vision. My balance seemed to shift, too, even though I was still sitting, as if my entire world had tilted on its axis.

"I have to go," I muttered, pushing back my chair and jumping to my feet.

Behind me, I heard the scrape of another chair. "Emily's right," Joe said. "This is obviously a private conversation. We'll just let you . . ."

His voice trailed off as I disappeared into the house. I didn't stop as I made it through the library and down the hallway, past the main hall. At the front door, I kept going, bounding down the steps two at a time. I followed a trail that led who-knew-where, gulping air, trying to get oxygen into my lungs without much luck.

"Emily!" Joe called after me, his words barely registering over the one thought pulsing with deafening thunder in my head—*I knew it. I knew it, I knew it, I knew it.*

I didn't turn back, thinking if I kept going maybe I could outrun the reality we'd both just walked out on.

But he kept following. "Emily, would you please stop?"

I couldn't stop. My hand clutched at the stitch in my side, and I still couldn't get a decent breath, but I kept going.

Joe jogged to catch up with me. Then he matched his stride to mine, walking at my side. "Are you okay?"

"Does it look like I'm fucking okay?" I snapped, startling him.

He didn't respond, walking alongside me quietly for several minutes.

Eventually, the phrase hammering inside slipped past my lips. "I knew it."

"Knew what?"

"That it was inevitable." Conversation was difficult with the lack of air, but somehow I managed short phrases. "That it was too good. To be true. I knew it. I *knew* it."

"What was too good to be true?" Joe honestly seemed to not be following. "You and Reeve? Please tell me you're joking."

I threw him a look that was meant to kill. "You know what? I don't need your fucking commentary on this."

"Hey. I'm not . . ." He grabbed my arm, stopping me. "Hold on, all right? You're going to pass out if you keep this up."

I yanked my arm out of his grasp, but I obeyed. He encouraged me to bend over, and I did, placing my hands on my thighs and letting my head fall between my knees as I forced my breaths to slow and even.

"Okay," he said, his hand patting at the small of my back. "I don't particularly like the guy. But I respect him.

Sort of. If he's really not into any of the shady dealings he seems connected to, then I definitely respect him. More importantly, I like you. So if this guy is *the guy,* then . . ." He couldn't bring himself to finish that statement. "All right. I won't go that far."

I peered up at him. "You suck at this."

He crouched down so he was at eye level. "Here's the thing. That guy is into you. If you're out here upset because you think you're losing him to your drug-addict friend—"

"That isn't who she is."

His features were soft but the look he shot me was skeptical. "You haven't seen her in a long time—are you sure?"

"Yeah. I'm pretty sure." I straightened. Now that I'd stopped walking, my body registered the cold, and I wrapped my arms around myself as I considered his question.

The truth was, there were things about Amber I was no longer sure of. But it didn't really matter. The one thing I did know was enough. "Even if she isn't," I said, "if she wants him, I have to step out of the way. That's all there is to it."

Joe rose to his full height. "Is this some fucked-up rule between girlfriends?"

"It's a fucked-up rule between *us.* I can't take a man from her. I won't." Any other explanation would be a waste of breath, and I still hadn't quite gotten mine back.

He gave a skeptical shrug. "Seems like she's the one taking the guy from you considering that you are the one who was here when I brought her back."

"I was only with him because of her."

"No, you weren't." He knew me better than I'd thought.

But the reasons I'd been with him didn't matter either. Nor did it matter that I would bend to him the way he liked. Because the more I thought about it, the more I was convinced that it was Amber's backbone that was what attracted Reeve to her. "He'll take her back."

"Don't be so certain of that. You're too blinded by her to see it for some reason, but she's a tragic mess."

"Doesn't matter. Reeve was in love with her."

Joe shook his head. "Not anymore."

As if he knew Reeve. As if he knew anything.

"He loved her so much he wanted to marry her, Joe." Saying the words out loud was liberating. Admitting the truth I hadn't wanted to face. That Reeve had loved Amber deeply, and that kind of love didn't just go away. "He loved her so much he kept her here and wouldn't let her go for weeks and weeks."

Joe put a hand up. "Whoa. What?"

Fuck. I hadn't been thinking.

And I didn't have the energy to try to cover my mistake. "That's why she called me. She wanted to leave him, and he . . . did his best to prevent that."

"Amber told you this?" He was back to investigator mode.

"She did. But Reeve told me first." I watched the wheels spinning behind his eyes. "He let her go in the end, Joe." His jaw tightened, and I pressed on with my defense. "I know what you're thinking—"

"No," he interrupted. "You can't have any possible idea what I'm thinking."

I let my mouth shut. It was appalling—I knew it was. Especially to a decent man like Joe. There was no way I could explain that I understood it—understood the other side, anyway. I understood what it felt like to want to be mastered and controlled and so it was much easier for me to accept that someone would want to master and control someone else and not be a sick person. Or, at least was as sick as I was.

Joe stared me down, though, as if trying to understand

the impossible. He shook his head back and forth, and finally he seemed to give up. "Let me tell you this, Emily—he has eyes for no one but you. And, fuck, I wish it weren't true. Especially after hearing how he treats the women he's into, like they're possessions . . ."

His voice trailed off leaving a silence filled with judgment so heavy I felt naked and ashamed.

Eventually he threw his hands up. "You know what? I can't do this with you. It sucks you're upset right now. Too bad it's not over someone who deserves it. Because, trust me, neither of them do."

He didn't wait for me to respond, turning to head back toward the house.

I watched after him, wishing that his disgust could move me. Wishing I was the type of person who would run after him instead of a person who was wishing that Reeve had been the one to follow after me instead.

CHAPTER

9

Despite the cold, I resumed my walk along the trail, following it over the ranch landscape until the sun got so low that I had to turn back for fear of getting lost and stuck out in the middle of nowhere.

The exercise had been good for my head, though, and, while I refused to steal a man from Amber, Joe's words had sunk in. Was it really stealing when she'd left him? Maybe she wouldn't even mind once I explained the situation. There were other men she would have willingly walked away from for my sake. Other men that she *had* walked away from. For me.

I didn't want to wonder if I could do the same.

I had to talk to her.

And I had to talk to Reeve. I couldn't know if her declaration had changed his feelings or intentions until I did.

It was dark when I made it back, and my thoughts were so turned in on themselves that I didn't notice the red butt of a lit cigarette or the man leaning against the side of the house until I was almost on top of him.

"Oh, hi! I didn't see you there." I sounded flustered and on edge.

"Sorry to have surprised you." The man's head tipped toward me. "Emily, right?" he asked, as he exhaled a puff of smoke.

I squinted at him, trying to place him, but I couldn't. In fact, I was certain I hadn't seen him before. He had to be one of the ranch guests, which didn't explain how he knew me. "That's right," I said tentatively. "I don't think we've met."

He tilted his head as he took another slow draw from his cigarette. "Nope. We haven't." Even in the dark, I didn't miss the hungry way his eyes groped my frame.

He took a step toward me, and I readied myself to run. Just then, the front door slammed open. I looked up to the porch to see a couple of Reeve's men leaving the house. When I turned back, the man wasn't there anymore. I glanced around and caught sight of him circling around behind the building.

A man didn't run off that easily if he hadn't had ill intent.

I shivered. I wondered if all of the guests were that creepy. No wonder Reeve was wary of them. Suddenly, I wanted to run and tell him about the encounter.

Then, at the top of the stairs, I noticed his door was shut, which meant he was in there. But what if he wasn't alone? What if the conversation with Amber at dinner had led them to his bedroom?

Before I let myself get worked up, I looked to Amber's door. It was shut too. It was the first time I'd seen it closed since her arrival, and my mind jumped to a hundred different possible conclusions. Maybe she was exercising her new babysitter-free status. Maybe she was puking again in the bathroom and wanted privacy. Or she was making out with one of the ranchers. Or crying over whatever Reeve had said to her after I'd left them.

Or she wasn't in there at all.

I could easily knock on her door to find out, but I wasn't sure I could face her if she answered, and I was absolutely sure I couldn't take it if she didn't.

Hoping I would be better equipped to handle the situation after a good night's sleep, I retreated to my own room with a sigh of resignation.

Though it was late enough to go to bed, my emotions were too frazzled for sleep. And I was cold. My evening walk had set a chill in my bones that lingered even in the warm house. While I wished it was Reeve warming me up, a hot shower would be just as effective at raising my body temperature and would also calm my nerves.

I stripped, tossing my clothes onto the chair in the corner of my room, then went to start the shower. I turned the water on without getting in, sticking my hand under the stream until it was hot enough. Then I crossed to the linen closet at the other end of the bathroom and picked out a couple of towels. When I shut the door, I turned back toward the shower and nearly jumped out of my skin.

"Reeve!" I patted my breastbone, trying to calm the thudding in my chest. "Goddammit, you scared the hell out of me." Between his sneaky arrival and the lurking cowboy outside, I wouldn't have been surprised if I was on my way to a heart attack.

His lip curled up with amusement.

I scowled. "I'm glad you think sending me to an early grave is funny." But I wasn't really irritated by his arrival in the least. I was glad, and I was certain the accelerated tempo of my heart rate had as much to do with his appearance at all as it did with the element of surprise.

He leaned his hip against the vanity and folded his arms across his chest, a position that highlighted both his broad shoulders and toned biceps. "You like it when I keep you guessing," he said dismissively, not an entirely inaccurate statement, though it was a bit discomforting that he knew it so well.

"And *I* like *you* on your toes," he added, his eyes dark as they slid the length of my body. I felt them like silk as they caressed over the slopes of my breasts, down the plane of my stomach, zeroing in on the landing strip above my pussy. Suddenly I'd warmed up quite sufficiently, the pool of moisture between my thighs as hot as the steam gathering in the room.

I met his scrutiny with ogling of my own, biting my lip as my eyes landed on the large bulge at the front of his pants. He was barefoot, and I tried not to wonder if that meant he'd been undressed once already in the evening. Tried not to wonder if it was his first or second erection of the night.

Bringing the towels in front of me as a much-needed barrier, I mirrored his crossed arms. "What are you doing here, anyway?"

He shrugged. "You wouldn't come to my bed so I had to come to yours."

It was surprising how easily happiness bubbled in my chest. Teasingly, I threw his words from the night before back at him. "This isn't my bed."

He was already walking toward me. "It's close enough." The towels fell to the floor as he seized my hips and turned my back to the counter. His mouth captured mine, greedily stealing my breath and sense of reason with his lips and tongue.

God, I was hungry for him. I roved my hands over his chest, wanting to touch all of his body at once, delighting at the hard muscles that met the underside of my palms. He was solid everywhere. A wall of strength and potency that could so easily overpower me. I was weak in his presence, incapable of anything except to yield.

A warning bell sounded in the back of my head, though,

urging me to get my wits together and address . . . something. It was difficult to remember what exactly when his hands were on my breasts, squeezing and pinching. The bite of pain sent jolts of electricity through my nervous system, signals that my brain read as pleasure. Pleasure I couldn't resist.

No. I *could* resist. I had to.

I pulled my head back, abruptly breaking his kiss. "Wait," I said—moaned, actually, as his mouth found the shell of my ear to torture instead. "What about—?"

"The only question you should be asking right now is how fast can I make you come." He relinquished a breast and slid his hand between us to tease my clit.

"Ah." I struggled to remain focused. "But, I need to know what happened after—" My back arched as he sank two long fingers into my pussy. "Oh, my God, that feels too good. You have to stop. We have to talk about earlier. I can't—"

With one hand still buried inside me, he clamped the other over my mouth. "Emily, if you don't shut the fuck up, I'm going to find something to gag you with." And then, as though ensuring I had no will to argue, he crooked his fingers and stroked them against that sensitive spot in my cunt, sending me into a dizzying state of ecstasy.

Maybe talking could wait after all.

Words dissolved on my tongue. The sounds that emerged from my throat were breathy gasps as he rubbed me toward orgasm. Then, when I got there, when I toppled over the edge, my head spinning from the magic of his fingers, he devoured my cries with a bruising kiss that magnified the intensity of my climax.

I was shaking, but eager for more, when he picked me up and set me on the counter edge. His hands were quick with his belt, yet it felt like decades passed before his cock was out and notched at my opening and another lifetime before he was pushing inside of me with a hard, merciless thrust.

He pounded into me, giving me no time to adjust or catch my breath before adopting a brutal tempo. He fit inside me so perfectly. His stroke hit every sensitive spot of my pussy even before I clenched around him. And the fierce way he impaled me . . . I adored it. He fucked me so savagely that I had to grip onto the counter edge for support. I held on for the ride, my eyes focused on his expression. Both cruelty and delight played on his features, and while it disgusted me to admit, it was the combination of those emotions that turned me on. He was ruthless, and he enjoyed being ruthless. And he enjoyed that his viciousness was what pleased me the most.

With no break in his assault, he placed his palm flat against my neck and pushed me back until my head was pinned to the mirror behind me. I couldn't swallow, couldn't get a breath in with his hand blocking my windpipe. Tension pulled at my insides and another orgasm stretched toward release, building, building, building . . .

But he let up too soon, and the pressure calmed to a steady buzz, while the explosion I desired was elusive and just out of reach. I clung to the dizziness of "almost there," wishing it was enough to send me soaring. "Please," I implored. "Please."

Reeve smirked—he loved it when I begged—but he didn't take me where I wanted to go. Instead, with his fingers pinching my chin, he twisted my face so that my cheek pressed against the glass.

"Look," he said in reverence.

The mirror ran the whole wall behind me then wrapped around the vanity so, facing this direction, I could see our reflections in the glass, half eclipsed by steam from the shower. He let go of me long enough to wipe the fog then resumed his grip on my jaw. I stared, transfixed by the sight of his cock driving into me over and over.

With my focus where he wanted it, Reeve rearranged my legs, bringing one foot up to brace on the counter and propping the other in the sink. Now I was angled so that my cunt could better be seen in the mirror. It was naughty and erotic and I couldn't stop staring.

"Look at that," he said again, his fingers jabbing into my skin. "The way you let me use you is so beautiful."

Beautiful. It *was* beautiful. The way he had me spread out awkwardly across the bathroom sink, naked while he was still clothed—it was vile and wicked and oh, so beautiful.

"I can't control myself when I'm inside you." His voice was ragged and threadbare. "I want to tear you apart. I want to rip you to shreds." He moved both of his hands to grasp my thighs, tilting my pelvis so that his thrusts hit even deeper. "I want to destroy you. Want to fuck you to pieces. Want to shatter you. Want to break you."

His awful, wonderful words set a storm to gather low inside me, and I could tell that this time it wouldn't back down. I shifted my hands from the counter to his forearms to brace myself for its attack. The movement drew his attention from the mirror to my face.

"Want to break you," he repeated, his words more of a rumble than actual speech.

"You do," I said, peering up under heavy lids, my voice a mere rasp. "You do break me. Every time."

Reeve's eyes sparked in awe, then the muscles in his neck grew taut and his rhythm stuttered. With a low growl, he froze and spilled into me, his fingers digging so deep into my skin I was sure they'd leave bruises on my thighs.

It was so hot how he defiled and wrecked me. So hot how he loved to see me devastated. So hot that I joined him in his release. My mouth fell open and my climax took over, coarsely racking through my body. Even with the mirror supporting my back, I was freefalling, spinning with pleasure. Only a thin layer of sweat and steam covered my body, but it felt like I'd been pulled underwater into a whirlpool of bliss.

Reeve put himself away, then watched me as I finished, as if completely enamored with my orgasm. As if completely enamored with me.

It was somewhat disconcerting to feel his eyes so heavy on me. He'd seen me come so many times before, but I'd never noticed him so intent. I lowered my gaze, but he lifted my chin, forcing me to meet his stare head-on.

With a gentle touch, he swept a lock of sweat-drenched hair from my forehead. "Every time?"

He'd been tender with me in the past, but it wasn't his usual M.O., and it startled me. Moved me as I realized it came from a place of concern.

"Yes," I answered honestly, because he *did* break me, every time that he stuck his cock inside me, every time that he made me climax, every time that he touched me. Outside of the moment, when the sex was over and we were people instead of sex-driven beasts, it sounded horrible. Who would want to be broken by her lover? Who would want to be destroyed?

I do. I always did. I longed for it and needed it. I needed *him*.

I caught his hand and pressed the back of it to my cheek. "It's the only reason I ever want to be someone who's put together. So that you can break me all over again."

Studying me intently, he skimmed his knuckles down around the curve of my jaw. His thumb grazed along my mouth, slowly. I held perfectly still, not wanting to break the trance, afraid even the rise and fall of my breath would end whatever moment we were having.

Finally, he leaned in and pressed his lips softly to mine. Again. Then again, and this time his tongue slid through the part in my mouth and the chaste caress turned deep and luxurious, but ever considerate. Even when his hands moved to pull my hair and claw at my neck, affection dominated the tone of our kiss.

It was frightening and perfect, the way we molded together, the way our tongues danced. As long as it lasted, I let myself be in it. Instead of analyzing what it meant or panicking about the intimacy or worrying about the woman in the room next door, I simply took what he gave, returning it in kind, forgetting everything but his taste and his touch and him, him, him.

When it was over, he pulled back, but not away, the connection remaining even when physical contact had ceased.

He glanced around the room, seeming to suddenly notice the shower running behind us. "Clean up." Was it my imagination or were his words as unsteady as the rhythm of my pulse?

"Are you joining me?" What I really wanted to say was *don't leave.*

He shook his head and my heart sunk. But then he said, "I'll still be here when you get out."

The water was lukewarm when I got in. I didn't even want a shower anymore, my initial reason for wanting one long gone. Still I stood under the nozzle for long minutes, letting the spray get cold enough to shock my brain back into cognitive reasoning.

What the hell was going on between us? Reeve acted like he knew. He acted like I should know as well, and if I read him right, maybe I did know. Maybe. Was it ridiculous that I needed clarification?

One thing was certain—I wasn't getting answers standing in here.

I shut off the shower and hurriedly wrapped a towel

around my hair and another around my body. He'd said he would still be there when I was finished, but all of a sudden I worried that he wouldn't be. When I opened the bathroom door and found him lying on my bed, his arm thrown over his eyes, I almost sighed audibly.

Then I stood in the doorway and stared in amazement. Because *he was still there*. And he'd undressed. His shirt and jeans had joined my clothes on the chair and now he was just in his boxer briefs, which meant he was staying. Which meant . . . ?

Seeming to sense me, he shifted his arm above his head and glanced in my direction. "I like it when you look at me like that. Almost as much as I like it when you look at me like you think I might slit your throat in your sleep."

I opened my mouth to respond then decided there wasn't any response appropriate. Instead, I asked, "Are we . . . *together*?"

"Well." He turned to his side and propped his head up on his hand.

And I held my breath.

"Right now you're over there and I'm over here. But when you come over here and we get into bed then, yes, we'll be together."

"Reeve!" Goddammit, this was hard enough. "I'm being serious, here. Please."

His grin faded. "What are you asking, Emily?"

"I'm asking about Amber." Amber, who was right on the other side of the wall. I could feel her presence in the room as if it were only a thin screen that divided us instead of a foot of drywall and insulation.

"Seeing as how she's not in the room, I'd say I'm even more not with Amber than I am not with you."

I let out an exasperated groan. "Why do you keep dancing around this? Do you not know what you want? If that's the case, just tell me." I'd never done this before—

never had to feel my way around a relationship that wasn't based on financial security. Strangely, this was so much more difficult than negotiating where I'd live and how much I had for living expenses and whether I'd allow double penetration or cum in my hair. This was my heart on the line, and until now, I'd had no idea how much I valued that.

Reeve sat up, and in the sincerest of tones, he said, "It's not the case. I know what I want. I want you." His lip curled into a half-smile. "Now come here."

My head fell with the weight of relief. Me. He wanted *me*.

It doesn't mean he doesn't want Amber, too, I reminded myself. There had been other men set on sharing us. That arrangement had worked once upon a time, but we were long past that, no matter who Amber was these days.

I pulled the towel off my hair and tossed it to the floor before starting toward the bed. I was nearly to him when I halted. "And what about Amber?"

"She'll have my protection as long as she wants it."

I nodded, glad for that, but it hadn't been what I was asking. "What did you tell her at dinner?"

Reeve sighed as if he were losing patience with the conversation, but he answered all the same. "I didn't tell her what I would have told her if you had stayed."

"Which would have been . . . ?" I gestured for him to fill in the blank.

He scooted to the end of the bed and reached for my hand to tug me closer. "That things have changed since she left," he said. He drew me closer still so that I was standing between his knees. "And that I'm currently in a committed relationship. With you."

My breath caught around the lump in my throat.

But then I noticed the flirty glint in his eyes, and, though his tone had seemed earnest, I didn't buy it. I couldn't.

I rolled my eyes. "No, you wouldn't have."

"Yes. I would have."

I pushed playfully at his shoulder. "Can you stop messing with me for half a second and be honest?"

In a blur of motion, Reeve had me pinned on the bed. "I am being honest." He narrowed his eyes. "Why is it so hard for you to believe me?"

Because no one ever chose me over Amber.

I couldn't say it out loud. As if that would jinx it. "It just is."

No sooner were the words out of my mouth than I realized what this was about for him. My trust. Or lack of trust. Again, he was seeking it. Again, I'd refused to give it. But this time it was totally unintentional on my part.

I searched his face, trying to predict what his reaction would be. I was afraid I'd ruined it. Ruined us. I was so desperate to undo whatever damage I might have done that I opened my mouth and prepared to tell him what he really wanted to hear instead—that I loved him.

Before I could, he broke into a smile. "Well, then you can believe it when you hear me say it to her."

"Okay." How could a word feel so soft on my tongue when it held so much? I couldn't even begin to name the emotions wrapped up in those simple two syllables, so many different shades and colors of relief and hope and affection and amazement.

Then reality came storming in, and I remembered my obligations and promises and all the reasons I couldn't let Reeve declare his love for me to my friend. "I mean, no."

His brow arched. "No?"

His grip weakened with his surprise, and I easily pushed out of his hold and stood up from the bed. I rewrapped the towel around me, gathering myself literally as well as figuratively, and then pivoted to face him. "I have to be the one who tells her."

This wasn't how things worked between us. He was the

one who decided how things would be; I was the one who followed orders. I didn't get to make demands.

This, however, was nonnegotiable.

I shifted my weight from one hip to the other, waiting for his response.

Reeve rolled to his side and eyed me carefully. "As long as you actually tell her," he said sternly.

"I will," I assured him. Then I frowned. "What do I tell her exactly?"

He cocked his head at me. "You know. *You* tell *me*."

It was a challenge, a test, and for half a second I was afraid that I'd fail because I didn't know what the correct answer was.

And then I did. "That I'm yours."

His features barely changed and yet his entire face lit up. "You're mine," he confirmed, pride thick in his tone.

I bathed in that pride. Let his words lick at my skin like the rough washing of a cat's tongue. I felt like I'd been re-made. Claimed. Newly wedded. Though my declaration and his acknowledgment were far from marriage vows, it was the strongest vow I'd ever made.

Well. Besides the one I'd made to Amber.

But this moment wasn't about her—it was about me and Reeve and this bond between us that she had no part of.

If there was any chance of letting her slip farther into my thoughts, it was gone a second later when Reeve yanked me to the bed and flipped me to my stomach.

"You're mine," he said again, this time with a growl as he jerked the towel away from my body. "And now I'm going to fuck you like I own you. On your knees. Ass up."

I scrambled into position while he stripped out of his underwear. Then he was inside me—bruising me, breaking me. Tearing me into a hundred pieces that all belonged to him.

And while he fucked me and used me and made me

beautiful, I stayed almost entirely focused on him. Almost. Because, unlike in the bathroom where the shower had masked our activity, here we were exposed with only that one wall between us and Amber's room. I would tell her about Reeve and me, but this wasn't how I wanted her to find out. So I swallowed my cries of pleasure and pain, and I buried my face in the mattress when I couldn't keep it inside.

He noticed, of course. With his cock buried in my cunt, he pressed his chest against my back and whispered at my ear. "Remember I'm the one who's letting you be quiet. If I wanted you to be screaming right now, you would be, no matter what you wanted anyone else to hear."

Was it wrong that this was his way of making love?

Was it wrong that it was mine too?

Later, like new lovers who can't get enough of each other's touch, we fell asleep coiled, our legs and torsos intertwined, unwilling to be parted even while we dreamed.

CHAPTER

10

The last time I'd shared a man with Amber I'd been twenty-one.

The last time I'd shared one willingly, anyway. Bridge had been after that, but I didn't count him for obvious reasons.

Bryan Crane had been nothing like Bridge. Amber had met him while we'd lived in Mexico. He'd been a guest at the resort we'd stayed at, but, though she'd been at his side the entire two weeks he'd been in the country, I'd been too wrapped up in my own affair to have a chance to meet him myself. When his vacation ended, Bryan had invited her to visit him anytime so, naturally, when we decided to head back to the States, he was the first person Amber thought of to take us in.

"He's so nice," she'd told me with a dreamy look in her eyes, "and really rich. But mostly just really a nice guy." After rescuing me from an abusive lover who had very nearly killed me, Amber had likely thought *a nice guy* was just what I'd needed.

She hadn't understood me back then. Eventually, she began to, but that came later, and, even then, she'd never understood all of me.

"I can't wait to meet him," I'd told her. And maybe I'd meant it. As horrible as my relationship with Aaron had been, he'd taught me some very important lessons about myself—that I had no limits. That I didn't know how to say *stop*. That I was incapable of deciding what was best for me in sexual situations.

A nice guy probably *was* just what I'd needed.

"Anyway, I know you're just going to love him," Amber had said for the fiftieth time as we'd boarded the private plane he'd sent to collect us. She'd been determined to sell me on him, not because I'd been reluctant to go, but because she'd thought it would be good for my morale to have something to look forward to. "Plus he can lick pussy better than any guy I've ever met."

"You're just as beautiful in person as Amber said," he'd told me when I met him in the foyer of his Atherton estate. I'd looked like I'd just been beat up by someone, because I had been, so I knew it was a lie, but he'd embraced me and kissed my cheek and made me believe for a fraction of a second that I actually was a beautiful person.

It had been immediately evident that Bryan was everything Amber had made him out to be—nice, rich, and incredibly good at oral sex. Every word that had come out of his mouth had been gracious and kind and, surprisingly, genuine. His house had been the biggest I'd ever seen, let alone lived in. And he could go down for hours.

He also turned out to be ordinary with a capital *O*. Except for the fact that he'd self-made his billions in the pharmtech industry, there was absolutely nothing notable about him. He was average age (midfifties), average looking, average height, average personality.

But Amber had liked him, and he'd welcomed us into

his life with no hesitation. He was newly divorced, and with his two daughters already grown and married, his fifteen-thousand-square-foot estate had probably felt large and lonely. It was to our benefit—living with him had been a paradise like no other. He'd spoiled us rotten, buying us gifts and bringing in servants to cater to our every whim, and never once did he act as though he'd expected us to pay him back in any way. He was just that nice of a guy.

We did fuck him, though. Of course we did. And just as he'd been outside of the bedroom, he'd been extraordinarily nice inside it as well. His generosity had been what Amber had liked the most about him. Not only did he give her several orgasms in a night, but he'd also caress her and massage her and lavish her with attention.

He'd caressed and massaged and lavished me with attention as well. I just hadn't responded to it the same way she had. The sex had bored me and it had very rarely been satisfying. Poor Bryan would lick me for what seemed like days, and I'd still go to bed frustrated. Each time was exhausting and embarrassing and not worth the effort. Early on, I'd considered excusing myself from the sexual activities altogether, until I'd discovered that Bryan also had difficulty releasing. Pretty much the only thing that could make him come was watching two women make out. More specifically, watching Amber and me make out. My participation had therefore been necessary. At least, it had been if I'd wanted to keep everyone happy, and I very much had wanted just that. So what if my own happiness was ignored? At least it was a much better situation than the one I'd left in Mexico, where orgasms were in abundance but so were bruises, fractures, and other assorted injuries.

Despite having several guest bedrooms available, we had all slept together in a king-size bed in Bryan's master suite. It was the first threesome we'd been in where Amber

and I had been treated equally, or, at least, where the fa-
çade was that we were equal. I didn't try to fool myself
that it was anything other than a ruse, and in case I ever
needed proof, I got it when I'd sit outside on the balcony
off the bedroom and listen to their conversations spill
through the vent, unbeknownst to them.

One night, I heard Bryan ask, "With Emily—am I doing something wrong?" His concern had been sincere
enough. Even though I suspected he was in love with Amber, he'd always sincerely wanted both of us to be happy
and cared for.

"She was raped," Amber had said in explanation for my
distance. "She's still recovering. Be patient with her."

"That must be it. Sure. I'll be patient." There had been
a brief pause before he'd asked, "Are you sure she's just
not more into women than men? The other day she got off
really easy when she was fondling your tits."

"I'm surprised you noticed since you also got off really
easy when she was fondling my tits."

Bryan chuckled. "True, true."

They grew silent and my thoughts turned to the occasion Bryan had mentioned. We'd been in a variation of
sixty-nine—Amber, sucking Bryan's cock while he went
down on her while, at the same time, he'd finger-banged
me. And I'd tried—I'd tried *so hard* to be turned on, but I
just couldn't get there.

Then Amber had let up on the blow job to turn to me.
"Touch my tits, Em."

I reached over and cupped a breast in my palm.

"Not like that," she'd snapped. "My nipples. Roll them
between your fingers. Do it now." She'd even taken my
hand and placed it exactly where she'd wanted it.

Amber had always been good about asking for what she
needed, but usually it had come in the form of pleading.
This time, she'd made demands. She'd ordered me and

used me for her own sexual pleasure. It was base and completely self-motivated on her part—she hadn't been concerned whether I was getting off. She'd been so consumed with her own climax that I hadn't even been sure she'd realized Bryan was working on me as well.

And I'd found that arousing. Very arousing.

"But you know," Amber had said, interrupting the memory, "I don't think that was the reason Em was into it." She said it if she'd been thinking about the scenario at the same time I had, and in retrospect, she'd realized something that she hadn't before.

A chill had run down my spine and my skin had started to tingle. It had felt like suddenly discovering I'd been being watched when I'd thought I was alone. It had been unnerving and comforting all at once.

Bryan hadn't seemed to have been struck with the same insight that Amber had. "You don't? What do you think it was?"

She'd hesitated. Then in her ultimate flirty voice, she'd said, "You. Silly." I'd known her well enough to recognize her cover. She hadn't really believed that it had been he who'd made me come. Either she hadn't wanted to hurt his ego or she hadn't understood enough about what she'd figured out to put it into words so she'd given him the credit. But I was certain that she'd had a moment of clarity and that she had finally glimpsed the animal that dwelled inside of me.

Whether that had been the first time she'd ever thought about what turned me on or whether she'd been trying to figure it out for a while, I wasn't sure. But after that, she'd been different with me, acknowledging the thing between us more than she ever had before. She'd always been slightly bossy, saying things like "Wear your hair in a French braid," instead of "maybe you should braid it" like someone else might. Now when she made her commands, she'd look me in the eye as if to say, *"I know. I know this is what you want and so that's what I'll give you."*

It tied me to her tighter than ever. Eventually I learned it tied her to me as well.

We'd been living with Bryan for almost a year when he proposed.

"I think you should marry me." It had come from out of the blue. I'd learned to tune out most of their conversations, and I'd been surprised I'd even caught it.

"What?" Amber had said, echoing my own surprise.

"Marry me." His tone was so sweet. So sincere. So romantic in its simplicity. "Yes, I'm more than twice your age, and my ex will have a field day with the news, but who the fuck cares? I love you. I can make you happy. Let's get married."

"I don't know what to say." Her voice sounded tight and I'd wondered if she was fighting tears or if she was already crying.

"Yes. You could say yes." His boyish exuberance in that moment endeared him to me more than anything before had.

"I love you, too, but . . ." She'd trailed off, and when she'd spoken again, her voice had been stronger. "What about Emily?"

What about Emily? Yeah, what *about* Emily?

"Emily too! I can only legally marry you, but for all intents and purposes, she'll be part of the family. As far as I'm concerned, you're a package deal. You love her, you know I'm fond of her, and she's an absolute essential part of our sex life. So let's make it official. We'll be scandalous and depraved—you, a knockout of a wife, and Em, our live-in mistress. Everyone will judge and talk about us behind our backs but mostly just because they're jealous."

I had to stifle a laugh. It wasn't funny, I was just happy. Happy for *her,* even as I knew that living that arrangement for the rest of my life would kill me. Even as I knew that I'd say yes right along with her. Because it was everything that she'd ever wanted in all the ways it was everything I'd never wanted at all.

But she hesitated. "I don't know."

"Are you worried Em will feel left out? I'll do everything to make sure she doesn't. I'll buy you both rings. She can wear hers on her right hand if she wants or around her neck. And I'll make sure she's listed as a primary beneficiary. After you, of course."

"Can I think about it?"

I choked back the lump in my throat. It was so obvious to me that she'd already made up her mind, but dear, sweet Bryan either didn't know her well enough or was too optimistic to see the truth.

"Yes. Think about it," he'd said. "Then when you're done thinking about it, say yes."

We'd moved out before a week had passed.

We'd left the cowardly way—packing up our belongings one morning while he was at work, not leaving so much as a note of explanation. "He'd try to stop us if we said good-bye in person," Amber had said.

"Tell me again why that would be a bad thing." But she hadn't even told me why a first time. Just like she hadn't told me about Bryan's proposal. And because I never challenged her decisions, I didn't push her.

Though we'd been taken care of for the better part of twelve months, we had no money of our own, so we had hawked some of the nicer pieces of jewelry that Bryan had gifted us, including a diamond ring I hadn't seen until it was on the counter before the loan shark. That baby bought us enough for two months' rent at a dump of a motel in Hollywood.

I hadn't said more than two words at a time to her between the pawnshop and the motel registration. Finally, in

our room, I couldn't hold back any longer. "I know he proposed." I didn't bother trying to hide how I felt. I'd been
angry that she'd walked away so easily from Bryan. Bitter
accusation streaked through both my words and my body
language.

Amber had furrowed her brow, never bothering to look
up from the drawer she was arranging. "He told you?" she
asked eventually.

"No. I heard you talking. I could hear every word you
said when I was out on the balcony, by the way."

"Ah." She'd nodded as if that were the end of the conversation.

"Amber." I had waited until she looked at me. "Why did
you say no?"

She'd sighed, but not so heavily that she'd actually relaxed her guard. "I didn't say no. I just didn't say yes either."

"Why not?" I'd stomped my foot, demanding for her to
take me seriously. "Why the hell not? He's the most decent guy we've ever been with. And I think he actually
loves you. I mean, besides just for what you do in the bedroom."

Her expression had tightened. "I know. I think so too."
She'd shut the dresser drawer and pivoted toward me. "He
wanted both of us."

It had been my turn to furrow my brow. "Is that why
you left?" I'd been so perplexed by all of it, I hadn't been
able to come up with a theory. Had it really been as simple as not wanting to share?

I'd taken a step toward her. "Amber, we don't have to
be a ménage à trois. If you had wanted him to yourself,
all you had to do was tell me."

She'd smiled. "It's not that."

"Then what was it?" I'd been beyond frustrated, desperate to understand her as well as I'd hoped she'd understand me.

"He wasn't what you wanted."

Her answer had taken me aback. Amber had always led me through life and I'd always followed. Not once had we ever stopped to talk about what either of us had wanted.

She really had seen me after all. It hadn't just been in my head.

I'd softened at that confirmation. "Maybe not. But he was offering a good life. Trust me, it wouldn't be settling."

She shook her head. "It would have been settling for you."

"Then I could have left."

"But that's just it—you never would." Now she was the one who'd sounded frustrated. Her words the ones streaked with bitterness.

Immediately she'd attempted to smooth me over. "And I wouldn't want you to. I love you, Em. One day things might be different, but right now if I have to choose between a boy and you, I'm going to choose you."

She'd met my eyes, and I saw the truth. Yes, she'd left because of me, but underneath that, I'd seen something else—fear. She's been afraid to stay, maybe because she hadn't known how to be happy or maybe because she'd been scared he'd eventually leave her and she'd wanted to be the one to do it first.

The minute she'd realized that I'd seen through her, she'd turned back to her task of unpacking. "It would have been weird without you, anyway," she'd said, stuffing panties into a drawer. "We already established our relationship as a threesome. Bryan wanted the things you gave him as much as he wanted the things I gave him. It doesn't work to go from sharing to not sharing."

I'd leaned my shoulder against the wall and continued to study her. There had been so much that we'd had in common. And so much that we hadn't. If I'd found the right guy, I'd have stayed through the worst of things.

When she'd found the right guy, she'd left while it was still good.

One thing had suddenly seemed quite clear—we couldn't go on like we had been forever.

I raised my chin and issued the challenge. "Then maybe we shouldn't share anymore."

"That's probably not a bad idea."

I don't know what I'd expected her to say, but it hadn't been that. "No, it's probably not," I'd agreed, more hurt than I should have been considering I'd been the one to suggest it.

Hostilely, I'd grabbed a dress from our suitcase and went to the closet to hang it up, determined not to let her see me get emotional.

But there'd been no hangers in the cheap motel room. I'd kicked the door, stubbing my toe so hard that tears pricked my eyes.

Amber had glanced at me over her shoulder. "Are you okay?"

"Yes," I'd hissed. Then I'd leaned my back against the wall, balled the dress up, and hugged it to my chest. "I didn't give anything to that relationship, Amber. You wouldn't have missed me as much as you think you would have." The words had felt like peanut butter in my mouth. They'd stuck and even when I'd pushed them out, there were still traces of them clinging to my tongue.

Amber had crossed to me then. She'd put a hand on my shoulder and with gentle eyes, she'd said, "He likes having two girls. Without you, he'd eventually want to bring someone else into the bedroom. He can't come without watching two girls go at it, and I'm not interested in having sex with any woman that isn't you."

They were excuses, and we'd both known it. "He wouldn't need another girl. Or you'd turn on a fem porn and it would be fine."

She'd shaken her head. "It's not the same." Then, with only the slightest bit of a breath beforehand, she'd said the words that had addressed the real issue. "Anyway, you wouldn't have left so it wouldn't have been necessary."

"I would have," my throat had caught on the lie. "If you had really wanted me to."

"Whatever," she'd grinned. "I wouldn't even begin to know how to get rid of you."

"Are you kidding me? Getting rid of me is easy—you just have to tell me to go." It had hurt to be that honest, in parts of me that I couldn't identify. It was as if I'd given up the key to my demise simply because the person who'd asked for it was someone I'd loved *that much*. So much that I'd been willing to clue her in on the one way she could destroy me.

I'd had to do it. She'd sacrificed for me. It was only fair I did the same.

At one point in our relationship, she would have refused the gift. She would have pushed my words away and told me that she'd never let me go.

But things had changed with Bryan. She'd seen what could have been possible for both of us. And, likely, she'd begun to grow weary of my needs and the trouble they'd caused.

So instead of denying, she'd embraced it. "I'll remember that next time."

Next time came a whole year later, but she did, indeed, remember.

C H A P T E R

11

Amber wasn't in her room when I looked for her the next day. Nor was she downstairs. Reeve also wasn't around. Despite the amazing breakthrough we'd had the night before, something inside nagged with suspicion and jealousy. Were they together somewhere? And if they were, did that mean anything?

Around noon, the anxiety began to crescendo, and I paced the house like a mother worried about her lost child. I was seriously considering asking Tabor, the bodyguard Reeve had assigned to protect me, to help me search the ranch, but then, on my third trip to the back deck, I spotted her.

She was standing about fifty feet away, by the shed that housed the ATVs and other large ranch equipment. Jenkins circled her feet as she chatted with a trim man in a button-down flannel shirt and jeans. He wore a cowboy hat so I couldn't make out his face, and, even though his description matched nearly every one of the men on the ranch, I tensed and began searching for clues that would tell me if it was Reeve or not. He was drinking a beer, something I'd never seen Reeve do midday. But Amber was so familiar with him. She grabbed the bottle from his hand and took a swig. With his hands free, the man retrieved something from his back pocket. Cigarettes, I realized. He lit one and handed the pack to Amber as she returned his drink.

Reeve didn't smoke. It wasn't him. And, when the man tilted back his head to take his next swig, I got a better glance at his face. I couldn't be positive, but it looked like he was the cowboy who'd approached me the night before. I tensed remembering how he'd eerily confronted me. I had no real reason not to trust him, but I didn't. His presence on the ranch felt wrong and his friendliness with Amber made me even more wary.

I was still shielding my eyes from the sun and squinting in their direction when he pointed up at me. Amber's gaze followed his gesture and, when she saw me, she waved. I smiled tentatively in return. A second later, she left him at the shed and crossed the yard toward the back of the house. Soon, she was climbing the stairs to the deck.

"Hey," she said, bracing her injured side. "Guess I should have taken those stairs with a little more caution."

"Are you okay?" There was really nothing for broken ribs except rest, time, and painkillers, and I doubted the small dose of methadone that Jeb gave her was enough to touch it. "Do you want me to help you back to bed?"

"Please, no," she said dramatically. "I'm so bored in that bed. I can deal with the ache in exchange for freedom."

Amber had never liked to be cooped up or stifled. When Reeve had forced her to stay at the ranch, she must have gone out of her mind. She was the type of person who needed to spread her wings. In fact, as I studied her now, I noted that her color was better than it had been in days, and the fog that had clouded her eyes was gone. It was surprising how different she looked from the meek woman I'd sat with in the bathroom only one day before.

"You look fantastic," I said, somewhat awkwardly. Talking to her still wasn't as easy as it had been once. I supposed that took time. "I'm guessing that you're feeling better?"

She eyed me carefully. "Maybe I should be asking that about you?"

"Oh, because of dinner last night?" I forced a smile that I hoped was just bright enough to be convincing. "I was fine. I was just giving you privacy."

"Thank you for that. I wasn't sure." Her expression didn't give away what other reasons she might have thought I'd run. "And, yes, I feel much better."

"That makes me so happy!" It felt false, but I meant it. I did want her better. I wanted a lot of things, though, and some of them were not straightforward. Some of them I wanted in degrees with conditions attached and some of the things I wanted were in direct contradiction to other things I wanted just as much.

But for that moment, I tried to concentrate on wanting her well and was glad that she was.

Well enough to traipse around with a cowboy, no less, which wasn't a judgmental thought, but a concerned thought.

I peered over the railing and saw that the man had disappeared, as eerily as he had the last time I'd seen him. "Who was that guy you were talking to?"

"Buddy, maybe?" She shrugged, avoiding eye contact. "That's his nickname, I think. I, uh, just met him. He bummed me smokes." She dug out a half empty box of cigarettes from her back pocket and held them up for me to see.

Years had passed in between us but I could still tell when she was keeping something from me. I didn't have to wonder what she was hiding—she'd shared that beer with the stranger when Reeve had already made it clear that he expected her to refrain from alcohol while she was trying to get over her addiction. While I wanted the best outcome for her recovery, I understood why she'd bristle at his attempt to control her behavior. And knowing Amber, it was only natural that she'd try to undermine him at every turn.

It was a war that the two would have to battle for themselves, I decided. But I was still concerned about the man—Buddy. "Be careful around him, okay? I saw him last night, and he gave me a creepy vibe."

Amber tilted her head. "Creepy how?"

He'd known my name, but that in itself didn't make him a criminal. "I don't know. I just didn't feel safe alone with him."

"You're a hottie who likes to do bad things," Amber said with a wink. "I imagine there are a lot of men you'd feel unsafe with."

It was an accurate remark—so accurate that I couldn't decide if it offended me. It was the kind of thing she could have said years ago, and I wouldn't have batted an eye. Now, there was too much distance between us and I couldn't pinpoint her motivation like I could then.

But that was the way with reunions—it took a while to settle back into the comfort of the past. At least she felt she could try.

So I decided I could as well. "Just as I imagine there are a lot of men who would feel unsafe with you."

"Touché," she said, beaming, and the sunlight caught in her hair, illuminating her so brightly she had a glow. Like an angel.

Angel. Reeve's name for her.

I ignored the pinch in my chest and concentrated on

what was right in front of me. My friend, looking vibrant and alive, the way I'd remembered her.

And if she was back to herself then that meant I had no excuse not to tell her all the things I needed to tell her, once and for all.

I took in a deep breath of mountain air and let it out slowly. "Can we talk a bit? Alone?" I almost hoped she'd say no. I almost hoped it so much that I gave her an easy opportunity to bow out. "If you're feeling up to it, because if you're not—"

She cut me off. "I'd love to spend some time with you. Have you been up to the attic yet?"

"No." I hadn't even known there was an attic.

"Fabulous. I get to show you. Nobody ever goes up there, and it's one of my favorite places on the ranch."

I followed her into the house and upstairs to the far bedrooms. I'd explored when I'd first arrived at the ranch, but I'd spent barely any time in this area after determining it was comprised of two rarely used guest suites. Between them was what, I'd assumed, was a linen closet. However, when Amber opened it, there was a hidden staircase.

"I'm warning you," she said before climbing up, "there might be spiders."

I shuddered dramatically. I'd always been horribly afraid of eight-legged creatures. "I'm guessing there might also be mice."

She mirrored my horror. "I'll take on the arachnids, you take on the rodents."

"Deal," I said with a laugh. Then we went up, one after the other, and we were two young, courageous girls again, out seeking our next adventure, like no time had passed at all. It felt easy, like getting on a bike after not owning one in a decade. It felt like the kiss of an old lover, lips fitting together as if made in the same mold. It felt better than I could have imagined.

It felt like coming home.

At the top of the stairs, I discovered the attic wasn't as dark as I'd expected. Light streamed in through a window on the east wall. It was there Amber led me, carefully stepping over an assortment of paint cans and brushes and worn suitcases and long forgotten Christmas decorations. This had been the house where Reeve had grown up, yet I'd seen nothing to indicate as such in the rooms below. Among the dusty boxes that lined the walls, I felt for the first time that a family had once resided here, and I had a pang of sadness for the parents Reeve had lost when he was only sixteen.

When she reached the window, Amber turned back to me. "The pane sticks, and I can't do any lifting yet. Would you mind?"

"Not at all." I traded her places, and, after flipping the latch to unlock it, I pushed the frame up as far as it would go. Outside the window, there was a flat section of roof that butted up to the eave behind it. "I'm guessing we're going out?"

"You got it."

I climbed out first, then turned to help Amber, who groaned as she hoisted herself up.

"Maybe this wasn't such a good idea," I said, wincing in sympathy.

"Nah. It's totally worth it for the view." She gestured behind me, and I spun carefully to look.

"Oh, my God," I gasped. The landscape was breathtaking. On the ground, there were too many trees surrounding the main house to see the green meadows beyond and the yellow flowers that blanketed the hills. Beyond that, snow-capped Rocky Mountains extended so high that the peaks disappeared into the nearly cloudless sky.

"It's why I always liked to come up here. It's peaceful." Amber sat down on the eave, and, when I looked at her now, she seemed less familiar than she had a moment before. In so many ways, she was still the woman I'd remembered. But in just as many, she wasn't. The Amber I remembered hadn't ever found beauty in nature—she'd preferred shiny jewelry and expensive cars. She'd been happiest in large crowds with her music turned so loud that she could feel it thunder her feet. Peace and quiet and solitude were things that had always made her restless.

Of course, we weren't kids now. But we were still young, not even thirty. And Amber suddenly seemed very old for her age.

She pulled a cigarette from the pack she'd gotten from Buddy and cupped her hand over the end to light it. When it was lit, she took a long puff, then sighed, smoke curling into the air as she did.

"God, I needed that." She leaned back against the roof, cradling her head in the crook of her arm.

"You know what this reminds me of?"

"Of course I do," she said, as if it were ridiculous that she wouldn't be thinking exactly the same thing. "I think about that night a lot."

I did too. It had been the first night I'd ever hung out with her. We'd snuck onto the construction site of an apartment building and smoked a pack of cigarettes on one of the balconies while we'd flirted with the men in hard hats and shared things we'd never shared with another person before. It had been the birth of our friendship.

Now, as our relationship was reborn, it seemed fitting that we were in a similar location.

I crossed to stand by her. "Can I have a drag?"

She held the cigarette out toward me, but asked, "Do you want one of your own?"

"I think a drag is enough." I took a puff and immediately had to stifle a cough. "Damn, I haven't had one of those in years. How the hell did we smoke so many of them?" I cringed as I handed the cigarette back to her.

She laughed softly. "We got used to the abuse."

Those were loaded words. Words that spoke volumes about so many aspects of our friendship and the men we'd chosen and the lives we'd lived. They were words that could be understanding but also very bitter. And when I looked her in the eye, I knew she meant them in every way they could be meant.

I had to tell her about Reeve. Now.

She inhaled her cigarette, staring up at the sky as I took a seat beside her. "Amber—"

"You know," she said, cutting me off, her voice tight as she held her breath. She exhaled before going on. "When I left you that message, it wasn't because Reeve wouldn't let me leave the ranch."

My neck prickled, and I had that sudden gut-dropping fear that I'd been lied to. "He didn't keep you here?"

She twisted her head to look at me. "No, he did."

Then Reeve hadn't lied.

"Oh. He did," I confirmed, trying my best to recover from the false alarm. Why was it so hard for me to trust him? I hated that I always assumed the worst where he was concerned. As if proving any of those assumptions true would change how I felt about him.

She nodded as she took another drag. "Just, that wasn't really that bad. I mean, it was. I wanted to kick him in the balls for it." Her eyes narrowed. "In fact, I think I did that too." She exhaled and smiled, as if enjoying the memory.

I drew my knees up to my chest and hugged them, uncomfortable with how it felt to hear her talk about Reeve. More specifically, *her* and Reeve.

She sat up and crushed the butt of her cigarette against a roof tile. "But he wasn't malicious. He didn't do it out of cruelty. He did it because he loved me, and he didn't want to let me go, and, yeah, it pissed me off, but I didn't feel like I needed to be rescued." She tossed the butt over the side of the house.

I swallowed a chiding remark about littering and asked instead, "Then why?"

She hesitated, her attention elsewhere. My eyes followed her gaze to her shoes—*my* shoes, rather. Her whole outfit had been borrowed from my closet.

And while I was marveling at how convenient it was that we'd always worn the same size, she said, "I called that day because I'd been thinking about not living anymore."

My breath caught as I realized what she was saying.

"I'd been thinking about it a lot. And, at the time, I thought you were the only person who'd maybe be able to talk me out of it." She glanced at me and grinned, as though that could lessen the severity of what she'd just said.

But it didn't in the least.

"Oh, my God, Amber, no." I had no other words than those. Even with years of acting under my belt, I couldn't improvise anything better. Because I'd never played this role before. I'd never in a million years imagined that I'd be on this side of a suicide conversation. With Amber, of all people.

Was this why she loved it up here so much? Had she stood up here, alone, trying to get the courage to step off the edge? Was she still thinking about it now? My mind flooded with worry while my body tensed with panic.

"Please. Don't." She waved her hand dismissively. "Don't make it melodramatic. It wasn't like that. I just . . ." She trailed off, and although she was silent for only a few seconds, the weight of them made it feel three times as long. "I don't know. Being trapped here gave me a lot of time to think, I guess. A lot of time for introspection. And I started to think what's the point? I was broaching thirty and had nothing to show for my life. I saw how far you'd come—"

"Hardly," I interrupted, mortified that she would have looked to my bland, empty life as a model of comparison.

But she ignored me, raising her voice to make sure I didn't speak over her again. "—while I was still living off someone else's handouts. No friends. No family. No one to miss me if I were gone."

"*I* would have missed you!" My throat was thick and my eyes watery. "I missed you *every day.*" It was such a relief to finally say that to her. Like it had been a shameful secret that I'd carried for years and now I was at the day of reckoning.

"And not just me. You had Reeve. He wanted to marry you." My voice caught, and I hated that it hurt to say that even now, when my sole focus should have been on comforting her. "How could you say you had no one?"

"He wanted kids." She said it as if that were an obvious explanation.

"So? You'd have kids." And somewhere in the back of my brain I thought, *Oh, he wants kids* and *God, do I want kids too? With him?*

Amber shook her head. "I can't."

I furrowed my brow trying to decipher if she really meant *can't* or if instead she meant *won't.*

"I can't have kids," she said again. "I've been checked out. I did too much damage to my uterus. Too many terminated pregnancies. And I can't have them." She gave a weak laugh. "Ironic how I did everything to not get pregnant before and now I'd do anything . . ."

She took a deep breath then let it out. "It wasn't fair to take that from Reeve just because I'd been reckless with my past."

I scrubbed my hands over my face not sure if I wanted to cry or scream. Or laugh. Knowing that whatever I did, this wasn't going to end well. It was one thing to claim Reeve as mine when she'd left him because they were wrong for each other, and quite another when she'd left him because she loved him.

It was unfair. And, irrationally, it felt somewhat spiteful.

Or maybe I was the one full of spite.

Steepling my fingers, I pressed them against my lower lip. "Did you talk to him about this?"

"No. I would have rather died." Her eyes met mine. "So I called you."

"Amber . . ." A thousand words died on my tongue before I managed, "I wish I'd been there for you." But, selfishly, I didn't really wish that at all. If she had reached me when she'd called, I wouldn't have had to go looking for her. I wouldn't have found Reeve. And while knowing him—*loving* him—might be the death of both Amber and myself, it was an end I would walk toward with my head held high.

"It all worked out okay," she said in a halfheartedly reassuring tone. "He let me go, and then I ran to Micha. Which was just as cowardly, and, in many ways, just as suicidal. Especially if he decides he isn't done with me."

My stomach lurched as Amber voiced the very thing I'd been concerned about. "Do you think he'll come after you?"

She shrugged. "I don't know. Probably not. I'm sure I'm just being melodramatic."

She sounded like she was trying to convince herself as much as me. "I'm just lucky Reeve is still willing to take me back in after I went to Micha just to piss him off."

Lucky, yes. Not loved, as I feared. Just lucky. "How did you even know that would make him mad?"

"It's a long story." She glanced at me and must have realized I wouldn't accept that for an answer, so she went on. "He'd been at a social event Reeve had taken me to. Reeve hadn't known Micha would be there, and they saw each other. There was a confrontation. Micha cornered me and said, 'If you're ever tired of him . . .' Blah, blah, blah. He was just another dirty, rich old man, you know? I blew him off. But then when I left Kaya, he was there. I mean he was right there, in town. Like he was waiting for an opportunity to, I don't know, get at Reeve. I made a snap decision. And I regretted it."

"He was waiting for you? That should have been a sign that he was not a good guy right there." I didn't hide my frustration.

"I had nowhere else to go, Em."

I shifted my whole body toward her. "You could have come to me." If she'd thought of me long enough to call, then she could have thought about running to me instead.

"I couldn't," she said emphatically. "Not after I sent you away like I did. I'd been horrible to you, and I didn't deserve your forgiveness or your pity hospitality, which was what you would have given me." She pointed a stern finger in my direction. "Don't try to deny it."

"I sure as hell will deny it. I would have helped you and it wouldn't have been out of pity."

"Yes. It would have. Then you would have been right where you'd been when I'd last seen you. Like you are now." She stood up and faced me. "You're so much better than this kind of life, Emily. I knew it, and that's why I pushed you away, and then you went and proved that it was the right thing to do. I never meant to drag you back here."

One phrase caught in my head: *"that's why I pushed you away."*

But she'd sent me away because of Bridge. Because she'd thought I'd stolen her boyfriend. Hadn't she?

The question that I'd buried for so long came to surface,

demanding to be asked, even though I already knew the answer. Even though I knew asking it now would change everything I'd held on to for these past six years. "You believed me when I told you Bridge raped me, didn't you?"

Her face screwed up, as if the truth were as painful for her as it was for me. "Yes," she said, her voice raw. "Of course, I believed you. He was a psychopath, and I left him ten minutes after you were gone."

And just like that, the fable I'd held on to for all those years crumbled in front of me. It was a truth I'd known somewhere deep inside but hadn't wanted to acknowledge. It had been easier to walk away when she and I had been at odds. If I'd let myself believe that she'd been on my side the whole time, I'd have never left.

I opened my mouth to speak, but she guessed my question and cut me off. "And don't ask me why. You know why."

It was another truth I hadn't wanted to face. Even now I had to hear her say it before I could accept it. So I shook my head and stayed silent.

She heaved a sigh. "Because you wanted to leave and I was holding you back."

I let my mind go back to that time, trying to see it from her point of view. I'd been pregnant. I'd gone to stay with her until I got on my feet. I'd been planning to get a job and take care of myself.

"No." I shook my head more vigorously. "You weren't holding me back at all."

"How can you say that? If you hadn't come to stay with me, Bridge would never . . ." She let her sentence trail away. Let the silence give us time to fill in the awful conclusion. *He would never have raped me. He would never have put scissors inside me. He would never have caused my miscarriage.*

"You can't blame yourself for that." My declaration felt

weak. How many times had I blamed myself? "You *helped* me. You were there when I needed someone."

"And you couldn't see that I was in no shape to be the strong one. You wanted me to save you. *Me*. A coked-out party girl who'd hooked up with a violent asshole. You thought I was the person to lean on?" Her tone was bitter and compassionate all at once.

She took a breath and her next words were softer. "You had enough money to set yourself up. You would have gotten a job in modeling and you would have had your baby." Her voice lilted up with emotion. "You would have been better off. You *were* better off."

"I wasn't better off. I was half a person. I was miserable." Every day without her had been a battle. Even when I'd gotten my life together, I'd been empty. I'd been alone.

She scoffed. "Well, you made out pretty swell for someone who was miserable."

I threw my head back and closed my eyes. All the horrible things I'd imagined about myself because she'd cut me off came flooding back. I'd told myself she couldn't handle my addiction to men who were bad for me. I'd convinced myself that my sexual proclivities were so terrible that she'd decided I wasn't worth the trouble.

"I'd thought I'd become a burden to you," I said, straightening to look at her. "So many times before you could have settled and been happy if it hadn't been for me."

She gave a brusque laugh. "That's not me, Emily. I'm not someone who wants to settle." She let a beat pass. "At least, I wasn't back then. When Reeve proposed, for the first time, the idea sounded kind of nice. I was just too scared to accept it."

Her words were knives, slicing at me and the visions I'd had of a future with Reeve. Wounding any chance of repairing our friendship. What I wanted warred with what was best and every option in front of me led down a road I had no desire to go down.

But there had been so much honesty in the air already. The floodgates were open, and truth flowed off my tongue, without me even feeling like I'd chosen it. "Amber, I seduced him." There it was—the worst truth of it all.

And wasn't ironic? For years, believing she'd blamed me for taking her man. My vow to never let it happen again. Me, forced to do the thing that had torn us apart so that I could get her back. Now I learned that she'd never thought that about me at all.

It felt like a catch-22. Like I'd never had a choice but to become the person she'd led me to believe I was. I didn't even get to enjoy the release of guilt before I had to admit that, even though I didn't deserve the blame she'd put on me then, I did deserve it now.

My excuses held no water, but, with my head hung, I made them anyway. "I had to. To get to you. To try to find you, I seduced him."

"I know." Her voice was steady yet soft. "I already know."

My head flew up in surprise. "You do?"

"Well, yeah," she said, as if it had been obvious. "You couldn't have gotten past that front gate any other way."

Exactly. Which was why I'd done it. And yet I still felt so terrible about it. "I'm sorry."

"Why?" Her expression was incredulous. "For doing what you had to in order to find me? I'm grateful! No one has ever done anything like that for me before. It's only because of you that I'm still standing here. I know Micha didn't hurt me enough to kill me that last time, but if I hadn't gotten out, he would have eventually. It's only because of you that I'm here." She corrected herself. "Well, and Joe, but he told me you'd hired him to find me so that still counts as you."

Now I knew what she meant about feeling unqualified to be a savior. Because I'd given up my search. I'd told Joe to stop investigating. He'd gone to Vilanakis on his own. "No," I protested. "It wasn't me."

Again, she ignored me. "And imagine what a total asshole I feel like. Because I made you be that person again. I made you return to the very thing I wanted you away from. Trust me when I say it's the last thing I wanted. I'm drowning under that guilt."

"Stop it," I said, standing, needing to meet her eye-to-eye. "Don't you dare feel guilty. You came after me so many times. Saved my ass. Got me on my feet again. I *owed* you."

She rolled her eyes so vehemently that her entire head swept with them. "You didn't owe me shit. We were even and now *I* owe *you*." She took one step toward me, taking a determined stance. "I'm going to pay you back, eventually. Someday. Somehow."

"You don't owe me." I still couldn't figure out how she'd thought we'd been even before. "There's nothing to—"

"There is and I will." Her tone said there would be no more arguing about it.

"Then pay me back by saving yourself, for once!" I snapped. "Stop with the bullshit life. Grow up! Think about your future. Make some goddamned plans."

Her expression said she was stunned, and frankly, I was as well. I'd never talked to her like that. Never tried to suggest I knew what was best for her. Never realized how fiercely I resented the lifestyle we'd both once called our own.

But a dam had broken inside of me, and I couldn't hold any of it back if I wanted to. She thought about killing herself? It broke my heart—it did. But if her life was so miserable, then why was she still repeating the same mistakes over and over? Why didn't she at least try to get out? It wasn't fair for her to talk to me about being scared of happiness, about being indebted to other people, as if she were the only person in the world who'd felt those things. As if she were the only one of the two of us that had it hard.

But I was a hypocrite.

Because even after I'd changed my circumstances, I'd still felt insecure and empty. So who was I to tell Amber about progress?

"I'm sorry." I turned away from her, not wanting her to see from my expression how much of a sham my life was. "It's not my place to lecture you."

"No. You're right." Her tone had an edge to it that wasn't there before, an edge that could simply be attributed to the rawness of her admission. Or maybe it was a sign that she was just as resentful of me as I feared she was.

Behind me, I heard her take a step, felt her moving closer toward me. Goose bumps rose along my arms and my neck tingled as I realized how near the edge I was. How easy it would be for her to push me off, if she wanted to. If she were *that* resentful.

It was a lunatic idea and I didn't really think she had any intention of harming me, but because the thought crossed my mind, I jumped when I felt her hand land on my shoulder.

I giggled nervously and pivoted toward her, wishing I had something solid to lean up against for no other reason but to steady the dizzy buzz of adrenaline.

"You're right," she repeated, her expression kind despite the hardness in her eyes. "And I've already come to the same conclusion. I have to be true to myself, once and for all. No more running away, no matter how scared I am. Time to 'grow up,' as you said. Time to be strong."

Her speech gathered conviction as it went on, each new phrase sounding more resilient than the one before. I wanted to be proud and assured with her, but the more her confidence grew, the more dread seeped into my veins, and

I wasn't sure if it was me being silly or insightful so I tried not to jump to conclusions.

Then she landed at her finale. "Which means I've got to fight for what I want."

With those words, I didn't have to jump; I just had to take the next step. "And you want Reeve." It wasn't a question. I knew the answer as sure as I knew anything.

"I do," she affirmed. "Maybe there's no future for us." *No future for us.* It echoed in my head. "We have our issues— I won't lie about that. You've heard some of it. He's nearly impossible. Well, you know him now. He's controlling and obstinate and difficult."

"Yeah. He's all those things, all right." My words sounded clipped, purposefully so. I had to draw back. Had to close myself off. Had to put up my guard. Because there was no way I'd be able to take her on if I let myself be compassionate.

And I *would* take her on. I was already preparing my attack. My only hesitation was in trying to figure out—did she really not know that I belonged to him? Or was her ignorance an act? If it was an act, did she think her hold on me was so strong that I'd quietly step out of the way just because she'd asked?

If she did believe that, I couldn't blame her. She was almost right. She did own me like that. Just, he owned me like that now, too.

"I love him," she said, sounding like she was a million miles away despite her bold declaration. "Love counts for something, doesn't it?"

"I wouldn't be here if it didn't." My smile was genuine. "You know that's why I came for you, right? Because I love you?" I hoped she truly believed that before I told her the rest—that I loved Reeve too. That he loved me as well.

"Yes. I do." She paused, and I was about to give my

thoughts on the subject when she continued. "Reeve told me he still loves me, too, you know. So I think we might have a real chance."

I hadn't heard her right. I couldn't have. "He told you he still loves you?"

"Yes. Last night." In that angel-like way of hers, she beamed.

She might as well have pushed me off the edge because I began to free-fall. Emotionally, anyway. I was still standing in the same place, my feet planted solidly on the roof, but inside, my heart sank like it was on an elevator, descending slowly and steadily, falling with no end in sight.

"What else did he say?" I didn't know how I'd managed the question, but I heard it, the words circling back to my ears, detached as if someone else had asked it, and I thought briefly how fitting it was that my voice had survived this crash. It was the most recognizable part of me, anyway. I could return to LA, to my life, to my job, and, as long as I could still say my voice-over lines on the set of my show, no one would ever know how completely I'd been destroyed.

This. This was why I never let myself trust.

"He didn't say a lot." Amber's image blurred in front of me. "Just, he apologized. And said he'd changed—which is probably a good thing. Maybe he won't try to keep me locked up this time." She laughed.

When I didn't join her in her amusement, she sobered. "Anyway. That's when he said he still loved me. I know love isn't everything, but it's more than I've tried to build a life on before. So I'm hopeful. It's the first time I've been hopeful in a really long time."

"That makes me really happy for you, Amber." It wasn't a lie, exactly. I did feel happy for her in some strange part of me that could separate us. Separate her man from mine.

That part of me was as hopeful as she was. That part of me was so excited and touched that it didn't seem odd that my eyes were watering.

Even though it wasn't that part of me that had the tears.

"You deserve it." I forced a smile.

She met it with a modest smile of her own. "I don't know that I'd go that far."

"No. You do. Everyone deserves to have hope." Even me.

And right now, my hope was that Amber was lying.

CHAPTER

12

After helping Amber back inside and down from the attic, I made some vague excuse to leave her and search for Reeve.

"He's out with the Callahans," Parker, the stable manager, told me when I found him out in the shed, putting gas in an ATV. "They're branding the calves up at the cowshed in the east pasture."

The doors of the shed were propped open so I squinted out over the property and pointed toward one of the trails. "That one? The one on the north side of the house?"

"Yep."

I was already heading out when he shouted after me, "It's a little more than a mile out there. If you want to give me fifteen or so to finish up, I can drive you."

"In fifteen minutes I'll already be there." I didn't wait for his response, half afraid he'd try to talk me out of going alone. It was already a bad idea to talk to Reeve about this while he was trying to work. At least, I could keep Parker out of it.

And maybe the walk would cool my head a bit.

It didn't. In fact, if anything, it stirred me up more. There were too many layers of emotions within me, and when I was able to come to terms with one, I'd lift it up to find another, more complicated layer in its place. And there didn't seem any way to organize them all.

If I started at the beginning, it would be with Amber. After all these years, there was still a bond between her and me. For that reason, I wanted to be able to give her what she wanted. But did that have to be Reeve? She'd left him. She'd said good-bye, and it didn't matter if she'd gone because she was wrong for him or because she was scared or if she regretted it. She was gone when I'd found him. He was fair game. What's more, he'd chosen me, and even though I was frightened, too, I was ready to be his.

Unless he'd lied to me. Unless he'd led me on.

Unless he'd chosen Amber, too.

He hadn't ever told me what he'd said to her at dinner. Only what he *would have* said had I stayed. Had he dodged because he hadn't wanted me to know what had really occurred? Could he have told her he still loved her—because he didn't want to hurt her or because he meant it—and then spent the night in my bed?

However hard I tried to stay away from that possibility, it kept circling back to face me. It bullied and chased all other conclusions until it was the only one in my head, and by the time I'd made the mile trek to the east pasture, it inhabited me so completely that I felt like a stranger in my skin. A stranger filled with rage.

I'd only been to the east part of the ranch once before. Reeve had taken me on a horseback ride that had led past the cowshed and the grassy fields that surrounded it. The pasture had been quiet that day, the air filled with the pleasant aroma of wildflowers, with only a few cattle moseying around.

Today it was filled with commotion and cowboys, and the scent of smoke and burning hide was so strong it made my eyes water. The cattle had been gathered into the corral, where they bellowed and snorted as men on horseback rode through the herd, disrupting their formation to round up the calves. Outside the pen, a fire blazed in a large pit. Surrounding the pit were several branding stations, each made up of a dozen or so men and women.

As I pushed through the crowd looking for Reeve, a woman opened up the gate and a horseback rider emerged, dragging a calf behind him with a rope. He pulled the animal toward me and I scurried backward trying to get out of his way, but crashed into a woman who gave me a spiteful look before brushing past me. I stepped to the side and bumped into someone's elbow so forcefully it knocked the air from my lungs and sent me tripping into the circle of ranch hands that had gathered to pin the animal down. I pitched forward, tumbling toward the end of a hot iron when two strong hands dug into my upper arms and pulled me back.

"Jesus, Emily," Reeve said, after he'd tugged me a safe distance from the branding station. "What the fuck are you doing out here? Are you trying to get yourself seriously hurt?"

I blinked, too stunned to speak.

Reeve didn't wait for an answer, clutching me to his chest. "It's okay," he said, and it sounded like he was trying to calm himself as much as me. "Just . . . breathe. Take a few deep breaths. You're okay."

I did as he said, staring transfixed at the scene Reeve had rescued me from. One woman used a piercing gun to tag the calf's ear while another man brought his knife toward the animal's scrotum. Then came the iron. I closed my eyes tightly, not wanting to see any more, but on the back of my lids I saw the red blaze of the brand coming toward me and the fiery end was a V instead of a K and even though I knew that Amber's tattoo hadn't been applied in that manner, it seemed just as vile.

I turned my head into Reeve, as if that would chase the frightening image away.

"Blue Eyes." He smoothed his hand over my hair, attempting to soothe me.

But the sound of his voice brought me back to reality, and with a jolt I remembered why I'd come out here in the first place.

I pushed away abruptly and hugged my arms around myself.

"What's wrong?" His voice was edged with concern that was probably left over from the near accident he'd rescued me from.

My adrenaline was still spiked as well, and so instead of starting the conversation in a rational manner like I should have, I pounced. "Do you still love Amber?"

"Excuse me?"

He'd heard me. I was sure of it.

We were face-to-face, far enough away from everyone else that it was unlikely that anything more than a few snatches of conversation could be overheard, and yet we were not at all in private. His warning was silent, conveyed simply in the arch of his brow, the reminder that there were rules and regulations I was meant to adhere to. Picking a fight in public was definitely not on the approved list of behaviors.

And I didn't give a flying fuck.

I repeated my question, speaking each word slowly and succinctly. "Do you still love Amber?"

"Do *you*?" His words were filled with as much accusation as mine had been.

It surprised me. "That's not the same."

"Really? How is it different?"

I opened my mouth to answer and realized I wasn't sure it really *was* all that different.

I rephrased. "Did you tell her that you still loved her?"

The three seconds between my words and his response were heavy and long.

Then, with his gaze pinned on mine, he answered. "Yes. I did."

When Amber had told me Reeve still loved her, I'd felt like I was falling. Now, I felt like I was fading. As if I were merely someone in a photograph left out too long in the sun, and although parts of my figure remained, I was no longer identifiable. I was no longer a person at all.

It didn't matter if there was more to his story or that he'd been honest with me when I'd asked or that he couldn't really be blamed for loving a person that everyone loved, even me. All that mattered was that he'd said words to her that he still hadn't officially said to me. I was the one who was supposed to belong to him. I was the one who deserved the sentiment, never mind my inability to say the words myself.

What mattered was that he'd said it to her, and that hurt.

I couldn't be there anymore. Spinning away from him, I took off.

"Don't walk away from me!" he yelled after me.

"This discussion is over!" I called back, not bothering to turn my head.

Again I felt his grip on my upper arm as he pulled me to an abrupt stop. "The conversation is over when I say it's over." The menacing warning in his tone caused my heart to flip. My breath stuttered, and I wondered if he knew it wasn't just because he'd startled me or because I'd exerted myself.

The gleam in his eye said that he did.

I couldn't stand that gleam. Couldn't bear what it did

to me, how it made me sizzle and melt like it was a branding iron on my skin.

I yanked my arm away. "I can't talk to you right now."

He grabbed me again, this time at both of my wrists. "You don't have to talk. You just have to listen."

Listening was even worse. He'd either say something I didn't want to hear, or worse, he'd say something that I did. So I struggled to get away.

"Stop fighting me." His grasp tightened.

But I was fierce. I was desperate. I had more on the line, and even though he would always be able to overpower me, I was determined to make him work for it.

Even in front of all the people around, he wasn't afraid to take me on. I raised my arm and twisted underneath so that I was facing away from him, my hands trapped behind me.

"Goddammit, Emily, sometimes I want to throw you down and tie you up like you're one of the calves." With a grunt, he tugged my back into his chest and crossed his arms around me like he was a straightjacket.

I pushed against him once more, but it was useless. He had me.

He had me in more ways than one. Even though I was upset, his embrace made my stomach spin and my head grow light, and the expert way he'd overcome me begged me to yield.

Yes, he had me.

"Are you done now?"

I huffed but I'd given up struggling. With him, anyway. I was still struggling with myself. Still fighting against my wants.

"Good," he said, his breath skidding against my ear. Thank God my shirtsleeves were long and he couldn't see the goose bumps on my arms.

"Now," he adjusted his grip, and I swore I felt his cock thickening at my ass. "Yes. I told her that I loved her. I told her I loved her but that *things have changed*."

Things *had* changed. Everything had changed when he said those words to her. And to tell me about it while he was hard against me? It was wickedly unfair.

He was silent for a beat, as if he thought that what he'd said or how his body reacted to holding me should have some impact.

When I didn't respond, he let out a sigh of frustration and released his grip.

I stumbled forward but managed to stay on my feet. It pissed me off as much that he'd let me go as that he'd restrained me in the first place. And it pissed me off that it pissed me off. I considered taking off again, but what would be the point?

So I stayed put, my back to him, rubbing my wrists, red from how tightly he'd gripped them.

"I told her I wasn't the man I'd been when she left, Emily." There was the barest hint of an appeal in his timbre. "And that she couldn't walk back in here and expect things to be the same."

I threw back my head and swallowed down a sob. If that had been all he'd said, if he'd left out the part where he loved her, maybe she would have heard it how he meant it.

But there's something about that four-letter word that's magical. It can erase everything else. So who could blame her for hearing only that? Who could blame me for noticing its absence when he spoke to me?

I twisted to look at him. "What else?"

He shook his head. "That was it. I didn't say anything else." His expression was unguarded. Open. It was maybe the most transparent he'd ever been with me, and even if his lips didn't say it right then, his eyes urged me to remember he had, in his way, told me he'd loved me too. I could have been moved, if I'd let myself.

But Amber had opened up to me today as well. Either I let her words move me, or his. It was like a tug-of-war with my sympathies. Who could pull harder on my heart-strings? I'd have to choose. And I didn't want to choose between them.

It was easier to just be pissed.

"Well, congratulations," I said, sarcasm spilling from my tongue. "You've sure created a mess, haven't you."

His body tensed as he cocked his head at me. "How exactly do you figure that I've made a mess?"

"You led her on!" Behind him, a couple of the ranchers watched our argument with interest.

Reeve kept his focus directly on me, seemingly oblivious to everyone else. "I think I was pretty damn straightforward."

"*Pretty damn straightforward* would have been you telling her that you wanted me." He should have been the one to decide. Not me. I couldn't.

I *wouldn't.*

"After you'd made it abundantly clear that *you* wanted to be the one who told her?" He threw his eyes toward the sky. "Jesus, Emily. I'm damned if I did and damned if I didn't. There is no winning with you."

I didn't have a comeback because he was right—there was no winning. Someone would lose, and I couldn't stand that it might be my fault.

Crossing my arms tightly over my chest, I pushed my voice past the knot in my throat. "Don't you dare turn this around on me."

He took a step closer so that he was practically hovering over me. "Why not, Emily? Because you can't handle your share of the blame? Because, just like always, you'd rather let things happen to you instead of taking any action so that you don't have to accept responsibility for the consequences?"

His words slaughtered me with their honesty. "That's cruel." My lip quivered with rage. I pointed an accusing finger in his direction. "That's how you *want* me. To be submissive and obedient. Then, when I am, you use that to blame me for being passive?"

His lip curled upward. "And that's how you want *me*, now, isn't it?"

To his credit, he couldn't hold his smile, as though he suspected he might have gone too far.

But was it really too far? Or just too accurate? It was precisely why men like Reeve were so bad for me—because I *wanted* them to be bad for me. And, when they were, it hurt.

Funny how then I wanted them even more.

"No," I said, making a decision, for once, on my own. The only one I could. "I don't want any of this. This is over."

"This is *not* over," he said, but I'd already turned away.

He might have come after me again, except, right then, Parker drove up on one of the three-wheelers, the expression on his face clearly upset.

Reeve's eyes darted from me to his stable manager, as if trying to choose which of us to deal with. Finally, he said, "We are not done talking about this, Emily," then turned to Parker. "What is it?"

"You're needed back at the house." He glanced at me and I could sense he was unsure whether he should say more in front of me.

Immediately, I feared the worst. "Is it Amber?"

Reeve arched a brow, seconding my question.

"I'm not sure. Come with me and you'll see."

It was vague, but the little bit he'd shared combined with

his anxious demeanor was enough to send chills down my spine. It was also enough to get Reeve moving. He jogged to one of the ATVs parked at the side of the corral. I turned back to Parker to ask for a ride, but he was already driving off toward the house.

Dammit. I'd have to hike back, another fifteen-minute walk.

But then Reeve pulled up beside me. He didn't meet my eyes. "Coming?"

I climbed on behind him, too worried about Amber to care that I'd just told him we were over. I'd meant it in the moment. But I wasn't so sure when my arms were wrapped around him, my body pressed tight against his solid frame. Wasn't so sure I could ever be over him.

We followed on Parker's tail to the shed, where I assumed we were parking the ATVs. But he pulled up short instead of driving all the way in. That was when I noticed the security guard standing by the open door, looking as though there were something of interest on the other side.

I hopped off as soon as Reeve cut the engine, but I let him take the lead, following two steps behind as he circled the open door. He halted suddenly, and I had to step to his side to see around him.

Joe was there, kneeling on the ground. A second security guard was at his side, and, between them, lay Jenkins. Vomit pooled around his mouth, and his eye was lifeless and glassy like a marble, and it only took me a second to realize he was dead.

But I wasn't a squeamish woman, and it wasn't his limp body that made me gasp. It was the word painted on his side in large red letters: MINE.

There was something utterly menacing about the image, and not just because the dog was dead. I had a feeling the word would have had the same impact if the dog had still been alive, and I found myself wondering if Jenkins's death was meant to be a message as well or if it was just easier to apply paint to an animal that couldn't move.

And if death was the message . . .

I shivered and casually took a step closer to Reeve. Whether we were together or not, I felt safety in his presence. Ironic, considering how often he scared the hell out of me.

"Time of death had to be recent," Joe said, delivering his report to Reeve, and, unless I was imagining things, avoiding all eye contact with me. "The body's still warm."

"Antifreeze?" Reeve asked.

"That usually takes a couple of days to affect the kidneys. Chloroform, maybe?"

Though he was trying to mask it, Parker seemed sullen. "He was completely fine when I fed him at dawn."

I'd forgotten that he'd taken an interest in Jenkins. Working on a ranch, Parker was surely used to dealing with animal deaths. He must have felt particularly close to this dog to be upset.

Honestly, I felt a bit unsettled as well, especially with all the other emotions festering inside me. It had happened so fast, too. "I just saw him about ninety minutes ago."

The second security guard, the one sitting with Joe, stood and addressed me. "Was he acting strange then? Did he seem thirsty or was he convulsing at all?"

I tried to remember if I'd seen anything unusual. "I don't know. I was too far away, but I'm pretty sure his fur hadn't been painted then. Amber was with him. I think she would have said something if he was acting out of the ordinary."

"Actually," I added, feeling oddly like I was about to get Amber in trouble, "someone else was there with her. Buddy is the only name I know. I think he's one of the Callahan men." There was still nothing to validate the creepy feeling Buddy gave me, but my gut sure felt like he was capable of murdering helpless animals.

Reeve and Parker exchanged glances. "What was anyone even doing up here on branding day?" Parker asked his boss. "I said it seemed suspicious how there were so many new guys this year. You thought I was being paranoid."

"Let's not make any rash conclusions. There are ways to get on the land back here without passing through the front gates. This could have been anyone." Reeve said "anyone" as if he might mean someone in particular. Someone who wasn't on the ranch at all.

He gestured at the graffiti on Jenkins's body. "Even if this Buddy person did this, he's not the one behind it."

The hair stood up on the back of my neck, and I had that eerie feeling of being watched.

Reeve nodded to one of the guards, who then pulled out his cell phone and made a call. "Yeah," he said, not bothering to step away, "we need a deeper investigation of everyone on the Callahan crew list, particularly someone named Buddy. That's the only name I've got, obviously it might be a nickname. Also, all recording equipment that has a view of the shed and the yard around it needs to be pulled and watched starting around noon. If you see the dog in any of the footage, mark that."

"The only cameras we have focused out here are on the shed itself," Parker said, shifting his jaw like he wished he had snuff tucked in his cheek. "We don't have anything watching the trees beyond."

Reeve's expression remained stoic. "We could get lucky. Security footage will at least rule out some possibilities."

Parker scratched behind his neck, then turned his whole body toward Reeve. "It's him, isn't it?" He didn't leave any chance for response, apparently confident in the *him* he guessed was responsible. "What do you think he means by 'MINE'? The land? Is he trying to stake some claim to Kaya?"

Reeve shook his head and I suspected it meant he didn't know rather than a firm *no*. He was still studying the animal on the ground. "Have you turned the dog over?"

"Right," Joe agreed. "We need to see if there's more." He grabbed Jenkins's front paws while Parker took his hind legs and together they flipped the dog to his other side.

As Reeve must have guessed, there was painting on this side of his body, too—SHES.

"Shes?" Parker pronounced the word with a short *e* vowel.

"It's missing the apostrophe," Joe explained as he stood, wiping his hands on his pants.

"She's mine," Reeve said quietly, putting the words together.

Parker squinted up toward Reeve. "But who's 'she'?"

Before anyone had a chance to speculate, another voice piped in behind us. "Me."

We spun in unison to see that Amber had joined us, her arrival unnoticed.

"It's me," she repeated, a distinct tremor in her voice. "It's from Micha, and he means me."

CHAPTER

1 3

Reeve's eyes hit me the minute I walked into Amber's room, knocking the wind out of my lungs. I pretended I was just out of breath from running up the stairs to get there, but the truth was I'd taken my time.

While Amber had been fairly composed when she'd first arrived at the scene of the dead dog, it didn't take long before she'd worked herself up to hysterics. Both Reeve and Joe had tried to calm her, to no avail. Eventually, after summoning for Jeb to meet him in her room, Reeve had swept Amber in his arms and carried her inside.

Joe had followed without a glance in my direction, essentially confirming my suspicion that he was avoiding me.

I'd lingered behind, feigning interest in the guard's investigation as they took pictures and looked for more clues around the shed. Mostly I hadn't wanted to be with Reeve as he attended to Amber. I hadn't thought I could stand it if he ignored me while caring for her.

I hadn't realized that his attention would be just as unbearable.

Amber didn't seem to notice my appearance with her face buried in Reeve's chest. She lifted her head. "He said he would find me if I ever left. He says that to all the women."

It was the same thing she'd said outside. She'd been repeating variations of it for the better part of the last hour, and every new rendition gutted me.

Reeve sat with her on the bed, his arm wrapped around her shoulder, but he kept his gaze locked on me. "He's not going to get you here."

His intense stare made my focus shift so that he was front and center in my vision, and everything else around him blurred and lost context. Yet, even though I refused to see his hand drawing soothing strokes up and down her arm, I could *feel* it. As sure as if it were my body he was caressing. Except that, instead of making it buzz with butterflies, my stomach curled. And instead of wishing it would last forever, I prayed that it would just end.

Jeb, who'd been at the dresser filling a syringe, turned toward the bed now. "Amber, can you give me your arm?"

Though she seemed barely aware of anything but the man holding her, she turned up her forearm, exposing it toward Jeb.

"This will make you rest a while," Jeb said as he emptied the medicine into Amber's arm. "So you can relax."

She nodded obligingly. Then she sat up with an anxious start. "He marked me, Reeve. He thinks I'm his! He's coming after me! He's warning me!"

"He's warning *me*." Finally Reeve moved his eyes to her, and my entire body sagged as though I'd been relieved of a heavy weight. "And I don't take warnings lightly."

Already I missed the burden of his stare.

"You have to keep me safe. You can't let him get to me."

Amber's pitch crept higher and it was impossible not to feel worked up with her. *For* her. My skin itched with agitation, and I kept shaking my arms, thinking I'd find something crawling on them but never did.

And Reeve—his expression was stoic and his voice even, but behind his eyes I saw a glimmer of helplessness. "I'll organize shifts again," he said, and in that moment I was glad he was there for her, no matter how torn up with jealousy it made me. "You won't ever be alone."

The words he'd intended to be comforting only stirred her up more. "No, I don't want babysitters," she insisted. "Micha had people watching me all the time. And you." She paused just long enough for her meaning to punch. "I can't live like that again."

I hadn't put that in perspective before, hadn't really thought about how she'd gone from Reeve's prison to Michelis's. I'd assumed she'd been rebelling against Reeve's authority when she'd demanded no more attendants the night before. Now I realized she was just trying to grasp at freedom that likely felt fleeting.

Reeve's expression fell as he absorbed the impact of her statement. "Then I'll double the guards on the house and at the gate instead. Is that better?" He managed a smile, but it felt strained.

I shifted uncomfortably, wishing I were anywhere else. My emotions and loyalties were tied up in knots. Even as my chest ached with sympathy for Amber, my blood also heated with resentment. She'd *left*. Reeve had treated her shamefully, but she'd made her own choices after that. Was it fair to add her sins to the load of guilt he already carried?

"That would be better," she said, snuggling into the crook of his arm. "I feel safe right now. With you here. Don't leave me, Reeve. Say you won't leave me."

I wanted to throw up. I wanted to scream. The best I

could get away with was rolling my eyes, and I turned around so that no one would notice.

Except Joe noticed.

I hadn't realized he was sitting on the arm of the love seat behind me and when I turned, his glare hit me as forcefully as Reeve's eyes had met mine when I'd walked in.

I groaned inwardly. Everywhere I looked there were thorns.

Well, Joe would probably be easier to deal with than Reeve and Amber.

I crossed over to him. "Did she say anything about Buddy before I got up here?"

"No," he said, his voice hard. "She's useless."

"She's scared."

"Yeah, I've seen quite a few addicts get 'scared' just like that when they wanted a dose of something."

I gaped, taken aback by the harsh judgment. "She's received a horrible message from a horrible man. She's upset!"

"You've seen her bruises and scars. I can't believe this is the worst that Vilanakis has done to her."

"Which is exactly why she's scared that he's back," I snapped. It was obvious his remarks had more to do with me than with Amber. With the day's events, the argument I'd had with him the night before seemed petty to me. Apparently, *he* was holding a grudge.

And I was already cranky. Cranky enough to let him have the fight he seemed to be intent on having.

"Don't forget you wanted to save her, too," I hissed, only half-heartedly attempting to keep my voice low.

Joe stood, and I followed when he gestured that we take our conversation to the hallway. "I wanted to get to Vilanakis's more serious crimes," he said, when we were outside the room. "I was hoping she'd be more helpful in that department."

My brows lifted with indignation. "Is that why you're really still here? Were you hoping that he'd be lured after her? You're probably ecstatic that you can continue your investigation now."

He drew back, appalled. "What? That's not . . ." He shook his head. "Okay, yes. I was concerned that Vilanakis would come after her. Would come here. So I stayed. But it wasn't because I wanted to draw him out and it wasn't for her."

"Sorry that Amber's life isn't meaningful enough for you," I sputtered, ignoring that he'd implied he'd stayed for me. "Next time I'll make sure that the person I hire you to save scores high on the Joe Cook barometer of worth."

He eyed me for a beat, a hint of amusement in his features. " 'Joe Cook barometer of worth'?"

He was mocking me. But hearing him repeat it, I realized it really had been a silly thing to say.

I let out a sigh. "I don't know what I'm saying. You're mad at me, and I'm irritated because I really need a friend at the moment."

"I'm not mad at you, exactly," he said, suddenly fascinated with the toe of his shoe. "You're just frustrating."

"So I've been told." Most recently today, when Reeve said he wanted to tie me up like the calves. I'd probably find that a turn-on if the rest of the conversation hadn't been so painful.

My chest pinched with the reminder of the heartache I was trying to ignore. I pushed past the urge to cry. "Anyway, I'm sorry for being difficult. I'm sorry for being someone who makes decisions that are rarely wise and generally impossible to understand. That's kind of the definition of who I am."

"Nah, I shouldn't have belittled your feelings like I did." He lifted his eyes to mine. "And there's definitely more to the definition of Emily Wayborn than 'rarely wise and impossible to understand.' "

His kindness was another thorn. It reminded me again of all the things I would never be, such as a person who could be loved by a decent guy.

I cocked my head and offered to shake. "Friends?"

He scowled. But he took my hand and shook it. "Friends."

We were still shaking when Reeve walked out of the room. Immediately he fixed on our clasped hands, as if he were jealous of Joe. As if he had a right to be jealous of anyone.

It infuriated me, and even as it did, I jerked free from Joe's grip. God, I disgusted myself. No wonder Joe was frustrated with me.

"She's sleeping," Reeve said, whether updating us on Amber's state or explaining why he'd left her, I wasn't sure. "Jeb's going to stay with her for now."

"She said she didn't want babysitters." I hated how spiteful I sounded almost as much as I hated how spiteful I felt. "Are you ignoring that?"

"No, but I think someone should be with her until I can get guards on the house. Especially when she's been given a sedative that should really be administered in a hospital-type setting." His reasoning was fair, but his tone was as nasty as mine.

The sound of footsteps on the stairs drew my focus. I looked to see Brent ascending. He perched on the last step and nodded at Reeve. "Branding should be done in a couple of hours. Our guests will be on their way by dinner."

"Good. No one knows there was an incident?" Reeve asked.

"Managed to keep it under wraps. The boys all think you're tending to a sick girlfriend."

I grimaced despite myself. A lot of those "boys" had seen Reeve fighting with me an hour before. They probably assumed he'd left to make up.

Oh, if it were only true.

"Thank you, Brent," Reeve said, and even though I wouldn't let myself look at him, I could feel his eyes on me. Always on me.

Brent leaned a hand on the rail post. "Have you had any e-mails from him since yesterday? Are you going to e-mail him back?"

I perked up at Brent's questions. It didn't take a genius to guess the *him* Brent referred to was Vilanakis. This was the first I'd heard about an e-mail, though. "What is he talking about?"

Reeve shot a warning look toward Brent before addressing me. "It's nothing you need to be concerned about."

Granted, it didn't take much at the moment to piss me off, but this legitimately pissed me off a lot. "Bullshit. That's my friend in there. What e-mail is he talking about?"

When Reeve didn't say anything I looked to Joe. "No idea," he said, his hands lifted in innocence.

I shot a glare at Brent instead.

"Not my business to say anything," he said. "Shouldn't have even brought it up."

"No, you shouldn't have," Reeve agreed. Then, with a conceding sigh, he said, "It was a taunt, Emily. That's all. A message meant to put me on edge and that's all you need to know."

I was beginning to feel as tired of babysitters as Amber did. "Will you stop sugarcoating and tell me what the damn message was already?"

He looked me firmly in the eye. "No. I won't." His tone and posture said the discussion was final. He turned to Brent next and said, "No, I'm not going to try to e-mail him. That's what he wants. I'm not letting him bully himself into my life. But if he attacks again, he'll regret it. He can't break long-standing rules without expecting me to retaliate. Do we have the manpower to double up on security?"

Brent nodded. "If we don't, I'll make sure we do."

The two continued to talk while I concentrated on holding it together. If I didn't, I would explode. I wasn't even sure what form my explosion would take, if it would be tantrum or tears. Anger, frustration, rejection—all were bubbling just under the surface, and it was all I could do to keep it down.

Brent's lip twisted up in a mischievous grin. "Sure you don't want to send him sort of message in return?"

"No message. He wants to play games, fine. I'm not stooping down to that level."

Any minute, I told myself, *Reeve will turn back to me and tell me about the e-mail.* He'd humiliated me by dismissing me in front of Joe and Brent. He'd shown he had the upper hand. Any moment he would realize he'd proved his point and he'd stop being an ass and answer my question.

"The security tapes are cued up in your office, by the way," Brent said. "Whenever you're ready."

"I'm ready now." Reeve didn't even glance at me as he crossed to follow Brent down the stairs.

In disbelief, I called after him. "Reeve?"

"Yes?" His expression was impatient, and his brow arched in question.

"Nothing," I said, biting back any emotion that threatened to show. I turned my back toward him. "Joe, I need to get off the ranch for a little while. Can you take me to dinner?" Admittedly, though my invitation was sincere, half of the reason I'd extended it was to ruffle Reeve's feathers. It was manipulative and defensive, but I couldn't help myself.

"Emily," Reeve warned from behind me before Joe had a chance to respond.

Feigning innocence, I peeked over my shoulder and imitated his recent address to me. "Yes?"

He made a sound of incredulous amusement, a sort of harsh laugh that suggested he saw right through me.

He probably did.

Then he said definitively, "You're not leaving Kaya."

I spun toward him. "What did you say?"

"You heard me." Though he'd left no room for argument, he didn't walk away. Instead, he held his position, as if he wanted to see how I'd react. As if daring me to challenge him.

There was no way I was turning down that dare. "You're going to try to keep me here?" I took a step toward him, hinting at his sins of the past. "You said you'd never—"

I wasn't surprised when he cut me off. "This isn't about anything but your safety. With what happened here today, this is not the time for you to be traipsing around town unprotected."

"I won't be unprotected. Joe will be with me. And, considering *what happened here today,* I'm not sure that you can say the ranch is safer than anyplace else."

His irritation was evident in the slant of his eyes, in the way he held his shoulders, in the heat that radiated from his body and hung in the air like a blanket ready to smother any opponent in his path. "I'm telling you not to go, Emily. You choose to do with that as you wish." Then he turned and descended the stairs after Brent.

"So," I said to Joe, swallowing the bubble of heartache in my throat. "Interested in taking me out?"

"Um. Sure." Joe's reluctant response told me both that he didn't much care to be a pawn in my argument with Reeve, and that even so, he was on my side.

"Awesome," I said with a smile brighter than I felt. "Give me thirty minutes to clean up."

Joe didn't ask where I wanted to go, and I didn't mind. We drove into town without talking. When he'd pulled over and I looked up, we were at The Four Seasons Resort.

"Brent recommended the grill," he said, as the valet

opened my door. "More meat and potatoes, but I think that's standard fare around here."

Joe respectfully let me brood in silence until we were seated and our waiter had brought our drink orders. Then he stretched and scratched at the back of his neck. "You made a great point earlier about the ranch being a potentially unsafe place at the moment."

"You think so?" It had sounded good when I'd said it, but not because I was particularly worried about safety. At least, not my own. "I'm only concerned about Amber. I'm not anyone's target."

"Not that you know, anyway."

I raised an inquisitive brow. "You think that article yesterday really makes me that vulnerable?"

"Maybe." He swirled the Wild Turkey around in his tumbler. "He's not coming after her because of affection. You don't win back the girl that you love by killing dogs."

"This isn't about love," I agreed before taking a sip of my merlot.

"Right. It's about exerting ownership. And I don't think it's just about him believing she owes him. It's about Vilanakis wanting to take away Sallis's prized possession."

I cringed inwardly at the label he'd given Amber. "Which is why she's not safe."

"Except Amber's not really the one who's his prized possession these days, is she?" He let that settle over me as he tossed back his drink in one gulp.

It was an arguable point, and my first instinct was to say that there was no way that Vilanakis could know much about me, but I realized that wasn't true. Someone had gotten to Jenkins, and that same someone could very well have seen Reeve and me arguing by the corral or embracing on the back deck or making love on the porch swing.

"No wonder Reeve hadn't wanted me to leave the ranch. Why did he let me in the end?"

"It's not because he doesn't care. If that's what you're thinking."

It irritated me that he could read my thoughts so easily. "Since you know so much, then why? Because he didn't want to cause a scene? I don't really think that Reeve cares so much about keeping the peace."

"My guess is that he doesn't want to worry you. Probably the same reason he doesn't want to tell you about that e-mail."

The waiter arrived then with our dinner and so the questions brought up by his speculation faded into musings that I mulled over as I cut into my fish. It was a nice thought—the idea that Reeve wanted to protect me from knowledge that might make me anxious. But it didn't fit his M.O. Reeve was secretive because he liked to hold all the cards. When he wanted to protect someone he gave them "babysitters" and brought in extra guards.

I glanced around the restaurant wondering suddenly if Tabor had been sent to follow me but didn't see him anywhere.

God, what was wrong with me? I'd been mad when he'd tried to keep me from leaving, and I was hurt when he'd let me go. Reeve was right—there was no winning with me.

I set down my fork, my appetite having vanished. "How long are you planning to stick around here? Around the ranch, I mean."

Joe took a swallow of his water before answering. "Trying to get rid of me?"

I smiled, but it faded quickly. "I was thinking maybe it was time for me to go home."

"Are you wanting to leave Kaya or leave Reeve?"

I didn't *want* to leave either. I *needed* to.

But I didn't bother correcting him. "Both?" It was only one word but it was harder to say than I'd thought it would be. I'd missed Amber, and I wanted so much to work on rebuilding our friendship. Especially after hearing how much she'd struggled with worthlessness and how vulnerable I sensed she was.

But if I were to stick around, I wasn't sure that I could resist Reeve. Even if he continued to love us both, as I suspected he would. It would torment me and shatter me to pieces, and I knew myself well enough to know that I'd very likely end up falling back into his bed or his barn or his porch swing. And when Amber found out—because she would—the discovery wouldn't help repair our friendship or her sense of worthlessness or lessen her vulnerability.

The only chance to save her was to leave. And wasn't that what all of this had been about anyway? Saving her?

"I just need to go home," I said, reinforcing my decision.

Joe nodded. "I want to go back to Chicago."

"You want to keep investigating Vilanakis."

"I do." He took a bite of his steak.

I tried not to be disappointed. Joe wasn't my only option to get home. He was just the easiest.

"But I need to go back to LA first. Take care of a few things before I head anywhere else. Wanna ride?"

"Really? Even if I might draw attention from the man you're after?"

"Sure. Why not?" He was a smart man. He knew what kind of burden I'd be. "When could you leave?"

Though I knew that it was the right thing to go, I still let myself search for reasons to stay, even one day longer.

I couldn't find any. "As soon as you like."

"Tomorrow?"

"I'll start packing as soon as we get back."

While Joe settled the bill, I told him I'd meet him in the lobby and excused myself to go to the restroom.

On my way out, my head was down and so I didn't notice the figure in front of me until I bumped into him. "Oh, excuse me." I stepped to the side to get out of his way, but he stepped with me. I laughed awkwardly and stood in place, gesturing for him to pass.

He didn't.

He stood solidly in front of me, like a barricade.

I raised my eyes to look at him. He wore a black suit. His hair and complexion were dark and the lack of wrinkles on his face suggested he was younger than I was. And though I was certain we'd never met, there was something familiar about him. Something I couldn't quite place.

"Ms. Wayborn," he said with a trace of an accent, the same Mediterranean accent that was present in many of Reeve's employees. So he'd sent a bodyguard after all.

"You're one of Reeve's men, aren't you? I'm here with Joe, and he can take care of me just fine, thank you very much. So you can go back and report to your boss, or don't, whichever you want. Just leave me be."

He took a step closer. "Are you entirely certain that Joe *can* take care of you? I don't see him around. In fact," he scanned the empty hallway, "I don't see anyone right now. Do you?"

My palms went clammy and my throat, dry. We were utterly alone, I realized, and he was standing close. So close that I wasn't sure I could get a scream out before he managed to clamp a hand over my mouth. And, besides, as the stranger unbuttoned the coat of his jacket, I could see the butt of a handgun at his waist.

I had no choice but to cooperate.

With my heart thudding in my chest, I stood up straighter, hoping to seem braver than I felt. "What do you want from me?"

My skin itched as his eyes swept crudely down my body. "How kind of you to ask." His cruel smile made the hair stand up on the back of my neck. "Unfortunately, it's not what *I* want that's important. It's what my *father* wants. And, at the moment, he'd like to talk to you."

"Who's your father?" I asked, studying his features. His expression was so familiar, that all of a sudden it clicked. I *had* seen him before, once. In the middle of the night. During an online poker game Reeve had been playing with his cousins.

So, though my heart skipped a beat and I suddenly felt drenched with sweat, I wasn't surprised when the man delivered his father's name. "Michelis Vilanakis."

CHAPTER
14

With the stranger's hand gripped tightly around my upper arm, he led me farther down the hall to a service elevator. There, he let me go to swipe a card across the access reader then punched the call button.

I studied him as we waited for the doors to open. "You're Reeve's cousin. Petros, right? Online poker."

"Good memory. Tell him he owes me a chance to win my money back sometime soon. He's been too busy as of late to join any of our games." His cordial temperament was both impressive and chilling. It was a trait that reminded me of the stereotypical mob men I'd seen on television. But there were things that were not at all what I'd have expected from a man with Mafia ties. For one thing, his scruffy face and coiffed hair made him look like an art student or grunge model rather than a hoodlum. And his boyish mannerisms made him seem innocent, and with Vilanakis as a father, I was sure he was anything but.

"I'll give him the memo." I laced my hands together in an attempt to stop their shaking while I tried to assess the level of danger I was in. With his tough guy demeanor and steely confidence, Petros would have been formidable even without a gun. But he interacted regularly with Reeve online, and he knew we were in a relationship. Surely he wouldn't hurt me. Out of respect, like Reeve had said.

Of course, that had been before someone—possibly even Petros—had snuck onto the ranch and killed a dog in order to leave a very pointed message.

"Where are you taking me?" I asked when the elevator doors opened and Petros gestured for me to go inside.

"My father's room is on the penthouse floor," he said simply.

I swallowed as I stepped in, glancing up to note the security camera in the corner, wondering what chance I'd have if I tried to signal for help or hit the emergency button.

But Petros was too close behind me for me to try anything. He pushed the button for the top floor then leaned against the elevator wall and cocked his head at me. "You don't need to look so terrified," he said with a sneer.

"Right. Because I'm completely safe and I can expect to walk away shortly without a hair touched on my head."

He chuckled. "Well. I didn't say that. But I'll tell you this." He leaned forward and lowered his voice to a heavy whisper. "The more scared you look, the more my father likes it."

My breathing grew shallow and I jumped as the elevator announced our floor. Again Petros laughed then nudged me out the door, following close behind. My eyes darted back and forth as we walked down the hallway, hoping to find a route of escape or a hotel maid or a guest who could help me. But there was no one, and soon we had stopped in front of a pair of double doors.

Petros raised his hand to knock, but I stopped him. "Joe

is just downstairs. He'll be worried when I don't return. He'll call Reeve and he won't be happy if anything happens to me."

"I'm sure that's true, Blondie. But, in case you haven't figured this out, my father doesn't give a flying fuck about anyone's happiness but his own." His words settled heavily over me as he rapped on the door in a peculiar little rhythm that I suspected was some sort of code. I also suspected it would be changed to something new the minute I left.

After a few seconds, the doors opened, and a petite, Middle Eastern–looking woman in a simple housedress stepped aside to let us in. She didn't say anything in greeting, didn't meet my eyes, and kept her head bowed as we walked in, and even before I caught the tip of the V tattoo on her collarbone, I wondered if she was there of her own free will.

The suite entrance opened into a luxurious grand room with a stone fireplace and a private balcony. To the left was a dining room large enough to seat ten. Beyond that, the circular-shaped kitchen was probably double the size of my own. In fact, the whole unit was probably double the size of my house in Los Angeles. At least that. To the right was a hallway that, I guessed, led to the bedrooms.

As I turned back toward my hosts, my eye caught on the stack of magazines and newspapers piled on the coffee table. Or, rather, on one magazine in particular—*Us Weekly,* an entertainment periodical that seemed blatantly out of place among the likes of the *Wall Street Journal, Forbes,* and *Business Insider.* I nudged aside the *New Yorker* that lay partially on top of it, and, there, on the cover, was a familiar face—Chris Blakely.

My heart sank as I read the accompanying headline: CHRIS TELLS ALL. *The actor spills about his upcoming nuptials, his struggle with addiction, and his theory behind Missy Mataya's death that includes cover-ups, government bribes, and the Greek mob.*

Goddammit, Chris, I muttered quietly. Despite running his mouth, I'd held out hope that he'd remained under Vilanakis's radar. Apparently not.

"Please, have a seat," the woman said in a thick accent, interrupting my fretting. I looked up as she swept her hand out toward the sofa and the oversized chair at its side. With her arm held out, I could see a trail of yellowed bruises running along her skin as well as a series of circular burns—from a cigar, maybe. If I hadn't been sure she was abused before, I was now.

My stomach churned. Ignoring her offer to sit, I bent to meet her gaze. "I'm Emily. And you are . . . ?"

The woman's eyes grew wide then flew from mine to Petros's, as if afraid she'd be punished because I'd addressed her.

Turned out she wasn't wrong.

He backhanded her hard across the face. "Did I give you permission to look at me?"

Rage and fear flared inside me, and I had to count silently to ten to calm myself before I did something else stupid, like, try to defend her.

The girl mumbled an apology and Petros responded with something in Greek, which I figured was a directive of some sort since she left the room then.

"Maya's a sweet girl," Petros said when she'd left. "Gives the best head too."

"Does she now? Hopefully next time, she'll bite your dick off." I sounded sure of myself, which was surprising. I prayed he couldn't see the sweat forming on my brow, couldn't hear the rapid firing of my pulse.

"Now that's uncalled for," he tsked. "It's her duty to suck me off, and she's never complained."

I blew out a stream of hot air and told myself to drop it.

But I was too pissed and worked up to be self-controlled. "Her duty, why? Because she owes you? What—did you take care of her ex-husband or pay for her mother's surgery or feed her drug habit and then tell her she couldn't leave until she paid you back?"

"Something like that."

I rolled my eyes, which he noticed.

"You really want to know about Maya?" His tone was sharp. "Then I'll tell you. Her father owed my family money. When we came to collect, he couldn't pay. He gave us Maya instead."

"Jesus," I whispered under my breath.

"So you see, she's ours." He circled around me as he talked, slowly, like a vulture. "She does what we want, when we want it. If I want her to make me a pot roast, she'll make me a pot roast. If I want her to answer the door, she answers the door. If I want to fuck her in the throat, then she'll swallow every goddamn drop."

"That's horrible. You're horrible, vile people." I couldn't bear to think of Amber in this situation, and yet it was the main thing on my mind.

"Sure. Whatever. Call names. I'm just telling you how it is so you won't be surprised when my father decides you're in his debt as well."

I bit back my gasp. "You're just trying to scare me."

He smirked. "Maybe so. Doesn't mean I don't also mean it."

"Petros," a thick masculine voice snapped from behind me followed by a string of conversation in Greek.

I turned to find a broad-shouldered middle-aged man had entered the room. I'd seen Michelis in pictures so I recognized him easily, but in person, he was both more formidable and more attractive than photos portrayed him. While his slicked-back hair was graying at the temples and his eyes were creased with age, he appeared to be in excellent physical condition. He was handsome, and I may have even thought he was sexy if I didn't know so much about him. If I didn't know what he was capable of. If I didn't know his hands could hurt and punish and break down.

It struck me—those were the types of men I was normally drawn to. Had I finally found a man who was a hard limit? Or was every man a hard limit if he wasn't Reeve?

"Emily Wayborn," Michelis exclaimed, crossing to me. When he reached me, he put his hands on my upper arms and greeted me in the European style with a kiss to each cheek.

Horror and adrenaline slid down my spine, automatically causing me to straighten my posture. I should have been prepared for that, and I hadn't been. But more concerning was how unprepared I was for all of it.

"Hello," I said smoothly, recovering as much poise as possible.

His lip curled up, and the gleam in his eye said he'd seen every beat of my reaction to him—my assessment, my apprehension, my regrouping. He'd seen it, he'd remember it. He'd use it if he could.

Despite all that, he was polite and hospitable. "I've heard so much about you, Emily—may I call you that?" He didn't wait for my response. "It feels like I already know you."

My skin prickled, and I had to scold myself to keep composed. *He doesn't know me. It's his way of manipulating the situation, making me feel both welcome and uncomfortable all at once.* I'd seen this trick played before. I wouldn't let it get to me.

"I wish I could say the same. I feel, however, like we're perfect strangers." I hoped it was a good move, dismissing any knowledge of him as if he were insignificant.

His smile fell slightly. "Well, we shall get to know one another now. For me, it's an honor to finally meet the face behind the name. Or should I say, behind the voice."

"I've heard that one before, I'm afraid." I sighed. As if I were bored.

"I'm sure you have." He lost the grin altogether now. "I wasn't going for originality. I was going for an icebreaker. Can Petros get you anything before he leaves? Coffee? A glass of wine?"

"Uh, no." At the last minute, I added, "Thank you."

"Water, perhaps?"

His persistence didn't necessarily mean he had ill intentions. He could simply have been attempting to put me at ease.

Still, I was smart about bad men. "I'm not going to accept anything you have to offer, thank you, Mr. Vilanakis."

"Call me Micha, please." With a nod of his head, he dismissed Petros, who disappeared down the hall.

And now we were alone.

"Have a seat, Ms. Wayborn. Make yourself at home." He thrust his hands in his pockets, relaxed but in command. He reminded me of a lion lying in the sun, his eyes half closed, comfortable as king. If a mouse tried to sneak past him, all he'd have to do was stretch out his paw, and he'd catch the sucker in its tracks.

All I had to do, then, was watch out for that paw. Easy enough.

I circled the coffee table, putting space between us, casual despite the cocktail of adrenaline and foreboding that hummed in my blood. Once I'd distanced myself as well as I could, I spun to face him. "Why am I here?"

"Ah, right to the heart of things. No beating around the bush." He'd beat enough around the bush for me, it seemed.

"That isn't an answer to my question."

"No, it's not. I'll get there momentarily. Please. Sit."

I remained on my feet. "My friend is downstairs. I'm sure he's looking for me already. Reeve will come looking for me as well."

"Only time for a short chat today, then. What a pity."

It was naïve to assume that a short chat meant he intended to let me go. But I clung to that notion all the same. He'd intimidate me, he'd bully me. But he'd let me walk away. He had to.

Michelis gestured at the armchair, wanting to put me at ease, I was sure. Wanted me to sit, unwind. Let him call the shots.

At another time, I might have played it that way.

With Michelis—I would never use the nickname Amber used—I didn't have the time or the patience. I would not sit. I would not unwind. He would not call the shots.

"Why am I here?" My tone was even but insistent.

"I wanted to meet you." He could have had a hundred different motives, none of them were clear.

I guessed at the most obvious. "Are you going to slip me your number and let me know you're available after I'm done with Reeve?"

"Amber's told you how we met. How dear of her." Sugar drenched his words, so much so that they became insincere. If he'd felt any fondness for her, it hadn't run deep. His eyes narrowed as he openly perused my body like a man checking out a horse. "She was an exception, though. I don't believe I'll make a habit of indulging in my nephew's leftovers."

"Then we're mutually not attracted to each other," I said brazenly. "That's perfect." As long as I was being bold . . . "Tell me something—why Amber?"

He tilted his head as if considering his answer, though I was sure he had a formulated answer at the ready for this as well. "We had a lot in common," he said carefully. "We'd both been betrayed by the same man."

"Reeve." I couldn't decide if *he* really believed that or if it were just the story he wanted *me* to believe.

"Beyond that, I found her entertaining."

I wrapped my arms around myself, hoping he didn't notice my shudder, "You mean you found it entertaining to abuse and demean her?"

Michelis frowned. "As her friend, I'm sure you well know Amber is a passionate woman. I'm also a passionate man. Perhaps we sometimes got carried away."

"'*We* got carried away'?" I practically laughed, a sound that was based as much in nervousness as scorn. "I don't see you nursing any injuries."

"Now, Emily. Please. I know you aren't a woman who believes that all wounds can be seen by the eye. Let's not pretend that you are." His attempt at sympathy failed.

He did, however, have me unsettled. He'd been in my presence for all of five minutes, and I'd already learned that he was a master at communicating in dual meanings. It was distressing that he could do it so easily and terrifying how he managed to see inside me so clearly. How did he know that I was someone who understood both physical and emotional abuse well enough to react to the hint of unseen scars?

Or maybe he didn't know. Yes, that was more likely. He was spouting vague lines that anyone could hear and hold on to like a well-written horoscope, applicable to thousands of people in an intimate way.

Well, fuck him.

"Let Amber go," I said, tired of his bullshit beating around the bush. "She might have wanted you once, but she doesn't anymore."

"She's back with Reeve now? I'm surprised that you support this since you'd rather be with Reeve yourself."

Even if he did have spies on the ranch, he couldn't know that. He was guessing.

"Wherever you got that, you should probably find a more reliable source." I kept my response smug—not too defensive. Not at all truthful.

But Michelis's brows rose as though he'd hit a jackpot. "My source is you, my dear Emily. You're very easy to read, you know."

He's trying to get to you. Don't let him. "Actually, no one has ever said that about me before."

"Then no one you've ever met has been very observant."

I opened my mouth and shut it again. As solidly as I understood that he was feeling around for the truth, his accuracy was startling.

But I'd also never let myself be surrounded by anyone who might see the real me. I was drawn to men who didn't care to find out anything beyond my willingness to submit. Even Amber had only seen as much as she'd wanted. Reeve had been the first person to peel away my thick skin and study the layers underneath.

Had he left me vulnerable? Could Michelis really see what he claimed he saw?

My hesitation gave too much away, and he slid into the opening I'd left him. "Seriously, tell me, Emily. I'm intrigued. How are things working out with the three of you?"

Don't answer. Don't give anything away.

"Are you girls sharing him equally? Or does he have a favorite?"

I shook my head ever so slightly—not an answer, but a plea for him to stop hedging, stop closing me in.

"It's you, isn't it? I bet that makes Amber crazy."

"Don't talk about us like you understand anything." But my breathing was heavy and my voice frail.

"Ah, I see." He grinned, as if he'd scored, and he had. "You don't want to share at all."

There it was, my biggest secret of all. My most shameful wound. I could blame Amber all day long for the reasons we'd given up our threesomes and never be lying. She'd been the one who'd decided that those were over.

But she wasn't the only one who wanted a man of her own. I did too.

And now all Michelis had to do was pour the salt. "You're not the first woman who's taken issue with his lack of loyalty."

Surprised, I responded before I had a chance to think about it. "He wasn't loyal to Amber?"

"I was talking about Missy Mataya."

"You're fishing," I said, aware that my composure had been shattered. "You're guessing at things that you think will upset me. It won't work."

"If you say so." He wore the triumphant air of victory.

Like the last soldier standing on a battlefield, I fired my remaining shot with little hope of hitting any target. "Leave Amber alone."

His eyes clouded momentarily with confusion or misunderstanding, and I almost thought he didn't know what I was talking about. But then he said, "People don't usually ask me for favors without offering something in return."

Of course, he'd want payment. I'd been willing to give my body to find her when I'd gone to Reeve. I wasn't willing to give that to Michelis.

Fortunately for me, I didn't have to. "You said you don't want me. I have nothing else to offer."

"*Au contraire*," he said, but I didn't let out the air I'd been holding because he took a step closer to me. Then another. Then he was so close he could touch me or strike me or reach out and strangle me.

He leaned in close so his cheek was near mine, and I had to force myself to swallow my scream. "You have much more to offer me than a trip to my bed, which, I'm sure you realize, I could have had already if I'd wished it."

Yes, I'd realized it. He could do almost anything he wanted to me here. He could kill me, and neither Reeve nor Joe would ever get to me in time.

Michelis sensed the extent of my fear. He fed on it. It aroused him, which made me hate him even more. He swept a hand through my hair—gently. So gently it was ominous, and I could no longer control the tremors moving through my body.

He liked that—enjoyed terrorizing me. I could smell the heavy musk of his interest as he pressed his mouth to my cheek. Then, he licked me, leaving a wet smear of saliva along my jaw.

Bile gathered in the back of my mouth. "You won't hurt me." It was myself I was trying to convince, and it was obvious. "You want me scared. But you respect Reeve and so you won't hurt me."

"Because you're his *woman*?" He pushed his nose against mine, giving me the most sinister view of his eyes. "But Amber's his woman, too, you said. And even if you share him, he can only claim one of you as his *woman*. I think it's really you. Which would make Amber free game, wouldn't it?"

"No. Not me." I wouldn't betray her even if it was true. But that didn't mean I wanted to put myself on the line. "It's both of us. We're both his women."

"Hmm." He pulled back to look at me, to assess if I were lying, maybe. "Unfortunately, Emily, I'm not sure my respect extends across two women. We'll have to see."

"What do you want from me?" The question was thick in my throat.

His hand stroked through my hair again, petting me as though I were a small animal and not a woman at all. "You can pass on a message."

"To Amber?" My voice cracked. I was sure any message he meant for me to pass would be given in physical form, and already my mind was racing with all the possibilities of injury and pain he could bestow. In what way would he rape me? Would I be able to walk out of here or would my message be delivered in the form of my limp body?

"Not a message for Amber," he said. "For Reeve."

"What's the message?" It was barely more than a whisper.

"I want to talk to him." He settled his arm around my shoulder and draped his hand low enough that it rested just above my breast, a reminder that he was the one with all the power in the situation, and for a quick second I could imagine how terrible it had to be for Maya to be his servant. How terrible it must have been for Amber to have been whatever she'd been for him as well.

"That's all you want? I tell him to talk to you, and you'll leave Amber alone?" Hope slipped into my words despite my attempt to keep it at bay. Could that really be all he wanted from me?

"No, no, no." He chuckled, his lips buzzing against my skin. "That would be too easy, wouldn't it?" He stroked my hair again and pressed his forehead against my temple. "I don't want you to *tell* him. I want you to *convince* him."

It sounded relatively easy, which was quite certainly deceiving. "Why doesn't he want to talk to you?"

Michelis considered. "Let's just say that Reeve's disloyalty doesn't only extend to women."

This was the second time he'd hinted at deception where Reeve was concerned. I twisted my head to meet his eyes. "He betrayed you."

Michelis smirked, and I knew he found too much satisfaction with my ignorance to give me anything more. He swept his knuckles across my jaw, the metal of his V monogrammed ring cold against my skin. "Convince my nephew to talk to me, Emily Wayborn. Face-to-face. You can tell him I'll be staying in the hotel for a week. Give him my room number. I'm available to speak to him at any time."

His hand dropped, and he stepped away from me.

My entire body sagged in relief, as though he'd been pressing a giant weight against my chest and now that he'd removed it, I could finally breathe.

"Our conversation is over, isn't it?" I was desperate to leave and find Joe. Desperate to get back to Kaya. To Reeve.

Before he could answer, a cell phone rang in another room. Michelis put up a finger, indicating for me to keep silent, as he seemed to try to listen to the conversation.

It was too low and muffled for me to make out a single word, but I was also pretty sure the language being spoken wasn't English. It was less than thirty seconds before the call ended.

"Petros?" Michelis called out.

His son stepped into the room. "It's done," he said, and though I had no idea what he was referring to, I felt a menacing dread settle on me like a heavy cloak.

"Wonderful." Michelis's eyes brightened as he turned his focus from his son to me. "Yes, Emily, our conversation is over. I trust you'll arrange for my nephew to meet with me soon. Petros will see you to the door."

A glance at the wall clock told me it had only been twenty minutes since I'd left Joe downstairs. He'd likely be about ready to tear his hair out when I found him again, but chances were he hadn't done anything too drastic yet.

Even knowing he'd be concerned, I halted my steps after Petros had led me only halfway across the room. "What if I can't convince Reeve to talk to you?"

"You can. You will." Michelis was much more confident than I was. "Besides, I've just done him a favor. Reeve isn't the type to leave a debt unpaid."

If his final words were meant to be reassuring, they were anything but, and even though I walked out of his penthouse suite alone, I took the cloak of dread with me.

CHAPTER
15

I spotted Joe pacing the lobby the second the elevators opened.

His eyes were moving constantly—checking his phone, the entrance, looking toward the restaurant, scanning the bank of elevators—so he saw me almost immediately after I'd started toward him.

"What the actual fuck, Emily?" He was visibly sweating, and his hair was disheveled, as though he'd run his hand through it several times. "Where the hell did you go? You've been gone for nearly half an hour. I was seconds from calling Sallis, and I promise you—"

He cut off, his eyes catching on something behind me. I swiveled to see Michelis with a man I hadn't seen in the suite getting off the elevator. He smiled, his expression cruel and taunting.

Joe put a firm hand on my shoulder, both protective and steadying, his eyes pinned to Vilanakis as he and his companion disappeared into the restaurant. "That was

Vilanakis," he said when I suspected he could breathe again. "You were with him? God, Emily." He began studying me—moving my hair off my neck, running his hands down my arms, searching for any signs of distress the way I'd searched him when he'd arrived at Kaya.

"I'm fine," I assured him. "A bit shaken up." I really was fine. But now that I was safe and with someone I trusted, my emotions surged to the surface. I put my hands up to cover my eyes. To breathe. "Just . . . I need a minute."

"Of course. We can sit."

He started nudging me toward the lobby couch, but I shook my head. "I'd rather get out of here. I don't want to be in that hateful man's vicinity one second longer."

"Understood." With an arm around my shoulder, Joe led me toward the front doors.

Before we reached them, though, I halted. "Maya!" He looked at me, confused. "There's a woman. Upstairs. In his room. We have to help her. She's a slave or a servant or whatever. She has the tattoo."

Joe dropped his hand from my shoulder and scrubbed it over his face. "We can't," he said after a beat, and the look on his eyes said he hated saying that as much as he knew I hated hearing it. "We can't just take her. We'll start a war that we can't win."

"But she's upstairs. She's . . . she needs help." Deep down, I knew he was right, but I wasn't ready to give up. "You took Amber. How is that different?"

"It was different," he said, practically at the same time. "Michelis left her for dead. And I took her to Reeve, who I thought could protect her."

"Then we'll take Maya to Reeve too!"

"If Reeve wants to take that burden on, then he needs to do that himself. Right now, I'm not even sure he can take care of Amber. I'm not going—"

"I thought this was what you wanted to do! You wanted to go after him. You wanted to help these women. Was that a lie?"

He sighed and tilted his head toward me. "I do want to help them. And I will, I promise. But right now, a rescue would be a suicide mission. You have to see that. You do, don't you?"

A fresh sob threatened, but I swallowed it down. "Yes. I do. You're right. Let's just go."

"Will you tell me what happened, at least?" Joe asked as he led me out the doors, his hand on the small of my back. "Are you really okay?"

"Yes. It was fine. I'm fine." If *fine* was defined as a jumble of fear and agitation, that was.

Joe glanced at me skeptically. "Then, you just talked?"

"Yeah. Mostly." My mind flashed back to Michelis's breath on my skin, the wet feel of his tongue. A shiver ran through me.

Joe noticed. He came to a stop, a few feet from the valet station, and faced me full on. "What happened, Emily? What did he do to you?"

"He didn't do anything, really, except try to creep me out." I hesitated, trying to decide how honest I wanted to be. Joe had made a good point about playing hero, and I didn't want him rushing to fight for my honor. From the urgency in his tone, there was a distinct possibility that he would.

"He didn't hurt me," I prefaced, then explained how I'd ended up in his suite. "He said he wanted to meet me. He didn't hurt me and he barely touched me."

"*Barely* touched you?" Joe looked ready to tear off someone's head. All I had to do was say the word.

"I'm fine," I insisted, nudging Joe toward the valet. "Everything's fine. He was manipulative and he made every effort to show me he was in charge and get me riled up and it worked."

I stood quietly until Joe gave the attendant his ticket. As we walked to the line to wait for his car, he asked, "But what did he want from you? Did he tell you anything about Amber? About Reeve?"

"Funny, you should ask." A breeze blew by, and I shivered, but it was quite possible I might have shivered anyway. "He wants me to convince Reeve to talk to him. I guess Reeve hasn't been receptive to such a conversation in the past."

"I wonder if that's what his e-mail to Sallis was about." Joe furrowed his brow. "Will you convince him?"

"To talk to Vilanakis?" It hadn't occurred to me that I had any other choice. "Yeah. I have to try. For Amber's sake."

Even as I said the words, I chided myself internally. *Always for Amber's sake.* When would I start doing things for *my* sake?

"It doesn't seem like this is about Amber at all, though. If she's just a pawn, then what is this really about?"

It was hard for me to think of Amber as anything less than a queen, but I put thoughts of her aside and concentrated on the feud between the men. "Michelis hinted that Reeve had betrayed him. Said it a couple of times. He wouldn't say much more when I prodded. Oh, and he said that he'd done Reeve a favor of some sort. Said I should use that to convince Reeve to talk to him."

"A favor?" The couple ahead of us drove off, and we moved up to the front of the valet line. "Remember once we thought that Vilanakis had taken Amber off his hands as a favor?"

"Yeah, but then Amber said she'd left voluntarily so that doesn't work."

Although she'd also said that Vilanakis had been right there in town, waiting for her. Which was somewhat odd. Maybe Amber thought she'd gone of her own free will, but could Reeve have arranged their meeting from behind the scenes?

And Vilanakis was in town *now.* He'd found me in the hotel the first time I'd gone there. As if he'd been waiting. Either the man was extremely well prepared, ready to pounce on every opportunity the minute it popped up. Or Reeve had made both meetings happen.

No. I refused to believe that. It didn't even make sense. But the thought added mass to the knot of doubt growing in my belly.

"Anyway," I said, ignoring the weight pressing against my ribs. "I'm not sure if it was a recent favor or something a long time ago or if Reeve even asked for it or if Michelis just took it on himself to give it. But I have a bad feeling about it, Joe. If I can't convince Reeve to talk to him, I think something very, very terrible is going to happen."

Joe's forehead creased. "Jesus, Emily. If Sallis is that adamant about not speaking to him, he's going to flip when he finds out you were with him."

"I didn't *try* to meet with him. I had no choice."

"I didn't mean to suggest you did. But he's going to be pissed that you left the ranch, and he's not going to be very supportive when you want to leave tomorrow."

"I hadn't thought of that." I would have been tempted to keep my Vilanakis incident quiet except that I planned to deliver his message. Besides, even after what had happened that day with the dog, Reeve did make me feel better. "I'll figure it out."

"*We'll* figure it out."

Joe meant to be supportive. Instead, it made me anxious. Because he and I were not a *we,* especially where Reeve was concerned, and that hadn't changed just because I'd said I'd leave the ranch with him.

Just as I started to correct him, an Escalade pulled up

in front of us. The attendant opened the door and gestured for me to get inside.

"This isn't our ride." The last word trailed off as my eyes met the driver's. My face went hot, my chest went cold. "Reeve."

His lips were a tight thin line and his eyes so sharp that his gaze was uncomfortable to stand under. The rigid set of his jaw and deep furrow of his brows were unfamiliar to me and completed his austere appearance.

Well, so much for worrying about how to tell him I'd met with Vilanakis. Ten to one odds, he already knew. It's the only reason I could imagine for him to show up out of nowhere with that look on his face.

"I guess this *is* your ride," Joe mumbled. His car pulled up then behind Reeve's. "Will you be okay?"

I paused, trying to decide who to ride with, but it didn't take long for my decision to be made. I wanted to be with Reeve—I always wanted to be with Reeve.

But I'd hesitated too long for Reeve.

"Get in, Emily," he ordered. His tone was just as tight as his lips. It confirmed what I already suspected about his emotional state. That he was beyond angry. That he was restrained, but just barely.

It was a mood that made me quiver, and I couldn't tell if I was scared or excited.

Both. I was definitely both.

"You're mad, aren't you?" I hated how shallow my breath had gotten, how rapidly my heart knocked against my ribs, how painfully my nipples peaked and pointed.

His lips curled upward ever so slightly. "Mad does not begin to describe what I am right now."

Most of all, I hated that I couldn't look at him anymore without seeing *her*. Without feeling her between us. Without having to acknowledge everything about her that wasn't me.

The smile I flashed him mirrored the strain in his. "Awesome. Because mad doesn't describe what I am right now either." I slammed the door and turned to Joe. "Let's go."

But Reeve had lightning reflexes. He was out of his car and blocking Joe's passenger door before I could reach for the handle.

Reeve's hand shot out and wrapped firmly around my arm. "You're riding with me."

The timbre of his voice, the tightness of his grip, the steel look in his eyes—I knew it wasn't in my best interest to protest.

"Guess I'll see you at the ranch," I said to Joe.

"Yep." He was the one with the tight tone now. His entire body was stiff as he opened his door.

"Oh, and Joe?" Reeve waited for his attention before going on. "It's time for you to move on from Kaya. We've appreciated all you've done to bring Amber back safely, and now your job is done."

Joe and I exchanged a glance. He'd been dismissed.

"I do agree," Joe said, with only the slightest hint of irritation. "Actually, I was already planning to leave tomorrow."

"Glad to see we're on the same page."

The only thing that made Reeve's smug smile tolerable was knowing that I planned to leave when Joe did. Something told me now wasn't the time to tell him.

As Joe's taillights faded into the distance, Reeve pulled me back to the passenger side of the Escalade. He opened the door, and half pushed me inside as he said, "Get in."

I climbed in with a scowl that deepened when he jerked the safety restraint across my body. "I can strap my own seat belt, thank you very much."

"Forgive me for not being confident in your ability to make wise decisions regarding your safety." He tightened the strap to the point of discomfort then, with a contemptible expression on his face, he slammed the door.

I'd expected he'd be mad. Reeve hadn't wanted me to leave the ranch at all and, even though my encounter with Vilanakis wasn't exactly my fault, it proved his concern had been warranted.

But the depth of his anger was uncalled for. Especially when I'd potentially been in danger. Especially when it had been *his* family that had come after me. Especially when I'd been mad first—before The Four Seasons, when he'd admitted that he'd told Amber he loved her.

We drove in silence. Every mile that passed without a word, I grew more and more incensed.

Finally, I couldn't stand it any longer. "Go ahead," I prodded. "I know you want to say something, so just say it."

He waited a beat. Then, with his eyes glued to the road, he said, "I don't think it's wise for me to say what I want to while I'm driving."

It seemed more like a tactic to manipulate control of the conversation than about controlling his temper.

It infuriated me. "More like you want to be able to manhandle me while you're talking. How else could you get your point across?"

"You're trying to provoke me."

"I'm trying to get you to ask me about Michelis." And, yes, I wanted to provoke him. I wanted to yell and argue and fight. Anything to break through the awful, terrible distance between us.

I studied his profile and waited, giving him a chance to respond. When he didn't, I said, "Since you won't ask, I'll tell you. He wants you to talk to him." I watched for any hint of a reaction.

But he was stoic and guarded and gave me nothing.

"A conversation, Reeve," I pleaded. "And then you can go back to hating him. I won't even try to figure out what all that anger is about. Just one conversation, that's all I'm asking for. That's all *he's* asking for. And then he'll leave Amber alone."

No response. But his jaw flexed and I swore his grip on the wheel tightened.

I shifted so I was facing him and nudged him again. "Isn't that what you want? For Amber to be safe?"

"Emily, I'm not discussing this."

"Not discussing this now? Or not discussing this ever?"

"As soon as I'm no longer operating a motorized vehicle, I'll happily discuss your absolutely foolish behavior this evening. As for—"

I cut him off. "Foolish why? You do understand I didn't leave to go meet up with your uncle, don't you? I didn't talk with him by choice. I am not Amber."

"I told you not to leave the ranch—"

Again, I didn't let him finish. "And you told me you'd never keep me trapped. Maybe you really did forget I wasn't Amber."

His eyes widened with fury. "Asking you to stay put so I can keep you safe is not even remotely the same." He was practically shouting, which was fair. It was cruel of me to keep bringing up Amber like this. And, honestly, I didn't know why I was doing it since I spent a lot of time fretting over how the two of us might compare in his eyes.

I redirected the argument. "You know, the real issue isn't that I left the ranch. It's that you haven't prepared me at all to be able to handle a conversation with your relatives. If I'd had even just a tad bit of information regarding the situation . . . or maybe that's not in the rules. Maybe I'm only good for sucking your cock and looking pretty." *Like Maya,* I thought then hated myself for imagining my situation was anything like hers.

He threw me a stunned glance. "What have I done to allude that my interest in you is only superficial?"

"You won't tell me anything!"

"You're so melodramatic," he muttered as he turned onto the road that led up to the ranch. Then, after he braked to wait for the guards to open the gate, he spun to me and said, "I've told you things that I haven't told anyone. Just because I won't talk to you about this *one thing* doesn't mean that I've told you nothing."

The light from the security booth streamed through the window, illuminating his features. His expression said he wasn't just frustrated and mad. He was also offended. And hurt.

I turned away. I didn't want to hurt him. I didn't want to know that it was even possible.

"You know what? This is beside the point." I forced myself to speak calmly and focused only on what was relevant instead of jabbing whatever I could think of in his direction. "The point is that you have the power to protect Amber and keep her safe from Michelis for good. All that's required is a conversation. Face-to-face. He'll be at The Four Seasons for the next week. You've made it clear that you still"—I grimaced, unable to say the word I really meant—"still *care* for her so I know that you'll do the right thing. Won't you?"

It was the best I could do. It would have to be enough.

The gate lifted and Reeve turned back to face the road, waving at the security guard as he drove past. Instead of driving on to the main house, he pulled up next to the manager's office and put the car in park. He shifted toward me again and narrowed his eyes. "Do the *right thing*?"

"Yes!" It was the first time since we'd left The Four Seasons that I felt he might really consider what I was asking. "Talk to him. That's all. Will you talk to him?"

He met my gaze head on. "No."

"Please, Reeve?" Blinking back emotion, I laid myself bare. "For Amber?"

His expression softened. "Not even for you, Emily."

His words hung in the air, with all the sweet and sting of a backhanded compliment.

And it dawned on me that it didn't matter if he loved both of us, because he didn't love either of us *enough*.

At least he seemed remorseful as he turned off the engine and unbuckled his belt. "Stay here," he said softly before slipping out of the car.

Numbly, I watched him unlock the office door and disappear inside. The blinds were closed so I couldn't see what he was doing inside, but I could tell he hadn't bothered to turn on the light. Darkness followed him—it was there, in the room where he'd gone. Here, where he'd left me. My eyes closed, and I let the gloom settle in like a pair of old shoes.

A phone vibrated with an incoming message, and I opened my eyes to find he'd left his cell in the drink holder. Curious, I picked it up and scanned the e-mail that had popped up on his screen. It was from someone I didn't know—a Lisa from KT & King Communications.

This went out across a nice list of gossip sites this morning. Hope it's what you had in mind.

The message was followed by a link to an online article. The headline appeared in the preview. I had to read it twice before I believed it said what I thought it said.

Luxury Resort Owner Reeve Sallis
Finds Love with the Woman Behind
Next Gen's Famous Voice

With my heart pounding in my throat, I clicked on the hyperlink.

Sources reported today that Reeve Sallis, heir to the world-renowned Sallis Luxury Resorts, has gotten serious with Emily Wayborn, the woman behind the voice of the house's computer main-frame in the hit TV show *Next Gen*. The two met while the actress vacationed at Sallis's Palm Springs resort and have been seen getting pretty cozy in the months since. A representative for the couple confirmed the relationship but declined any further comment.

"Oh, my God." I was alone in the car, but I still said it out loud.

It was the first time I'd ever seen a press release about a Reeve Sallis relationship. And the note from "Lisa" sug-gested it was Reeve himself that had requested it. It was surprising to say the least.

And confusing.

If I was being honest, when I'd seen the headline, a thrill had run through me. *Love* and *Sallis* and me all in one sentence—it made my chest flood with warmth.

But the release itself was cold. Concise. Clinical. The first time he really declared any feelings for me, and it was like this? I'd already been angry. I'd already felt shut out. Now I was heartbroken as well.

His phone still in hand, I undid my seat belt, got out of the car, and went inside after him.

The office was dark, but a door on the far wall was open and enough light spilled from there to see that the room was empty. I crossed to the door and peered inside. The back wall was covered with monitors displaying various locations on the ranch. It was the second security room, I realized. There was another in the main house, smaller than this one, and while a single guard generally manned that one, there were two sitting here.

One of the guards glanced up as I walked in. If he was surprised to see me, he didn't let on.

"He's in there," the guard said, nodding toward another open door on the opposite side of the room.

It was as if he'd given me permission to enter, and so I dropped my tentativeness and marched over to where the guard had pointed.

This room turned out to be a large closet. Reeve was facing away from me, but he peeked over his shoulder in my direction and frowned. "I told you to stay in the car."

I ignored his comment and addressed his back. "What the hell is this?"

Reeve didn't look at me when he answered, "What the hell is what?"

"This." I held out his cell even though he hadn't turned around. "This statement from your *representative*. Did you send out a press release about us?"

He took a Glock off the wall in front of him—a wall that was lined with weapons, I realized now. It was a startling sight, even without Reeve personally handling the firearms. . . .

"Yes." He glanced toward me, then seeing his phone, he took it from me and slipped it in his pocket. "I did." He slid down the wall to a cabinet. There he opened a drawer and pulled out a magazine. "Stating that you and I were in a relationship."

"Why the hell would you do that?" I'd already known what his answer would be and I was still astonished and outraged and bewildered all at once.

I came up alongside him. "Did you not believe I'd tell Amber? Was that your way of ensuring the truth got out?"

"It had nothing to do with Amber. It was damage control."

"Damage control?" I was flabbergasted. "What if she'd seen it before I'd had a chance to talk to her? What damage would that have done?"

He swiveled to face me. "I was less concerned with protecting your fragile relationship than I was about protecting you." He let that sink in.

Except, even after a few seconds to process it, I still didn't understand.

Before I could ask, he explained. "An official statement from my publicist trumps the gossip going around about you and Blakely. If anyone were to think that you might be involved with his ignorant ramblings to the press, they also needed to know that the only way to you was through me."

It could have been the most romantic thing he'd ever said to me, especially paired with the fiercely possessive gleam in his eyes. It was a look that had the ability to make my chest tighten and my legs quiver.

But right now it only made me want to lash out. And not just because every declaration he made came with the baggage of the declarations he'd made to her, but also because I didn't trust his motives. Was it really the only way to keep me safe? Or was it just an asshole, overprotective gesture—a jealous attempt to publicly claim me as his?

"You had no right to say anything about us without asking me." I could barely keep my voice level. "No right."

He loaded the gun with a magazine. "I was protecting you."

"Your method of protection sent a bad man looking for me!" I was practically screaming.

Reeve stuffed the gun into an inside jacket pocket and slammed the drawer shut before turning around to face me. "He was going to come after you anyway, Emily. Connecting

you to me made you purposeful instead of just a liability.
I very likely saved your life." He brushed past me and left
the closet, switching the light off as he did.

With a huff, I chased after him and nearly bumped into
him when he stopped to talk to the guard.

"I'm taking a Glock and a magazine," he informed the
man. "Here's the serial." He pulled out the piece from his
jacket and read off a number while the guard wrote it down
on a clipboard.

"Got it checked out," the man said.

"Thanks." Reeve continued out to the office with me on
his heels, ignoring the guard's fish-eye as I passed.

"Seriously, a gun? That's helpful. So much better to put
out press releases and carry a gun than have a fucking conversation. One simple conversation and all of this could
be over."

He was midway through the room when he stopped and
spun around toward me so fast that I nearly bumped into
him. "A simple conversation? There's no way you're that
naïve, Emily. Do you really believe that's all it's going to
be?"

"I have no basis to believe anything else since you refuse to tell me—"

"Bullshit. You don't need to know anything other than
what you already know. He killed a dog to prove a point.
Those bruises on your friend? Those broken ribs? That
drug habit? And you think that a few minutes of my time
is all he's after? I know you're a smarter woman than that."

He straightened. "Or maybe you're not that smart because you talked to him." His voice escalated as he spoke.
"What the fuck were you thinking?"

"*Petros* approached *me*." I matched his volume as if I
were confident, as if his anger didn't have me shaking in
my shoes. "He had a gun! He told me to be scared!"

"You wouldn't have been in that position if you'd stayed

put like I'd told you to in the first place." He put a fist on his hip and stared at the ground, shaking his head as he let out a breath. "When Petros told me you were there . . ."

Petros? He'd been an utter asshole, and *he'd* been the one to tell Reeve?

I didn't have a chance to ask because just then Reeve brought his fist from his hip and slammed it on the top of a nearby desk. "Jesus Christ, Emily, you make me so fucking furious. I can't even think, I'm so goddam angry. I want to—"

He cut himself off, but his body language said he was only just barely restraining himself.

I should have let it go. I shouldn't have challenged him. But I was out of control too. "You want to . . . what?"

He lunged for me. I automatically put my hands up, thinking he was going for my throat, as if I were strong enough to push him away. He grabbed my forearms and pulled me to him so that the length of his body pressed against mine, and I could feel the rigid bulge of his cock at my pelvis. My legs went weak, and I prepared for him to kiss me, but instead he twisted my arms behind my back. Gripping my wrists with one of his hands, he circled around behind me, put a hand on my back, and pushed my torso down to the desk, hard.

"You're hurting me," I said, struggling to get free.

With one hand still securing my wrists, he reached under my dress to tug my panties down.

"Don't you fucking dare," I seethed, but I was already wet, and, even though I was still fighting him, I was most definitely aroused. "I mean it, Reeve."

He ignored me. Bracing his leg against mine to hold me still, he flipped my dress up, exposing my bare ass. Then, with a loud smack, his hand came down on my sensitive skin.

"Ow!" I tried to sit up, but he pressed his upper body

against mine and spanked me again. And again. And again. Several times in succession until my eyes were watering and my ass was burning and I was so turned on that moisture was dripping down my legs.

I'd stopped struggling by the time he finally paused. I could hear him breathing heavily as he adjusted his grip on my wrists. He didn't let me go, and I imagined him behind me, staring at my naked backside, red with his palmprint.

After several long seconds, I felt his hand slide across my stinging ass, lower, between my legs.

I bit my lip, embarrassed about how wet he'd made me, desperate to have him find out just how wet.

He paused at the rim of my cunt. "You frustrate me beyond belief, Blue Eyes," he rasped, then plunged his fingers inside me.

I gasped, vaguely aware of the guard in the security booth, the door wide open between both rooms. I knew Reeve hadn't forgotten that his employee could hear everything going on between us. Why did that turn me on so much?

Reeve crooked his fingers and stroked in and out of me. "Do you know what a man like Michelis does with people who frustrate him?" He paused, but I didn't know if he really wanted an answer. I couldn't give him one if he did—my thoughts were too blurred for speech. The lingering sting on my ass muddled with the pleasure of his hand job.

"He takes things from them," he said, answering his own question. "Things they care about. People. And that's when he's in a good mood."

I shuddered, both from his words and from the new spot he'd found to rub.

Suddenly, his fingers were gone and I jumped when he smacked me again. He hit me twice more before shoving back inside of my pussy. His strokes were slower this time, and my orgasm began to build, so leisurely, so steadily that I knew it would knock me off my feet when it fully bloomed.

Reeve leaned over me, pressing his chest to my back as he massaged me. "He has a reputation for a reason, and what people say about him is kind. He's an expert at pain and suffering. And, when he's done with a person, he doesn't bother with a conversation. He just kills them."

"I . . ." I choked on a sob. "I didn't . . ." *I didn't realize he'd come after me.* I couldn't speak, too distracted, too worked up.

Reeve rubbed his nose against my cheek. "He could have hurt you, Emily," he said, his voice raw and threadbare. "In order to hurt me."

I squeezed my eyes shut, as if that could keep away the emotion that I was sure would swallow me up when my climax hit me. Soon. It was so close.

Reeve sensed it too. "All I'd have to do is brush your clit and you'd come, wouldn't you?"

I nodded.

Abruptly, he stood, releasing me and removing his hand from my cunt at the same time.

I blinked, confused and desperately wound up. Propping myself up on the desk, I twisted to look at him. "Why did you stop? I was almost there."

He wiped his hand on his pants. "I'm not going to let you come. I'm mad at you."

The rage I'd somehow forgotten while he'd had his fingers inside me returned with a vengeance. "You are so manipulative." I pulled up my panties. "And mean. I hate you and I never want you to touch me again."

I started to storm past him, but he grabbed my upper arm and pulled me to him. "I will allow you your space while you work through whatever conflict you imagine exists between us, Emily, but I will not tolerate being lied to."

"I'm not lying. I really do hate you." And I did. As much as I loved him, I hated him.

He didn't even flinch. "I'm sure you do. But you most certainly want me to touch you."

I hated him even more for that—for knowing me that well.

No longer able to look at him, I wrenched my arm away and stomped out to the car. I got in and pressed my face against the window and kept it there until we'd driven into the garage by the main house.

When we'd parked, I unbuckled my belt, and without looking at him, I said, "I'm leaving with Joe tomorrow. Don't tell me to stay. Neither of us wants to find out if I'm able to ignore you." I threw open the car door and hurried into the house.

I'd meant to head straight to my room, but Brent and Joe met me at the door, each of them somber and serious.

Panic rose inside me. "What is it?"

"You haven't heard?" Joe asked.

"I was with you all night. What could I possibly have heard?"

Joe started to answer, then stopped as Reeve came in behind me.

I'd wanted to be away from him by the time he got inside, but now I didn't care. The air was tense and charged and all I could think about was Amber, sure that something terrible had happened to her and I had to know now, before the worrying ate me up. "Will someone please fucking tell me what's going on?"

"It's Chris Blakely," Joe said without any further hesitation. "He's dead."

CHAPTER
16

I didn't sleep well.

The few times I started to doze, I dreamt. Vague nightmares where images of Chris faded into images of Reeve then Michelis then Joe until all of them morphed into one man who was one minute trying to make me come, and the next, trying to kill me.

It was still dark outside when I gave up on sleep. I tossed the covers aside and got out of bed to pack my suitcase instead.

Joe had heard the news about Chris on the radio as he drove back to the ranch from The Four Seasons. Although the police weren't releasing any information yet, he'd called a friend on the Los Angeles force and learned the cause of death appeared to be an overdose. Chris had been shooting a guest role on a nighttime soap and was found dead in his dressing room earlier in the evening.

I'd had to lean against the wall when he'd told me, the edges of my vision having gone black and fuzzy. Reeve had pulled me into his arms, and I'd clutched onto him and cried as Joe and Brent explained what they knew, which wasn't much.

"It will be nearly impossible to prove that the drugs weren't self-administered," Joe had said. "If they weren't."

Brent piped in next. "Even if they weren't, we don't know that Michelis had anything to do with it."

"We know," Reeve had said.

I'd let him hold me for a few minutes longer before I'd gotten over enough of the shock to remember that I didn't want to have anything to do with Reeve. Then I'd pushed him away and excused myself, running to my room, where I'd locked my door and thrown myself on the bed and cried until I was dry.

Chris's death had a numbing effect on me. It was as though I'd found the eye of the storm, the cyclone of emotions that had hit me still present and around me—but calm for the moment. It felt like I was moving through slow motion. My thoughts took effort. All I could concentrate on was one step at a time—first, pack my bags.

After an hour, and a break to shower and dress, I zipped up my suitcase and looked at the clock. It was half past six, but the ranch woke early and I could already hear activity below me. Joe and I hadn't discussed what time we were leaving. Hoping it would be sooner rather than later, I carried my things downstairs and left them in the hall while I set out to find him.

Joe's room was on the main floor and, to get to it, I had to cross through the den. Usually this part of the house was empty, but, despite the hour, I heard voices as I rounded the corner. Reeve's voice, specifically. I didn't want to see him, so I started to turn, but then I heard Joe.

"Is the house part of the resort?" he was asking.

"No, it's on the opposite side of the island," Reeve answered. "A five-mile walk along the shore. There's also a wall around the perimeter of the resort to discourage guests from wandering."

The conversation wasn't necessarily friendly, but it was more than I thought Reeve would share with Joe after the night before. I slipped into the back of the room quietly and discovered Amber and Brent were there as well. Amber was still dressed in pajamas, curled up on the couch with her feet underneath her. Joe sat away from her on the opposite end. Reeve was sitting on the coffee table directing his talk to both of them.

Brent stood off to the side, seemingly an observer like I was. He nodded when he saw me, drawing Amber to peer back at me. Reeve followed her line of vision and his gaze slammed into mine. An electric jolt ran through my body, like a cable trying to jump-start a car. I was numb, I was void, but Reeve could get me running. If I let him.

I refused to let him.

Unable to look at him for long, I pinned my focus on Amber. "What's going on?"

She leaned her arm on the back of the sofa. "We're going to Reeve's island for a while. It's safer there and it will give his men time to work things out with Micha."

So they were going somewhere too. Good time for me to leave, then.

Though, it didn't *feel* good. It felt far from.

I forced a small smile. "I think that's smart. I'm really worried about you after . . ." *After the dog, after meeting Vilanakis, after Chris Blakely.* I couldn't say Chris's name without spiraling into anxious, guilt-ridden grief. "Well, yesterday."

She reached up and gave my hand a squeeze. "I heard about your friend. I'm so sorry, Em. I don't know what to say."

When I'd thought Amber had died, I'd felt deep, gut-wrenching sorrow. I hadn't been close enough to Chris for that, but I was still sad. And I blamed myself for stirring up suspicions he'd long put to rest. If I hadn't brought up questions about the past, would he have started blabbing about Missy to the press? Would he have ever made the mob connection?

I shook the thought away. "It's okay. I don't know what to say either. Except, stay safe. If going to the resort is how Reeve thinks you'll be best protected, listen to him." I meant what'd I'd said, but I didn't want to think about the efforts Reeve was going to in order to keep her from Michelis. And I was still upset that he wouldn't agree to talk to his uncle, even though he was convinced it was hopeless.

"Anyway, I'll let you get back to planning." I hadn't told Amber yet about my plans to go. This wasn't how I'd wanted her to find out, but I needed to make sure others knew I was still firm in my decision. "I just stopped in to ask—what time are you thinking we'll leave, Joe?"

Though my eyes were directly on Joe, I was ever aware of Reeve in my periphery, ready for his protest. Part of me wanted that—wanted him to fight for me to stay, even though I'd told him not to.

But if he didn't, if he planned to just let me go, it would break my heart a little.

It would break my heart a lot.

Joe didn't answer me. Instead, he looked to Reeve as if asking for guidance. Reeve responded by shooting a look at Amber, a look that I knew and understood as though it spoke in a language that had been scratched on my bones at birth. The look told Amber to *do* something—something that they must have previously discussed. And the look she gave him in return was the one I was most familiar with—it was a look of acquiescence.

"I need to make arrangements," Reeve said. He stood and left the room with Brent in tow.

Exhaustion fell over me like a curtain. I knew what was coming and, in some hidden remote place inside where I was still capable of strong emotions, I was outraged and on guard. This was not how I wanted him to fight for me. It wasn't what I wanted at all.

But mostly I was just tired. Tired of fighting and hurting and loving. Tired of always needing to please.

Amber watched as Reeve left the room then smiled in my direction. "Come sit by me."

She hadn't even blinked when I said I was leaving. She'd already known. Of course she'd already known.

I didn't move. "Just out with it. I'm ready." Or, rather, I was resigned. Resigned to listen, resigned to this feeling of betrayal. I was *not* resigned to agree, but, if experience told me anything, I probably had no other option.

Amber pursed her lips, unhappy that I'd refused her invitation. "You're going to be difficult, aren't you?" she teased.

When I didn't answer, she sighed. "It's not just me who needs protection anymore." She said it softly, breaking the news gently.

"You think I don't know that?" It had been the more selfish of my current worries. If Vilanakis had killed Chris because of what he knew, what would he do to me? I was half sure the only reason I'd been able to leave his hotel room alive was because I still had a possibility of proving useful. What would he do when he realized I didn't have the power over Reeve that he imagined I had?

What would he do when it became apparent that I wasn't even with Reeve anymore?

"I'll hire protection," I said, resolutely. "Joe will help. Won't you, Joe? Or direct me to someone who can do the job?"

"There will be quite a few things I'd want to put in place before I felt you were safe back in LA." He appeared sincerely contrite as he added, "Going away to a private island for a few weeks while I arrange that isn't a bad idea."

"You didn't think my leaving was such a bad idea last night. Last night when Reeve *kicked you off the ranch.* Remember that? Now you're on his side?" Apparently, I was still capable of expressing emotion after all.

"A lot has happened since then," he said patiently.

I let out an exasperated groan, tears of frustration brimming under my lids.

"Sit by me." Amber patted the cushion next to her. "Hear us out."

Us. The word referred to her and Joe, but I knew all the power behind it was Reeve. This conversation had been arranged by him. This intervention. I'd told him not to tell me to stay, and he'd found a way around it.

Frowning, I circled the couch and plopped on the spot between the two of them. "I'm listening."

"The island is secluded," Amber began, as if reciting from a travel brochure. "He owns all of it. Besides the resort on the opposite shore, his private compound is the only developed land. He's personally informed when anyone lands or docks and, unlike here at the ranch, his home there is not shared with any guests or seasonal workers."

"The security system there is the most advanced of all his properties. It was apparently designed to be a safe house of sorts." Despite his encouragement, Joe's tone belied that a man who needed such an asylum was not the kind of man he approved of.

"It will only be for a couple of weeks, Em. Just long enough for Reeve's men to negotiate some sort of peace." Her argument was sound and convincing, but, like Joe, her expression showed a lack of enthusiasm for her viewpoint.

I pulled my legs up to my chest, rested a cheek on my knees, and studied her. I hadn't seen her since Jenkins had been found dead, and I hadn't spoken to her since we'd been on the roof together. So she knew that I'd had a relationship with Reeve. I'd been ridiculous to ever think she wouldn't figure that out immediately.

"Don't you want time alone with Reeve?" It was harder than I thought it would be to make the suggestion. "A secluded island paradise—it sounds awfully romantic."

"It's definitely romantic," she agreed. "He took me there for a getaway once last year."

It wasn't my imagination that she was boasting. Reminding me of the relationship she'd had with him before me. Reminding me that she'd had him first.

I had things to remind her of as well. Like how easily I could see through her. "You don't really want me there." It wasn't an accusation. It was simply the truth. I understood where she was coming from—I didn't want her on that island with Reeve either.

For a second, she looked like she might deny it.

Then, she didn't. "It's not that I don't want to be with you."

"I know." I was so sincere in that statement that I said it again. "I know."

There was a strange comfort in the confirmation that our friendship was important and separate from Reeve, as separate as it could be with the entanglement we'd found ourselves in.

"It's just . . . you know, PGR." She winked.

PGR—Pretty Girl Ratio—was an Amber-created term that I hadn't thought about in years. It was used to refer to the ratio of attractive women to attractive men in any given social situation. When we were between men and in search of a new one, we'd choose which opportunities were best for the possibility of finding one based on the PGR. At the bar of a luxury hotel, for example, if a peek inside showed a high ratio of pretty girls to wealthy men, we'd find another bar. *Why stack the odds against ourselves?* she'd say.

Her use of the term now was obvious. The two of us to Reeve—someone was guaranteed to lose. And even when I would surely be that loser, it would be a bitter victory for her. She was the girl who always won, but she wasn't heartless.

I bit my lip. "If you don't want me there, then why are you asking me to come?" I knew the answer so I didn't wait for hers. "Because Reeve told you to ask me, right? That's not like you to let someone else make your decisions for you."

Her grin was coy, saying she was both proud and a touch embarrassed to be called out on her reputation as a diva. "You know how to play the game," she said. "Sometimes when you're trying to win the guy, you have to forget who you are for a minute and be who he wants you to be."

I sat with her statement, unsure how to let it settle. Somehow I'd forgotten that about her—forgotten that, even though she was a natural princess, she could play submissive when she needed to.

And what a time for her to remind me.

She was honest, at least. I was grateful for that, and, if I had any inkling to begrudge her for taking that position, I knew I had to swallow it. Because flexibility had been one of the most basic rules of our man-hunting. I'd focused on that very idea when I'd prepared myself to go after Reeve—*be who he wants you to be*. And I had been.

But then I'd fallen for him, and when I had, it had been genuine and the ways I'd won him had been honest. It bothered me that she had to pretend in order to fight for his affection. Almost as much as it bothered me that he'd taken advantage of her willingness to do so.

I lowered my feet to the floor. "I'm sorry he put you in this position." I cringed at my words as soon as they were out. I couldn't apologize for him, and I didn't want to. "I'm sorry *I* put you in this position," I corrected. *God, what a mess.*

"Not any more sorry than I am for dragging you into this to begin with."

Oh, yeah. That.

We'd shift blame all day if we didn't stop now. Blame wasn't productive.

Thankfully, she knew it as well as I did. "No more apologies." She started to get up, and then paused to place a hand on my knee. "It's early and I haven't had coffee or a smoke. We can talk more about this later, if you want. But, come to the island with us. Okay?"

She gave me the same look that Reeve had given her. The one that said *I know you'll do what I want so I don't even need to hear you agree.*

At that moment, I hated seeing that look on her face as much as I'd ever loved seeing it on Reeve's. My hatred for it, as much as the power it held over me, kept me from answering—I didn't want to and I didn't need to.

But I did have one more thing that had to be said. The thing that I hadn't truly decided until just then. Because it was the hardest thing. "I'm not playing the game anymore, Amber. Not with Reeve."

There it was—my official relinquishing of the man we both loved. It seemed like it should have been a bigger moment than it was. Like, the dark cloud above me should burst open and light should shine down with the heavens recognizing my good deed.

But it wasn't that. It was almost not even a moment at all. Especially when Amber's acknowledgment of it was simply to nod and say, "I know you don't want to." She stood and then turned back to me. "But I'm not sure you have a choice." Then she left the room.

With a soft groan, I threw my head back against the couch.

"That was one hell of a strange conversation," Joe said. He'd been so quiet, I'd almost forgotten he was there.

"It's complicated." Why I kept defending our relationship, I had no idea. "The best thing for all of us would be for me to leave, and you know it. So why do you want me to go with them? I know you don't like Reeve."

Joe leaned forward and leveled his stare at me. "I don't have to like him to recognize his strengths. He is more powerful than I am, Emily. He has resources and connections at his fingertips that I don't. You're vulnerable right now. It pisses the shit out of me that he's the one who put you in this vulnerable position, but that doesn't negate the fact that he's the best option for your safety."

He considered for a moment then added, reluctantly, "Also I actually believe that protecting you is a priority for him."

"So you think I should go to the island." I already knew I was going to go. I was only fighting it because I was unhappy about it. "How long am I supposed to stay there?"

"Until Reeve works out a truce with Vilanakis. Meanwhile, I'll take care of making your home back in LA secure so that it will be ready for you to come back to."

I pinched the corners of my eyes, fighting again against the tears.

Joe apparently assumed it was because I was scared. "Hey. You're going to be fine. Chris blabbed, and that's what got him in trouble. We're not even entirely sure it was Vilanakis behind his death. It could have been an accidental overdose."

Considering Chris's previous drug problems, that was certainly a possibility. But the timing of it had been too coincidental. I was 99 percent sure that Michelis had ordered a hit on Chris and that the phone call Petros had taken for his father when I'd been with them was someone telling him that the job had been completed. He'd wanted me to witness that. Wanted me to be an alibi and, at the same time, wanted to give me a message—*This is what I'm capable of. Watch how easily I can get rid of a problem.*

It was a scare tactic, and it worked.

An idea occurred to me. A very much unwanted idea that had to be voiced. "You know, Reeve took that article about Chris and me better than I'd expected. He's been much more jealous than that in the past. All he said was that he'd handle it instead of getting mad like I thought he would."

"He did handle it. He leaked that article about you and him in response. It was a smart move." The Google alert must have finally reached Joe's in-box. "You knew about it, didn't you?"

"Yes. But . . ." I decided not to bring up that I hadn't known about it until after the fact. I was still angry about it—it just wasn't foremost on my mind.

What *was* foremost was much worse, and I didn't know quite how to say it. I swallowed, then rushed through. "What if that article wasn't the only way he handled it? What if getting rid of Chris was the favor that Michelis referred to doing for Reeve?

"Or what if Michelis had nothing to do with it and Reeve wanted Chris to stop blabbing because of the risk it put me in? What if killing him was how he thought he could keep me safe?"

Joe pressed his lips together in a way that suggested he'd already been through these scenarios in his mind. "Do *you* believe that Reeve is behind it?"

I didn't want to believe that Reeve had killed my friend. But there was a sliver of a part of me that *could* believe that he was capable of a myriad of horrible things, including this. He'd even told me once that he could take someone's life, if it were the *right* life. He didn't go so far as to explain what would make a life "right." Could jealousy be enough of a reason for him to commit murder?

"I don't know what I believe," I admitted. "I guess I'm surprised that you're so sure I'd be safer with Reeve when you know he could be behind Chris's death."

"Honestly? If he's the type of guy who would kill because of you, then that's exactly who you'll be safest with."

Less than thirty minutes later, Joe drove away from the ranch without me. I stood on the porch and waved and watched after him until he was only a speck on the road.

When I went back into the house, my luggage was missing from the hall. Presumably, it had been returned to my room for me. It pissed me off. Wasn't it enough that I'd stayed? Reeve had to rub it in that he'd known all along that I would?

As if to further gloat, Reeve was standing at the top of the stairs when I climbed up.

"Congratulations," I said before he could speak. "Looks like you succeeded in 'keeping' me too."

I stomped off to my room before he could respond, and shut the door behind me, leaving *him* to stand in the hall alone for once.

CHAPTER

17

It took three days to prepare to leave for the island. There were all sorts of arrangements to be made. The compound house had to be opened and the kitchen needed to be stocked. Clothes were an issue. Amber had been sharing my clothing since she'd returned to the ranch, and neither of us had anything that would be suitable for wearing on a beach in the South Pacific. Reeve didn't allow us to leave the ranch to shop, and even if he had, Jackson, Wyoming, in the spring wasn't likely to have the items we needed. We resorted to choosing items over the Internet and giving our lists to one of Reeve's men in LA, who picked them up and met us at the airport there when we stopped to refuel.

I spent more time with Amber in those three days than I had since she'd returned, and almost no time at all with Reeve. When I wasn't with him, my emotions were manageable. If I didn't have to engage with him, I could stay numb and resigned. Without his eyes on me, I could hold on to my resolve to let him go.

Fortunately, he made it easy to avoid him. He locked himself away in his office from the time he woke until the time he went to bed, taking meals on his own. Whether he was too busy with his planning and organizing or staying clear of me, I didn't know. I supposed it was a bit of both, but I tried not to let myself spend much time thinking about it. Or him.

The morning we were set to take off, we loaded up the Escalade and made our good-byes before the sun came up. Two of Reeve's security men were appointed to accompany us and another two drove in a separate car. Anatolios, Reeve's main henchman, stayed behind.

When I mentioned it to Amber, she said, "He's going to handle negotiations with Michelis."

She had to have learned that from Reeve. Then it was only me he was avoiding. I wondered if my face gave away how much that bothered me.

"What exactly is he going to negotiate? Shouldn't Reeve just negotiate?"

"Reeve will never talk to Micha," she said with certainty. "He'd have him killed before that happened." She climbed into the back of the car, sliding to the middle, where she would be seated between Reeve and me.

I hung behind until I could convince myself that her last statement sounded more like supposition than wishful thinking. Michelis scared me, and I'd shed no tears if he ended up dead. And, truth be told, if it were Reeve who made the order, I could likely handle that too—Michelis was a bad man and deserved the worst.

But there was something manipulative about Amber's presentation of the idea. And that bothered me more than I wanted to admit.

Since we were flying to the island on a private jet, checking in at the airport was quick. After making it through security, Reeve stopped at a gift shop to get a paper.

"Do we have gum?" Amber asked as we stood waiting with the security men.

"No. I'll grab some."

I met Reeve at the counter and handed him a pack of Trident. "We need Dramamine too. Amber gets airsick."

He held up a tube of pills. "Already got them."

"Of course you know her needs. I don't know what I was thinking." My voice was thick despite my smile. I turned away and headed back to Amber, ignoring him when he called after me. Ignoring him again when he joined us a minute later, his searing gaze on me as he handed the bag of purchases to Amber.

When he finally moved his attention to his men, I let out a sigh of relief. Was this what the next few weeks held in store for me? Constantly avoiding and ignoring? All the while, pretending I wasn't miserable?

I wasn't sure I was that good an actress.

On the plane, Reeve sat with his men in the cabin nearest the pilots. Amber and I took seats in the next cabin, she at the window, and I at her side. Ginger, the stewardess who'd also been on the plane when I'd flown into Jackson, served us mimosas and then disappeared to take care of the men.

Amber and I chatted a bit, then, about half an hour after we'd been in flight, she yawned and said, "Dramamine always knocks me out." She leaned her chair back and, with earbuds and the iPod that she'd borrowed from me, she turned to her side and fell asleep.

As if on cue, Reeve emerged from the first cabin, and every nerve in my body came to life. I buried my head in my Kindle and resumed the ignoring game from earlier. Or resumed pretending to ignore him. He was impossible to truly ignore.

I definitely couldn't ignore him when he took the seat across from me, but I tried, keeping my eyes down as he silently studied me, his gaze lighting up every inch of my skin.

Finally, he spoke. "So. Are you officially not speaking to me?"

Officially, no, I was not speaking to him, except for when absolutely necessary. But that was childish. Even I recognized that.

"I'm speaking to you," I said. "I spoke to you in the gift store earlier."

"I think, counting that, you've said all of twenty-five words to me since Joe left."

It had been forty-seven, to be precise. I'd counted.

With my chin still down, I shrugged. "There's nothing to say." It wasn't exactly true. There was plenty to say, but I was tired of being the only one talking.

"Hmm," he said. Then he went quiet, and I continued to stare at the screen in front of me, reading the same sentence over and over without comprehension. All I could focus on was his nearness. How his presence affected me so greatly that it felt like he was touching me. How he was only sitting a few feet away from me and yet was farther than he'd ever been.

I closed my eyes and wondered if it would ever end—this yearning for him. For all of him. For any of him at all. I'd grown so used to how that desire completed me, I wasn't sure who I'd be if one day it actually did.

"The Vilanakis family—*my* family—"

I opened my eyes at the sound of his voice.

"Has been involved in organized crime of some sort or another since God knows when," he continued, and I stopped breathing. "It's a complete culture, like being raised in a religious family. A baby born into our family is automatically raised in the lifestyle. There's no leaving. Vilanakis blood is a tie that can't be undone."

I lifted my head, slowly, afraid that if I moved too quickly, I'd interrupt the spell. It was the first time he'd admitted his connection to Michelis. The first time he'd volunteered information without me prodding.

His eyes grazed mine, but he quickly shifted his focus out the window. "My mother, as I'm sure you've figured out by now, was born *Elena Vilanakis*. Her grandfather was . . . a don, of sorts. Powerful. His children and their children were practically royalty. Crime was their birthright. It's a patriarchal system, but women do have their places and their duties. My mother was the oldest of her siblings so her role was significant. Whoever she married would be adopted into the family business. It was expected that she would wed someone with economic or political strength. Someone like Daniel Sallis, who had built a fortune and name in luxury resorts. Their union was blessed and encouraged by her parents."

"But your mother wanted to leave." It came out before I could stop it, and his stare flew back to mine, his eyes wide as though he'd forgotten I was there.

Immediately I tensed, sure I'd spoiled his confession.

Instead, his lip curled up in an impressed smile. "Yes. She did want to leave." He settled back into his chair and crossed his ankle over his knee. "Ironically, the level of power that her parents required in an intended husband was the same level capable of making a Mafia princess disappear."

He seemed to have relaxed a bit, which made me less wary to ask, "Did your father know what he was getting into?"

"Yes. My father loved my mother. I believe that he would have committed to the Vilanakis Empire if she'd asked him to. But she wanted nothing to do with her family, and so he committed to that instead."

His features brightened when he talked about his parents. So much that I felt warmth in my chest for the first time in days, like sun hitting a patch of snow.

"But your father was high profile. He obviously didn't vanish."

"Right. He couldn't. But he managed to hide my mother. He arranged for her to take on a fake identity before they were ever wed so he was never officially tied to the Vilanakis name. He never traveled with her. Made sure he was never photographed with her. And he purchased the ranch in Wyoming secretly. It was a place no one would ever look for a businessman like Daniel Sallis. Certainly it wasn't where anyone would look for the granddaughter of a Greek mob boss. Essentially, the only people who knew that my father's young bride had any other name than Elena Kaya were her parents."

"Her parents *knew*?" That surprised me, especially after he'd said there was no turning away from the mob. "Were they mad? Did they put out a hit on her or something?"

Reeve tilted his head, clearly amused. "Did you get that from television?"

"Excuse me for not having a lot of personal experience with the mob."

He chuckled. "Well. You're not entirely off base. Her grandfather would have 'put out a hit' on my father." He used his fingers to indicate quote marks when he said, "put out a hit." "Then he would have dragged my mother back home where she belonged."

"Okay, that's only half as horrible as I thought." I caught myself before I smiled back at him. But just barely.

"Or he might have killed her as well. My great-grandfather did have a reputation for being ruthless."

I almost thought he was joking. Goose bumps shot down my arms when I realized he wasn't. "Your parents protected her and didn't tell great-granddaddy Vilanakis what happened to her."

"Exactly. Her parents—my grandparents—were like most parents. They loved their daughter, and, even though it was against everything they believed in, they wanted her to be happy. And alive. So when my father proposed a believable scenario for an accidental death, they clung to that."

"They cut off all ties?"

He nodded. "The night she slipped away with my father, her parents hugged her good-bye and that was the last they ever saw of her." He sobered. "They kept tabs, distantly, though. They knew she'd had a son. And so they also knew to reach out to me after my parents were killed."

"Which is how you ended up in Greece with your grandmother." The puzzle pieces were sliding together easily now. It was so satisfying that I nearly missed what he'd said. "Did you say 'killed' on purpose?"

"I did."

My heart tripped. I'd known his parents had died in a car accident when he was sixteen, but never once had he or any of the Internet sources I'd referred to suggest that it had been murder.

Much like Amber when she'd tried to comfort me about Chris, I didn't know what to say so it took me several seconds to manage, "How?" and another few seconds to add, "Why?"

I assumed he was going to say his grandfather had found them, but instead he said, "Your television shows probably taught you about rival branches in organized crime rings."

"Yes. They probably did."

"We have a rival branch. Distant cousins. The Lasko family. One of them discovered my mother was still alive. I don't know how they found out. Maybe my mother blabbed to a friend. Maybe one of the Laskos got wise and did some research. I'll probably never know. What I do know was my mother was an easy target." His voice was even, but his eyes spoke volumes of pain and grief.

"Oh, Reeve." I wasn't naturally very sympathetic, but the hurt I felt for him was genuine. All the time I wanted to be in his arms, it was the first time I longed to wrap him in mine.

He shook his head once, and I knew he was dismissing the memories rather than my compassion. "Anyway, I was vaguely aware of relatives on my mother's side back in Greece so it wasn't a complete surprise when my grandparents found me. I was sixteen. My parents were dead. My father had no family. I didn't have a choice when they offered to take me in."

"And you didn't know about their business?" Whatever his answer was, where this was going was inevitable.

"I didn't have any idea at all," he confirmed. "But I learned quickly." He leaned forward, emphasizing his next words. "Because that's how the family works. There's no tiptoeing along the edges of the life. It's full immersion. For me, it was baptism by fire."

The hair on the back of my neck stood up as the truth sunk in, the truth I'd both suspected and denied since I'd first discovered his picture with Michelis. "You're mob, too."

"I *was* mob," he clarified.

"You said there's no leaving."

"I guess I'm the exception."

He was quiet while I sunk back in my chair and processed. One of the reasons I'd always been attracted to Reeve was because he'd seemed dangerous. He'd always suggested that I wouldn't want to find out that he actually was. I wasn't sure that he'd been correct. I wasn't sure that he hadn't been.

"You aren't part of the family business? Not at all?"

He leveled my stare. "What do you want the answer to be, Emily?"

No. Of course the answer was *no.*

I swallowed the ball in my throat. "You said you weren't. You said you left."

He nodded ever so slightly.

Propping his elbow on the armrest, he leaned his chin in his hand. "But I *was* in it. Really in it. I didn't even realize it in the beginning. First, it was just running errands for my uncle Nikki with my cousins. Then it was accompanying him on what he called 'negotiation visits.' After a few of those, I retitled them 'scare jobs.' I'm sure you can guess the nature of what those entailed."

If those TV shows I watched were at all based in reality, then, yes, I could. My dark side was curious, though. It wanted to hear the details. But more importantly, I wanted to know, "Were you a participant on these scare jobs or just an observer?"

His eyes narrowed. "What do you think?"

I think you don't want me to know. "I think you like it when I think the worst."

He laughed. "Touché."

He considered for a minute, and it occurred to me that he was as torn about what he wanted me to believe about him as I was. Part of me wanted the truth, wanted him to tell me the truth no matter what it was. Another part of me wanted to never know that he was as dangerous as I thought him capable. Never wanted to know that he wasn't.

If he wasn't torn himself, he at least understood that I was. So he admitted nothing, and hinted everything. "I fit right into the life, Emily," he said. "It fit me like my skin. As though it were written in my genetic code, which, I suppose, it was."

It did fit him like his skin. He wore it well. He looked good in it, too.

But I had to stop thinking about how he looked. It wasn't helping me any.

I rubbed my hand over my face, getting myself back on track. "What happened next?"

"A few things, actually." He uncrossed his leg and leaned forward, propping his elbows on his lap. "Michelis took an interest in me. He was my mother's oldest brother and he'd been close to her growing up. He made it his mission to groom me as thoroughly as he'd one day groom his own son, Petros. He gave me scare jobs to handle on my own. Then, when I turned eighteen, he told me he had a present for me."

The plane bumped as it hit a patch of turbulence, but I was pretty sure it was only part of the cause for my sudden queasiness. I'd spent all of twenty minutes with Reeve's uncle, and it was enough to realize he was a terrible man. I didn't want to know what kind of present he would give to a favored apprentice. But considering how vivid my imagination was, it was just as bad not knowing.

Reeve noticed my discomfort. "Are you okay? The bed's in the back cabin if you'd like to lie down." There was only the slightest hint of mischief in his tone.

Now my stomach was twisting in new ways, deeper ways, that shot memory sensations down my upper thighs. The last time we'd been on this plane, he'd taken me in that cabin and used me to distract him from Michelis. Oh, how I would love that distraction now.

But no. "I'll be fine, thank you. Go on. This present."

"Let me know if you change your mind," he said suggestively. Then he returned to the seriousness of earlier. "We'd had suspected the Laskos as the cause of my parents' accident, but no one could confirm it. Michelis kept digging, though, until he not only confirmed their involvement, but he also found out exactly which Laskos had set up the hit. On my birthday, he gave me a name—Broos Laskos."

My breath caught. "He wanted you to kill him?"

Reeve pointed a finger at me, a silent "bingo" gesture. "He said I could do what I wanted with the information, but it was time to prove my place in the family."

Time to prove his place.

So it was the first time that such an act had been required of him. Whatever awful things he'd done before that, it hadn't involved taking a life.

I tried to imagine it—a young Reeve, only two years after his beloved parents had been killed, asked to undertake such an awful, important task. With the support of his family, it had to feel less like a burden and more like an opportunity.

Yet, it was still murder. It would taint him. It would be a line that, once crossed, was crossed forever.

I met his eyes now and, despite the weight of them, I forced myself to hold his gaze. If I looked hard enough, could I see the scars on his soul? Because killing someone—that had to leave a mark that was visible somewhere, somewhere deep and hidden maybe.

Or, maybe not hidden at all. Maybe all his scars were in plain sight and sitting right in front of me.

"See anything interesting?" he smirked.

I'd studied him so long that he'd become amused by it. "I'm not sure. Do I?"

"I wish I knew the answer to that." His tone was wistful and solemn, and it struck a chord that reverberated so hauntingly through me, I was near throwing myself at his feet and confessing in detail every interesting way he affected me all the time.

But I hesitated, and the moment passed.

"I did what was expected of me," he went on, his voice absent of whatever melancholy I'd heard there before. "I made the arrangements. I knew where Broos would be alone and when. I had it all planned.

"Meanwhile, my parents' will had specified a few things to become available to me on my eighteenth birthday. Some stocks and a few personal items, including a letter from my mother that had been written to me when I was only eight. She'd saved it for those ten years, intending to give it to me when I turned eighteen, not knowing she'd be dead by then. It arrived at my grandmother's house a week or so after my birthday, a few days before I'd planned to take care of Broos. I read it and everything changed."

He didn't have to say more for me to understand what he meant, but he did anyway. "I didn't go through with my plans."

The relief that swept through me so was great and so unexpected that I had to bite back a laugh. Here I'd been searching for signs of the murder that I was so sure he'd committed, and he hadn't. I was smart enough to realize that didn't mean he'd never killed anyone after that, but I was grateful that this one story, at least, ended differently.

"Does that surprise you?"

I shrugged. I was more surprised at my reaction but wasn't about to admit that.

"Let me rephrase then—does it disappoint you?" He seemed more than just curious about my answer. He seemed desperate.

No. I'm not disappointed. I'm still very much interested.

But I couldn't tell him that either.

I redirected, instead. "What did the letter say? It had to reveal something significant."

"Yes. And no. She told me everything. Her life story, how she'd fallen for my father, why she'd left Athens. Everything. I already knew all of it now, but not from her point of view. Before that, I hadn't gotten a clear picture of why she'd left. It was biased information, pieced together from her family, and I didn't have any understanding of all the trouble my father had gone to in order to change her life. Or why. Until I read that letter."

I nodded, trying not to think about how charming he must have been. This young mobster with a natural knack for danger and lawlessness and, also, a sentimental streak. No wonder I loved him.

"The letter didn't change any of my beliefs," Reeve assured me, as though he were afraid he'd get a soft reputation.

"Of course not," I said, smugly.

He chuckled. "God, I was eighteen, I didn't know what I believed. But I knew that I'd loved my mother. At least as much as my father had. And she said in that letter that the true proof of his love had been how fully he'd stood against the Vilanakis way of life, for her. She ended it by saying she hoped I'd do the same."

"So you walked away. For her." And I'd begged him to talk to Michelis, something that might possibly undo all that he'd left behind. I'd wanted him to put Amber—to put *me*—before his mother. Boy, did I feel like an ass.

Except I'd seen him in pictures with Michelis when he was older than eighteen. "How did you get out? You said people couldn't leave."

"Michelis, actually. He became the head of the family when my grandfather died, and he allowed me to remain completely detached. He said it was a shame that they'd lost so many years with my mother, and that we should learn from those mistakes. When I moved back to the States, I stayed close to him and a few of my cousins. He advised me when I took over Sallis Resorts. He connected me with men capable of fighting against the Laskos or any other Mafia-related attacks I might encounter. He provided trustworthy people to work close to me."

More puzzle pieces fell into place. "The V monogram

on your driver in Los Angeles. He was one of your uncle's men. Do you pay him or does he serve you out of some debt to your family?"

Again, he seemed impressed at what I knew. "I pay him. I told you, I left the business."

Next to me, Amber shifted to her side. But she settled again quickly, her breathing adopting the even rhythm of sleep.

I looked up from her to find Reeve staring at me intently, as though he were done with his story and was waiting for my verdict.

But he hadn't explained everything yet. "He told me you betrayed him," I said.

"Did he? I suppose from his point of view, I did."

"By leaving the business? You said he was supportive, though." How did Michelis the father figure turn into Michelis the man who beat Reeve's ex-girlfriend? The dots weren't connecting.

"He was supportive. But his support had a price, and I didn't realize that until later. When I was dating Missy."

I gestured for him to go on.

Reeve heaved a sigh, as he seemed to begrudgingly enter territory he'd hoped would remain off-limits. "At first, it was small favors. He wanted connections. He supplied Missy and her friends with drugs, which was fine. But then he asked me to launder the money for him through the resorts."

Reeve reconsidered. "*Asked* is the wrong word, actually. Demanded is more appropriate. Said I *owed* it to him and the family. Said it was my role to play." He lowered his eyes and frowned. "We were still arguing about that when he started talking about taking one of Missy's friends."

"*Taking*? Like, kidnapping?" I shouldn't have been as shocked as I was. I knew he was involved with human trafficking—where did I think those women came from?

Reeve's mouth tightened, and he didn't have to affirm my question. His expression said it all. "I kicked him out of my life then. He's tried to talk to me a few times since. Petros said he's still set on getting me to launder for him. I suppose it wouldn't be the worst thing I could do for him. But my father held out, and Sallis Resorts was his baby."

"No. You can't bend to him." Though, really, I didn't know what he could and couldn't do. Reeve was a Vilanakis whether he wanted to be or not. His choices could have consequences that I couldn't begin to fathom.

Now I definitely felt like an ass about pushing him to talk to his uncle. And I was frustrated for him. I wished there was an answer that he hadn't thought of yet. "What about Petros? Who's side is he on?"

"His own. He works for his father but he's also sympathetic to my desire to stay out of the business. So he throws me a bone now and then."

A bone. Like telling Reeve when his girlfriend had stupidly left herself alone with his father. Petros had told him about other women, too, I realized. "He's how you knew Amber wasn't dead."

"Yes." He leaned toward me, his eyes narrow. "But how did you know I'd ever have reason to believe otherwise?"

The last time he'd asked me, I'd dodged the question. It seemed pointless to lie about it any longer. "I looked at your e-mails one night. You can't be surprised."

"I'm not." He sat back with a satisfied grin. "I just wanted you to admit it." He was especially cute when he got cocky, and he knew it. "What else did you see?"

"Pictures of you and Amber together. You looked happy."

His smile faded. "Maybe we were." He moved his focus to her and studied her intently, as if he could find something he'd lost if he just looked hard enough.

I regretted bringing her up, and I didn't all at once.

Because, just like he was a Vilanakis whether he wanted to be or not, Amber was a part of our lives, whether I wanted her to be or not. And whatever Reeve felt for me, he'd felt it first for her.

The warmth that had bloomed during the last hour of conversation began to fade away, and my body stepped back into familiar heartache.

"Who have you told about all of this?" I asked, a bitter edge to my question.

"Almost no one." He wanted me to realize his candidness was a gift.

I wouldn't accept it. "Did you tell Amber? Did she know all of this before she went to him?"

A beat passed. "Yes."

"Why didn't you just tell me too?" My pain was apparent and raw. If he'd just told me the truth from the beginning . . .

"Do you think it's some sort of validation of my affection? To have heard this story?" He kept his voice low, but it was thick and full of emotion. "Every time I've brought someone into that part of my life, things have ended badly. Look at Amber. Missy. Chris!"

"We can't be sure about Chris." It was a lie—we were sure. But I was looking to poke holes in his excuses, because there was no excuse he could give for why he hadn't told me things he'd told Amber that would satisfy me. "And you think your uncle was involved with Missy after all?"

"I don't know what happened to her. But I do blame him for who she was in the end. He seduced her with his drugs and power the same way he seduced me. Eventually he would have expected payment. Is that what you wanted me to open you up to?"

"I wanted you to open up, period!"

"I have. More than with anyone else. I've told you this."

His body language, his gravelly voice, the way his eyes pierced into my very being—he was desperate for my acknowledgment.

"What did his e-mail say?" I challenged, likely proving his theory that nothing was ever good enough for me, but really I was looking for reasons to stay mad. It was so much easier to hate him when I was.

"Nothing," he said, as I'd expected. As I'd half hoped.

"That's what I thought."

Then he surprised me. "Your name," he said softly. "Your real name. Nothing else."

He'd played the higher card. I had nothing that would compete. He should have been the winner.

I laid my head back against the seat and gripped the armrests tightly, as though I might fall out of my chair if I didn't. The world was spinning and my stomach felt like it was dropping and I knew that, no matter what I said from here on out, it was too late to save myself from being loved by Reeve Sallis. Really loved. Everything I'd thought he'd done to protect Amber he'd done for me.

How could I push that away?

But Amber had done those things for me, too.

I closed my eyes and concentrated on breathing in and out so that I wouldn't do something stupid like cry.

"I miss you," he said, his voice a near whisper.

I shook my head. "Don't say that."

"I miss your body."

I opened my eyes and the expression on his face was primal. Hungry. "You miss what it will let you do to it."

"Yes," he admitted. "But I miss you too."

His words sliced through me, cutting me into shreds of the person I'd once been—a person who knew who she belonged to and who she loved.

Needing to be reminded of who I was, I turned my head toward Amber and back to him. "You can't have both of us." And according to his uncle, he couldn't save both of us either.

"I don't want both of you."

No. I couldn't hear that. I wouldn't. "She's the only one you can have."

He sat stoic for five seconds. Then he bolted out of his seat and leaned his hands on either side of me in my chair. "You don't get to decide that, Emily." His chest rose and fell heavily. "That's not how this works between us."

He held his stance for a moment, his jaw ticking, his body tense. Then he pushed off the armrests and disappeared into the bedroom cabin behind me.

I curled up in my chair and pretended I didn't miss him too.

CHAPTER

18

Even though we stopped in LA to refuel, we still had most of the day ahead of us when we arrived on the island because of the five-hour time difference. I'd moved over to a window and watched as we approached, the tiny speck of land growing larger and larger, but still small enough that I glimpsed the opposite shore before we touched ground.

The airport consisted of a runway and a hangar with restrooms and a vending machine. Two cars pulled up alongside the plane as we landed, and the driver of one got out and met us at the bottom of the stairs.

"Filip!" I exclaimed, recognizing him as Reeve's driver from LA.

He smiled cordially as he helped me down the stairs. "Welcome to Oinopa." His accent, though Mediterranean, somehow seemed fitting in the Pacific setting. "Alex and I will get all the bags. Please take a seat in my car."

Amber and I climbed in the backseat while the plane was unloaded. A few minutes later, one of the security guards got in the front seat along with Filip. Reeve joined us in the back. This time, I was in the middle, and even though I kept my body as small as possible, the length of his leg pressed against mine as we rode, sending bolts of electricity through me.

To distract myself from his nearness, I kept my eyes out the window in front of me and asked questions about the island. "What does Oinopa mean?"

"Wine-dark." I swear Reeve pressed even tighter against me. "It's how Homer described the ocean in *The Odyssey*. My father thought it made a good sound bite for the marketing brochures. 'Experience your own odyssey on the island of Oinopa.'" He proclaimed the last sentence like a television announcer. "It loses its effect when I try it."

Amber let out a laugh, and I recognized it as the one she used when she was flirting. "I think you sounded sexy."

"Nah. I'll leave the voice-over work to Emily." The glint in his eyes said he wanted to add something about me being sexy.

I pursed my lips, praying he'd read my mind and keep his comment to himself.

He got the hint, but other than a soft sigh, he didn't show any other signs of disappointment. He spent the rest of the thirty-minute drive giving an overview of Oinopa, pointing out the resort as we passed by, specifically where the spa was and the shopping mall, and explained where each of the side roads led when we came upon them.

"That's the hillside trail," he said. "It's a nice run from the house. The view at the top is amazing. On a clear day, you can see from one coast to the other."

I didn't think it was an accident the way his arm grazed against my breast as he leaned across me to point it out. I held my breath, pissed at how aroused I was and how he had to know by the way my nipples stood up, reaching for the brush of his limb. And if I hadn't been sure before, I was certain now that we might be in paradise, but being here with Reeve, whose touch was torturous and hot—was the closest thing to hell I'd ever known.

Reeve's private compound wasn't beachfront property as I'd imagined it would be. Instead, it was on the mountain, inaccessible except through a secured gate and a tree-lined driveway that wound up the cliffside. At the top, the canopy broke into a clearing with the house on one side of us, and on the other side, a view so spectacular I couldn't believe that there were any more incredible on the island.

The positioning of the house was brilliant as well. It had been built on an outcrop of land so the ocean could be seen on three sides. It was grander than Reeve's Los Angeles home, but still simple and clean in its design. The sprawling one-level with its various courtyards throughout was the safest layout, according to Reeve, and I had a feeling he meant safe from more than just hurricanes. Either way, it was easy to see why he considered this his most secure property.

As soon as we were out of the car, Reeve became preoccupied with business and, I suspected, news from Anatolios regarding measures he was taking with Michelis. He disappeared into his office and so Filip offered to show Amber and me to our rooms.

"That's not necessary," Amber said in the typical uppercrust manner she used with servants. "I'm guessing Reeve is putting us in the east suites?"

"He is," Filip said, his head bowed in deference to her. "I'll make sure your bags are brought immediately."

I thanked Filip as I passed him, since Amber didn't, then followed her through the front doors.

"This is the main living space," she said, gesturing to the area in front of the entryway. "And behind it is the kitchen. The entire perimeter of the house is surrounded by these open walkways."

The open walks referred to were basically hallways missing an outer wall. I trailed behind her as she followed the hall to the left. "There are three main parts of the house with courtyards in between. Here's the first."

The inner wall of the walk continued here, but it was lower, and in the area behind was an additional dining room and entertainment area that extended from the first building.

The next building we passed wasn't open like the first, and I couldn't see what rooms were contained inside.

"This is the office and master bedroom. There's a mini-kitchen on the opposite side. Basically this is Reeve's area."

I tried to ignore the prick of awareness I had, knowing that he was just on the opposite side of the wall. "There aren't any windows. I'd think the master would have the best view in the house."

"Right? But it's the most secure area on the compound so it's supposedly surrounded by thick, impenetrable walls. It's practically a safe room. But the outer wall here on the office can be raised like a garage door. Reeve almost always keeps it closed, though. You know him—he likes to be all secretive and shit."

Yes, I did know him. I hated that she did as well.

The walls opened again and this time we turned into the courtyard. "This pool is heated and there's the hot tub off the master." She gestured to the last building. "And these are the guest quarters."

There were two doorways leading into this part of the house. Between them was a bank of showers and, I guessed, dressing rooms behind them. She took us through the closest door, and, after we got inside past the back wall of the pool changing area, the building opened up to a large common space.

"These are all bedrooms," she said, pointing to the

doors that surrounded the main area. "Except that area on the back wall, which, you can see, is the exercise area. And we'll have the two suites on either side. The best rooms in the house."

She opened the door to one of them, and I gasped. The entire back wall was open to the outside, giving a breathtaking view of the ocean. Outside the bedroom was yet another patio area. A second pool ran the length of the building and spilled over the cliff beyond.

I walked in further and surveyed the scene. "This is . . . amazing," I said, unable to find appropriate words for the spectacular setting.

Amber joined me as I walked out onto the covered lanai. "These walls close, too, like the office. In case you want to shut them at night for privacy. That room on the opposite end will be mine. We're practically neighbors."

I had to swallow past the ball suddenly lodged in the back of my throat before I could speak. "Just like old times."

Once upon a time, I fantasized that she and I could live like this forever. Together in a luxurious location, both of us taken care of, nothing lacking.

"Yes." The breeze blew in and lifted her peroxide-blond hair off her cheek, revealing the entirety of the grin that lit up her face. She turned from the view to face me. "Well, not *just like*."

Because this time only one of us would get the guy. For half a minute I'd forgotten.

"No, I guess not," I agreed, and I managed to keep beaming despite the sinking feeling in my chest. A slow sinking, as though a paper airplane had been tied to my heart or my hope or the ball of optimism that I kept trying to nourish and sustain inside, and now had been tossed out into the wind. Little by little, it made its descent, carrying everything wonderful between us with it.

Behind us, footsteps could be heard across the stone tile of the common area. "Filip," Amber said. "I'll tell him whose bags are whose." She turned to go.

"For what it's worth," I called after her, "I think the parts that *are* like old times are really nice."

"Me, too." She disappeared into the hallway and I reminded myself that, while there was beauty in this fall, paper airplanes never stayed in flight for long. Eventually, I'd hit the ground.

We spent the rest of the day settling in. Reeve was absent for both lunch and dinner, but with the four security guards, Filip, Alex, and two women house servants, the house didn't feel lonely. While everyone else dined inside, Amber and I took our supper on the lanai off the kitchen, and, when the sweet Polynesian girl left the bottle after pouring my glass of merlot, I passed it to Amber.

"You're very naughty," she said with a wink. She dumped the water from her glass on the stone ground and replaced it with wine. "Reeve would not approve."

"I'm sure he wouldn't." I knew she assumed that my disregard for his rules meant that she still held the highest position of authority over me, and I let her believe that.

In truth, I wasn't sure what my motive was. It might have had more to do with Reeve than with Amber. There was a stab of satisfaction at the idea of riling him up, even if he didn't ever find out.

After dinner, we hung out in Amber's room like old girlfriends at a sleepover. I'd commandeered a second bottle of wine from the kitchen and by the time we'd finished it off, I was feeling more tired than tipsy.

Seeming to sense that I was fading, she stood up from her bed where we'd been lounging and stretched. "I think I'm going to take a bath."

"Okay."

"Or I can soak in the hot tub instead, if you want to join me."

I stifled a yawn. "I'll take a rain check. I didn't sleep on the plane like someone else I know, and this time difference is killing me."

"You're going to call it a night then?"

"Just as soon as I can work up the energy to get off this bed."

She pulled a pair of panties out of a drawer and a slinky nightie out of another, and I tried not to think about the reason she'd picked out something so blatantly sexy in her online shopping spree.

Don't think about it, I told myself. So she was planning to seduce Reeve. I'd have to get used to her sleeping in his bed sooner or later.

"No rush," she said. "You're welcome in my bed as long as you want. Make yourself at home."

Yeah, because she probably isn't expecting to sleep in here herself.

At the door, she paused. "But if you aren't here when I get out, I love you and sweet dreams."

Her declaration of affection caressed and scratched, like a beloved fleece blanket that had lost its softness from one too many times in the wash. I knew she loved me, and hearing her say the words warmed me, but they felt uncomfortable at the same time, and I didn't know what to do with them or how to react.

She lingered, and after a few seconds I realized she wanted me to return the endearment.

The best I could manage was, "Same here."

Fortunately, it was enough. She grinned then disappeared into her bathroom, and a minute later I heard the sound of water filling the tub.

With a weary groan, I pushed myself up to a sitting

position then froze, my eye catching on an item sticking out of the travel bag open on the dresser.

I'd generally been one to respect Amber's privacy, even when she didn't always return the favor. But curiosity and concern overruled that consideration, and before I could think twice, I'd crossed to the bag and pulled out the object that had attracted my attention—a full prescription bottle. Two bottles, actually, one hiding under the other. Without removing the caps, I recognized the round, white pills inside as oxycodone.

Goddammit, I swore quietly.

And if I wondered where she'd gotten them, one look at the labels told me. Both had been prescribed to Bud Greenwood—*Buddy*. He hadn't just given her cigarettes; he'd loaded her up with drugs.

I counted the seconds by the tick of the wall clock as I debated what to do about my discovery. One hundred twenty ticks passed before I decided that I'd thought about it for two minutes too long. Two bottles of oxy was serious. This wasn't the same as secretly sharing two bottles of wine.

With both containers in hand, I took off in search of Reeve.

I crossed the courtyard between the east wing of the house and the center building. Seeing that the office light was off, I traipsed through the open door of the master bedroom, already making my announcement as I entered. "You won't believe what I just found in Amber's room."

The words were out before I realized that the room was empty.

And then it wasn't empty. Reeve stepped out of his bathroom, his hair wet, wearing nothing but a towel around his hips. "What was that?"

"Oh." My eyes slid down, across the sculpted planes of his chest, to the deep creases at his waist that angled and disappeared under the white terry cloth. Inches and inches of bare skin before me, wet and glistening, begging for my tongue to dart along his dips and bends.

My fingers tingled as though from muscle memory. I could practically feel his toned body beneath them.

Except my hands weren't holding him—they were holding plastic bottles full of narcotics found in the bedroom of the woman who really should be holding him.

I turned, averting my eyes. "I'm sorry. I didn't realize you were in the shower. I'll come back."

"I'm not in the shower now." His smirk was apparent without looking at him.

"It's fine. This can wait until tomorrow." I started toward the open door, my feet seeming to move through molasses. Had the distance doubled since I'd walked in?

I'd barely made it three steps when he said the word I both dreaded and longed for—"Stay."

I shook my head, but my feet were planted. "I need to leave."

"I told you to stay."

He'd used that voice, that one that rasped with demand. That one that turned my insides into jelly and made my pussy throb. That one I couldn't even dream of denying.

But I *had* to deny it. I had to be strong.

"Reeve . . ." It was a plea, but I didn't know what I was asking for. For him to let me leave? Yes. But, also, no. Because no matter how much I believed that was the right thing to do, I didn't want to beg for that. It was one thing to walk away. It was quite another to ask him to send me. And I couldn't do that—could I?

It didn't matter. He wouldn't listen if I could.

"Turn around," he commanded, and like a trained performer, I did.

I kept my eyes down, studying the tile beneath his feet. Unglazed ceramic-like throughout the rest of the house, but there were more grays and dark browns in the flooring here, while the flooring elsewhere stuck to the color of sand.

"Look at me, Emily."

I lifted my gaze, slowly, as if it were heavy, as if the weight of it took all my strength to hoist. In reality, I just knew what I'd find when I raised my eyes high enough, and that knowledge made me hold the reins and sent shivers down my spine. Shivers of fear because I didn't want to see what he wanted to show me. Shivers of anticipation because I didn't want to see anything else.

Then I was there, staring at his bold erection, the towel abandoned on the floor at his feet.

My breath slid out in a slow sigh. Just the sight of him, naked and hard in front of me, and I was instantly aroused. My nipples tightened and rose into sharp peaks, and the thin cloth at my crotch felt damp and oppressive. And the night that had felt almost too cool just a moment before was suddenly hot and stifling.

Reeve brought his hand down and slid it down his length before circling it at the base of his cock. "Watch me," he said in that tone that forced me to comply. That voice that wasn't even necessary because I was already glued, my focus cemented to his rhythmic stroke.

"Should I tell you what I'm imagining while I do this?" His voice was like an intruder, an unwanted narrator in an already hard-to-watch scene.

I couldn't look away. I couldn't move. But I could manage one faint word. "No."

"I think I should." His teasing had an edge of cruelty that ratcheted up my desire another ten degrees. "Don't you want to know what gets me this hard? What kind of thoughts?"

"No. I don't." More than anything I wished that I meant it.

"Hmm. I don't believe you." His hand slowed, this time

tugging all the way to his crown where his palm rubbed across a drop of pre-cum before sliding down his length again.

God, it was so hot. And the door was wide open. Anyone could come in. *She* could come in. What kind of person was I to be even more turned on by that possibility?

"You want to watch," he said, his stroke adopting a lazy tempo. "But you're not sure if you want me to say I'm thinking of you while I'm touching myself. Or if you want me to say I'm thinking of Amber. That's it, right?"

I shook my head, unable to even say *no* anymore.

"Well, this might be a disappointment. But I'm not thinking about Amber." He took a step toward me and automatically I took one back. "I'm not imagining her lips wrapped around my cock." Another step toward me, another away from him. "Or her tight pussy milking me to orgasm. It's not her blond hair I'm picturing twisted in my hand."

His stride sped up, and each step pushed me back, back, back until I hit the wall behind me and couldn't go any farther.

He gave a smug smile that reminded me of a cat about to pounce on a caged canary. "It's not Amber making that sweet little sound in the back of her throat."

I shuddered every time he said her name, my eyes darting to the open door, half-expecting to find her standing there, half-disappointed when she wasn't.

"That soft one that's completely a cry of pleasure but it's so near the sound of pain—you know which one I'm talking about. Do you even notice when you make it?"

Was I making that sound now? I had no sense of myself anymore. All I knew was everything about this moment was pure torture.

"It's not Amber begging for me to be inside her."

I dropped the pill bottles to the floor and slammed my hands over my ears. "I'm not listening to this."

He was only a few feet from me now, but he halted abruptly. "Put your hands down." The teasing edge had vanished and was replaced with bitterness. "Or I'll tie them behind your back."

It was meant to be a punishment, and it was, only the punishment was not in the threat, but in how difficult it was to deny him.

"Don't touch me," I begged. "You *can't* touch me."

"I can't?"

I shook my head, fiercely this time, even though it didn't matter how furiously I protested—if he wanted to touch me, he would. And it wouldn't ever be nonconsensual, no matter how many times I said no, because he and I both knew that, despite my objections, I wanted him to touch me. More than anything.

He closed nearly the entire distance between us. "You don't mean that. You don't mean to tell me what I can and can't do with what belongs to me."

My entire body went weak. If I hadn't had support behind me, I would have collapsed.

He placed a forearm on the wall next to my head and leaned in so that his mouth was only an inch away from my ear. "Tell me I'm right."

I swallowed, my eyes watering. "Yes."

"Good girl." His lip curled up. With one arm still braced on the wall, he glanced down between us where his other hand continued to jerk himself off. "For being such a good girl, I'm going to give you a reward. I'll let you stop worrying about what I'll do to you. I'm not going to touch you. I'm not going to fill your mouth with my cock even though I could. You know I could. I'm not going to squeeze your breasts or stick my fingers in your cunt. I'm not going to lick swirls around that pretty little clit."

Each word out of his mouth pinched and bruised and slapped. I ached for the touch he talked about, the physical touch he'd denied thus far. And I knew him well enough now to understand that he wouldn't give me anything until I asked for it. That was his secret weapon, what made him different from all the men I'd been with before him—he wouldn't allow me just to take what he gave. He made me want. He made me accept.

"All I'm going to do is make you watch." The low rumble of his voice so near my skin made the hair stand up on my neck. "Watch me stroke myself."

"Stop!" I cried, surprising even myself.

He stilled.

I closed my eyes and tears slid openly down my cheeks. "Please, stop. I can't do this anymore. You know I'll do whatever you want me to. You know you have that power, but I'm begging you, please, stop."

He was silent, but I could feel that he hadn't moved. Gathering my courage, I opened my eyes again and focused on an imaginary spot behind his ear. "If you keep on doing this," I said, my voice choked, "she's going to find out that we still have feelings for each other and it's going to break her. And that will break me. And not in the way you want me to be broken."

It was everything I had laid bare in front of him. What he chose to do with it was up to him. I wouldn't fight anymore. I couldn't. This was the last bit of restraint I possessed, and my resolve was quickly deteriorating.

He let another several seconds pass before he lifted his forearm off the wall and then slammed it back down in frustration. "Goddammit, Emily," he rasped. "I don't want to lose you."

"I know. And you couldn't ever lose me." Just like Amber could never lose me. "That's why I'm asking you to let me go."

He straightened, and I could see the war behind his eyes as he scrubbed his hand over his chin. "No," he said after several long seconds. "I can't do that. I'm sorry. I won't let you go."

"Reeve . . ." I wasn't pleading anymore. I was his to keep or discard as he chose, and he'd decided to keep me.

Except then he went on. "I can't let you go, but I can continue to give you space. If that's what you need."

"And you won't do this anymore? You won't come on to me?" I wasn't sure if I felt optimistic or destroyed.

"I won't come on to you." He sounded as ruined as I felt. "Until you say I can."

"But what if that's never?"

He met my eyes, and with all the solemnness of a vow, he said, "It won't be."

He held my gaze for a moment longer, then turned his back to me and walked toward the bathroom, stooping to pick up the towel he'd discarded on his way.

I didn't wait a second longer before swiping the bottles off the floor and darting out the door.

My legs shook the entire way to my room. I dumped the pills in the bottom of my suitcase, turned off the light, and climbed into bed fully dressed. A second later, I jumped up and locked my door. Reeve had let me go tonight, but I didn't trust him to be able to stay away.

To be fair, I didn't trust myself to stay away either.

CHAPTER
19

Several days passed, and we settled into a manageable routine. I spent most days lounging on the lanai off the wing I shared with Amber, reading terrible scripts that my agent had sent over. If I could book something even halfway decent before I had to be back to the *NextGen* set in August, maybe I'd have a chance at a career that utilized more than just my voice. It was the start of planning for what came next. When I got back to LA. After Reeve.

For now, I avoided him like I had before we'd left the ranch. It was obvious he was avoiding me as well. Amber, on the other hand, tried to spend as much time with him as possible. Fortunately, she didn't want me around when she did. The two typically ate breakfast together. I had her for lunch. On the few occasions that Reeve joined us for supper, I slipped away early, leaving them to enjoy whatever after-dinner activities they wanted to without me. Then I'd take a swim in the heated pool, the one in the courtyard by the master suite, always sure to disappear to my room before Reeve and Amber finished their meal. I didn't ever want to know what time She came back to her room. Whether she came back to her room at all.

We'd been on the island almost a week when she finally mentioned the prescription bottles. I'd just closed my computer on the latest script my agent had e-mailed, and I was in a bad mood. Partly because the script had been terrible. Partly because Amber was late coming back from breakfast with Reeve. Partly because I was tired of trying not to think about Reeve, a task I managed with a lot of effort during the daylight hours and didn't manage at all in the dark, in my room with the door locked, where I thought about him incessantly. And missed him. And pretended I didn't hear his nightly footsteps on the tile outside or the soft knock on my door or the rattle of my knob.

It was wearing. All of it. Needless to say, I wasn't sleeping well either.

So when Amber stomped up to my chaise lounge chair, an hour after she usually returned from breakfast, I was already on the verge of snapping.

With no greeting, she said, "You found my pills." It was already an accusation, her tone blatantly confrontational.

I slid my sunglasses down my nose and peered up at her. "*Your* pills? They didn't have your name on the label."

Her sigh reminded me of a snotty teenager, tired of her overbearing parents. Or of an addict who'd ran out of believable excuses. "Buddy gave them to me."

I took off my sunglasses and gave her a look that clearly said *tell me what I don't know.* When she didn't volunteer anything, I asked, "In exchange for what?"

Another sigh. More exasperated than the first. "Does it matter?"

"It does. He might be working for Vilanakis. He could have killed that dog. Those pills might not even be safe." Not that they were any safer if they'd come from someone else.

She rolled her eyes, another gesture so teenager-like I was beginning to feel old. "Buddy isn't working for Vilanakis."

"How do you know that?"

"Trust me. I know." Something about how certain she was told me that she'd been a lot closer to Buddy than I'd first imagined. I would have bet money that the favors she'd given in exchange for his pain meds had required her to be on her knees.

Which only added to my foul mood. If she'd genuinely wanted to work things out with Reeve, she shouldn't have been sneaking around his back, especially not to score drugs when he'd been so committed to help her get clean.

I almost put my sunglasses back on just so I wouldn't have to look at her anymore.

But then she plopped down on the lounger next to me, her feet planted on the ground so she was facing in my direction. "Anyway," she said, gentler than before, "that's not why I brought it up."

I cocked my head to study her. "Then why did you?" There was only one reason she'd bring them up. If she didn't think I knew where this was going, she was an idiot.

She shrugged, embarrassed. "I just wanted you to know that I'm not taking them. I didn't plan on taking them."

She was earnest and remorseful and my heart went out to her despite the wreckage between us. Throwing my feet over the side of my chaise so I could meet her eye-to-eye, I asked, "Then why did you have them?"

She took a deep breath in and let it out, a much different sigh than the immature ones she'd delivered a moment ago. This one was sincere. It was a woman with a heavy load as she sat down to rest for the first time in a decade.

It took her a handful of seconds to look at me, and a few more before she answered. "Just in case. You know. In case it was too hard."

"Too hard to what?" I tried to be compassionate but all I could think about was what she'd told me on the roof in Jackson, how she'd called me because she wanted to not live anymore, and if that was her motivation for holding on to those bottles, I needed to know so that I could be good and pissed with her. "Too hard to stay clean? Or stay *alive*?"

She winced as if I'd slapped her. Then, immediately, she was on the defense. "Don't be hostile with me. I'm trying to be honest."

I forced myself to take a deep breath of my own. "Sorry. I'm . . ." *I'm still mad, and I don't know how to stop being mad.*

But anger wasn't the solution. "I'm worried about you. That's all."

"I know." She reached over to take my hand in hers. "I'm sorry. I really am. Like I said, they were an insurance policy. That's all. They made me feel safe. I didn't ever have any intention of using them."

"Good." I even mostly believed her. I squeezed her hand. "I'm really glad to hear that."

She smiled. "And thank you for not telling Reeve." I furrowed my brow, wondering how she was so sure I hadn't when she explained. "If you'd have told him, he'd have been the one who brought it up, not me."

"Good point." I chuckled down at our joined hands, glad I hadn't gotten the chance to tell him about the pills after all. Also, a little ashamed for thinking I knew where the conversation was going.

But then she said, "So?"

And I looked up again, my brow raised, even though I knew exactly what she wanted. She'd have to ask. If she were going to be so ballsy, she couldn't just hint around about it. She'd have to come right out and ask.

And she did. "Can I have them back?"

I considered telling her I'd dumped them already. The lie would be easier. But, instead, I just said, "No."

"Ha ha. Funny."

I let her laugh. Because why wouldn't she? I'd never stood up to her like this before. In fact, I wasn't sure I'd stood up to her ever.

But when she'd finished her chuckle, I made sure I was completely somber when I said, "I'm not joking. I mean no. You can't have them."

She pulled her hand from my lap. "You can't keep them. They're *mine*."

"No. Actually, they're not. And if you want to refute this with a third party, we can take this up with Reeve." I was surprised at the confident sound of authority in my tone. And proud.

Amber twisted and sat back in her lounger, her knees up and her arms crossed over her chest. "You're on his side. Typical."

Maybe I'd given her too much credit when I'd thought of her as a teenager. This behavior was much less mature. "I'm not on his side, Amber. I'm on your side."

"I don't know what the hell crack you're smoking, but whatever side you're on, it's definitely not my side."

"Then I'm on my side. For once." I stood up, needing the composure that towering over her gave. "I don't want you to have those drugs. I don't want you to destroy yourself little by little, and I don't want you to have the option *just in case*. Because that would hurt me. A lot."

She glowered off in the distance, her lips shaped into a pout.

I hated it—hated her being unhappy, hated her being displeased. At me.

But I resisted the urge to run to my room and dig out

the bottles from my luggage so I could return them to her and beg for her forgiveness. I'd done that for far too long. It was past time that ended.

"Go ahead and be mad at me if you want," I said, feeling more courageous as the seconds passed, "but you should remember that this is who you wanted me to be. When you let me go all those years ago, this is who you created. Someone who can stand up for herself." Sure it had taken until just now to get there, but I still counted it. "If you were expecting anything else, I'm sorry to disappoint."

She continued to mope. She continued to ignore me.

The longer I stood there, the more my anger dissolved into something kinder, something less assertive. I needed to get out of there. "I'm going to go for a run." Again, I waited for her to respond. "Amber?"

Finally she glanced up. "What? Do you need permission?"

"I need to know that we're okay." But I already sensed that it was a pointless question to ask. We'd been far from okay for quite some time.

With the tightest smile imaginable, she said, "As okay as ever."

Yeah. Exactly.

I'd been out on a few runs since we'd arrived at the island, and I already had a course that I preferred. I'd discovered it when I'd gone exploring one of our first days on Oinopa. The trail began on the estate's lower grounds, an area accessible down a set of stairs leading down from each of the courtyards. The lower level of the compound was practically a resort in itself. There were tennis courts and stables, as well as a lush tropical garden featuring a fountain with freshwater fish. Our compound prison certainly had plenty to keep us entertained, but, since Amber seemed

uninterested in much besides laying poolside, I hadn't utilized many of the amenities.

The unpaved trail off the garden, however, was a perfect place to have time alone. The difficult course—down
the side of the mountain and back up—kept my thoughts
at bay. I had to concentrate on my rhythm and form to have
any chance of finishing the five-mile loop in a semi-decent
time.

Usually, the run cleared my head and improved my attitude, at least enough to return to being civil. Today, I was
in just as bad a mood when I'd finished as when I'd started.
So instead of going back up to the house, I decided to ven-
ture down another path, hidden with foliage beyond the
garden fountain.

The trail wound through dense tropical trees for no
more than a quarter mile before opening up to a small
clearing with a stone seating area and a fire pit. At the far
end of the stretch, the hillside dropped dramatically. It was
a serenely beautiful location. The kind of spot that lent
itself to meditating or reading. And it was romantic—
secluded and quiet. Perfect for a picnic or a roll in the grass.

It was so charmingly peaceful that I wasn't even bothered by the thought of Reeve there with past lovers. Or,
not *that* bothered, anyway.

Maybe it was better not to think about that.

I walked to the ledge instead, braced my hands on the
security railing, and took in the view of the ocean below.
The craggy cliffside dropped fifty feet or so, ending in
sharp pointed rocks that jutted into the water. To one side,
a sandy beach stretched out for as far as the eye could see.
Late morning fog clung to the mountain wall just beneath
me. It felt spectacular, if not a little overwhelming, to be
that high, like being on top of the world. A breeze blew
across my face and the smell of sea hit my nose, and I wondered how it was possible to be this alive in the world and

yet feel so alone. How it was possible to recognize there was so much beauty in everything and yet not feel part of it at all.

Was this how Amber had felt when she'd left that message? Was this the way she felt when she held on to pills "just in case"?

If so, maybe I understood. Partially.

The difference was the feeling didn't make me want to die. It made me want to march back up to the house and figure out what I needed to do to start living, to stop feeling alone. To seize the beauty. It was a new emotion, one based in action rather than reaction. Was I turning into someone who didn't just let things happen to me? Like Amber?

If so, that was new too.

A glint of gold on the ground nearby caught my eyes. It was partially covered with grass, so I'd missed it at first. I bent down to look at it now and found a plaque buried in the ground engraved with Missy Mataya's name, birthday, and day of death.

My pulse slowed as I realized what this place was—it was the cliff Missy had fallen from. The rocks below, the security railing that looked to be fairly new. Even the foliage that had grown over the path, as though it had been a trail neglected in recent years. It all fit.

I stood back up. Being there where she'd been and feeling the way I'd imagined Amber felt, I wondered for the first time if Missy's death had been a suicide. Jumping off the side into nothing would be a very thrilling and tragic way to end things. Like flying.

Maybe that was too dramatic. She could have just as easily fallen. If the railing hadn't been there, in the dark and if she'd been drunk or high or upset or all of the above.

Or someone could have pushed her, relying on the probability that her death would be ruled an accident.

Reeve had told me he hadn't been anywhere near her when it happened. He'd been on the beach, making sex tapes. There was proof that that was where he'd been. But there were still pieces of Missy's death that felt unsettled. Things Chris Blakely had mentioned that didn't have an answer in the story Reeve had told me.

Rustling leaves interrupted my reverie and drew my focus to the path behind me. The glimpse of white moving through the trees told me someone was coming. A few seconds later, Reeve emerged into the clearing. And, as though the sun had just moved from behind the clouds, my world got abruptly brighter.

I watched as he approached, feasting on him with my eyes for the first time in days. His casual island look somehow made him seem more dangerous than usual. Gray drawstring linen pants were paired with leather sandals and a cream button-down shirt that he'd left open, and damn if he wasn't devastatingly attractive.

I turned away, unable to stare at him any longer without feeling physical pain. It pissed me off that he looked good. And that he was intruding on my privacy. And that he looked so good intruding.

"Why are you here?" I asked, not bothering to hide my irritation.

He cocked his head. "Why am I here on my property?"

I gave an exaggerated sigh not unlike the teenager-style sighs Amber had given me earlier. "Why are you here where I am when I'm here? The whole island is your property. You don't need to be where I am." I glanced back at him.

He seemed to debate between a few responses then finally responded with a question. "You want the honest answer?"

I wasn't sure I did.

He took a few steps toward me, his hands in his pockets—damn, why did he always look so hot when he did that?

"The honest answer," he said casually, "is that I saw you come down here, and it made me uncomfortable."

He stopped several feet from the security rail. "I'd be considerably more comfortable now if you'd back away from the railing."

His discomfort bothered me, but I didn't move. While I believed that my proximity to the edge caused him anxiety, I didn't necessarily believe that his telling me so was without ulterior motive. Like, mostly he wanted to be sure I knew he still cared. It might not have counted as making an advance, but it had the same effect on my psyche. It pulled at me, made my heart pinch, made me consider possibilities I'd already put to bed. I'd accepted that I wouldn't stop caring about him anytime soon. But it would be so much easier if he'd stop caring about me. Or, at least, if he let me believe he'd stopped.

I was bitter. I wanted him to be bitter with me. Curiosity and the urge to bicker prompted my next question. "Was Missy killed because she knew your family was mob?"

"No. A lot of my girlfriends knew my family had mob ties. That wasn't unusual. Move away from the ledge, Emily."

I paid no attention to his request or to the fluttering in my belly that accompanied his worry. "But were all your girlfriends talking to Interpol about it?" It was the first I'd asked him about Interpol. I'd forgotten about that detail when he'd told me his family story on the plane.

His brow pinched in surprise. "Where did you hear—?" Understanding dawned across his features. "Chris Blakely?"

"Does it matter?" It *had* been Chris. He'd told me he'd overheard Missy and Reeve arguing on the night of her death. She'd mentioned Interpol, and Chris had speculated that she'd been killed to keep her from testifying against Reeve and his Mafia relatives.

But I didn't want to think about Chris. I definitely didn't want to imagine that was the information that very likely had gotten him killed. I did, however, want to know. "Could you just answer the question?"

"No. Missy wasn't talking to Interpol. I was."

I didn't bother to hide my surprise. "But why?"

"Do you want to sit and talk about this? Preferably over there." He nodded to the seating area. "A safe distance away from the railing."

"We should go back up to the garden where we can be seen so you aren't tempted to touch me." I'd thought I'd made the comment so that I could feel like the change in our locale was my choice and not because it was what he wanted. But maybe I really just wanted to provoke him into saying something that proved he actually did still want to touch me.

"Ah, Blue Eyes," he said with a wicked smile and an equally wicked gleam in his eye. "Lets you and I not pretend that an audience would ever be a deterrent for me touching you."

Yeah, something like that.

"Fine." With a sigh, I pushed away from the railing, feigning to concede reluctantly when, in truth, I would have done anything he wanted after a line like that. "At least button up your shirt."

I crossed with him to the stone bench and let him sit first. Then I sat in a spot that was more than a respectable distance from him.

As if a few feet of space between us was any better a deterrent than an audience.

"Okay. Talk." I crossed a leg over the other, trying to ignore the fact that he hadn't done up a single damn one of his buttons.

He gave me a tight look that suggested he didn't like being given orders. But then he began. "The week I was out here with Missy—the week she died—Michelis and a few of my cousins came out as well. He'd been pressuring me more and more, and I'd, foolishly, thought that we could all come down here, have a good time, and put an end to our disagreements. Instead, that was when he began talking about taking one of Missy's friends.

"I didn't tell Missy that," he clarified. "She was too doped up, and I didn't want to scare her. But I knew I had to deal with my uncle's business once and for all. I told you before that you can't leave the mob."

"Right. And yet you left." Did his olive skin shine like that in the sun naturally? Like it was slick with oil. Or sweat.

"I didn't leave fairly, though." He seemed simultaneously proud and ashamed of the fact. "A team from Interpol had contacted me before that, asking a bunch of questions about the Vilanakis family and what I knew about them. I'd blown them off. But I'd started collecting proof of illegal dealings. In case I needed it. That week here, I decided I needed it."

"So you told him to leave or you'd go to Interpol?"

"Basically."

A few more pieces clicked into place. "And that's why he says you betrayed him."

"I would presume so. Yes."

I couldn't imagine the amount of proof Reeve must have had to feel confident making such a threat. "Why isn't he afraid that you'll still turn him in now?"

"He's found my weak spot." When I raised a questioning brow, he explained. "I didn't have people I cared about then like I do now."

I took in a shaky breath. *He means Amber.*

But I wasn't an idiot. I knew he also meant me.

"Anyway." I forced myself to focus on something other than the possessive way he was staring at me. "How did Missy get involved?"

He smirked, suggesting he knew how he got to me, then launched back into his tale. "She overheard part of the conversation. She already knew that my family was mixed up in illegal activity, but she didn't understand the extent. When she realized I'd kicked them out of my life, she thought it was an extreme tactic to cut off her drug supply. She was mad. She couldn't believe I'd go to Interpol."

"You fought. Chris heard part of it."

"I'm sure everyone heard parts of it." Hence why half the world was convinced he'd killed Missy even though he'd never had charges brought against him. "I was angry that she didn't support me. Granted, I didn't give her all the information. I didn't feel I should have to."

Apparently lack of disclosure had always been a problem in his relationships. But he was sharing with me now. And I knew in my gut these were not things he'd shared with anyone else. With Amber.

The realization made it hard not to love him a little bit more.

I rebelled against the urge. "And that's how you ended up on the beach fucking two other girls while she was . . . up here." It was snotty and unfair and cruel and the only defense I had against falling completely at his feet.

"Thank you for the recap." His voice was even, but his eyes showed the sting. "In case I'd forgotten."

"Right. Exactly. In case you'd forgotten." I folded my arms across my chest wishing there were a more substantial barrier between us. Wishing there were no barriers between us at all.

He twisted toward me, and I could see him warring with himself. Shaking his head, he seemed to decide it wasn't worth it. He stood, looking as though he would leave.

Good. I'd pissed him off. That was . . . good.

Abruptly, he turned back. "As if the way I treated Missy was any worse than the way Amber treated you."

I was genuinely shocked. "It was a hell of a lot worse. Amber took care of me."

"You think I didn't take care of Missy?"

I didn't think that at all. But I needed to lash out. I needed to be mean and hard. "You weren't there for her when she needed you most."

"Amber wasn't there when you needed her most either."

I shook my head realizing he still believed Amber had ended our friendship because I'd stolen her boyfriend. "That's not true. I thought it was, but it wasn't. She knew it was the only way I'd leave her behind and make a better life for myself."

"By letting you blame yourself for being raped so violently that you lost your baby?"

I jumped to my feet to defend her. "She knew what was best for me."

"Jesus, Emily, do you hear yourself? Tell me, I'm curious—were you open about this hold she has on you? Did she make you wear a collar?"

I didn't need that from him—didn't need him to challenge our relationship. My role with her was already shifting, and the only way I knew to survive was to cling to the few truths that I kept sacred.

"She knew what was best for me," I said again. "She knew how to keep me safe. And it wasn't just by imprisoning me." It was a hit below the belt. He considered keeping Amber locked up at his ranch the worst thing he'd ever done. He'd trusted me when he'd admitted it, and I'd just thrown it back in his face.

I rightfully deserved the callous expression he gave me in return.

Callous and chilling.

He took a careful step toward me, his eyes hard. "What did you say?"

I wasn't dumb enough to repeat it. And I was smart enough to run.

He lunged when I did, catching me immediately. With his hands gripped on my upper arms, I bent my knee up, hitting him in the gut.

That only enraged him more.

He spun me outward so that I was facing away from him, twisting my arms behind my back and holding them firmly at my wrists. "You've been acting like a royal bitch for far too long, Emily. If you're going to act like one, it's time you learned, you're going to be treated like one."

He pushed me forward, toward the railing, and panic rushed over me even though I knew *without a doubt in my body* that he'd never do anything to seriously hurt me.

But wasn't it thrilling to think that he could?

I struggled with everything I had, knowing that I didn't have a chance of escape. Knowing and loving.

"Let me go," I said as he used his entire body to pin me against the metal railing.

"No." He shifted my arms so he was gripping my wrists with just one of his hands.

I twisted my neck to see why he needed a free hand and found him shrugging out of his shirt. Jesus, he was hot.

I turned away, afraid my face gave away how aroused I was. Which didn't mean I wasn't mad too. Especially now that he'd forced me to the ledge, the same spot that he'd admonished me for being in earlier. Then, when my hands had been free to grip the railing, the view had been exhilarating.

With him in control, his body position pressing my gaze down, the view was terrifying.

I jerked my shoulders up suddenly, hoping he'd let go from surprise.

"Hold still." He yanked my wrists down so sharply, I cried out.

"I'll scream."

He laughed. "Go ahead. No one can hear you down here, and screaming is a turn-on. Even more than struggling."

And now I was wet.

"You're a fucking asshole," I said, meaning it with every cell in my being.

He switched his hold on me to his other hand. "Sorry to disappoint, but fucking you in the ass wouldn't be a good idea today. I'm feeling too spiteful. You wouldn't be able to walk after and I'm not carrying you up that mountain."

"Jesus, you're unbelievable."

"I'm taking that as a compliment."

I was sweating now, my heart pounding so hard my chest hurt. Suddenly, he let go of my hands. But before I could think fast enough to figure out what to do with my freedom, he wrapped his shirt around my neck. And pulled. Hard. Choking me.

He leaned into my ear and rasped. "Beg for my cock when I let you breathe."

My hands flew to my throat. I scratched at the material, clawing, using up the air in my chest with my frantic wrestling.

Of course I couldn't get free. His hold was too tight, too secure. Seconds passed. Several. Then several more. Black spots dotted my vision by the time he loosened his grip.

I gasped, desperate to heave air into my lungs. I'd barely gotten in a good breath when he was choking me again.

"Too slow," he said with a tsk. "I'll give you another chance. I hope you're ready."

Once again his grip loosened. I blinked, disoriented and confused and definitely unprepared for whatever it was he wanted me to do. "Uh . . . uh . . ." I stuttered.

Again he pulled the shirt around my neck, tighter than before. So tight, I didn't even care that I couldn't breathe because I was sure the pain would kill me before the lack of oxygen.

"I mean it, goddammit, Emily," he said, and somehow I understood what he was saying, despite my muddled ability to think. "Tell me you want my cock or I'm walking away right now."

I hated him. Hated every terrible wonderful emotion he inspired within me. Hated how completely and perfectly he mastered me. Hated how he could be absolutely brutal and yet still required my consent. Hated how much I could never stop loving him.

This time when he let me breathe, I forced the words out as I gulped for air. "I want your cock!"

His shirt disappeared from my neck, and then he was tugging my shorts and panties down my thighs. "What do you want me to do with it?"

I imagined him undoing the drawstring of his pants and letting them fall silently to his ankles. Imagined that his hands were absent from my body because they were freeing his erection.

I grabbed the railing, ready for him. Desperate for him. "I want you to fuck me."

"I know you do. I always know." His voice was sweet, soothing, the way a parent calmed a child. He pressed close to me and I could feel the head of his cock rub against my slit. Then at my entrance. Then he was shoving inside, sliding in with no resistance, I was so wet.

I whimpered as he stretched me and filled me. And

when he pounded into me with fierce abandon, the tears that fell down my cheeks were from sweet relief.

"You feel so good," Reeve murmured against my ear, making my knees weak. "It's been so long, and you're so tight."

It had been *too* long, and every stroke he drove into me felt new and invasive and amazing.

"Bend over the rail." He pushed my torso down over the metal, bending me in half. Draping me over the same precipice that his former girlfriend had fallen over.

It was sick. And wrong. Sick and wrong how that thought didn't disgust me, didn't turn me off. Didn't scare the hell out of me.

I reached down and grabbed onto the lower bar of the railing—not because I thought I might fall but to stretch me open even wider. To let him in as far as I possibly could.

"Yeah," he grunted. "Just like that." He was deeper than I'd ever felt him, hitting places inside me that I swore had never been touched. He leaned over me and grabbed my ponytail with both hands, pulling my head back. "I wish you could see this, Emily. You're so beautiful like this. Bent over and open for me. I'm watching my cock fuck your tight cunt, and there's never been anything sexier."

Then he let loose, drilling into me with rapid fire.

Sensation besieged me.

The bite of my pulled hair. The railing digging into my waist. The feel of the wind in my face. The dizziness from the height. The smell of the sea. The smell of sweat and sex. The tension fraying in my belly. The crass words spoken behind me. The slap of balls against my thighs. Reeve's delicious stroke in and out and in and out.

I had no choice but to surrender. No choice but to give in. No choice but to let go. I was a kite and Reeve held the string, tugging me this way and that until I was soaring on a gentle breeze.

I cried out as he jerked my hair back sharply, causing electricity to jolt through my body. "Tell me this isn't what you wanted," he challenged. "Tell me."

"I wanted it," I gasped, grateful I could give him my assurance. Grateful I could give him myself, if even for just this once. "I wanted you so much."

"You did. I know you did." He let go of my hair, wrapped his arm around my waist, and wrenched me up against him. Pinching my chin, he forced my head back against his shoulder. "You know what this is, Emily?"

"Mmm?" I couldn't talk if I wanted to, and I didn't want to. I wanted to do nothing but feel and relish and savor.

He pressed his nose to my cheek. "This is me taking care of you. How you need to be taken care of. Whether you want to admit it or not. I know what you need. This is me doing what's best for you."

Men had said similar words to me in the past, usually as some form of justification for having just treated me badly. For abusing me and destroying me in irreparable ways. It was always a lie. Pretty prose to convince me that their sadistic behavior was only for my benefit.

But this time, when Reeve said it, the words sounded different to my ears. They felt different in my body. They reverberated through my skeleton with truth and recognition and clarity. And even though Reeve had been harsh and savage, and even though his actions fed some primal hunger in his own soul, he was absolutely correct in knowing it was exactly what I needed too.

With one hand still gripping my chin, he lowered the other toward the strip of hair between my thighs. "You don't deserve it," he said, his fingers brushing ever so gently across my clit, "but I'm going to let you come so that you'll remember that I love you."

He pressed his thumb against the bundle of nerves, and I exploded. My entire body convulsed as tears washed my face and colorful bolts of lightning danced across my vision.

"Ah, that's it. Good girl," Reeve murmured against my cheek, coaxing me, cheering me. "Feels so good, doesn't it?"

So good that I'd lost perception of what my body was doing. Was I standing or being held? Was my climax starting or ending? Was I dying from ecstasy or was this the process of rebirth?

Just as I began to get oriented, his thumb returned to my clit. "Again," he said.

And there I went again. Lost. Spinning. Flying higher. But with him, this time—he jutted deep into me and stilled, emptying himself inside me and we came together.

Aftershocks shook through me until long after my breathing had returned to normal. I put myself back together as best as I could, but I was sure that parts of me were broken permanently. Dark parts of me. Parts that I'd held on to for far too long.

I was so high postorgasm that it took me a minute to realize that Reeve was eerily silent. He was standing at the railing, peering out over the ocean. He'd done up the buttons of his shirt, and while it probably meant nothing, it made him seem closed off. Or maybe he *was* closed off. And so very distant.

"Reeve?"

He said nothing.

I stepped up behind him, my hand hovering just above his back. But the barrier around him was so obtrusive, I couldn't bring myself to touch him. I let my hand fall to my side. "Say something."

"I broke my promise." He didn't even glance at me.

"It's fine. I wanted you to." I'd wanted him to fuck me then almost as badly as I wished he'd wrap me in his arms and hold me now.

"I know." He turned to face me, his expression cold and resolute. "But I'm not doing it again. This is the last time I'm fucking you until you decide we're together." Without another word, he crossed the clearing and disappeared up the trail.

As though he'd shut off the main breaker to my buzz, my world dimmed. The hum in my body silenced and the cloud that had lifted in our interlude returned, darker than ever.

Numbly, I trudged up the path toward the house. There were things to process and absorb—the last hour, the last six months. My entire life. But I didn't have the bandwidth to even try. I was tired. I was incapable.

I'd assumed Reeve had gone back to the house, but when I got to the top of the path, he was in the garden with Filip. And Amber.

He was bent over the fountain, as if examining the contents. In my anesthetized state, I couldn't tell if the air was tense, or if it was just me. But one look at Amber's face, her expression both distraught and horrified, told me something was wrong.

"What's going on?" I asked tentatively.

It was Filip who answered. "The fish are all dead."

"What?" I peered into the fountain and immediately started to tremble. The water in the basin had been emptied, but all the fish that had been inside, maybe a hundred of them, were dead on the bottom.

The sight was chilling. More chilling was the gut notion that it had been deliberate.

"I came by here on my run earlier," I said, trying to remember if I'd seen anything odd. "Shit. I didn't pay attention to the fountain. I don't know if they were alive then or not." They weren't flopping around now, but they didn't smell yet. How long did it take for fish out of water to die?

"Whatever happened, it was an accident, I'm sure," Reeve said. "A leak in the drain." His body language said he didn't believe that.

"No. It's not. It's a message," Amber cried, and while I thought she was being a bit histrionic, Vilanakis had been my first thought too.

"It's not a message," Reeve snapped. "It's a coincidence."

Filip shook his head and held up a portion of the hose that recycled the water from the bottom of the fountain to the top basin. There was no way it hadn't been cut. On purpose.

Amber's crying escalated sharply. "He wants me dead! Don't you get it? That's what he's been saying. Like the dog. Now the fish."

"It's not possible. He couldn't get here." Reeve seemed truly baffled, although it was hard to get a true read on him since he was doing his best not to make eye contact with me.

"Somehow he did," Amber insisted. "Maybe he got to one of your men. But he's here. I know it." She thrust herself into Reeve's arms. "You have to go after him. There's nowhere I'm safe anymore. He won't stop until he gets to me."

I tried to be compassionate. I tried to remind myself that she was sincerely scared.

Reeve patted her back consolingly. "Shh. I won't allow that."

"If he could get here, he could get me in my room," she said, her voice muffled as she cried into his shirt. The shirt that had only recently been wrapped around my neck while Reeve had ordered me to beg him to fuck me. "He could kill me in my sleep."

"He won't. I won't let him." Reeve continued to soothe her.

I couldn't help it—I rolled my eyes.

Amber couldn't see me from her angle, but Reeve could. He narrowed his gaze in my direction, his features hard and heartless. "Filip," he said, still looking at me, "please take Amber to get her things together. Then move her into my room so I can keep her safe."

CHAPTER
20

After that, the loneliness of the island became unbearable.

I rarely saw Amber. She didn't have any reason to come to my part of the house. The pool by the master bedroom was more convenient, not to mention nearer to the office where Reeve spent his days. More than once, I considered joining her there with my laptop or a book, but really, there wasn't any point. She barely spoke to me at lunch, and whenever I was close to her and Reeve at the same time, the tension stretched my insides so taut I wasn't pleasant to be around anyway.

The nights were the worst. I stopped locking the door to my room, hoping that Reeve would turn the knob and find it open. Hoping he'd sneak in and take me in all the ways he liked. Hoping he hadn't meant it when he'd said he wouldn't try anything until I asked him to.

But the knob never turned. And now, Amber was more of a barrier between us than ever.

I couldn't stop myself from thinking about the two of them, together, in his bed. I understood why he'd moved her in with him—the master bedroom was the most secure room in the compound. The walls were thicker. Other buildings surrounded it. An intruder couldn't make it there without going through the other parts of the house, which would trigger the alarm long before the master was encroached. And, of course, if someone did manage to get to her there, she wouldn't be alone—he'd be with her.

It was a safety measure. Maybe that was all it was. It was possible that their nights together were innocent. The bed was large. They could sleep next to each other without ever touching.

But I knew Amber. And I knew Reeve. And they'd been in love once. Was it likely that they would share a bed and not be intimate?

No. Not likely at all.

I could manage to keep it from my mind in the daylight, but once the sun went down that was all I thought about— him and her. Him touching her. Him kissing her. Him fucking her.

It made me itch for him in places I didn't know could itch—inside my body and out.

After three days like that, I forced myself to come to terms with two things—I'd been the one to encourage Amber and Reeve to be together, and, now that they were, it was time for me to leave the island.

I debated joining the two of them for breakfast. I could discuss leaving with both of them at once and get it over with, but it was so hard for me to be near either of them at the moment. Together I'd be distracted by the way they were with each other, searching for innuendo and pretending I didn't notice when I found it. So, instead, I waited until Amber was snoozing on a lounge in the courtyard and slipped by her to Reeve's office.

The wall to his office was open and his back was to me while he worked at his L-shaped desk. It was tempting to watch him for a minute before I made myself known—the muscles in his neck were tight and his shoulders seemed slumped but he was still so magnificent to look at.

But he always had an uncanny way of sensing my presence, so I only gave myself a few seconds to take him in before I forced myself to stroll in confidently. "When can I go home?" I asked with no other preamble.

His head ticked up abruptly, either surprised by my question or surprised to see me in his office. Both were possible.

I didn't allow myself to search for any signs of disappointment in his eyes as his gaze met mine. "That's up to you." He leaned back in his chair. "I'll arrange transportation the minute you ask. I'm not *keeping* you here."

He was so solemn, so matter-of-fact. So emotionless. There wasn't even a trace of bitterness as he emphasized the word "keeping." And he hadn't argued, which was unexpected. And disappointing.

"So, is it safe for me to leave now?"

"You'll have to check with Joe to be certain. He and I have talked quite a bit through e-mail. He said he'd found a suitable place for you to move into last week. A gated community. Last he mentioned, he was checking to see when he could get in and test out the security system."

"I suppose I don't have any say in this, do I?" I'd wanted to be stoic like he was but failed. I was too irritated. I just didn't know if it bothered me more that Reeve had been talking to Joe or that Joe had been talking to Reeve. I'd assumed the latter would leave me out of my own life planning, but not Joe. Yet it was Reeve's lack of disclosure that hurt me more than Joe's.

"Of course you get a say. I figured you and he were in contact. I apologize for assuming." Reeve hit a few buttons on his keyboard and I tried to remember a time that I'd heard him say he was sorry. Though he'd shown regret in his actions, I couldn't think of any time he'd actually given an apology. Somehow hearing it now made the distance between us widen, even as he swiveled his laptop toward the side and beckoned me to come around his desk to look at the screen. "This is it."

I bent to click through the images, seven different shots of a one-bedroom apartment. It was nice, actually. Similar to the location and style of the place I lived in now. I clicked Escape and was taken to Joe's e-mail. It was short and concise, and said pretty much exactly what Reeve had just told me. It also listed the rental price, which was reasonable.

I glanced at the address line of the message. "He copied me at my other e-mail address." He'd sent it to the account I'd set up strictly for corresponding with him. "I guess I haven't been checking that one." I cleared my throat as I straightened. "I'm sorry for overreacting."

"I didn't think you were overreacting at all," he said sincerely.

The last time I'd spent any time with him, after he'd left me on the ledge both literally and figuratively, he'd barely been able to look at me. Now his eyes sought mine out at every opportunity. I wanted to believe the change meant he missed me. That he couldn't stand to keep from staring into me for long, the same way that I couldn't stop from staring into him.

It made me want to say things I hadn't come to say. Made me want to apologize for more than overreacting. Made me want to ask him to do the things to me that he'd said he wouldn't do unless I did.

All of which was counterproductive. I shook his gaze away. "What about Michelis? What's going on with him?"

"Actually, he sent something just this morning." He closed Joe's e-mail and clicked on the top line in his inbox.

The message opened and Reeve gestured toward the screen for me to read.

I peeked at it somewhat thrilled he'd chosen to share it with me. Until I realized it had been written in Greek. "I can't read it. What does it say?"

"Oh. Right." He chuckled at himself as he tilted the screen where we could both see it. "Basically, *I have not done these things of which you accuse me. I have alibis for all events. One alibi even your own beautiful Emily.*"

Your own beautiful Emily.

I snuck a peek at him after he said my name, wondering how he felt when he called me his, if it felt anything like how I felt when I heard it.

He swallowed, suggesting that it at least made him feel *something.* But that something could have been irritation, because then he launched into a rant about what he'd read so far. "It's ridiculous. Alibis prove nothing, and he knows that. He never does his own dirty work. Blakely's toxicology report is going to say overdose, we're sure of that, but Joe's been investigating and he's found one of Michelis's men spotted on the set's surveillance camera. There's no way that's a coincidence."

"Then they'll be able to press charges against someone?"

"Doubtful. There's not any evidence pointing to foul play. And even if we could prove that it was murder, someone else would take the fall for Michelis. There are people who would be heavily rewarded for that kind of sacrifice."

"That's how it works in those mob TV shows I've watched too." The muscles in my smile felt stiff, like it had been forever since my lips had moved in that direction.

The smirk he returned felt just as foreign. Had it really been that long since we'd exchanged friendly banter? It would be so easy to fall back into it. I had to remind myself why that was a bad thing.

Sobering, I asked, "Who discovered Chris? Do you know?"

"The assistant director on the show. Don't know her name."

"Do you know the time? Was it when I was with Michelis? There was a phone call while I was there. Petros answered and said, 'It's done.' It could have been a call about anything, but I swear it was about Chris. He wanted me to hear it. He dismissed me right after." Not that it made much difference to find out. It wouldn't prove anything in a criminal case, but it could at least settle the question in my own mind.

"That sounds like the manipulative bullshit he'd pull. I'll have Joe look at the phone records into his hotel room. It's unlikely to tie him significantly enough to murder, but it's worth a shot."

"Thank you." I leaned against his desk, facing him. "What else does the e-mail say?"

He narrowed his eyes, picking up where he'd left off before. *"Be assured that your possessions are safe from my hand."* He glanced up, his expression apprehensive. "He, uh, means you and Amber."

"Yeah, I got that." I bit my lip. "Does he actually consider Amber to be yours anymore? His messages thus far seem to indicate he thinks she's his."

Reeve shook his head. "I'm not sure it matters. I don't trust him either way." He put his finger on the screen at the next line in the e-mail. *"Anatolios and Petros can't work out the issues between us. Please consider face-to-face meeting. It's time we figure out how to put things to,* um, *peace between us."* He concentrated for a moment on correcting the translation. *"Put things to rest between us."*

Reeve cleared his throat before adding, "There's a post-script. *Here's the favor I did.* And he includes a link."

"Where does the link go?"

He pushed the screen toward me. "Click on it if you want."

I scooted back so that I was sitting on the desk. Then I picked up the computer and set it on my lap. I followed the link to a Greek news site and clicked the Google bar at the top requesting that the page be translated into English. The paragraph was short and didn't read clearly, but I still got the gist. It was a report on a recent body that had been found dead, causes unknown. The victim had been iden-tified as Broos Lasko—the man who'd killed Reeve's par-ents. The man whom Michelis had wanted Reeve to kill in revenge.

"Oh, Reeve." My throat felt tight. "I don't know if I should say *congratulations* or *I'm sorry.*"

"Both are probably appropriate," he said quietly. Then he blew out a frustrated breath of air. "He's pretending he did this for me. He did it for himself. He's hoping it will obligate me to him. It doesn't."

"He did the same thing to Amber. He killed her father and told her it was a present for her. Then held it over her head so that she felt like she couldn't leave."

Reeve cocked his head, his brow furrowed. "Did she tell you that?"

"Didn't she tell *you* that?"

He shook his head, his expression guarded. "No. She didn't tell me any of it. I knew, because Petros mentioned it. In his version, Amber begged Michelis to do it for her."

I considered the possibility, which mostly meant trying to decide what I might have done in her place. If I'd known a man who had that power, if it were unlikely he'd ever get caught, would I have taken advantage of that connection?

I didn't think I could do it. Which was a little surpris-

ing considering how attractive the "dangerous man" type
had always been to me. Or maybe it wasn't surprising because it would require me to make a choice with significant consequences, and that was not my strong suit.

Amber was another story. She'd been able to hit Aaron
over the head in Mexico and then leave him for dead, but
that had been in order to rescue me. "What do you think
is the truth?" I asked, curious what Reeve's opinion was.

"Your version makes more sense," he mused. "It's
further proof of how my uncle twists everything to his
benefit."

I shrugged. "Or it's proof that Petros can't be exactly
trusted either."

"Also possible."

There was something intimate about Reeve listening to
my ideas and taking them seriously. It made my cheeks
flush for absolutely no reason at all.

I lowered my head to examine the laptop, hoping Reeve
didn't notice. My forehead creased as my eye caught on the
sender's line in the heading of the message. "This isn't from
the same address as the other e-mails." I'd seen two from
the other address—one had included the picture of Michelis
and Amber from the casino in Colorado, the other had attached the autopsy report of the woman I'd thought had
been Amber.

"Like you, I'm sure he has more than one. Makes it
harder to track him."

"True." Besides the one I had for Joe, I had an e-mail
for junk, an e-mail for publicity, an e-mail for personal.
But I tended to keep all my correspondence organized. If
I e-mailed someone from a certain account, I didn't later
e-mail that person from another account.

There was another thing that was odd. "Why is this one
written in Greek when the others were in English? What's
his language preference with you?"

"Greek." He lifted a brow, catching my drift. "Do you think they've been sent by different people?"

"Probably not. The ones before could have been sent by an assistant or something." That was a comical idea—having some hired goon send your threat letters. But maybe it hadn't been someone he'd hired at all. What if Petros had sent the previous e-mails? Maybe it hadn't even been malicious. Petros could have simply wanted Reeve to know what was going on with Amber.

Whether Reeve was thinking along the same lines I was or not, I couldn't tell. But he was obviously thinking something. "I'll have Joe check into that as well."

He seemed to disappear into heavy thought. He threw his head back against the chair and closed his eyes, his hands gripped tightly on the armrests at his side.

My chest tightened. I'd seen Reeve upset before, but I hadn't ever seen him like this. I hadn't realized until now that the situation was taking a toll on him as well. It was self-centered and pretentious to have been so oblivious. Sure, my heart was being torn over the two great loves of my life, but so was Reeve's. And, on top of that, he had to deal with the stress of protecting us while trying to keep his family at peace.

Even with his eyes closed, his face wore the lines of stress. I studied him—studied his long dark lashes, the chiseled sweep of his jaw, the tight line of his mouth. I wanted to press my lips on each feature of his face, wanted to cherish it and distract him from his pain. I wanted to kiss his lips—how long had it been since I'd done that? Forever, it seemed. Since the night he'd made love to me back in Wyoming, when he'd slipped into my room while I was getting in the shower.

That felt like a lifetime ago now. I couldn't stop staring at his lips. Couldn't stop yearning for the taste of his tongue on mine.

His eyes opened, and mine flew up to meet his. He knew I'd been staring, I was sure. And the way he was looking at me now, it seemed he knew what I'd been thinking too. I wondered how long he'd stare like that before staring turned into something else.

I had to say something. "Are you okay?"

"I haven't gotten much sleep lately."

Because he was worrying? Or because . . .

The nighttime images attacked me—the ones with Reeve and Amber tangled up in each other. Of course he wasn't sleeping well. Not with her in his bed.

It suddenly felt hard to breathe, the air lodged in my lungs, unable to recirculate the way it was supposed to. Stuck like I was on this island, in this heartache, in this love.

"Right," I managed, my voice clipped. "None of my business." I set the laptop down and scrambled from my perch on his desk. "Anyway, thank you for sharing this information. I'll e-mail Joe and let you know when you can arrange for me to leave."

I rushed to leave, knowing he'd call after me.

It was still unbearable and amazing when he did. "Emily—"

I turned around, but I didn't give him a chance to speak. "Are you going to meet with Michelis?" I honestly wanted to know, but I also just wanted to look at him one last time and asking him the question was a good excuse to keep my focus pinned to him.

He opened his mouth then closed it, and I would have bet money he was trying to decide if he wanted to answer or if he wanted to say something else. After a few seconds, he asked, "Do you still think I should?"

"No. I don't." Not at all. It would mean a war, I knew it in my heart, and even if I couldn't have Reeve for myself, I still wanted him safe. I still wanted him alive. I hoped he understood that from my body language, because I couldn't say it any clearer without breaking down, but it was something I needed him to know.

"Anyway," I said, pushing my hair behind my ear, "I was just wondering what you were thinking."

"I was thinking that if I met with him, I'd have to kill him."

My stomach dropped. He'd always led me to believe he was the type of man who could do that. But now that I was faced with the possibility that he might, that it would be partially because of me, I couldn't bear it.

Something about his expression told me he wanted me to give him my opinion. Wanted me to support him or talk him out of it.

I couldn't be the one to do that.

With my eyes lowered, I gave him the best that I could manage. "You'll do what you have to. It's one of the things I admire most about you."

"Emily—"

I didn't turn around this time. I wondered if I would ever turn around for him again.

The phone was easier than e-mail, and after the long days of avoiding my island companions, I needed to hear a friendly voice.

"I picked up keys for the place this morning," Joe said after we'd exchanged greetings. "My guy is coming out to check the alarm system tomorrow."

"You have a guy?" That sounded more like something Reeve would say, and the idea of Joe having minions made me chuckle.

"Well," he admitted, "he's an ex-con with a record for getting past some pretty stellar security. If there's a hole in the system, he'll find it."

"Okay then." Maybe Joe was more like Reeve than I realized. Both certainly had questionable associates.

"Have you read any of my e-mails?" Joe's tentativeness put my guard up.

"I haven't been online much. Why? Is there something else I should know?"

"Nothing like that. I, uh, took the liberty of moving your mother to an institution closer to your new place. There's one not too far with excellent care. You'd mentioned you wanted to do it sometime anyway, and the facility she was in before didn't protect the names of their patients as well as I would have liked."

I rolled my neck from side to side. The mention of my mother made my shoulders tense. I'd come to terms that we were long past any meaningful reconciliation—her alcohol-induced dementia prevented us from connecting on that level. But she required care, and though I couldn't be 100 percent responsible for her on a day-to-day basis, I wanted to be involved. Just dealing with her was emotionally trying, and I avoided her as much as I avoided most anything. It would be harder to continue that with her close by. It was so much easier to make excuses about how rarely I visited when she was over an hour away.

Joe misread my silence. "I should have waited until you got back to me before doing anything. I'm sorry."

"No, no," I assured him. "It's fine. It's necessary. I just need a minute to get used to the idea." At least I didn't have to worry about the mechanics of the transfer. "Thanks for doing that for me, Joe. Thanks for all of it. You've been a really great friend." One of the only ones I had at the moment.

My gratitude seemed to fluster him. "It's my job," he said after a few seconds.

It was more than that, but I didn't need to argue with

him about it. He knew I appreciated him. "Anyway. I'll let you know when my flight is arranged."

Saying it out loud like that made my leaving a reality. It felt like I kept coming back to this same place. Kept making the decision to go and yet never ended up seeing it through. This time would be different. It had to be.

I couldn't bring myself to talk to Reeve a second time in one day so I pushed off asking him to make my travel arrangements. I didn't bother joining Amber for lunch either, and, after grabbing a sandwich late in the afternoon, I had a valid excuse of not being hungry enough to show up for supper.

When I was sure that Amber and Reeve were dining, I put in thirty minutes in the pool by the master bedroom. I hated being so close to his room—*their* room—but the pool by my room wasn't heated, and the water was too chilly for my taste once the sun began to set. The rhythm of swimming laps was comforting. It got me out of my head and forced me to concentrate on the basics—my form, my breathing, not drowning.

It was dark when I got out. I wrapped a towel around myself and slumped into a deck chair in the shadows and brought my knees to my chest. My workout had brought me to a Zen state. I felt, not numb, but subdued. The thoughts that had taken front stage in my mind all day were now background noise, eclipsed by the hypnotic sway of wind in the trees and the distant crash of ocean waves.

The sound of splashing water interrupted my daze, and I looked up to find Reeve in the pool, swimming laps at a steady speed. My breath hitched, both because he'd surprised me so completely and because he looked, as always, so damn good in the water. His stroke was perfect. The muscles in his body flexed and stretched fluidly, as if he were a part of the water. He was beautiful to watch, magnificent and strong and graceful all at once.

It felt voyeuristic to watch him like this. He didn't know I was there—I was sure of it. I was too curled up in the shadows for him to have noticed me easily, and his form was too natural and uninhibited to have been a performance. Which was why it was so hard to look away. I told myself just a few more minutes, just one more lap, and then I'd slip inside without him ever knowing I'd been there.

But one more lap turned into two more. Then three. And I hadn't left. I couldn't tear myself away for any other reason than I didn't want to stop watching him.

Then the curtains at the door of the master bedroom parted, and Amber stepped out onto the patio. I was too late to sneak away unseen.

And I really didn't want to be here anymore.

Amber took a seat in a deck chair at the pool's edge, crossing one leg suggestively over the other, and watched Reeve as intently as I had. She was clearly in seduction mode. Her hair was pulled to the side in a loose braid, and the nightie she wore was more sexy lingerie than sleepwear. She looked alluring and provocative and, just like when I'd first seen her in my neighborhood, I felt plain and drab in comparison.

I pulled my knees tighter to my chest, wishing I could disappear. Wishing I could love her enough to truly want this for her. Wishing I could love her enough to forget how much I loved him.

"You look good out there," Amber said when Reeve popped his head up from the water.

He paused. "Thanks."

Even from where I sat I could tell he hadn't expected her to be there when he'd broken his lap. But there'd been some reason he'd come up. Had he expected me instead? Could he sense my presence the same way I'd sensed his when I'd swam in his Palm Springs pool that first day I'd met him?

It wasn't a good idea to wonder about that. Or him.

"I've always loved watching you in the water," Amber cooed. "I love being in the water with you, too. I could join you."

My gut twisted as images flashed in my mind of times he and I had been in his LA pool together, naked. But now, like in a dream, I saw them from a distance and she was in my place.

I closed my eyes, not wanting to make those pictures any more real than they already were in my head.

But then Reeve said, "I'm getting out, actually," and the knot in my stomach loosened ever so slightly.

I couldn't help but stare as he climbed out of the pool, distracted by the sight of his firm body, nearly completely exposed in his black swim trunks. I didn't have to look at Amber to know she was as focused on him as I was.

Reeve grabbed a towel from the shelves and began to dry himself off, his back turned to both Amber and me.

She peeked over her shoulder to ask, "Have you heard from Micha?"

"I hate it when you call him that."

"Sorry. Michelis."

He was slow in answering. "Nothing recent."

Had he already told her about the e-mail that had arrived that morning? Or had he chosen not to tell her about it altogether?

She uncrossed her leg and twisted her body in his direction. "You'll feel better when you decide how you're going to handle this." When he didn't say anything she went on. "You know what I think you should do."

Reeve's shoulders fell as he let out a sigh. "You know as well as I do that there would be serious repercussions." His tone was even despite the irritation in his words.

"Every member of my family would be affected. It's a last resort, not a choice I'm going to make lightly."

So she wanted Reeve to meet with Michelis. I hadn't talked to her about it, and, for some reason, it surprised me that this was her position. She knew what her last lover was capable of better than anyone. Why would she want to ask anyone to have to face him?

As though in answer to my question, she said softly, "He's not going to let me go as long as I'm alive."

Reeve spun toward her, his head cocked. "But why is that? You told me he wasn't really invested in your relationship. Petros told me the same thing. Michelis has broken up with other girlfriends without harassing them. Why is he so desperate to hold on to you?"

"He doesn't want you to have me," she said, confidently. "You know how he is."

"Then the solution is to distance myself from you."

"No. That's not . . ." She trailed off.

"It's not?" Reeve left the question open and crossed to the liquor cart to pour himself a drink.

Amber ran her hand absentmindedly across the base of her neck. "He'll still come after me, Reeve. He's afraid I'll tell people what he did with my father. He'll silence me the way he silenced that friend of Missy's."

"Every one of his ex-girlfriends could testify to his criminal involvement. He's hung up on you for some reason." He sank into a chair and slipped his feet into his sandals.

Amber rose and moved over to him. "Bourbon?" she asked, eyeing his drink. "You really must be stressed. We won't talk about it anymore. Let me help you relax." She circled around behind his chair and began kneading his shoulders.

The scene that had been beautiful before she'd arrived had turned dismal. I'd been breathless watching Reeve in the water, so taken with his presence, but now the tight feeling in my lungs felt more like suffocation. I willed myself to close my eyes, but I wasn't that strong.

"Oh, God, you're tense," Amber said, her words turning my chest into cement. "You should lie down and let me rub you all over. You need a real massage."

He scrubbed his face. "I need sleep." The mere mention of sleep made me want to sob. "I should get to my room."

And then the desire to cry evaporated, and my ears pricked up. *My room,* he'd said. But his room was her room too. Wasn't it?

I sat completely still, anxious, afraid to even think. Afraid I'd miss something if I stirred even that much.

She ran her hands over the taut muscles in his neck. "You should stay," she purred. "I feel bad for taking your bed. It's the best one in the house."

Taking your bed.

"All the beds are the same."

"When they're empty they are. We could make it the best bed. Together." She leaned forward and stretched her fingers down his damp chest.

"Amber," he warned as he clamped his hand around her wrist, stopping her from moving her touch lower.

"What?"

He glowered at her, and she drew her hand back with a huff.

I clasped my hand over my mouth, stunned. Relieved. I couldn't believe what I was hearing. They weren't sleeping together. How was that possible? Amber was most definitely staying in the master bedroom. Where the hell was Reeve staying? Had I misread the situation somehow?

Amber crossed back to her chair and moved it to face him before sitting in it. "I know what you said," she said quietly. "You think things are over between us."

"Things *are* over between us." He was insistent but kind. He'd said he still loved her, and it was apparent in his tone that he did, but it was nonetheless a rejection.

She nodded, accepting. "Yes. I get it. That's my fault. I left. I ended us." She scooted to the edge of her seat. "But— just hear me out before you say anything. Yes, things are over, but that doesn't mean we can't begin again. We both made mistakes before." Her voice grew stern. "*Both* of us, Reeve."

"I've already apologized—"

She cut him off with a raise of her hand. "I'm not asking for another apology. I'm saying we could both do better. And this could be a great opportunity to clean the slate. Try again." There was nothing manipulative in her declaration. Just a gentle plea, and I understood in that moment exactly how much she'd really loved him too.

I clutched my hand to my chest, hoping to ease the cramp at my breastbone.

"We were ready to spend our lives together," Amber said, somberly. "Remember?"

Reeve responded with a bitter edge. "*I* was ready to spend my life with you. I don't recall that *you* were."

He'd surprised her with a wedding. No warning. No proposal. It was probably one of the most dominant things I'd heard he'd done.

"I was scared," she said. "You didn't give me time to prepare. You know that." Her voice caught and she had to clear her throat before going on. "Then *you* were scared. Scared to lose me, remember?"

She'd tried to run, and that was when he'd kept her from leaving, against her will.

"I remember all of it, Amber." Regret thickened his voice. "And like any good history lesson, I've learned what not to do again."

"Then let's not repeat our past. Let's be something new."

She fell to her knees in front of him, her hand on his thigh. "I could be different for you now. I've learned how to be different. I can be what you want now."

I'd never seen her that submissive, that demure. Her hand moved up his thigh, nearer to the bulge in his lap.

This time he grabbed her upper arm. "I think you can see that I'm not interested."

She glanced down in the area of his cock, which I assumed was soft. "Because you're so tense. Let me fix that." She rose and returned to massaging his shoulders.

"Amber, I'm tired." *Too tired to argue*—I could hear it in his voice. So tired that he'd let her seduce him?

I didn't want to watch.

Dammit, I didn't want there to be anything *to* watch. So she wanted him. So she would be good for him. Well, I'd be good for him too. And I wanted him more than anything I'd ever wanted. I wanted him to push her away once and for all. I wanted him to be mine and only mine.

And I had the power to stop what was happening. All I had to do was stand up and decide to use it. All I had to do was claim him.

But I was transfixed with the spectacle in front of me, unable to act. Amber was stroking down his arms now. Even from where I was sitting I could tell that her touch was too light. Reeve preferred firm. The gentle caress would never help him relax.

Still he let her continue. And then she was leaning down to kiss his ear. And his neck. And his jaw.

And he wasn't moving or brushing her away because, somehow, he'd found me in the darkness.

His eyes widened and they locked with mine, sending a bolt of electricity through me so heavily charged that my pulse thrummed everywhere along my veins. His gaze was a prison. I couldn't move my focus from him, couldn't move at all. Like a wild animal caught in the sight line of a predator, I was frozen and alarmed.

He sat forward, his legs tensing as if he were ready to pounce. Ready to chase me. My heart knocked louder against my rib cage. So loud I was certain that any second she'd hear it and discover me.

But she remained oblivious, while, in my periphery, I was aware of her still—of her hands sliding down his chest, of her voice when she exclaimed, "Looks like you're interested now."

So he was hard. And his eyes were still fastened stubbornly on mine.

It was less decision and more primal instinct that knocked me from my stupor. I leapt from my chair and darted noiselessly through the closest door of the building behind me.

He would follow—I practically felt him bound out of his chair after me. But he had to make his excuses to Amber then he had a pool to circle around and I had a head start. Once I was through this hallway, it was only a quick diagonal sprint across the common area before I'd be safe in my room. Not that a locked door could stop Reeve if he were determined.

I emerged from the hall and was three steps into the room before I saw him. He'd come in the other door, cutting me off. He stilled, ready to give chase if I fled from him.

But I didn't run away. I walked toward him.

He met me and our mouths crashed together. He devoured me, and I consumed him. I inhaled him. I took him into my very self in deep gulps of tongue and lips, my hands wrapped so tightly around him, they were a vice grip at his neck.

He walked me backward until my back hit the wall and

pressed firmly against me, locking me in place, his erection throbbing against my belly through the thin cloth of his swim trunks.

Gripping my ass in his hands, he tilted my hips to stroke his cock. "This is for you," he said against my mouth, breathless. "Not her."

"I know." I pushed my body into him. "You moved her to the master bedroom," I said, sinking my teeth into his jaw. "I thought you were sleeping with her. Why didn't you tell me you weren't?"

He gathered the damp strands of my hair and pushed them behind my shoulders. "I might have wanted you to think that I was."

"You wanted me jealous." I could have kicked him if I wasn't so busy tasting every inch of his skin.

He lowered his forehead to mine. "I wanted you to realize that you still want me."

I pulled back so he could see my eyes. "I always realized that I wanted you."

"Shh," Reeve mouthed, putting a finger over my mouth. I listened and heard a loud knock sound from the hallway he had entered through. Someone—Amber—rapping on a door.

He pulled me around the corner, hiding us in the opposite hallway. "She's at my room," he whispered. "The door's locked. She won't know I'm not in there."

He'd been that nearby. Those nights I'd wished for him at my door, imagined he was fucking her, he'd really been sleeping alone, just a hallway away.

I shared my appreciation by licking up the line of his neck.

His cock pulsed against me in response.

I froze at the sound of another loud rap. Silence followed. Then waiting. Then footsteps sounded in the common room.

Reeve peeked his head around the wall. I held still, slowing my breath until I heard a door fling open a few seconds later.

He returned his focus to me, pinning his eyes on my lips. "She's in your room now."

I wondered if she'd worry where I was. If she'd automatically assume I was with Reeve. I wondered if I cared.

"Did she see me outside?" I asked, assessing the situation.

He shook his head. "She couldn't have."

I bit my lip, torn. I was so completely taken with the man in front of me. He was the master of my heart and my body. Maybe even the master of my soul.

But she still held parts of me in her clutch, still had power over them like a voodoo queen in possession of a doll in my likeness.

Reeve brought his hands to rest at either side of my neck. "I need you, Emily." It was sweeter than any admission of love he'd ever made. It was honest and real and raw.

I brought my fingers up to touch his face. "I need you, too." And it was the most honest and real and raw I'd been with him. The most I'd ever admitted. It was a promise to admit more.

But not while she was waiting for me in my room.

"I have to talk to her, Reeve." I couldn't stop staring at his lips, wanting them everywhere on me, imagining them so vividly I could feel them. Then I was feeling them because he was kissing me, owning my entire body with just his mouth.

I was tired of fighting it—no matter what I did or said, I belonged to him. I always would.

Summoning strength that only came from knowing we'd be together again shortly, I pushed out of his arms.

"I'll come to your room," I promised, already heading toward mine.

In a hushed voice, he called after me. "Will you actually come?"

"Yes." I was even pretty sure I meant it.

CHAPTER
21

I'd seen Amber around the neighborhood for some time before I ever learned her name.

The guy next door, Doug, had been a dealer. Nothing serious—pot, LSD, 'shrooms, X. He was a sixty-year-old hippie with hair twice as long as mine and a different person or set of people camped out on his couch every week. I had no access to cash in high school. My mother spent everything she earned on booze and taking care of her as well as myself hadn't left anytime for a job, so I rarely was able to take advantage of the plethora of recreational drugs on the other side of the duplex wall.

Until Amber showed up.

I'd see her outside smoking when I took out the trash or sometimes I'd bump into her at the 7-11 down the block. Every time she'd say hello or wave, and the best I'd ever manage in response would be a shy smile before I ducked my head down. I'd been sixteen and awkward. I'd had acne, and my breasts were embarrassingly large, and communication was not an area I'd had any skill in. Amber, on the other hand, was beautiful and put together and charismatic. I'd been envious of her from afar. I'd also had more than a little bit of a crush.

"You swim a lot," she'd said to me one June day the summer after my junior year. She'd been sitting on Doug's front porch steps, smoking when I'd gotten home from practice. Of course she'd be there when I had forgotten to bring my bag with my towel and change of clothes. I'd dripped for most of the six-block walk.

As always, her hair and clothing had been perfect. I'd been mortified to be seen in my still-wet ratty one-piece. "I'm on a team," I'd said, covering myself by hugging my arms across my chest.

I'd hurried on, hoping to get in my front door before she talked to me again.

But she'd called after me. "Any good?"

I'd stopped and turned back to her. "Our team? Not really."

It was a neighborhood league. Our coach was the mother of one of the team members. I'd only been invited because they'd needed another swimmer to have enough members for relay competitions.

Amber had smiled, her glossy lips shining in the afternoon sun. "I bet you're being too hard on yourself." She picked up the pack of cigarettes on the porch beside her and held it out to me. "Want one?"

I'd smoked before, but I hadn't been good at it, and I hadn't liked it much.

Still, I'd said, "Sure."

She'd lit my cigarette for me then I'd spent the next several minutes feeling stupid because I couldn't think of anything to say.

"I'm Amber, by the way. Emily, right?" she'd asked, blowing a ring of smoke in my direction.

"Yeah." I'd never told her my name, but it had made me feel cool that she'd known it.

"I've heard your mother yelling it," she'd explained.

"Oh. Sorry about her." I'd dropped my head at the mention of my mother, as embarrassed about my parent as I'd been about the way I'd looked in my swimsuit.

Then, worried she'd want to talk more about my mother, I'd asked, "Do you live with Doug?"

"For now."

"Cool." And we'd returned to silence that was awkward—for me, anyway. I'd just met her, but I was already sure that Amber had never had an awkward moment in her life. I'd racked my brain to come up with something to say—anything. Finally, when she'd opened her purse to drop her lighter inside, I'd found an opportunity. "I like your bag."

It had been a Gucci. Too nice to be a knockoff.

"Thanks. My uncle gave it to me." It was much later before I'd learned that her uncle was her married lover. That day, she'd said *uncle* and I'd assumed she'd really meant *uncle*.

She'd stood up then and pulled her blond hair back to show off her ears. "He gave me these too. Like?"

I'd leaned in closer than necessary to study her solitaire diamond studs. She'd smelled good, like menthol smoke and expensive shampoo. "They're gorgeous," I'd said, fingering one of the jewels, and I'd really wanted to say *you're gorgeous*.

She put her cigarette out and cocked her head at me. "What are you doing now, anyway?"

"Just going to change."

"After that. Wanna get high and hang out?"

It hadn't dawned on me until then that she was likely working for Doug. An associate dealer, or something. She'd probably only talked to me so she could sell a bag.

"I don't have any money." It hurt to admit, not because I'd been embarrassed about being poor, but because I'd figured that would be the end of our conversation, and I hadn't wanted to stop talking to her yet.

So I'd lit up like Christmas when instead of blowing me off she'd said, "No worries. My treat."

We'd spent the rest of the afternoon together, smoking pot and dining on junk food. Later, she'd taken me to an apartment building construction site a few blocks away. It had been late in the day and most of the workers had gone home. The few that lingered had paid us no mind when she pulled me inside one of the stairwells and up to the top floor. I'd followed her through the maze of drywall and exposed pipes to what would eventually be a balcony. There hadn't been a railing installed yet, so we'd sat at the edge, dangling our feet over the side. It had only been three stories up, but it had felt like so much higher, and not just because we'd been stoned.

We made our own little nest up there, smoking cigarettes and drinking Diet Coke and for the next few hours, time stood still as we talked and got to know each other.

Mostly, it had been *Amber* getting to know *me*. She was good at asking questions and even better at making me feel comfortable enough to answer them.

"What's with all the baggy shirts you're always wearing?" she'd asked, tugging on the oversized Dodgers T-shirt I'd changed into after stripping from my swimsuit. "You have great tits under there."

"No, I don't," I'd giggled, my cheeks hot. "They're . . . too big."

"Baby, there's no such thing as too big when it comes to tits. Show them to me."

"Okay." I hadn't known what else to say. I'd figured she was kidding anyway. But then she was staring at me, waiting. "Right now?"

"Yeah, right now." She followed my gaze as I surveyed the men working below. "Ignore them. You'll make their year. Give them a new fantasy to whack off to later."

"Okay." I'd never done anything like strip in public. I was nervous and scared, but I wanted my new friend to think I was cool and brave like she was. So I grabbed the hem of my shirt and pulled it over my head.

"All of it," she coaxed, when I paused before removing my bra.

A second later, I was topless, my DD breasts on display.

Hollers and catcalls came from the construction crew, but it was Amber's response that had goose bumps puckering my skin.

"Jesus, Em, they're incredible!" She leaned toward me, and, without asking, plumped a breast with her hand. "If I had your tits, I swear, I'd . . . I don't know. I'd make all the men happy. No more of this sports bra shit." She snagged my bra out of my hand and tossed it to the ground before I had a chance to stop her. "You need nice underwear for a premium rack like this."

"But I don't own any other kinds of bras." I hurried to put my shirt back on, in case she got the idea to toss it as well.

"I'll take you shopping. I have an open account at Nordstrom's. I'll buy you something sexy."

I hugged my knees to my chest, strangely bashful *after* I'd put my clothes back on. "You have an open account? How the hell do you have that?"

"My uncle. He's rich."

"Nice uncle." I'd been tentative about asking Amber questions, afraid I'd say something wrong and piss her off, but my curiosity got the better of me. "Why isn't this rich uncle putting you up somewhere better than Doug's house?"

She leaned back on her elbows and gave me an even look. "Good question. I guess I haven't earned it yet." It had been an interesting response, one that raised more questions than it answered.

I didn't get a chance to find out if I was brave enough to ask anything further, though. Because apparently Amber had questions of her own, and she launched into a series of them, shooting them off one after another. "Have you had sex?"

"Yes."

"More than oral?"

"Yes." Once. It counted.

"A boyfriend?"

"No."

"Do you shave your pussy?"

I blushed again. "I trim."

"Have you ever kissed a girl?"

My blush deepened. "I have not."

"Would you?"

"Yes. Probably." But I was afraid she'd think I was gay and that she'd feel uncomfortable so I added, "But I like dick."

Then I was afraid she might be a lesbian herself, and what if I'd just made her not want to be my friend because I'd said I liked dick?

I needn't have worried.

"Yeah," she'd said. "I like dick too. Have you fucked an older guy?"

"Yes. Two months older."

"That's not older," she laughed. "Would you fuck an older guy?"

"Like how old? Like Doug?"

She cringed. "No. Not like Doug." A second later, she reconsidered. "I mean, if Doug had something better to offer you than drugs, then maybe, but otherwise, do not fuck a guy like Doug."

"Okay. I won't." It had been strange advice, but everything about her was so wise and mature that I'd figured I was just unsophisticated.

"Would you fuck my dad?"

"No!"

"You don't even know what he looks like!"

"Oh." I chewed my lip, unsure what the correct answer was. "Is he hot?"

"No." She shrugged. "I don't know. Maybe. People say he's good-looking."

I studied her, again trying to guess at the right thing to say. Much later, when I recalled that conversation, I didn't remember anything unusual about the tone she'd used to talk about her father. It had been casual. A bit bored, maybe. The way any teenager talked about a parental unit. There'd been no hint of animosity or fear or resentment or even attraction.

When Joe had located her father in a California prison, I'd finally gotten to see a picture of the man. Surprisingly, he actually *was* hot. It made sense—his daughter was beautiful. Genetics usually played a role in that. It stood to reason he'd be attractive as well. But by that time, I'd already known for a while that he'd been a pedophile who'd raped his own daughter for years before she'd gotten the guts to run away to live on Doug's couch. I'd just figured that, since he was so much of a monster on the inside, he probably looked like a monster on the outside.

It was a ridiculous assumption. Hadn't I learned early on that the people with monster insides were always the most beautiful on the outside?

That first night, though, I hadn't known much about monsters at all. And I certainly hadn't known that Amber's father was the monster that hid under her bed. Even if I had, I don't know if I could have guessed how she wanted me to respond to her line of questioning. In the end, I had asked point blank, "Do you *want* me to say I'd fuck him?"

"Yes."

I'd gaped at the unexpected answer. I'd known nothing about her, though, so my expectations were based on absolutely nothing. My imagination flew with scenarios of what her life must have been like to lead to that response: She thought her father was lonely. She hated her mother. Her mother was dead and she hated her stepmom. She'd run away because of her stepmom. She wanted *me* to be her stepmom. Because she liked me. Because she wanted me to be tied to her forever.

Hope, I think, was what led me to ask, "Why would you want me to fuck *your dad*?"

She looked at me like I was an idiot. "How else would you get close enough to kill him?"

I'd laughed. It was funny because it was so startling. And it was revealing. Without details, it told me that he was the reason she'd run away. She hadn't wanted to talk about it, but she'd wanted me to know.

Then she moved on. "Would you jump from here if I asked you to?"

I didn't even blink. "Yes." I was pretty sure I would have done anything she'd asked at that point. Even jump off a balcony that was three stories high.

"Damn." It was nice to surprise her for a change. "I think I love you."

"Really?"

She didn't hesitate. "Yeah. Really."

My throat suddenly felt thick. No one had ever said they'd loved me. Not my mother. Not any of the casual friends I'd made in my life. Not any of the boys who'd put their dicks in my mouth and not the one who'd taken my virginity.

So even though I'd known that she might not have meant it the way most people meant it, and that I might very well never see her again after that night, it had affected me to hear her say it. It had affected me to hear her say anything. To just spend time with me. It was honestly the most attention anyone had ever given me.

It was a big thought, a big emotion, one that needed space.

So I scooted back from the edge, stretched my body out on the floor, and stared at the framing of the balcony roof.

"Which quality do you find most attractive in a man?" Amber had asked next.

"Hmm." I didn't have to think long. "Power."

"You really would like my father," she'd muttered. "Why power?"

"I don't know. It's sexy, I guess." I hadn't known how to articulate the appeal. My entire life, I'd felt powerless. With my mother and her drinking. With my body and its abundant curves. With the swim coach who considered me a team filler and never bothered to time any of my laps or check out my form. Power was an enigma to me. I was fascinated by it—by what it could do, by what it could inspire, by what it could create.

"Personally, I like a guy with money," Amber had said. "Which is a lot like power, but not really. I want the guy to have the money and me to have the power."

"Yes. That's what I mean," I'd said, wanting to be liked more than to be understood.

But Amber had already understood me more than I'd realized. Propping herself up on her side, she'd said, incredulously, "You wouldn't know what to do with power if you had it. You don't know what to do with the power you do have."

"I don't have any power."

"Those knockers!"

I shook my head. "You're funny."

"You're naïve."

It hurt because it was true—I *was* naïve. My ignorance

was one of the reasons I'd felt so powerless. It was a side effect of not having anyone. Who was going to teach me how life worked? I'd had no friends. No father. An addict of a mother. A mediocre education.

There wasn't any way to hide my naïveté. It was who I was. But I'd hated that Amber had figured it out so quickly. It embarrassed me, more than my abundant chest size and my cheap clothing.

All of a sudden, Amber was on top of me, her weight propped up with her hands at either side of my head. "Hey," she'd said. "I wasn't saying that to hurt your feelings. I like that about you. That you're green."

Before she'd ever spoken to me, I'd been enamored with her. She'd been a falling star that I'd been lucky enough to catch sight of—far away. Too beautiful and fantastic and special to engage with or touch or truly look at. Too special to notice me.

But here she was, her face just inches above mine, saying that she liked the thing I hated most about myself.

It felt like the light had just gone on. Like the black-and-white story I'd lived in all my life had an Oz. It was a remarkable moment, completely different from any other I'd had before. So if it was odd that she leaned down and placed her mouth on mine, I didn't notice. It just added to the singularity of the occasion.

At first, her lips only dusted against mine, soft and full and cherry-gloss flavor. Then they nudged my mouth to open so they could wrap around my bottom lip and press. Less than five seconds later, she'd pulled away and it was over. Short, but unabridged. Complete. Exactly as long as it should have been.

And while it was somewhat arousing, that was only one component of the kiss—a kiss that had so many layers, all of them dependent upon each other, none of them significant when dissected alone. It didn't leave me questioning my sexuality or hers. It didn't leave me questioning anything. It was the kind of kiss that answered. Everything.

After, she sat up, straddling me, and smiled triumphantly. "There. We're bonded now because I was your first."

Then she rolled off me, lit a cigarette, and flitted on to the next item on her brain.

In the next few weeks, we became nearly inseparable. She opened my eyes to so much, but she let me keep them closed a lot too. She let me be naïve so she could be powerful, and I was attracted to her for that, like I was attracted to so many powerful men after her.

We never kissed like that again, not just the two of us. Our sexual interactions were always about the men involved, not each other, and almost five months would pass before that phase of our life began.

But she'd been right—we *were* bonded. Because she was the first girl I'd ever kissed. Because she was my first everything.

CHAPTER
22

I stood outside my bedroom door for several minutes, centering myself. The words I needed to say to Amber—the ones I'd needed to say for so long—were no longer stuck in my throat, but they were still jumbled and thick on my tongue. There were so many ways I could start, so many different narratives I could deliver, and I didn't know how to decide which way to go.

Just tell her you love him.

That was what it came down to. Telling her I loved Reeve. Everything else was just decoration and excuses.

So, after several deep breaths, I put on a smile and went inside.

"Hey," I said, then immediately frowned at the scene. My suitcase was open on the bed. A stack of my T-shirts had been dumped inside, and now Amber was returning from the dresser with a handful of shorts.

She glanced up at me as though I'd interrupted her, adding the clothes in her hand to the shirts in my bag. "I haven't seen you in a one-piece since the summer we met."

"Yeah, I thought conservative would be most appropriate for this trip." I folded my arms across my chest and watched as Amber, back at my dresser, opened up a drawer and pulled my suits out, one by one, seemingly impressed that there was only one bikini.

"Thoughtful of you." She crossed back to the suitcase, where she heaped them on top of my shirts. "There's no hiding that body, though. You're still every man's wet dream." Her tone was both complimentary and accusatory.

"I've been trying to do my laps when no one was around." My defensiveness was automatic, but it was also a stall tactic. Even if the tension in the air was in my head, the packing was not. I had barely been prepared to come in and upset her with talk of Reeve. I had definitely not been prepared for her to already be upset.

"I know you have. You can't help being born to look like sex on a stick. You'd think I would have learned already." My mouth opened, but I didn't get a chance to say anything before she turned from her task and asked point-blank, "Where were you?"

"Just now? Sitting outside. Thinking." Again, I was defensive. It had been true. It just hadn't been where I'd been last. And, though I meant to talk to her about it, I didn't think Reeve should be the first item of discussion.

No, the first item we needed to address was the underwear she was now stuffing into the outside pocket of my suitcase. "Amber, what are you doing?"

She sighed, a deep, remorseful sigh that seemed to empty her completely. "You have to go, Em. You can't be here anymore so I'm helping you pack. I'll arrange to have you on a flight back tomorrow."

"Okay." But what I really meant was *give me a minute to process.* "I don't understand what's going on. Did something happen?" Had she seen me in the hall with Reeve after all?

"What happened is you're in the way and I need you gone. You being here has ruined everything." The intensity of her voice increased abruptly. Hints of accusation became full-out blame so quickly it was obvious that she'd been holding these feelings for quite some time.

Well, I had feelings I'd been holding on to for a while as well. "You're the one who talked me into coming!"

"You know why I did that," she seethed, her eyes narrow. "And I shouldn't have. I should have realized that nothing's changed, that you'll always come between me and whoever I love."

"Wait . . . what? When have I ever . . . ?" The only other man who'd been an issue had been the one who'd raped me. "You said that you knew I didn't go after Bridge."

She shook her head dramatically. "It doesn't matter if you went after them or not," she said, heading into my closet. "They always wanted you more. You were always the prize."

I followed after her. "What the hell are you talking about? That was *you*. Which one of any of the men that we've been with didn't want you the more?"

She spun toward me. "Oh, let's see. Bridge, Rob, Liam, Bryan." She ticked the names on her fingers as she named them. *"Reeve."* She turned back to her task, jerking sundresses off hangers and piling them over her arm.

I was flabbergasted. "Bridge was a sick asshole. Rob was *your* boyfriend. Bryan—Bryan proposed! To you!"

"Bryan only wanted me if you were part of the package. Liam liked playing house with me, but he wanted you. And Rob? Are you serious?" She paused to read my reaction. "Rob was the whole reason I found you in the first place." Then she trekked back out to dump the clothes she'd gathered into my suitcase.

I hesitated for a second before trailing after her. "What are you talking about?" Her last statement, as incomprehensible as it was, also resonated with potential. Like, discovering a connection that had always existed but had never been fully realized.

Her jaw tensed, and I suspected she regretted bringing it up.

But it was too late to take it back now. "Tell me what you're talking about, Amber. What do you mean Rob was the reason you found me in the first place?"

She folded a dress into a square, the same dress she'd just folded. "Did you think it was my idea to bring someone else into my relationship with him?" she asked, quietly.

"You wanted to share him with me. Because we were friends." It was what I'd believed for so long, but saying it out loud, it felt hollow.

"You're as naïve now as you were then."

I leaned against the foot of the bed, my head spinning. "That night we first hung out . . ." The questions she'd asked—would I go for an older man, had I kissed a girl, wanting to see my breasts. "What was that? A screening?"

"Ding, ding, ding!"

"That night was everything to me. It changed my life." I sounded like a kid who'd just discovered the truth about Santa Claus. I felt like one, too—stunned, disappointed, betrayed. "And that was just for him?"

"Yes," she snapped.

She closed her eyes and pinched the bridge of her nose. "No. That's not true." Her voice was softer. She dropped her hand and met my eyes. "I mean. He wanted me to find someone to join us. But I found you because I needed to find you. And I didn't take you to him at first because I wanted you to myself. Then I wanted you with me everywhere."

My legs felt weak, so weak. I sunk to the ground, my back pushed against the footboard for support. Our friendship, the one relationship I'd built my entire life around, and it was based on a lie.

Amber dropped to the floor beside me. "That night meant everything to me, too, Emily. It wasn't just for him. I didn't mean that. I meant that I wasn't looking for friends back then. And he forced me to go out and it ended up being the best thing because I found you."

I hugged my knees to my chest, as if, by curling up into a ball, I could somehow close the wound she'd opened.

"Please believe me, Em." She scooted closer, her expression sincere. "If it had been just for him, would I have kept you around for all those years after?"

"Well, I don't know," I retorted, my throat tight. "Maybe you *kept me around* to get the men since they 'always wanted me more'."

"You still don't see it, do you?" Her tone was gentle, affectionate. "This isn't something I made up to make you mad. Think about it. Really look back and think about it."

I didn't need to think about it. I remembered everything. Our past lived in my head with startling clarity. I could recall it at any time without any prodding.

Still, I found myself looking at it again now. Because she'd challenged it and because I suddenly didn't trust anything, including my memory.

But try as I might, I didn't see what she wanted me to see. "I was always the third wheel. You were captivating and dynamic. You were the main girlfriend. I always had the spare room."

"You always *chose* the spare room."

I twisted to look at her. "Because I thought that's what you wanted!"

"It was!" She smiled, and I could see it was a tactic to fight tears. "It just wasn't what any of them wanted."

I dropped her gaze. It was too hard to hold all the pain and sadness buried in her eyes. Pain and sadness that she was inferring I'd caused.

I stared at my kneecaps, not really seeing them. Instead,

I saw Rob, the "rich uncle" she'd taken me to meet as a birthday present. *"She brought you here for me,"* he'd told me when he'd made his moves. He'd told me outright, and I still hadn't gotten it. Hadn't *wanted* to get it.

"Liam," I said, thinking out loud. Amber had played doting wife, but maybe she'd given herself that role. It was me he'd loved to spend hours talking with over a bottle of wine. It was me he'd buy gifts for, little presents he'd find around town that reminded him of me.

"He was so in love with you. You were so detached. So unattainable. When you decided we should leave, I figured you'd finally realized that he would have been the one for you, if you'd let him."

My head snapped up to see if she was serious.

Her expression said she was. "I could never decide if that bothered you because he wasn't what you wanted or because you were worried about me."

"I don't know." I was numb. Had I known Liam had felt that way? Deep down somewhere, had I known?

I'd wanted to leave because he'd scared me. He'd made me understand things about myself, how I liked to be treated, how I liked to be fucked. He'd made it easy to be that way with him—because he'd loved me? Because he'd loved even the bad things about me?

"Things were better when we stopped sharing guys," Amber said, and I wondered if she were taking her own trip down memory lane or if she were just guessing the places I was visiting myself.

She'd resented me. For so long. It was apparent now, so clear I couldn't believe I'd never seen it.

It triggered my own resentment. "Then the real reason you ended our friendship wasn't because you thought I was better than that life. It was because you were afraid I'd get in your way with your next boyfriend."

"It was both," she admitted. "You can't tell me there

aren't things you've done for me that didn't have a benefit for you as well."

Reeve. I'd gotten involved with him because of her, but also because of me. "No, I can't." It wasn't enough of an apology. I just didn't know what exactly to apologize for.

I tried to imagine what it must have been like for her, to feel like I'd always been between her and the various men she loved. "You should have gotten rid of me earlier."

"Emily," the word was thick. "I never wanted to get rid of you at all. You were my touchstone. I kept hoping that some-how, someday it would work out, and we'd both find whatever happy ending we were looking for. But then Bridge . . . not only was I not enough for him—not good enough for that fucking useless asshole—but he also ended up hurting my best friend. So bad." Her voice cracked, and my gaze followed a tear dropping down her nose.

"You pushing me away hurt almost just as bad." My eyes were dry, but my chest ached.

More tears fell, wetting her cheeks. "I know," she said. "It hurt me too."

She sniffed, wiping her face with the back of her hand. "Ending things with you didn't work anyway. You were still there in the middle of my relationships, even when you weren't physically present."

I shook my head, not understanding.

"Like, with Reeve. I'd finally found a guy who really loved me. *Me*. And the whole time, I couldn't stop won-dering whether or not he still would have picked me if he'd known you."

"That is not my fault." But it made me feel sick because she'd been right. It made me sick because I understood—I'd done the same thing, imagining her there through so much of my relationship with Reeve.

"I'm not blaming you. I'm telling you how it is." She

swallowed. "I'm telling you I know there are parts of him that are better suited for you."

She shut her eyes as a slew of new tears fell.

"Amber . . ." I reached out for her.

But she stood up, pulling away from me. "I can't do this with you anymore, Emily." She rocked back and forth on her feet. "I can't. Blue raincoat. I quit. Because I don't want to compete with you again. I want to love you and I want to love him and I don't want those two things to conflict with each other like they have over and over and over."

I scrambled to my feet. "Don't you see I feel the same way?"

"Yes, I do! That doesn't make this any easier."

No. This made it harder. Knowing all of this, and I still hadn't said what I'd planned to say. But how I felt didn't seem to matter as much at the moment as how *he* felt. If we both loved him, then he needed to be the one to decide. And he had.

"He wants *me*." I didn't say it triumphantly, but I said it proudly. I said it definitively. I said it knowing it was what needed to be said most.

As heavy of a declaration as it had been, it didn't faze Amber. "He wants you because they always want you. Because you're an option. If you weren't here anymore, he'd come back to me."

I gaped. "And you want that? To be his second choice?"

"I was his first choice, first."

It was a truth that slammed me in the gut. How ironic that I'd been wrong all those times that I'd thought she'd been the star of our relationships, and now, when I finally wanted to be the star, I was merely an understudy.

She turned him down. I kept coming back to that. She'd left him. For reasons that she could justify until she was blue in the face, and it still didn't change the fact that she'd let him go. She'd forced him to move on. That wasn't something she could just take back.

Except it wasn't that simple. Like she'd told him earlier, Reeve had made mistakes too. He'd pushed her to run.

And I'd made mistakes as well. I'd gone after him for me, not her. If I'd walked away when I'd thought she was dead, if I hadn't pushed him for a relationship, maybe his reaction to her return would have been different.

None of that was relevant, though. The whys and the hows and the blame—it was all rough water under a very high bridge. The only thing that mattered now was who would back down. Who would give in. Who would give up.

Our history did not bode well for me.

I shook my head, my neck tense as I struggled to temper the threatening sob. "This is the worst thing you've ever asked me to do, Amber. He's the only person I've ever loved besides you."

"And he's the only person who's ever loved me besides you." She was hard and unwavering. Set in her decision.

And the more resolute she grew, the more I fell apart. "You're really going to do this, aren't you? You're really making me go."

"If you stay, can you really be happy knowing I'm not? It's not like I have the choice to leave like you do. Not with Micha after me. It will be like this, like it is now, day after day after day. Can you keep living like this? Because I can't."

She used pretty words. I'd feel for her if I had anything beyond what I was feeling myself. Right now, my primary emotion was contempt.

"Say it," I demanded. "I need you to say it again. Tell me exactly what you want from me." If she couldn't say it, I wouldn't have to obey.

She didn't even hesitate. "I love you, Em. And I want you to leave."

Funny how being so let down felt like falling, and I

wondered if this was how Missy had felt, tumbling through the sky, seeing the bottom get closer every second of her descent.

"There's a flight tomorrow off the island," Amber said. "I've already checked. It leaves in the morning, and I know the manager at the resort. He'll be able to get you a seat. It's never a full flight." There was more, words that made sense but sounded far away and out of tune.

I hated that she assumed I'd just do as she'd asked. But more, I hated that I would. She had power, and I kowtowed to it. It was what had drawn her to me. It was what had drawn Reeve to me, too, and it wasn't a trait that I could suddenly shed, no matter how much I wanted to. No matter that it brought me here, plummeting to the ground.

"I should let you get some sleep," Amber said, drawing my attention after she'd finished talking. Or maybe she'd been silent a while. I'd stopped paying attention. "I'll give you all the info you need in the morning."

I perked up as she started toward my door. "Let me change and I'll walk you. I don't think you should be roaming the compound alone."

The bathroom clock flipped to nine thirty-three as soon as I shut the door. I allowed myself one minute—exactly sixty seconds—to crumble and break apart. When the clock on the counter flipped to nine thirty-four, I gathered myself together, stripped off my conservative one-piece, and put on the robe that had been hanging on a hook next to the door.

We were quiet as I walked her down the hall, past the room that I now knew was Reeve's, to the courtyard.

"Good evening, ladies," said Tabor, one of the security guards. "Headed to your room, Ms. Pries? I'll escort you."

"I'll watch you from here," I said, even though it wasn't necessary with Tabor there. "I'll stay until your light goes on so I know you're okay."

Amber turned to me, her expression soft and grateful. "Thank you, Em. For everything." She leaned in and pressed her lips to my cheek.

And I smiled tightly and tried not to compare it to the kiss Judas had given Jesus that night in the Garden of Gethsemane, a kiss of betrayal. Tried not to focus on the sacrifice that she had forced upon me. Tried to pretend that this last kiss of hers was not one that brought quite so much pain.

Then she and Tabor were walking away, and her light went on, and the guard took his post in the courtyard, and I wondered if instead it were I who was Judas and she the betrayed. Because, as soon as I turned from her, I went to Reeve's room. And, without knocking, I opened his door, threw off my robe, and fell naked at his feet.

Then I gave him the three words he'd been wanting to hear for so long, the three words I could no longer give to Amber. "I trust you."

CHAPTER

23

Reeve had been lying on top of his bed when I walked in. He'd changed from his swimsuit into pajama bottoms, and the smell of body wash erased the smell of chlorine, suggesting he'd showered since I'd seen him.

Now, as I knelt naked in front of him, he stood and looked down at me.

"I trust you," I said again, wanting him to hear it as much as I wanted to feel the words on my tongue. From me, they were equivalent to an *I love you*. They were bigger, even. They were the strongest words I could ever say to someone, and I needed Reeve to know this more than any other thing I left him with.

He looked down at me. "I was going to go easy on you." God, his voice was raw and textured. It scratched along my spine, straightening my back and waking every nerve ending in my body. "You know that I can't now, right?"

My stomach flipped and a thousand hummingbirds let loose inside. "You can do whatever you want with me." I'd always meant it—any time I'd given myself to anyone, it had been true.

But it was so much more thrilling to give myself and know that the man in front of me would take me and push me and be exactly what I needed and would protect me as well.

"Yes," Reeve said, stroking two fingers along the curve of my jaw. "I can." He moved his hand to my shoulder as he circled around behind me. Then, with a hand coiled tightly in my hair, he jerked me to my feet. I shivered as he bit into my neck then soothed his mark with his tongue.

"The question is," he said, his mouth hot and wet at my ear, "can you take it if what I want is to love you?"

My entire body tensed as adrenaline shot through my veins. My heart thumped against my chest and thrummed in my ears and throbbed at my pulse points. No. I couldn't take that. I wanted to shake my head, wanted to refuse, but I'd said he could do anything. And I wanted to mean it.

He knew what he was asking, how hard it would be for me. He ran his hands soothingly over the slopes of my shoulders and down my arms. "I think that might be the one thing that would truly break you," he murmured. "The one thing that will truly destroy you."

It would. It would break me so sweetly, so deliciously, so completely. This man had held me down, controlled my breath, threatened danger that made me fear for my life. But this—to be truly loved, to truly let myself take it and accept it and *feel* it—this was the most frightening thing he'd ever put upon me. The most terrifying slope he'd asked me to climb, and I didn't have a safety belt or a net or anything to catch me but him.

Then I would leave, and he wouldn't be there, and I'd keep falling. Forever.

"Can you take that?" he asked again.

The answer was no. The answer was definitely not. But

it wasn't mine to decide. It was his because he owned me, and he could do with me as he pleased, and I trusted him.

So I didn't answer him. Instead, as he bent to kiss and nip the side of my throat, I told him that I liked how it felt. I told him, "Yes."

His hands were all over me then, sweeping over my skin with the attention one would give to polishing fine silver. His stroke was firm and purposeful, and everywhere his fingers grazed I was revived. Dissolved. Little by little, like sun touching on one mound of snow and then another and another, melting and thawing into beads of sweat and anticipation along the nerves of my body.

I turned my head toward him, a spring flower reaching for the nourishing light. He hovered his mouth over mine. "Where do you want me to touch you?"

His breath brushed across my lips and even that—even just that—sent bolts of fire to my core.

"You choose," I pleaded with him. If he was going to destroy me, I wanted him to decide what the method would be.

"No. Tell me or it will be everywhere." He licked across my bottom lip, and I had to reach my hand up to clamp around his neck to keep from falling.

Everywhere, then. If that's what he wanted, then that's what I'd endure—his touch, everywhere.

"Yes," I purred. "Yes."

He wrapped his arms around my torso and pulled me tighter against his body. The rigid outline of his thick, hard cock pressed into my backside and his hands lifted my breasts, heavy from need.

"Here?" He bent over my shoulder to watch as his palms spread over my skin and plumped my tits. "Is this where I should love you?"

"Yes." If it was the only word I could manage for the rest of the night, it would be enough. I'd say it over and over, to everything he asked. *Yes, yes, yes.*

He narrowed the grasp of his fingers, bringing them in close to pinch and tug my nipples so hard I squirmed. "Your body is mind-boggling, Emily. So round and soft yet firm and strong." He rubbed his cock in the crevice of my ass with a groan. "It's like crown jewels, and I can never decide if I want to show you off proudly, to let everyone see the beauty of my most prized object or if I want to keep you locked away only for myself."

I panted, the pressure of his fingers on my nipples enough to bring me near climax.

"Please," I croaked, because his words were killing me. He'd told me before that there were other beautiful bodies, that mine was nothing special, and I'd been so turned on to be just his receptacle, just this thing that he used for his own pleasure.

But I'd never known this. Never known how aroused I could be from his love, from hearing how I was a place to put his cock but I was also *more*. How I was someone he wanted to look at and please and adore and command. I'd underestimated the possibility that the two could coexist, never quite believing that I could be both used and cherished. Both owned and valued. Not to this extent. Not this completely both.

Without warning, Reeve spun me around and threw me backward to the bed. I raised myself up to lean on my elbows. He still had his bottoms on, minus any underwear, I realized from the way his erection tented out from his body. And as he stood above me, staring at me, eyes dark with lust and devotion, he stroked his cock through his pajamas. It had to be painful with how strained and large he was, with how he pulsed under his palm.

"Wider," he said, his teeth gritted. "Spread your legs wider so I can get to all the places I'm going to be."

I bent my legs, widening until I was completely displayed for him. My breathing grew heavier, and I curled my fingers into the sheets, anticipating his next move. He'd strip. He'd brace himself over me. He'd jut into me and I'd be destroyed.

But the devil teased me. He taunted. Leaving his clothing on, he bent over me and flicked his tongue across one nipple. Then, he moved to the other, closing his teeth around the sensitive area and jerking his mouth up until I yelped in ecstasy.

"Where should I touch you next?" He bit down over the curve of my breast down my belly, hard enough to leave a trail of teeth marks as he lowered himself down my body. "Here?" He thrust his tongue into my navel, and I writhed as intense shock waves rolled through me.

He slid to kneel on the floor, wrapped his hands around my calves, and pulled me to the edge of the bed. "Or how about I touch you here?" He brushed across my clit with the tip of his nose, and my thighs clenched.

"Don't worry, Blue Eyes. I'll spend plenty of time touching you here. But first . . ." He inhaled deeply, his lip curving up into a naughty grin. "I could bottle your scent. Wear it as cologne."

"You're so dirty," I grated, enraptured with how he sprinkled filth over his romantic odes. It was a brilliant technique—extending my torture, giving me vulgarity like footholds to keep me climbing toward our final destination.

With his eyes pinned to mine, he stuck out his tongue, slowly, deliberately drawing out the anticipation before flicking it across the head of my clit. Pleasure zapped down my legs and throughout my lower belly like an electrical storm, and I bit my lip to keep from bursting.

My response seemed to delight him. He stroked a thumb down my seam, gazing at it with admiration. "I'd never thought I was fit to glimpse heaven until I put my head between your thighs." Circling the rim of my cunt with his thumb, he licked across my clit again. And again. "The taste of you should be forbidden. It's the fruit that causes gods to war."

"God. Reeve." It was excruciating how he drew it out, how he lapped at me leisurely, while his fingers explored farther inside my hole, never hitting the spot where I wanted him most.

He wanted me to tell him, I was sure. Tell him exactly where to stroke, tell him how hard to press and how fast to go. "There," I urged when his touch got closer. "Almost, almost."

I was so close, too, and I wouldn't come until he got there, until he caressed me just so.

Except I was wrong. Because he never got right to the spot, the spot that I knew he had memorized better than I did, and his tongue never did more than tease, and yet I fell over the edge, my orgasm nudging through me at a snail's pace. It was almost more affliction than relief, the way it never quite exploded, the way he never let it fully end.

"Good girl," he praised me, trailing his fingers to the rim of my other hole. Using my moisture to ease their entry, he pushed into me, two digits at once. At the same time, he plunged his tongue into my pussy, again only brushing near the most sensitive spot of my vaginal wall.

It was overwhelming—the orgasm that plodded along without resolve, the increase in sensation from both areas at once. I whimpered and tried to pull away, but Reeve put his free hand on my belly to hold me in place.

He continued to torment me like that for several long minutes. Or maybe it was hours, time was lost to me in that state of suspended bitter bliss. I threw my head back in agony. Eventually, he moved his hand from my torso, and I felt him shifting. I lifted my neck and found him wrestling with his bottoms, pulling them down so he could stroke himself while he fucked my cunt and ass with his fingers and his mouth. The sight was so hot, so arousing, and when he added a third finger to my tighter hole, I exploded, coming so hard that my legs and arms and neck muscles all strained and shook.

Still he kept up the punishment.

I wriggled away, unable to bear it. When he grabbed my hip to stop me, I turned inward, to my belly, trying to close myself off in whatever way possible.

Immediately, he pulled his face and hand away, and smacked me hard across my ass cheek. "You aren't done until I say you are," he said so gruffly, so brutally it made my insides dissolve.

Gripping my thighs, he twisted me to my knees and pulled me back to the edge of the bed. His mouth found my cunt again, and this time he added his fingers to hit my G-spot, instantly spiking my orgasm up even higher, higher than I'd thought possible, until I was crying and drowning in ecstasy.

He brought me down slowly, gently, easing up with his attack little by little until he'd wrenched out every last bit of my climax.

"This isn't all," he said behind me, almost apologetically as he rubbed the cheek he'd spanked. "It will be easier on you if you tell me how to touch you next."

I didn't think I could stand to be touched anymore at all. My body was fire and ice all at once, a ball of sensation that flared with the slightest aggravation. Exhaustion pulled at the edges of consciousness and, if he had let me, I would have succumbed to it without a second thought.

But I knew he wouldn't let me go yet. And, as sure as I was that I couldn't take anymore, I was also sure he wouldn't be happy until he'd annihilated every part of my being.

So, with my face pressed against the bed and my ass in the air, I picked my poison. "Touch me with your cock.

Put it inside me." Because I knew he'd demand a more specific location, I clarified. "My cunt. Put it inside my cunt."

"My girl," he said, scooting me forward. The weight of the bed shifted as he climbed behind me and thrust his cock inside.

He wasn't as relaxed as he'd been with his mouth, but his tempo was more moderate than it could have been. I sighed into the bed, grateful that he'd taken me this way, from behind, where I could let the emotional connection between us fade away and simply enjoy being used. Enjoy him, the length of him, the pressure of him, how full he felt inside me.

I scooted my knees in to tighten the hold around his cock, and, soon, he pulled my arms back, using them to leverage his weight as he bucked against me. Sounds fell from my mouth, soft rhythmic mewls that echoed his thrusts and spurred him deeper inside of me. I cherished each noise—the slap of balls against my thighs, the sand-papered texture of his voice as it praised and cursed and grunted and groaned.

"You're so easy to ride," he commended. "So easy to maneuver. I can bend you so easily, shatter you."

"You already did," I sighed, still weary from the orgasms he'd forced upon me.

"Not all the way." He tugged me back so my back pressed against his chest. Wrapping his hands around to fondle my breasts, he raked his teeth across my collarbone. "I want you destroyed. I want you completely annihilated."

I didn't have the energy to disagree, but I felt edgier in this new position, exposed, open for him to play like a musician strumming his instrument.

"Rub your clit," he instructed. "Rub it like it's me rubbing you. Firmly. Faster." An orgasm began to build, and

Reeve moaned as I tightened around him. "Just like that. Good."

He increased his speed, clutching onto my breasts as handholds, and I closed my eyes and let myself just feel and enjoy.

"I love you," he whispered harshly at my ear, and my breath caught. He'd said it in so many ways, but never directly. Never so forcefully. Never in such a way that I had to take it as a gift rather than a fact, where I had to accept it and languish in it. Every thrust of his cock painted the words inside me. Every rock of his pelvis against mine.

"I love you," he said again, like a creed. "I love you so thoroughly it feels like you're in my DNA. Like you must be part of my genetic code because there's no part of me that isn't linked to you. My love for you is so consuming on the inside that there's barely room."

He moved a hand to my throat and pressed it against my windpipe ever so slightly, slowing the oxygen just enough to make me heady and weak.

Or maybe that was from the sweetness of his talk.

"My love for you is so ferocious, so dominating that I'm possessed by it. It changes who I am. It makes me someone different and yet I'm more who I've always believed I am than I ever have been."

Tears slipped out from under my lids. I'd never been loved like this. My mother hadn't been capable of coming close in her alcohol-fed state of existence. And Amber—her love had been complex and had conditions. But it was a love I knew and understood. The rules were clear in my head and ingrained in my responses.

Reeve's love was simpler, but heavier. It wanted me to change like he'd changed. It wanted me to belong and be free all at once. It wanted me to grow up and be brave and trust. And while I'd only felt the fringes of it, I knew it was glorious and incomparable and that it demanded more than I'd ever given before.

And I wasn't sure I was capable of that kind of courage. The kind it took to be loved like this all the time. Which was why I was crying, and why, after the night faded into morning, I would leave Reeve's bed and his island and his life.

"Look at me."

I twisted my neck toward him, opened my eyes, and fastened my gaze on his. My eyes were blurry but I could see him perfectly. Could see everything he felt, the depths of his emotion. For this moment, this brief moment, while he was inside me and around me, I could hold it. I could shoulder the weight and love him and be loved.

"There you are." His murmur tensed and then he was shooting into me, his face straining with release. I tipped over the edge after him, like I was falling off a cliff, soaring for the briefest span of time before I hit the rocks below.

I let him hold me after. I let him caress me and say things that didn't burn so much in the dark of his room, with my eyes on his chest and not buried in his gaze.

"This isn't the only part of you I want, Emily." His chest rumbled under my cheek. "I want the other parts too."

"What parts?" I asked, drunk on every word he said. I'd beg him to say the alphabet just so he'd keep talking.

"Every part. I want the part of you that smiles and teases. And the part of you that argues. The stubborn part. The sassy part. The submissive part. And the parts of you that everyone knows. The famous parts. The private parts."

I glanced up at him, laughing softly. "You've had all my private parts."

"I want them again. I want them forever. I want them to be only mine." He brushed his lips across my brow. "Anyone else who owns a piece of you—I want to take their share. Whatever I have to do to make that happen, I'll do it. If you'll let me."

It seemed inappropriate to even think her name when I was pressed up against him, naked, our bodies still sticky with sweat and sex, but I knew he was talking about Amber. It was her shares of me he wanted to own.

And he did. He owned all of me, even if he never knew. She'd relinquished her rights to possession earlier in the evening, when she'd told me I had to go. Perhaps it was paradoxical, that I could only truly be his when I was about to leave him. But this was what we had, and I'd take this one night over never belonging to him at all.

"I've already let you," I hummed. "I'm yours."

His arms tightened around me. "I know. There's nothing that can come between us, Blue Eyes. Anything that tries, I'll handle it. Just like I always handle it."

I could believe him—for one night, I could believe anything. I could believe that he was the prince who would rescue me. That ours would have a fairy-tale ending. That love could be all and save all and redeem all.

So I believed and I reveled in his plans. "More," I spurred him. "Tell me more about how it's going to be."

"It's going to be like this. Always." He kissed my forehead then the spot between my brows. "I'll cherish you and make you beg and make you scream. I'll be the one who breaks you, and I'll kill anyone else who even tries."

I closed my eyes so he could press his lips to my lids, one by one.

"I'll dress you in my come," he said, kissing the tip of my nose. "I'll mark every part of your body. Your face, your breasts, your neck, your belly."

I felt him in all those places as he mentioned them. Felt him all along my skin, even in the spots he wasn't touching and had never touched. I felt him in the places he could never reach—in my spine and in my ribs and in my veins.

"Everywhere." His mouth found mine, and his lips, firm and demanding and without any more words, told a thousand other tales about a future that we'd never have. He lingered and he loved. He shared dreams he'd never spoken of and showed me how they fit with mine. He rebuilt me for all the times he'd broken me before. He claimed and made me new.

And I pretended it was the kind of kiss that could make all that possible. The kind of kiss that could seal and bind and change and forgive. A kiss that couldn't fade. A kiss that could go on forever. A kiss that could last.

Instead of what it really was—a last kiss.

CHAPTER
24

I slipped out of Reeve's room early the next morning, without a message, without good-bye. He'd assume I didn't want Amber to see me in his room, which was true. It didn't need to be discussed. More importantly, I'd already said good-bye to him in the way I'd wanted to say good-bye.

The sun was still low on the horizon when I'd finished packing my bags. I didn't want to see her, but Amber hadn't given me any details about my flight. Waking her early would at least feel satisfying.

But when I got to her room, it was empty.

What's more, her bed, though rumpled, didn't look really slept in. Like, maybe she'd gotten in, but hadn't stayed there. And when I looked around the room more closely, I saw that the vanity was clear, and her makeup and toiletries were in disarray on the floor nearby.

The hair on the back of my neck stood up. It was too soon to panic, but I had an uneasy feeling in the pit of my stomach.

Then I remembered Tabor. He'd been on guard all night, and I hadn't seen him as I'd gone into her room. I headed outside to look for him.

I found him relatively soon, on a deck chair at the side of the house. "You're asleep?" I screamed, shaking him awake. "What the fuck?"

"Sorry!" He sat up abruptly. "Sorry. I must have just dozed." He stifled a yawn.

"*Just* dozed?" I was almost too livid to speak coherently. "Are you sure? Because Amber's not in her room."

"You're kidding me, right? She was there last night." He looked worried but I wasn't sure if it was because she was missing or because he thought I might get him in trouble.

"How long was she—" I stopped midsentence. "Jesus, I don't have energy for you."

I left him calling after me, heading straight for the one place I thought I'd never be again.

"Reeve. Wake up," I said, perching on the edge of his bed. He opened his eyes immediately, and I got right to the point. "Amber's not in her room,"

He blinked several times. "What time is it?"

"Half past six." I forced myself to speak slowly even though my mind and heart were racing. "Her bed doesn't look slept in. And Tabor was asleep when I went looking for him."

"Tabor was asleep? I'll fucking kill him." He sat up, his body on high alert as he flung the sheets off him and opened the drawer next to his bed. From there, he pulled out a black cloth bundle and unwrapped it as we spoke. "Last night, when you talked to her . . . ?"

"It was fine. We were . . ." I let the sentence fall away. I didn't want to tell him about the conversation I'd had with her before coming to his room and right now those details seemed lengthy and irrelevant. "She wasn't upset when I left her. Everything was good." Good for her, anyway.

Reeve paused, his tone hedging on reproach. "Then you didn't tell her—?"

I cut him off. "I did. I told her about us. I promise. But she and I were settled when we parted." His expression said he knew there was something fishy in my report. "We were fine, Reeve. Just, find her. Please?"

He stood up and nodded, accepting even if not convinced.

The object in his hands, I saw now, was a handgun. I shivered at the sight of the black steel, not because I was afraid of guns necessarily, but afraid of what it might mean. Reeve, however, moved with confidence and no hesitation, like he knew what he was doing. He clicked a magazine into place and crossed to his dresser, where he grabbed a belt from the top drawer. After threading it through the loops of his jeans, he strapped on a holster.

"Was there any reason in particular you were trying to find her so early?" There was no suspicion in his tone. He was merely a man sorting out the details.

"I was up and thought I'd catch her before breakfast." Guilt stabbed through my chest, but I wasn't sure if I felt bad because of what I was keeping from him or because of what I'd kept from her.

He nodded again, returning to the nightstand, where he grabbed a walkie-talkie from a charging dock. He turned the volume knob and static sounded over the device until he pushed the talk button. "All security meet in the main courtyard immediately."

He put on shoes and gestured for me to follow him as he headed toward the bedroom door.

I paused, suddenly realizing something odd. "Reeve?"

He turned back with a raised brow.

"When did you get dressed?" I'd been too distracted about Amber to notice he was already wearing jeans and a T-shirt when I woke him up. When I'd left him earlier, he'd been naked.

"What?" He seemed baffled by the question. Or he was stalling. "Oh. I woke up a while ago and got dressed. Come on. Let's get out there."

Gotten dressed and then fell asleep again, fully clothed?

But getting his story clear wasn't high on my priority list at the moment. So I dropped it and followed him out to the courtyard.

"Have you looked anywhere else besides her room?" he asked as we walked toward the guards gathering outside.

The early spring morning was cool, and I wrapped my arms around myself to ward off the chill. "No. I came to you first."

"Good girl."

The phrase set my body to vibrate with unwitting memories of the night before, beautiful memories, and it occurred to me that if something had happened to Amber while I'd been wrapped around Reeve . . . well, I'd known it was a betrayal when I went into his room. But I wasn't sure I could live with that level of betrayal.

"What's up?" Alex asked when we were close.

"Amber's missing." Reeve sent Alex to search the house and another guard to search the lower grounds. With Filip and a few other guards in tow, Reeve headed to check out the master bedroom.

I trailed behind, feeling like deadweight but too invested to stay out of the way.

Reeve quickly scanned the room and the bathroom. At her vanity, he squatted down to examine the items on the floor.

Filip hovered over him. "Looks like someone got mad and swept them to the ground."

"Agreed." Reeve peered up at me.

"It could have been her." She'd been angry when she'd gone to find me. Neither Reeve nor I had any way of knowing if she'd been to her room after he'd left her at the pool. She could have gone in and made the mess herself.

"It could have not been her, too," he said, and my stomach knotted so tightly that it nearly caused me to double over. He eyed me sympathetically, like he wished he could hold me, and I wished he could hold me too. Wished that was all it would take to make this anxiety ease.

But both of us knew that whatever would erase this dread, it wouldn't be found in each other's arms.

Reeve rose from the floor. "Tabor," he said, pointing at the guard cowering outside the door.

The bodyguard once assigned to protect me, stepped into the room. He didn't say anything, his expression conveying his distress and remorse.

Reeve seemed apathetic to Tabor's anguish. He strode up to the young man, murder in his eyes. "How long were you asleep? Tell the truth and the only thing you'll lose today is your job."

The message wasn't directed to me, and it still caused me to shudder. The man in front of me was a version of Reeve Sallis he'd hinted at, but I'd never seen. It was the version of Reeve Sallis that deserved the reputation of danger. It was a version that, I imagined, had been good at the jobs that his Mafia uncle had once assigned him.

If I hadn't been so upset about my friend, I might have been impressed.

"I don't know," Tabor said, his spine straight. "A while. I saw her to her room and when the light went off, I figured she was out for the night." His bottom lip trembled slightly. "I fell asleep soon after that." Then he broke. "I'm sorry. I'm really sorry."

Reeve looked like he might punch a hole in the wall.

"She better turn up fine, you shithole, or I swear to God you'll really understand sorry."

Shooing Tabor aside, Reeve stepped out to the courtyard and addressed his staff. "Everyone's on full search. Filip, call over to the resort and see if anyone there has heard from her. Talk to the housekeepers and the cook as well. Then get on the phone with the mainland and see what Anatolios can find out. Alex, check out the cameras on the outer walls of the compound starting at ten last night. The rest of us will divide up in teams to go over the grounds and then move outside from there."

The staff immediately dispersed, everyone to their assigned tasks. Reeve started toward the stairs to the lower grounds then stopped when he caught sight of me.

I wrung my hands together. "Where do you want me?"

"Either you stay locked in the master bedroom, or, if you insist on searching with us, stay glued to me. Your choice." It had been hard for him to give me that option; the difficulty was written all over his face.

It changes who I am. My chest pinched as I recalled those words from the night before. He hadn't been that man when I'd met him, a man who could offer alternatives. He'd been a man who said how things were, and I was expected to go along.

Alternatives, options—it was much more than Amber had given me.

I appreciated the choice, and to show him how much, I selected the one he wanted me to select. "I'll stay here. I'll look through her things and see if there's anything unusual. And I'll call Joe."

"I like that plan." His relief was palpable. "It's a safe plan." He turned back to the stairs.

I called after him. "Reeve?"

He paused, his expression encouraging me to go on.

Did she know? That was the question pressing most at

my thoughts. Had she realized what I'd done? That I'd spent the night with Reeve? Had she run away as punishment?

But I couldn't ask his thoughts because then he'd wonder why it mattered if she and I had sorted everything out. And I'd have to explain the agreement we'd come to, and maybe I'd have to explain it eventually anyway, but, at the moment, I didn't know how.

His face softened, and he closed the distance between us with two long strides. "We're going to find her," he said, kissing my forehead. "She's fine. Trust me."

And since I did trust him, I said, "Okay."

I called Joe first, from her room—from the room that had been Reeve's. The conversation was brief. I apprised him of the situation and told him how I'd meant to leave the island that day without sharing much of the details. "I don't know when she disappeared or if she made the arrangements for me to leave or not. If she did, that might at least give us a time frame."

"And you haven't told this to Sallis because he didn't know you were going? Are you planning to tell him?"

"I'm sure I will eventually. Right now, though . . ." I was too tired to explain anything, not just because I'd barely gotten any sleep but because my reasons were so fuzzy now I could barely explain them to myself let alone to someone else.

"Keep it to yourself," Joe said. "I'll see what I can find out. Hang in there."

After I hung up, I looked through her belongings. All that she owned had been purchased for the trip and even though her perfume was the same brand she'd worn for years and her lipstick, the same burnt red color she'd loved since she was a teen, everything felt impersonal. I told myself I was searching for clues like a grown-up Nancy

Drew, but what I was really looking for was her. I wanted to find her in her clothes, in the vanity drawers, in the items strewn across the floor—a swimsuit, her eyeliner, a manicure set, a bottle of aspirin.

None of it felt like her or smelled like her or vibrated of her except the near empty pack of cigarettes I found tucked in the back of her dresser and a half empty container of methadone. Those items I clutched to my chest and curled up on her bed where I could smell the faint scent of her shampoo on the pillow, and I prayed—to God, maybe. Or her. Or to the universe. To whoever or whatever might be out there listening to the prayers of desperate and despondent souls like me. "Please, let her be found. Please, please, please, let her be found."

"You weren't slated to be on that flight," Joe said when he called back later. "I talked to the manager at the resort—discreetly, don't worry—and he said he hadn't heard from her."

I let out a long, heavy breath. "So either she changed her mind or she didn't get a chance."

"What is your gut telling you, Emily?" Joe was like my conscience, saying out loud the questions I was asking myself silently.

"She didn't change her mind." When I'd last seen her, she'd been firmly decided. There had been no swaying her.

"Then you think something happened with Vilanakis?"

"Yes." I paced out into the courtyard, smiling at Filip, who'd stayed behind to watch after me along with the housekeeper and cook. "Unless it was someone else."

"Like who? Like Reeve?"

"I don't know. I'm being paranoid." I spun around, retracing my steps back inside.

"Be paranoid. It's a good investigative technique."

"It's silly. Just." There was a boulder of worry on my

shoulders. A boulder so weighted that I couldn't be in my right mind, and, really, it couldn't be expected that I would be.

So I spit out the idea that had tossed around inside my head all day. "He told me last night that he'd . . . well, he said he wouldn't let anything come between us. He said he'd handle anything or anyone who did. Amber wanted me to go home and that was going to come between us."

Again, he asked, "What's your gut telling you, Em?"

"My gut says that something fucking happened to her. I'm scared out of my goddamn mind."

"About Reeve. Do you trust him?"

I rubbed my fingers across my forehead, remembering that he'd been dressed when I'd come to him that morning, remembering how he'd dismissed me when I'd asked about it.

Remembering the night I'd spent with him and the things he'd said and the things I'd felt.

I'd been in this quandary once before—torn between loving him and the things Reeve was capable of. I didn't need to examine the conclusions I'd come to again.

"I do trust him," I admitted honestly. "But that doesn't mean he didn't do something to her."

I didn't eat or sleep all day. Filip was on and off the phone speaking in Greek so I was only able to catch bits of information. I gathered he was talking to Anatolios most of the time, and that Anatolios was attempting to reach the Vilanakis clan, but Filip didn't share anything with me voluntarily.

"Well?" I asked after the third phone call.

He frowned, his eyes darting as he seemed to debate whether he should confide in me.

"Don't keep me in the dark on this," I said bitterly. "Please."

His shoulders sagged and he let out an apologetic sigh. "Michelis won't talk to anyone but Reeve."

"And Petros?"

"Knows nothing. I'm sorry."

Reeve called as well, every two hours, to give me updates and make sure I was all right. He and his men came back to the house when it got dark but went back out with flashlights after they'd refilled their water and food.

I managed to doze for a couple of hours during the night with her pillow clutched tightly in my arms and the feeling of loneliness in my bones.

It was just after dawn when they found her.

Reeve woke me, waited for me to sit up and wipe the sleep from my eyes, then delivered the news, straight-faced and even.

She'd washed up onshore with the tide, her body bloated, her face so swollen and deformed she was hardly recognizable. The damage to her bones suggested she'd hit the rocks, either because she'd fallen from the cliffs above or because the ocean had slammed her against them. Her arm had been scratched or cut, deep enough that she'd bled and not long enough before her death that she'd scabbed over. Despite how deteriorated her remains were in just one day in the water, the message was clearly legible—*Not Yours*.

Not Reeve's, I supposed it meant. Not mine either. Not anyone's. Not anymore.

When the tears began, silent torrents that flooded down my face, Reeve reached for me, put his arms around me, and held me as I drowned his shoulder in grief.

CHAPTER

2 5

I'd mourned Amber's death once before, in private, mostly, with no one aware of my pain except for Joe. It had been nearly impossible to put on a happy face when my insides had felt like they'd been ripped to shreds.

This time, I had full support in my heartache. I had a shoulder to cry on. I had someone to grieve with me. And all I wanted was to be alone.

We went back to the mainland the day after she'd been found. My new apartment was ready, but I had a feeling Reeve would protest if I told him I wanted to be there, and I didn't feel like arguing. So I stayed with him in his LA house. I slept with him in his bed. I spoke as little as possible, in one-word sentences and grunts and nods. I did nothing but try to survive.

The funeral was held four days later. Reeve arranged everything with austere strength, encouraging as much or as little input as I felt up to. Numbly I picked out flowers and an urn and selected a charity for guests to donate to in her name. There were more people at the service than

I'd expected. People I didn't know. Friends and acquaintances of Reeve who had met her when they'd been together. Besides a few men from the ranch and Reeve's staff, the only people I knew in attendance were Reeve, Joe, and my mother.

Her mother was invited but didn't show. I guessed it was easier for her to pretend that Amber had died long before, or maybe that she hadn't ever existed at all. I didn't mind Mrs. Pries's absence. I liked being the sole representative of Amber's family. We hadn't shared DNA, but as far as I was concerned, we were as close to family as it gets.

"She called me," my mother whispered during the service. She patted my hand, a gesture I supposed she thought was comforting. "The other day. She left a message on my machine. I saved it for you."

"I know, Mom. I heard it, remember?" It was the message that had brought Amber back into my life. It had been left on my mother's old answering machine late the previous summer. Months passed before she even mentioned it to me. Now it was May and it was both frustrating and upsetting that her dementia made her think that Thanksgiving was "the other day."

Her brow furrowed in confusion, an expression she wore often these days. "I don't know where the machine is since the move. It was important, I think. We need to find it." She began to stand, and though I pulled her back down, she seemed on the verge of a public tantrum.

Reeve put a hand on my knee, silently asking if he could help. It was Joe that managed to calm her. "I think I know exactly which box it's in, Ms. Barnes. Let's watch the rest of this beautiful service. I'll help Emily find it later."

I mouthed a *thank you* to Joe and spent the rest of the hour thinking about that message, the one where she'd said Blue Raincoat, and I changed my world to come to her rescue. I wondered what would have been different if I'd never heard it. Then I wondered what would have been different if I'd heard it earlier or if I'd not gone after her or if I'd never met her in the first place. I wondered if I'd ever actually known her like I thought I had. I wondered if I could have fixed her if I'd been less broken myself.

But I could spend hours and days and years on what-ifs, and whatever better scenarios I created in my head, it wouldn't change anything, and I'd still be without her now.

There was no reception when the service was over. The guests left and I sat by myself in the room with her ashes while Reeve settled up with the funeral home. Just her and I alone together for the last time. I didn't know what to say to her. We said so much to each other the last time I saw her. So much and yet not enough. All those years apart she'd been alive in my head, always present even when she wasn't there physically. Her voice had been as clear as my own when I'd gone about courting Reeve, and there had been many times that I'd wondered if she weren't already dead, wondered if it were her ghost speaking to me.

But now she was really gone, and her voice was silent and I'd never felt so lost or alone.

It was a sign of what needed to happen next in my life. It was finally time to move on.

Footsteps sounded behind me, and when I heard someone sit two chairs down, I didn't need to look up to know it was Reeve.

I let out a long slow breath. "It's over."

"Yes. It's over." He sounded as tired as I felt. "We just have the scattering of the ashes, if you still want to do that, but when you're ready. No rush."

I looked at him, really looked at him, for the first time in weeks. Maybe the first time ever. When I first saw him, I'd thought of him as mysterious and dangerous, a playboy who cared only about himself and his own wants and needs.

That wasn't the man sitting with me now, a man who cared for me in ways that I'd never imagined a man would. Ways that weren't sexual or materialistic.

"I mean us, Reeve. I mean it's over between us."

If he were the type, I imagined that he would have rolled his eyes. "Don't be—"

I shifted to face him, cutting him off. "I'm not." I was calm, in control. Barely, but it counted. "I'm not emotional or ridiculous. I'm not being melodramatic. I'm not making snap decisions. I'm not being anything but completely serious. This is over. We have to be over."

"Why?" He was equally calm, and it suddenly seemed absurd that he'd even have to ask and that either of us could be so restrained as we talked about the woman who'd been such a crucially important person in both our lives.

I burst up from my chair. "Because she's dead! Because I was with you when I should have been with her." I'd barely spoken since her death, but that had given me plenty of time to think. "Because I can't be certain you had nothing to do with it."

His eyes widened then immediately narrowed. "You think I had a hand in Amber's death?"

"Why were you already dressed that morning?" I'd turned that fact over and over in my mind and hadn't been able to come up with a satisfactory answer.

He sighed. "I told you. I woke up. I couldn't go back to sleep."

"So you got dressed? And then went back to sleep? Why would you do that?" I wouldn't let myself imagine what else had happened—how, while I was packing, he might have woken and slipped into her room. I wouldn't imagine it but it sat there in my head, like a door with a spotlight above it, begging for me to put my hand on the knob. Whatever was on the other side was as pervasive in my mind with the door closed as it potentially could be wide open.

Reeve stood, strengthening his response. "I went to my office, okay? When I got back to my room, I was tired, and I didn't bother getting undressed again."

"You didn't notice Tabor wasn't around when you went out?" It was an unfair accusation—I hadn't noticed the guard absent from duty when I'd first gone in to see her either.

"No. I didn't. Forgive me for being distracted." There was bite to his words, the first hint of bitterness he'd shown me since her death.

"Distracted by what? Me?" *By the fact that we'd just spent the whole night fucking?* "So it's my fault?"

"No." He took a step toward me, a bit softer now. "I'm not blaming you. Of course I was still thinking about you. But I was distracted by what I was doing. I went to my office to send an e-mail and that's all I was thinking about."

I didn't want him soft. I wanted him hard. I wanted to fight. "What e-mail? To who?"

Frustration flooded his features. "Does it matter? Even if I opened up my account and showed you a time-stamped e-mail, it would only prove I sent an e-mail. I could still have done whatever it is you think I did to Amber then, isn't that right?"

There it was. Point-blank. "Well, did you?"

"I shouldn't have to answer this."

There was a familiar glint of pain in his eyes. I'd seen it before, when I'd questioned his involvement with Missy's death. It made me feel cruel to ask again, but I didn't feel like I had a choice.

Which was the whole problem between us.

"You know what, Reeve?" I pushed back the lock of hair that had fallen from my bun. "It doesn't matter what your answer is. Because whether you never tell me or whether you tell me you did or you didn't, there will always be this dark cloud hanging over us. She will pervade any bit of happiness we have. We will always be star-crossed and impossible."

He moved toward me again. "That's emotion talking right now, Emily. That's going to go away. Right now we need each other. Don't push me away. Please."

He was right there, in front of me, asking me to reach out or let him reach out to me. Pleading for me to accept his love, again. Always.

But as warm and tempting as he was, I couldn't accept. His love was the sun, and I was ice, and even though it felt so good to melt in his presence, I didn't recognize what he'd changed me into. I didn't know who that person was. All I'd ever been was what Amber had made me into. I didn't know how to be anyone else.

I folded my arms across my chest and took a step backward.

Taking that one step said everything it meant to say. The pain in Reeve's eyes spread throughout his entire expression and posture. "You said you trusted me!" he snapped. "Was that a lie?"

"I don't trust myself anymore, Reeve! I thought I knew what I was doing. I told her I loved you, and she told me to leave, and I said I would, and I meant it, but then I spent the night in your bed anyway." I was spouting stream of consciousness, barely recognizing this was the first time I'd actually admitted to loving him or to the secret I'd kept from him since she'd told me to go.

He toughened, the fwitch of his left eye the only sign of emotion. "You were going to leave? After we were together on the island?"

I didn't even consider backtracking. It was time to lay everything out on the table. "Yes."

"Why?"

"Because she told me to and that's how it worked between us—she told me what to do, and I did it."

"I don't get you, Emily." That simple statement pushed the knife farther into my gut. I'd thought that he was the one person who had understood.

"And that just validates why we don't belong together."

He shook his head, rocking backward as though he were too angry to continue the conversation. Just as I thought he might turn to leave, he twisted back at me. "How do you still let her have that much power over you? She's gone. You've been released. But you're like a victim with Stockholm syndrome, still defending her, still looking to her to tell you what's 'allowed.' When will you see that you don't need her to tell you how to feel about things?"

I hadn't cried throughout the entire service, and suddenly, now, my eyes burned and my throat constricted. "You're one to criticize someone for using their power."

"You're right. I like having things my way and there are certain places in my life I demand that. And if that's what you need, someone to tell you how to dress and what to say and where to live and what to drive and how to fuck, then I can be that for you."

He bore into me with wide eyes, a single finger raised to enunciate his point. "But I'm not going to manipulate you into choosing things that will make you unhappy. I'm not going to allow you to stop being a woman who can think and decide for herself. If that's what you get off on, then you're right, we need to be over."

Once again he turned as if to leave, then spun back around. "She didn't die because you loved me, Emily."

A tear rolled down my cheek. "But maybe she died because *you* loved *me*."

"Oh, Jesus. This is talking in circles." With an abrupt burst of rage, he kicked at one of the wood-slat folding chairs. "I loved her, too, remember?"

I twisted my lips, trying to hold in the sob. "It's not the same."

"It doesn't matter if it was the same. I loved her, and I wouldn't have done anything to hurt her like this."

"How am I supposed to believe that?" The shitty thing was I *did* believe him. I'd always believed he loved her, but our argument had spun out of control, as arguments do, and I was speaking out of pain. I was picking at the places that I knew were his weakest. "You let her go off with Michelis in the first place."

"And how was I supposed to stop her?" His subtext was clear—*I'd kept her and you weren't happy, I let her go and you're not happy.* "Do you want to hear that I blame myself for this? Because I do. I do, and I have to live with that, but I don't believe that my punishment should be living without you."

I flinched because I *did* believe my punishment should be living without him.

He walked toward me. "Do I need to prove myself? Should I go after Michelis to show you how upset I am? He's the one who was responsible, and we both know it. Should I meet with him? Settle things once and for all?"

I folded my arms tighter around myself. "It's what she wanted you to do. Maybe you should."

"What do *you* want me to do?"

I didn't know what to say because I didn't know the answer. Did I want him to avenge her? Maybe. Did I want him to start a war with a man who had more power than he did? Maybe not.

"See, that's what this is really about. You said it earlier—you don't trust yourself." He closed the distance between us as he spoke, cornering me. "You don't have faith in your own opinions. You don't think I had anything to do with her death, and you don't think I should confront my uncle about this, but you still can't speak up, can you?

Your whole life is a reflection of this. It's why you waited so long to put your mother in a good facility. It's why you have a job that's beneath you. It's why you can't get the guts to go audition for something you believe in. It's why you're stuck, and why you'll always be stuck because you're not capable of making your own decisions."

His words were bitter and painful in their accuracy. I raised my hand to slap him, but he was faster than I was, and he caught my wrist before I made contact. He held me like that, his fingers both heat and ice where they touched my skin, his eyes searing into me with righteous indignation and conviction.

I held his stare. I held it, my lips tight, my body rigid. *See*, I said with my eyes. *You use your power against me too.*

He understood, either because he realized it for himself or he really could read me that well. His gaze fell, and he released his grip on me, a silent surrender.

With his guard lowered, I slapped him.

"How was that decision for you?" My hand stung, but I refused to let on. "And how's this one—I'm going home. To my new apartment. Without you. You do whatever the fuck you want about your uncle. I won't tell you what to do because I don't care."

"If that's what you need to do, then that's what you need to do." It was the coldest he'd ever been with me. "And I'll take care of Michelis. He's taken too much away from me, and it's time for me to stand up and make him pay."

It was a challenge, a last attempt to get me to tell him not to go, not to start a war, to stay and be safe.

But I was incapable. I was numb. "If that's what you need to do, then that's what you need to do."

He left in a cab. Filip drove me to my new home. Joe had given me keys and a security code, but it was the first time I'd been there. My furniture had been placed in

logical locations. The basics had been unpacked for me—
my kitchen was organized, my clothes were hanging in my
closet, my bed was made. Unopened boxes were stacked up
in the living room, the less important items that made up
my life. My books. Pictures. The few knickknacks I owned.

I stood at the door and surveyed the apartment, a place
with no memories, no emotional attachment. It was as cold
as I was, and it was my new home.

So I'd rebuild. Without Reeve. Without Amber.

It's not the worst thing in the world, I told myself, in a
voice that was completely my own. *You've done it before.
You can do it again.*

CHAPTER

2 6

It took two days before I could spend any real time out of bed. Three days before I managed to get dressed. On the fourth day, I forced myself to be productive.

I spent the morning on e-mails and reading a new script from my agent that was, for once, not terrible. Then I began working through the boxes. It was early evening, and I'd finished unpacking almost half of them when Joe stopped by.

"I wanted to make sure you were eating," he said, holding up two boxes of Chinese take-out.

"I'm more interested in that bottle of wine you have tucked under your arm. But, please, come in." I gestured toward the dining room and headed to the kitchen for a corkscrew, plates, and wineglasses.

"Sorry, I wasn't really dressed for company," I said when I returned, referring to my ensemble of yoga pants and a tank top.

"I don't know, I think you look pretty cute."

"Oh. Well." I tucked a hair behind my ear and studied

him as he uncorked the bottle of Riesling. His hair had grown out since I'd met him, and he'd grown a goatee. He had almost ten years on me and wore more than a few scars, but, I had to admit, he was very much an attractive man.

An attractive man who wouldn't be my type even when—or if—I ever decided I was ready to date again.

"Calm down. I wasn't hitting on you," he said, handing me a glass. "I'm just saying you look good."

"Then I'll say thank you. And you look good, too."

We ate together, the first meal I'd really tasted in more than a week. When we finished, he helped me clear the table and load the dishwasher.

"What's up for you next?" he asked, leaning against the counter.

I finished pouring detergent into the machine and pushed Start before turning to answer. "Production for *NextGen* starts up again in August. So there's that." I remembered what Reeve had said about how I'd been too scared to make any real change happen in my life. He'd been right, of course, but I was determined to change that. Starting with my career. "I've got a contract for the season, but if I could book another job before that, it might give me options so I don't have to sign the next contract."

"Good," Joe said encouragingly. "I'd love to actually *see* you in something."

"Yeah. So would I."

I wiped my wet hands on a dish towel then together we walked out to the living room that was a mess from unpacking.

Joe surveyed the scene. "You're settling in here. I'm surprised."

"Why? You didn't think I'd like it here? I think you picked a nice place, actually." Not that I'd been out of the apartment to explore the neighborhood yet, but from the window it seemed nice.

"I know I picked a nice place," he said as though his taste would never be in question. "But Reeve asked me what the lease terms were. Wondered how fast you could get out of it if you moved in with him instead. I figured that's what you'd decided to do."

"What?" Reeve and I had never once discussed moving in together. "When did he ask that?"

"Last week. He e-mailed me. The same day Amber disappeared, actually."

I immediately thought about the e-mail Reeve had claimed he'd gotten dressed to send. "Did he message you really early? Like, maybe the middle of the night island time?"

Joe sank onto the arm of my sofa, considering. "Maybe. It was in my in-box when I woke up. I didn't check when it had been sent and then we got wrapped up in Amber so I didn't think much about it. Why?"

So, Reeve and I had spent the night together, and after I'd snuck out, he'd had to get up immediately to make arrangements for me to possibly move in with him. It was . . . sweet, actually. And typical—making serious plans without consulting with me. No wonder he hadn't wanted to admit to it. In the light of day, he'd probably realized he'd acted impulsively.

In some other universe, maybe there was another Emily Wayborn née Barnes who got to be delighted about a man who'd do that. A man who loved her so much he couldn't even wait until the sun came up before looking into ways they could be together more permanently.

My chest pinched at the thought, and I had to take a seat in my armchair before answering. "I don't know. It doesn't matter, I guess. We're not together anymore."

Joe cocked his head, not surprised, but curious. "You still feel he might have had something to do with Amber?"

No, I didn't. Even knowing about the e-mail to Joe didn't make me believe Reeve had done something to her.

But there were a hundred reasons not to dwell on it too much. "I think there're too many questions that will never be answered. And other than that, I don't really want to talk about it."

"Fair enough." He squinted, as if trying to decide to say more on the subject. "For what it's worth, I should mention that I've done my own investigating, and I've been in contact with Sallis's team, and no matter how I look at it, I just can't figure out how Vilanakis would have managed to get into that compound. Every one of the staff checks out clean. The flight itineraries and hotel records off the island show no one suspicious at first glance. I can keep digging if you want, but I don't know how deep I'm going to have to get before I get anywhere."

"Well, that just points more to Reeve, doesn't it?" *All* the evidence seemed to point to Reeve. Which was exactly my reason for not wanting to think about it.

Joe shrugged. "I guess. But there's something that still doesn't add up, and, if I am to continue investigating, he's not where my focus would be."

"Where would it be instead?" I asked, actually interested in the answer.

"Not sure yet. I guess I'd start looking harder at Amber, figure out who she had relationships with and see if I could make a link that way. Dig deeper into the things that don't make sense. Like, for example, did you know she got that tattoo on her own?"

"What do you mean?"

"In my investigating, I found the place she had it done. The owner of the tattoo shop said Amber came in with a picture of the V and paid for it herself. She was alone. He also said that was the only tattoo like that he'd ever done. And when I showed him pics of Vilanakis, he claimed he'd never seen him."

"Do you believe him?"

"I'd have to dig deeper to know that." He frowned. "It's just odd. Why would she get a tattoo that stands for something so specific and terrible? Did she have feelings for Vilanakis? Did she get it to impress him? Was it just another way to piss Reeve off?"

There was something about it that definitely didn't make sense, and with all the questions, it was tempting to want to continue the investigation.

But just like Reeve had suggested, more proof wouldn't change how I felt in my heart. "You don't need to dig anymore. I'm ready to be done with all of that."

"I think that's probably smart."

We grew silent, and I wondered how long it would hurt like this to talk about Reeve. Would I ever actually be able *to be done with all of that?* Be done with *him*?

The question was exhausting. "Anyway," I said, dismissing the subject of my ex. "You came here for more than just to feed me. What's up?"

Joe scratched at the back of his neck. "Very perceptive. If this acting gig doesn't pan out for you, you should consider joining my team."

"Your team," I chuckled. "You're a solo kind of a guy and you know it."

"Maybe that could change," he said with a wink. "But yes. I'm glad you've decided to end the investigation, because I came to say that I'm leaving town for a while. I wanted to make sure I gave you a proper good-bye before I did."

I gave him a knowing smile. "You're going after Vilanakis, aren't you?"

"I'd rather not say anything more."

"That's not at all obvious," I teased, then paused, debating whether I should say more.

I decided I owed Joe everything I knew, even if it some of it hurt to talk about. "You should probably know that Reeve is planning to go after him as well. I don't have any details, but it was his intention when we last spoke."

"Damn," he said, stunned. "That's not going to start a war or anything, is it?"

"Not my circus anymore." But my stomach churned, and I was pretty sure it wasn't just my dinner digesting.

"Well, even if Reeve manages to take care of Vilanakis without getting himself killed, it won't free any of the women he's helped enslave."

"So they'll need to be rescued," I said definitively, ignoring that he'd just put a label to the cause of my stomach pain. "Like Maya."

"I think so. Yeah." His brows furrowed and he stared at his hands, growing somber. "Though it seems I'm not always good at recognizing which women need to be rescued from the ones who don't."

He peered up at me, his expression asking. And I realized it was an apology of sorts, for once thinking that Reeve had been a danger to me. For warning me away when I'd been dead set on pursuing Reeve's company.

So I hadn't needed rescuing. But maybe if I'd listened to him, it could have prevented the awful heartache I was feeling now.

"I don't know," I said. "I think you're better than you realize."

We said our good-byes after that, making promises to stay in touch that I was pretty certain neither of us would keep.

Then I poured a second glass of wine and settled down on the floor to tackle more boxes. The very next one I opened caused my heart to skip a beat. It contained items from my mother's house, one of several that didn't go with her to her new facility. On the top of the pile was her old answering machine, the one that had Amber's message from last summer on it.

If it was still saved there . . .

I'd listen to it. It would tear me apart, but I would listen because I missed her voice and her presence. Mostly I just missed knowing she was somewhere in the world, and maybe hearing her again, even just that small clip, would bring her back long enough to fill the hole she'd left in me.

Picking the machine up cautiously, as if it were delicate and might break if I mishandled it, I got to my feet and began searching for a place to plug it in. The outlets in the living room were all in use or behind furniture, so I took it into the dining room, plugged it in, and set it on the table.

The display lit up showing zero new messages. I held my breath as I flipped through the menu to the saved items. Then, when the automated voice said, *"You have two saved messages,"* I pushed the button to play them all and held my breath again, hoping one of them was her.

The automated voice announced the first message's time stamp, and I sighed with relief and melancholy when I realized it was hers.

"Emily." Tears slipped down my face. I couldn't believe it had only been a week since I'd last heard her say my name. *"It's been ages, I know. But I've been thinking about you. God, I'm not even sure if this is still your number. Anyway, I wanted to ask—do you still have that blue raincoat? Miss you. Bye."*

I sank down into a chair as my crying strengthened. It was such a little thing, listening to a silly ten-second voice mail message, but it was a gut punch. Knowing I wouldn't ever again, hearing her say blue raincoat (our safe word), realizing it couldn't keep her safe—it brought on an onslaught of emotion that had needed to be released. I pushed Play again, put my face in my hands, and sobbed.

I was too absorbed in my blubbering to stop the message when it finished the second time. The automated voice moved onto the next saved recording, and I was semi-aware of another time and date being announced. But then it started playing, and my breath caught.

It was her voice again. Amber's. A second message.

I restarted the message, and my heart started to pound when I realized it had been left on the night I'd last seen her. The night she'd died.

"Hi." There was a beat. *"Hi,"* she said again and every part of my body tensed. *"I'm in my room on Oinopa. I left you about half an hour ago, I think? Maybe longer. Anyway, I wanted to tell you I changed my mind. I don't want you to leave the island tomorrow. I was wrong to ask you to go. I was selfish. I'm selfish a lot. I know."*

Sinking. I felt like I was sinking, sinking, sinking.

"I went to tell you that. Went to tell you to stay. Went to your room." If I'd thought her first revelation had been overwhelming, this was earth-shattering. Heartbreaking. She'd gone to my room, and of course, I hadn't been there.

"Surprise! Your room was empty." She laughed bitterly. *"I was worried. Or maybe curious. So I went to Reeve to see if he knew where you were, and when I got to his room, right before I knocked . . . well, except for the master bedroom, the walls here are thin."*

"Oh, no," I gasped out loud. "No, no, no."

But yes. That's exactly what had happened—she'd heard Reeve and me together. Heard us making love.

"I was upset. And I went back to my room to think about it and I got more upset." The items on the floor by her vanity. She'd thrown them there. *"Lucky thing I snagged those pills. I saw them in your suitcase when I was helping*

you pack. And right now I'm just super grateful you hadn't dumped them down the toilet."

Fuck. The pills.

I'd forgotten all about them. The ones I'd taken from her the day we arrived. I'd hidden them in my suitcase, and, now that I thought about it, they hadn't been there when I unpacked. Why the hell hadn't I thrown them out?

"I've had a few of them now. Maybe more than a few. I'm going to have a few more in a bit. Or a lot more. Whatever. Just, first . . ."

She let out a long labored breath, and I closed my eyes, wanting to block out her voice, wanting to avoid the ending where this conversation inevitably led, but not able to cover my ears or shut off the machine. I *had* to keep listening, as horrible as it was to hear. I had to know all of it.

"This isn't a blue raincoat call." How ironic was it that the safe word she'd made for me had only ever been used by her? *"You'll get this when it's too late to do anything to help me. Honestly, it was probably too late for you to help me when we met. But maybe that's why I loved you so much—because you didn't try. You didn't try to fix me or take me back home or tell me that my life was on a downward spin. You only wanted to make me happy. I think you're the only person who ever really did. I'm sorry it was such an impossible task.*

"And now it's my turn to return the favor. If I can't have Reeve, there isn't anyone else I'd want him to be with except you. I just can't be around to see it happen. I hope you understand."

She was quiet, and I thought she might be done, but I could still hear her breathing. It grew slower and slower over the next several seconds. *"Okay,"* she said finally, possibly jerking herself awake. *"I'm getting tired. I'm gonna go for a walk now."* Her words were starting to slur.

"It's such a nice, nice night. And you know how I love high places. I'm letting you go, Em. I let you go."

There was a rustling sound as she moved to hang up, then a click. Then a beep, and the automated voice returned to say, *"You have listened to all your saved messages."*

I stared at the machine for a long time, the pounding of my heart the only sound in the now silent room. I stared and stared and stared.

The sadness I'd felt when I'd heard her first message had completely disappeared, I realized. It was gone and had been replaced with something not quite as identifiable. Something darker and deeper. Something more hostile. Something full of spite.

The something inside sparked hotter and soon it was fury, red and hot and blazing through me. My breathing quickened and my hands balled into fists, my fingernails digging into my palms as my ire became an inferno.

Then I couldn't contain it anymore.

With an angry sweep of my arms, I shoved the machine on the floor, letting out a low, guttural sound of pain and rage.

" 'Let me go'?" I shouted bitterly to the empty room, to her ghost. "How dare you!" It was shitty when she'd done it to me the first time.

To do it to me twice?

And the way which she'd decided to cut ties—to take her own life because she couldn't have the man she wanted—it was manipulative and selfish. And mean.

I just can't be around to see it happen.

"What you really mean was you couldn't stand to see me win!" Again, I yelled to the room. "Were you really that sore a loser? That you'd rather kill yourself than deal with trying to put your life back together?" Instead she'd left me to put *my* life back together. Left me to pick up the pieces and grieve and be the one who *lost.*

Rage propelled me up, and I stood so quickly my chair knocked over. "God, you were such a selfish bitch." The tears returned, partly because I was that mad and partly because I'd still loved her, no matter how egocentric and mean she'd been. "Selfish and conniving. You knew that killing yourself would ruin anything I had with Reeve. You might have done this for me, but it wasn't to give me a gift. You wanted to make sure I didn't have him either."

I swiped at my cheeks, pissed at my tears, pissed that I couldn't say all of this to her face. Pissed that she got the last fucking word.

"You know what? No." I paced the room with furious strides as I spoke. "You don't get the last word. *I* do. You can't let me go. You're dead, and you can't do anything to me anymore. But I'm still here, and I can let *you* go." I laughed, an acidic choked laugh that might have been just a variation of a sob. "Did you hear that? *I let you go.* You don't get to have a hold on me anymore. I let you go!"

My last words echoed off the walls and the Spanish tile floor, resounding through the room as clearly and effectively as if I were in the recording studio and someone had turned up the echo on the soundboard.

Appropriate, I thought. It was a statement I was sure would reverberate for a long time, not only in my dining room, but also in my life.

I felt good. Really good.

For about five minutes.

Then I started to shiver. I leaned against the wall and slid down to the floor. Then I wrapped my arms around myself and cried—really cried. Sad tears, angry tears, but mostly just cleansing tears. I sobbed until my face was wet and my eyes swollen and my head pounding. I cried until I was dry, until I was empty, until she was completely gone from inside and all that was left there was me.

* * *

I dozed there on the dining room floor. When I woke up, it was dark outside, and my arm ached from how I'd been laying on it.

I stood up and stretched then headed to the kitchen for a drink. At the sink, I filled a glass with water then leaned against the cabinet while I took a long swallow and picked up my cell phone from where it was charging on the counter and checked the time. Half past nine. And I had one missed text from Joe.

What if she wanted Reeve to THINK V gave her the tat?

I chuckled. He couldn't really give up an investigation. He'd probably always have it in the back of his mind, just like I would. Just like I'd always have Amber in the back of my mind.

And then I was thinking about his text. Why would she want anyone to think she was indebted to Vilanakis as his servant? Especially when she wanted Reeve back. What would she have to gain from that?

Nice try, Joe.

I set my water and phone down and started to the living room. Halfway there, I stopped. *If he thought she was in danger, Reeve would want to protect her.*

It was actually an excellent way to try to win him back. To be vulnerable, like he liked.

But it was silly to think she would be that manipulative.

Except . . . was it? She'd manipulated me. More than once. And I'd seen her exploit many men over the years. *"Forget who you are . . . be who he wants."*

So, what if Joe was on to something?

I sank onto the sofa, playing a possible scenario out in my head. Amber had run to Vilanakis willingly, but when she'd realized that punishing Reeve came at a price and decided she wanted him back, maybe the only way to minimize the extent of her betrayal was to become a victim. Get the tattoo. Pretend she was in more danger than she was. She could have been the one to send the other e-mails to Reeve, the ones in English. Could have posed as Michelis and sent the Jane Doe autopsy to see what Reeve would do if he thought she was dead. See if he still cared. She'd had to know that Petros would tell him the truth eventually. Maybe she hoped he'd come after her then.

But he didn't come. Instead, Joe did. And she'd insisted he take her to Reeve.

Then, if Vilanakis hadn't been the one to tattoo her, if he hadn't considered her a belonging, he would likely not have come after her. He'd never had a history of going after his ex-girlfriends before. It would explain why he'd eventually told Reeve that he wasn't responsible for terrorizing her, which could also still be a lie. But wasn't he the type to take credit for his bad deeds? Denying it would have defeated the point.

But the dog. And the fish.

Well. She could easily have cut the line to the fountain. Maybe she'd even seen Reeve follow me down to the cliff. She would have wanted to draw back his attention and another "incident" would do the trick. That's why Joe couldn't find anyone else to blame.

Except she was with me when the dog likely got poisoned.

But Buddy wasn't. Amber had been so sure that he hadn't been working for Vilanakis, but she hadn't said anything about him not killing the dog. She could have convinced him to do it—given him a hand job in exchange or maybe even just batted her pretty eyes. There had been paint cans in the attic. Surely there had been poison for pests around the ranch as well. She could easily have supplied Buddy with the items he'd needed. And the message "She's Mine" led Reeve to believe it was from

Michelis and that he'd keep coming after her. It ensured that Reeve continued to keep her close.

It had happened the morning after Reeve had told her things had changed. So maybe she did really understand, and the whole "he said he still loves me" was just a show for me. To make me step aside. And I did, like she knew I would.

My heart was racing now; my palms, sweaty. Everything was fitting together so perfectly.

She'd probably leaked the press release about Chris Blakely and me too. There'd been computers at the ranch. And a laptop in Amber's room. *Reeve's* laptop. She could have easily found the picture of Chris Blakely and me in his e-mails. She would have guessed Reeve had been pissed when he saw them, could have used the same pictures and released them on social media to remind him *how* pissed he'd been. She probably hoped it would cause a fight between us. I had actually been surprised when it hadn't.

I sat forward and rubbed my hands together. Was I really considering this? Was it really possible that Amber had staged . . . everything?

The scratches on her arms—*Not Yours* . . . That couldn't possibly have been Vilanakis who made the marks if he hadn't been the one to kill her. So, at the very least, she'd done that herself.

And the rest was possible. Maybe not probable, likely never provable, but it made sense somewhere deep inside, in the parts of me that had known her so well they didn't require proof or reason. They just *knew*.

I should have been mad.

I *was* mad, but I should have been *so mad* I couldn't feel anything else, but I wasn't. Because it was also actually kind of funny. Desperate, for sure. And more than a little bit impressive.

I flung myself backward into the cushions. "Amber, you little devil," I said, with a hint of a smile. "So conniving. You really did want all the power, didn't you?"

I wondered if she ever realized she hadn't been quite as powerful as she'd thought she'd been. Or that she might have had so much more if she hadn't abused the power she did have. Seemed like that might have been a lesson she should have learned from Vilanakis.

Vilanakis!

I sat up abruptly. Reeve was going after Vilanakis because he thought he'd killed Amber. Reeve already had the odds against him, but when his motive was based in a lie, he had even less of a chance of coming out of the feud alive.

Cursing, I jumped from the couch to go grab my cell. *Dammit, dammit, dammit.* I had to try and stop him. And where the fuck was my phone?

The kitchen. Right.

I ran for it, chiding myself the whole way for not trying to stop him when I'd had the chance. I'd never wanted for him to get himself killed. I'd never wanted him to start a war. And I hadn't told him . . . why?

I couldn't think of the reasons now. All my emotions had been hazy then, like a thick fog had kept them shrouded and elusive. Now that I'd let her go, Amber wasn't clouding my feelings. Everything was so much clearer. And I needed Reeve to be safe. I needed him in my life.

With phone in hand, I chose his name from my contacts and paced circles around my bedroom while I waited for it to ring.

It only rang once before going to voice mail.

"Fu-uck," I said, drawing out the word as I hung up and redialed. Again, voice mail.

His house. I should call his house. Except I'd never had his house number, and there was no way it was listed.

I'd have to go to his house instead. Even if he wasn't there, his men would know how to reach him.

Swearing up a storm, I slipped on some shoes, and ran to the kitchen to grab my car keys from the hook by the fridge. I had no idea where my purse was so I decided to leave it, anxious to get to him as soon as possible.

In the hopes that he'd answer eventually, I redialed his number as I opened the door.

And then I froze.

Because there he was, standing right in front of me, his hair messy like he'd run his hand through it a thousand times and his eyes wide and warm the minute they locked with mine.

I dropped my hand from my ear, my mouth gaping.

"Hi," he said cautiously.

His voice shocked me into action. "I was just calling you," I said, clicking End on my cell.

With his forehead creased, he reached into his pocket and pulled out his cell. "Oh. It's on airplane mode," he said, pocketing it again. "Why were you calling me anyway?" Though wary, he was so obviously hopeful.

I was focused on his lips, the way they curved up with the slightest hint of a smile when he spoke. The way they were just barely parted, as if preparing for a kiss.

"Emily?"

I blinked, instinctively wetting my own lips. "Oh. To tell you not to go to Chicago." But now I didn't have to because he was here, in my threshold, looking sexy and smoldering with the most absolute perfectly kissable lips.

And then he said, "I already did."

"You already went to Chicago?" It was hard to talk with my heart in my throat.

"I just got back."

Did that mean . . . ?

My vision got dim around the edges, and I had to put

my hand on the doorframe to keep me standing. It had been four days since I'd seen him. It had been enough time for him to . . . to do a lot of things.

"Emily." Gently, he gripped my arm, trying to help support me. "What's wrong?"

"It wasn't him. Your uncle didn't kill her."

He bent down to meet my eyes. "Do you know something? Or are you saying it's me again?"

"Not you." I took a deep breath to clear the cloud of dread. "Amber left a message. You should hear it. Come in. Please."

Reluctantly he let go of me so he could walk through the door. When it shut, he locked the deadbolt behind him, and, if I weren't so worried about what might have happened with Vilanakis, I might have chuckled at the gesture. Once upon a time, that sort of behavior from him would have frightened the hell out of me.

Now, I knew he was simply concerned about keeping me safe.

"She left a message?"

"Uh, yeah. This way." I indicated for him to follow me to the dining room, and as we walked the handful of yards to get there, I chided myself again for not stopping him sooner and fretted over the awkward tension between us and also reveled in his presence, how just being near him made me feel all jumbled and dizzy and agitated.

I stopped short at the entrance of the dining room, not remembering that I'd thrown the answering machine to the floor until I saw it now on the floor. "Just one sec," I said apologetically as I leaned down to pick up the device, praying that I hadn't broken it during my tantrum.

I set it on the table, and with shaky hands, cued up the saved messages and skipped to the second one. It started playing—thankfully—and bit my lip, not wanting to hear her message again but wanting to be there for Reeve when he did.

I watched him as he listened, following every shift in his expression. I could tell when he realized she'd heard us by the slight twitch of his eye. And when the color left his face, I could tell he'd figured out what she'd done.

Before she'd finished, he sank into a chair. Then, when it was over, he sat motionless, processing.

"My God," he said softly after what seemed like forever. "I had no idea. That she would do that. Did you?"

"She'd mentioned that she wanted to end things once before." I didn't add that it had been when he'd kept her on the ranch. He didn't need that extra guilt. "That had been in the past, though. I had no idea she still felt that way."

"We couldn't have known," he said emphatically, as if he feared I would blame myself.

"No. We couldn't have known." I leaned against one side of the arch that served as the entrance to the room, hating that the distance between us was a barrier when there were already so many other less tangible barriers between us as well. I wanted to hold him. *Shouldn't* I be holding him? Shouldn't we be consoling each other and comforting each other and loving each other at a time like this? Shouldn't we be doing that all the time?

I supposed that's what he'd been trying to do all along. And I'd pushed him away.

Damn, did the truth ache.

Reeve glanced at the answering machine. "Was that message the reason this was on the floor?"

I blushed. "Yeah. It, uh, made me mad." I furrowed my brows trying to figure out how to explain how I'd felt and what I'd realized in the last thirty minutes of my life. I knew that getting the words right wasn't as important as just getting them out. "It made me mad because it was so damn manipulative."

His head lifted slightly. "Oh?"

"It was all manipulative. Everything she did. I see that now. She controlled me, and I let her." I avoided his eyes and scratched absentmindedly at my collarbone. "You were right. All the things you said about us—about *me*—they were right."

"I shouldn't have—"

"No, you should have," I said, interrupting him. "I appreciate that you said it. I mean, I didn't at the time, but I do now. I'm sorry I didn't get it earlier." I braved a glance up at him, and when my eyes met his, so full and earnest, I thought I'd melt.

But Michelis. "So Chicago! What happened?" I barely dared to ask.

"Chicago." He stood, drawing out the word as he walked toward me, and for a minute I forgot I was waiting for him to talk and instead hoped he was coming to me, finally. Hoping he would finally put his arms around me.

I swore, if he did, this time I'd never let him let me go.

But he passed by me, ending up at the opposite wall of the arch. He leaned against it, mirroring my stance. "I just got back, actually."

"You said that. Did you . . . ?" It worried me that he hadn't just come out and said what happened already. "Is it bad?" I wrung my hands, waiting.

"Emily," he said softly. "I didn't hurt him."

Relief filled my chest so fully I was surprised my bra still fit comfortably.

"I couldn't," he continued. "I know you want me to be that kind of man. The kind who could kill someone, and I could. But not him. Not for this. I thought I could. But then I was there and I realized . . ."

I was still and composed on the outside, but inside, my heart was running a million miles a minute and my belly was twisting, coiling with anticipation. "Realized what?"

He pinned his eyes to mine. "She wasn't you."

"What?"

"Amber wasn't you. I could kill someone if they took my whole life away. But he didn't. Because he didn't take away *you*."

The only reason I wasn't already running to him was because I was too stunned and overwhelmed with emotion.

"I came here to get you back, Emily. I came here to get what's mine."

Then I *was* running to him, because I couldn't go another second without touching him, without kissing him. His arms wrapped around me and our lips locked and he tasted faintly like bourbon and mints and salt because, it seemed, I was crying and my tears had mixed into our kisses.

When I could bear to release his mouth—or, rather, when I had to come up for air—I cupped my hand against his cheek and said, "That's not the kind of man I want you to be. I know it seems I like I might. But you're dark and dangerous enough for me just as you are."

He searched my face, as if trying to decide if I were telling the truth.

"And I'm so glad you came back here for me, but even if you hadn't, I was coming to look for you. Not just to stop you from going after your uncle, but also to tell you I want you. I want the things you give me. I want to be yours."

It was the first time I'd ever remembered making such an important decision for myself. It felt good. Really good.

"Oh, Blue Eyes," he sighed, and I pressed tighter against him and into him, wanting to be as close as possible, to be inside him, for him to be inside me.

Abruptly, he spun us so that I was the one with my back against the wall and he was the one pushing into me. He caught my wrists in his grip and pinned them above my head. My breasts perked up in this position, and his gaze flicked down to them, searing through the flimsy material of my tank top, arousing me as though I were already naked and he was already sucking my nipples into his mouth.

"What now?" I asked hoarsely, and I meant *how are you going to make love to me now,* but I also meant *I'm yours— now teach me how to belong to you.*

"Well." His expression darkened. "Now I'm going to fuck you against the wall."

My chest rose and fell heavily against him. "Then what?"

"Then, if we make it to the bedroom, I'm going to fuck you again. If not," he glanced at the apartment around him, "we'll do it there on the floor."

"Yes," I gasped, moisture pooling between my legs.

"Tomorrow," he let my arms go, and his hands came to play gently at my neck, "I'm moving you into my house, and you're letting this place go. Then, in a few days, few weeks maybe, I'm going to give you a ring. And you'll wear it. And when you agree it's appropriate, I'll take you to a church, and you'll tell everyone that you're mine once and for all."

I clutched onto him. "I want that."

"I know." He always knew. Knew me better than I knew myself.

"And babies? Do I want babies?"

His lips crept into a smile. "You do. At least five."

"Five?" It was half exclamation, half *no fucking way.* "I think I maybe want two."

"That's not what you want."

"Oh, really?"

"Really. I know, remember?"

I raised an eyebrow, the extent to which I'd argue with him at the moment. Later we could hash it out, and just the idea of a *later* with Reeve did the funniest warm things to my insides.

He leaned forward and pressed his forehead against mine. "Right now, though, you want me to tell you I love you."

"I do. But I already know."

"And you want to tell me that you love me too."

I choked up and my voice barely made it past the lump lodged in the back of my throat to finally tell him what I'd felt for so long now. "I do. I love you."

His eyes shut briefly, as though he were relishing the sound. When they opened again, he said, "That's the first time you've said it." His words were gruff and thick and affected.

"Yes, the first," I admitted, staggered that I'd waited until now, astounded that I'd *been able* to wait when it felt like it was bursting from every part of me, desperate to be set free. "I promise it won't be the last."

And his love *was* heavy and hot, but not at all the burden I'd imagined it would be because he carried it for me, I realized now. He held it around me like a blanket. Like a nest that had been built just for me.

And the love I felt for him was weightless, like a feather, like a beam of light, like falling forever and never touching the ground.